COUNTERSTRIKE'S RUIN

The Naplian Stratagem

Steve Rzasa

Kgruppe, LLC

CONTENTS

TAKAMO

TA'KA'MO   (High   Radnian,   Radnia--Central continent from TAI (Universe) and KHA'MO (ebb and flow) 1.Gestalt, the wholeness of the universe. 2. History. 3. Conflict.

- Vol. 234, file 451- Sepal's Unabridged Galactic Dictionary

What is Takamo Universe?

Takamo started as a massive multiplayer science fiction game in the early 1980s. It had a newsletter where players and staff published descriptions and stories about their alien empires. That generated spin off publications for fan fiction and stories rooted in Takamo lore. Over the years the stories and worldbuilding took on a life of its own and for decades we collected and curated the stories of others along with our own writings. In 2014, Kevin J. Anderson and Wordfire Press published our first novel Empire's Rift, by Steve Rzasa. Now Takamo is a science fiction imprint with about twenty titles by various authors, all based in a shared universe.

We like to say that Takamo is the ancient language of space. Any moment in the Takamo timeline is one part of a whole - a spark in a complex, limitless, gestalt universe. You'll find that Takamo stories are set along a historical timeline. The books are filled with easter eggs and references to events and characters in other stories. Different tales are told by diverse authors in separate adventures, yet each book is connected to all of the others.

This book is a part of that shared universe.

If you want to know more, please visit
www.takamo.com

PROLOGUE

Classified Facility
Ursoq System
June 2685

C orporal Tenett Tyn Durrad averted his gaze as
he walked the corridor leading past the assembly
labs. He knew quite well what to expect from the sights
and sounds. No need to remind himself that the aliens
inside were being reassembled into killing machines.

He couldn't remember the name of the species. Urq-
something? Probably the same as the system since they
didn't strike him as terribly creative. The furred aliens
had only two dozen cities scattered across their arid,
desolate planet and hadn't even achieved rudimentary
spaceflight when the Advanced Technological Research
Unit (ATRU) had received the coordinates. Fourteen
hours. That's all it took for the Briddarri task force's
ships to destroy military bases with coordinated orbital
strikes and land assault teams that obliterated anything
left of the Urq's armies.

No sense in beginning a harvest with warriors
standing in your way.

"Corporal." One of the researchers in charge of

the assembly unit, Dr. Jurrot, approached him. Durrad found the stocky scientist arrogant. Likely, he was compensating for being a head shorter than every Briddarri soldier manning the facility. His lack of height and green skin two shades too light for a true son of Barra Bridd, but all Durrad cared about was not spending another day past the three months he'd been stuck guarding this abattoir. "Get your commander in here."

Durrad smirked. "Sorry, Doctor, but I'm not at liberty to summon the colonel to anything. That's not how the chain of command works. Problem with your comms?"

"Of course not. I calibrate the communications myself." Dr. Jurrot looked offended by the suggestion of malfunctioning technology and by Durrad's existence. *The feeling is mutual.* "I have test results he needs to see in person."

Durrad's curiosity got the best of him. He peered beyond Jurrot into the laboratory. Thanks be to the honored ancestors that work seemed to have halted for the moment. The Urq varied in height from two to three and a half meters. Big, furry bruisers. Their coats ranged from pale blond to rich muddy brown, some bearing light speckles, others sporting thick stripes.

All eighty-four subjects in the sprawling laboratory had been ripped apart, cybernetic limbs implanted as replacements. Some had a single appendage swapped out—where there had been a three-fingered hand on the end of an arm, there was a set of metal pincers mounted on servos. Others were further along, with half their bodies turned into nothing more than chassis for weaponry.

The subject on the pedestal in the center, though, must have been what Jurrot was excited about. Durrad couldn't tell if anything of the Urq remained because the bulk of what stood there was a sleek cybernetic warrior with shoulder-mounted particle weapons and clawed hands that looked able to tear through even the thickest battle armor Durrad and his fellow troops possessed.

"We're getting closer," Jurrot said. "It's not quite a Truppen. There's not the seamless integration of the original being's consciousness that makes them so effective as cybernetic soldiers. This one, though. .." He tapped the transparent wall. "This has potential. We've suppressed what's left of the Urq's mind with a combination of software enhancement and pharmacological inputs. The central nervous system has been repurposed as a redistribution network for—"

"I don't need to know all that." Durrad shuddered. He was trying not to imagine his brains plucked from his skull and shoved into a mechanical frame meant for combat. There was no way he'd ever submit to a procedure that would leave him a robotic slave. But he supposed that's why the ATRU was harvesting the alien species no one would miss. *At least this way, they'd contribute to the war effort against the one-eyes.* "Fine. I'll go grab the colonel, but next time, report it up through the proper chain of command."

"Don't be so dismissive." Jurrot wagged a finger under Durrad's nose. Durrad longed to shoot it off. "One day, these beings will flood the Naplian's front lines, and then you won't have to do anything but point them in the direction of an enemy you want obliterated."

"What good's that going to be to a warrior?"

Durrad turned away and stalked down the corridor. *Farrudd.* His grandfather would have smacked him if he'd heard that kind of language or even suspected Durrad of using it.

Alarms blared throughout the halls. Emergency lighting flashed on. Barriers clattered as they dropped into place.

"What is it? A power failure?" Jurrot grabbed his arm.

Durrad yanked free and thumbed his comm. "Central, this is Durrad. What's the word, sir?"

"Suborbital intruders." Colonel Kadran's voice rose a pitch. Durrad could hear shouts in the background. "A squadron of mixed interceptors and bombers are strafing the fuel depots. We don't know where they came from. In-system satellites reported no unusual activity. All outbound communications are jammed. We think they're targeting—"

A thunderous roar filled the signal with screeching static. Durrad winced. "Colonel?"

No response.

Durrad seized the front of Jurrot's lab coat. *Let's see how he feels about it.* "Evacuate your staff, now. Get to the transport hangar."

"Evacuate? I'm not leaving this work behind!"

A nearby explosion shook the corridor so badly that Durrad had to brace himself against the transparent wall. He let Jurrot toppled. Green blood spattered the deck plates. Jurrot wiped his forehead with the back of his hand. He looked astonished.

"Listen, Doctor, I don't like you in the slightest, but if you want to survive, you won't question my demands," Durrad snapped. "Clear out your lab—of your coworkers, *not* your science experiments! The hangar is shielded against the weather and is the best hope you've got if we're being bombarded."

Jurrot stood, his legs shaking, and opened his mouth for what Durrad assumed was another argument.

"Move!" Durrad shouted.

Another explosion sent them both reeling, but when Durrad peered through the smoke now drifting from the overhead vents, he saw Jurrot fleeing into the lab. Didn't matter whether he took Durrad's warning seriously. He'd been given his instructions.

Durrad sprinted for the stairwell beside the lift shaft. There was a lot of shouting upstairs, but he couldn't see much beyond the shadows of people scrambling around. He forced his mind to slow down so he could think through the situation. The hangar should be a decent shelter, but if marauding one-eyes were intent on disabling or destroying the base, they wouldn't let transports flee.

A blast threw him from his feet before he could complete his thought. The shockwave mingled quik-crete, reinforced plastics, and metal in a cloud that cut across his skin. He slammed onto the floor, sliding across its slick surface.

He blacked out long enough that when he recovered, he could see open sky.

The planet's sickly-orange clouds whipped overhead. Durrad tried to get up, but a sharp pain lanced through his midsection. He clutched at his side. His hand came away covered in his blood. The floor around him was smeared in the emerald liquid. That was what he'd slid upon.

The lab was demolished. Cybernetic limbs jutted from between collapsed walls and shattered transparent metals. He realized one of the limbs was Briddarri and recognized the communications unit strapped to the severed appendage as belonging to Doctor Jurrot. He wondered, in his addled state, if Jurrot would consider himself a candidate for the cybernetics harvest.

Smoke rose from the back corners, where Durrad knew the database's physical backups were stored. He wasn't sure how much information had survived the raid, but given the continued rumble of explosions and sudden silencing of the alarms, he didn't have high hopes for survivors digging out what was left.

Fighter craft roared in the distance. Durrad grimaced as he pulled himself up the rubble. The pitch was all wrong, though. Naplian starfighters had a particular shriek to their engines while they were racing through the atmosphere. These vehicles...

Durrad's eyes widened as he saw their tiny silhouettes expand on the dusty horizon. They didn't belong to the Naplians. He stared as an AF-32G Raider fighter-bomber wheeled past the wreckage of the base with two SF-107 Warhawk starfighters in escort formation.

Humans?

Impossible. The Terran Republic and other human governments in that region of the galaxy had joined the Grand Alliance in the past few years, spurred by the Naplian conquest of the Baedecker System and its serjaum reserves. These spacecraft were painted drab colors with no markings.

Durrad tried his comms. No signal. Only static. He puzzled as the craft banked over the ruined landscape. The fuel depots were aflame, a thick column of billowing smoke reaching far above the hills enclosing the plains around the base. Every structure —fuel depots, comms array, laboratories, command bunker—were destroyed.

It didn't make sense. Pirates wouldn't destroy a base. They wanted loot or immediate payment. Unless they were working for someone. Hired by Naplians? Absurd. The Naplians had plenty of their own curved-winged fighters.

Durrad coughed. More green blood smeared the torn front of his uniform. His only hope was a transport, maybe one buried beneath the rubble. He and other survivors could get even a damaged one in working order. Given the right supplies and enough time, they would get it aloft and—

The pitch of the starfighter engines shifted again. They were coming back.

Fatigue rolled over Durrad as the reality of the situation sank in. This wasn't a raid. This was an obliteration. Whoever was up there was intent on wiping the cybernetics facility from the face of the planet.

He wouldn't be denied the chance to face his enemies, though, whoever they might be. Durrad tugged his pistol free of his belt. The carbine he'd carried on patrol was gone, probably crushed beneath the rubble. Only the shredded strap remained.

Durrad aimed the pistol at the onrushing bomber

and its fighter escorts. It was a futile gesture, but someone would know a valiant *rinndda* had shown his soul worthy of Barra Bridd.

For the glory of the kingdom.

He shouted a wordless, ragged cry skyward and drained his weapon's powerpack as he fired at the ships. The acinic glare from the blasts made his eyes water.

The heat and light from the dropped bomb turned the universe around him into a supernova long before he felt the pain of his death.

* * *

The raiding aircraft swept past the final flurry of explosions. Nine more aircraft, separated into three flights of three apiece, regrouped past the lopsided hills that framed the plains for kilometers in every distance. Eight Warhawks and four Raiders became a seamless squadron once again.

The squadron leader took his flight on a final recon pass over the base. No transmissions had escaped the surface—jamming ahead of the attack had assured that. Sensors indicated zero sentient life forms and no power signatures. Every structure had been at least leveled, if not turned into a glassy crater.

The last anti-matter warhead dropped on the base ruins had scoured even those broken buildings, ensuring no life remained and no data.

All that remained was a quick withdrawal.

"Virry Two to Virry One. Negative for signs of interception. Nest reports no signs of ripwave or jump activity. Clear skies."

"Roger that, Nine." Major Taggert "Tag" Wester

allowed his muscles to relax. He felt as if he'd been clenching his entire body since the home ship had arrived in the Ursoq System, through the approach and drop, and most definitely during the attack. "Withdraw to rendezvous coordinates in orbit and standby for ripwave to Nest."

"Confirmed, One. Two out."

He smiled at the dry but coolly professional tones of Captain Naomi "Princess" Wyss, his squadron executive officer. It was reassuring to have her watch his back for what had grown from a crazy idea into a covert operation.

It wouldn't please anyone in the Grand Alliance to learn that Terran Intelligence was sabotaging Briddarri cybernetic experiments. They'd shown a lot of promise.

Tag wanted to spit. *Promise.* Exact word from the official reports. The Briddarri were secretly enslaving entire alien worlds they thought no one would miss, so they could create bastardized versions of truppen warriors who'd helped to smash the Naplian invaders on more than one front.

That wasn't the fight Tag signed up for. "Not by a long shot," he muttered to himself.

He glanced at the word "Scrape" etched by a plasma torch onto his weapons console. His flight suit and fighter were unmarked, but Tag had insisted his former wingman's call sign be added to the cockpit.

"For Baedecker," he said, "And so innocents don't have to suffer."

The green indicator light told him the squadron had reached safe distance to ripwave. Tag spun up the generator, and seconds later, the twelve fighters raced away from Ursoq Six toward the rendezvous with their carrier and the next mission.

CHAPTER ONE

July 2685
Andresen System
Cometary Cloud

Crossing nearly thirty sectors in three weeks made for rough travel for any passenger, though Tag didn't mind the downtime. It gave him time to repair to his secondhand Warhawk.

Virry Squadron was housed in the cavernous cargo bay of their ersatz carrier, a converted Liberty Freighter. Tag didn't know how Terran Intelligence had procured one of the thousands of these newly constructed ships that had been launched in the past year, but given the battle damage they'd left unrepaired on the hull, it appeared the ship had been captured by enemy forces and then, ironically, liberated.

Tag had christened it *Aox*, an Audrian word for a spacebound creature that drifted between stars, soaking up interstellar radiation for hundreds of years before gorging on a sun's strength. That was all part of the plan, and as he stripped out the last of the fizzled fire control linkage circuits in the cockpit of Scrape, he had to admit it was his favorite—using varied alien terms to throw off anyone who might catch wind of their covert action.

The cold packet nestled in his jumpsuit pressed

against his bicep as he straightened from underneath the weapons console. Any self-congratulation he felt dissipated. Sure, it felt good to be fighting quietly against the Briddarri harvesting, but the reality was that the whole operation was unsanctioned.

There would be no getting caught.

"If you're not too slathered in grease, Tag, the captain reports our escort is due to arrive."

Tag winced as he worked a kink out of his shoulder muscle. He leaned out of the cockpit. Naomi Wyss stood at the bottom, wearing the same drab gray jumpsuit he and the rest of the Virry pilots sported. No names, no insignia. Heck, they didn't even have manufacturer labels inside the collar. But as boring as they were, Princess somehow made the garb seem elegant. Her lithe body fit the jumpsuit better than anyone aboard, and her dusky complexion, coupled with eyes as green as Briddarri blood, was a bold contrast.

Briddarri blood. The blood and the green took Tag back to the bombing runs. His scanners had obliged him with dispassionate recordings of casualties, but that sickening jolt faded almost as quickly as it arrived because Briddarri Green also recalled Lira Lin Reen.

Stars, I miss her.

"Thanks, Princess." Tag clambered down the ladder. The converted hangar bay tinkled with the sounds of maintenance as Virry pilots and their bots affected final repairs to their fighters and bombers. Tag sniffed the air. "Are the air refreshers offline again?"

Wyss wrinkled her nose. "I'm fairly certain

that's your odiferous self, Major."

"Oof." Tag grinned. "I suppose I'd better shower off before we shake hands with the boss, XO. No sense in getting kicked off our mission because of body odor."

Wyss led him into the main access corridor but apparently couldn't resist a final taunt over her shoulder. "If that were a true threat, he'd have sacked you and promoted me months ago."

Tag chuckled. He needed a good laugh. A decent joke. Something. Fighting the good fight was one thing, but destroying those harvesting facilities was a morale-sucker—especially when he wasn't sure he wanted to continue that fight. Or any fight.

What he wanted above all was to find Lira and convince her to leave the galaxy behind. Run off to a paradise planet somewhere a thousand parsecs away and grow old together.

He allowed himself a bemused frown. *You sound like an old man, Tag. Father would find it hysterical.*

The realization didn't cure him of his hope, though, that he'd catch up with Lira again. Their contact had been sporadic since he'd helped her escape Briddarri clutches so she could live a full life— and get herself out of the Blue Kitt crime syndicate. They were criminals with hearts of minimally tarnished gold, but it was hard to contemplate enjoying civilian life when one had a "Wanted" marker on one's data profiles.

The bridge was in the center of *Aox*'s forward quarter, nestled between bulkhead after bulkhead of armored reinforcement. Sensor modules were crammed into that part of the ship, too, along with enough missile tubes and railgun emplacements that made a standard Liberty Freighter's armaments seem like cheap kids' toys.

Captain Desmond Wu nodded to them as they entered. "Glad you could join us, folks. Sensors confirm the task force will make rendezvous in forty-five minutes."

Tag gazed at the holographic navigation display. *Aox* was a blue pip nestled against one of the thousands of cometary fragments littering this arc of the cloud surrounding the Andresen star. It helped conceal their presence, as did the background radiation pouring off the blue giant at the center of the system. White dots appeared at the display's fringes, growing in number until sixteen vessels filled it. "I'm guessing we didn't pick up any other contacts. You'd be growly if we had, Dez."

"I'd also be terrible at my command if I let us get followed to every meetup." Wu shifted his stance, the blue lights overhead gleaming off his bald head. He scratched at the trim black goatee and mustache combo he'd been cultivating this last deployment. "Adding extra jumps to an otherwise straightforward course makes it more difficult for anyone to track our trajectory."

"Yeah, I get that. Appreciate all your hard work at keeping us from getting blown out of space."

"You're welcome," Wu said, his tone dry.

"These Terran Intelligence types really don't have much in the way of a sense of humor." Tag exaggerated his whisper to Wyss so it was plainly audible.

"Does that mean you assume you're the expert

to educate them in such matters?" She feigned a horrified expression. "Heaven help us all."

"Chatter," Wu said. "Less of it, please."

"Captain, encoded transmission incoming," the comms officer announced. "Running it through the filters. Commodore Ram sends his compliments and looks forward to receiving his two guests."

Wu, who was shorter than both Tag and Wyss by a few centimeters, glanced up at the pilots. "I suppose you won't mind a brief shuttle ride back after all the cockpit time you've accumulated."

Tag shrugged. "What's another five minutes after six months of ops? But I'm glad we've got those —" He peered at the countdown timer to rendezvous. "Forty-three and a half minutes until I've got to be presentable. Comms, send to Commodore Ram my compliments to his compliments. We're eager to report."

"Understood, Major."

Tag winked at Wyss. "Got to go scrub down."

She rolled her eyes. "You might consider the pressure sprayers in the hangar."

It was funny enough, but as Tag left the bridge, he thought he heard Wu murmur, "Was that smell *him*?"

Speaking of smells. .. The hangar bay of *TSS Confiance* reeked of the same pungent combo of lubricants, ionized particle discharge, and human odors that Tag remembered. It smelled like home.

"There they are," Princess murmured.

A row of gleaming delta-winged starfighters sat beneath extended catwalks, where jumpsuited technicians clambered for better access to vital systems. Their scurrying mimicked the twin-horned mesa bison on Baedecker that he'd buzz in training fighters before his superiors had figured out he was causing undue stress on the local breeding population.

Tag was more impressed by the sleek appearances of the SSF-90 Sunsabers. He ran his hand across an extended wing as he and Princess passed. His pride swelled a tad. He'd helped to secure the contract from Pallas Industries, a Union of Planets corporation, for naval procurement after the Union had joined the Grand Alliance against the Naplians.

That had been his induction into the shadowy world of Terran Intelligence and the last time he'd been in the same room as Lira and their android friend, Dyston Ashteo.

His memories flashed back to their self-congratulatory dinner at an upscale restaurant on Kayna Two's moon. They shared food and drink and laughter—well, mostly he and Lira did. Dyson, being artificial, didn't partake.

They'd formed a bond of friendship amid calamity, one that had helped them stand against Briddarri corruption even when they knew it might mean altering the fortunes of war.

And in Lira's case, I was hoping for a lot more.

He snapped himself from his reverie in time to acknowledge salutes from the *Confiance* crew as a deck officer led him and Princess through the warren of corridors to the command section. His more advanced rank was still an odd adjustment. Sure, while he was out on patrol or skulking around hunting cybernetics labs, rank wasn't as big a deal, not when sequestered away with his fellow fighter jocks. They were more of a brotherhood—and sisterhood. A family.

Here, though, ratings and uniforms mattered again. Tag couldn't quite get used to the wide-eyed younger officers gazing at him with what he suspected was a bad case of hero worship.

Younger officers. Tag snorted. It had been seven years since the Naplians conquered Baedecker. Seven years since he'd had to fight them off his planet and lost that battle. Sometimes, it felt like decades.

But if that hadn't happened, he wouldn't have come to respect the man whose station he was approaching.

Commodore Sobban Ram's office was perched right behind the bridge. This, too, had the distinct feel of a place Tag hadn't seen in a long time and yet had never left. Gray and black. Newly refurbished plastics and metals. He got a whiff of cleaning solvent, but he was pretty sure the chairs hadn't changed position in months.

Ram sat behind the antique desk, its mahogany sheen so fresh Tag wondered if the commodore spent what little free time he had polishing it. Ram looked up as the trio entered the office, a smile on his face, though Tag thought he looked exhausted.

"Major Taggart Wester and Captain Naomi Wyss, reporting as ordered, sir." Tag thought his salute was damned sharp. He'd been practicing for weeks. What else was he going to do during downtime aboard a covert ops freighter in the backwater systems of the Great Desert Rift?

Besides daydream about Lira, that is.

"At ease." Ram plucked a withered leaf from one of the pots of violets lining half his desk surface. Tag noted the collection had expanded by two, bringing the set of purple flowers up to an even six. "Have a seat."

Tag plopped into one of the chairs and dragged a second nearer using his boot heel, the chair's magnetic fasteners dragging on the deck plates. That made for a nice footstool.

"By all means, make yourself at home." Ram seemed bemused even though he frowned at Tag's apparent ease.

"It's nice to take a load off now and then." Tag grinned and clasped his intertwined fingers behind his head. "You should try it."

Princess made a choking sound. She had remained standing nearby. "All due respect, Commodore, I'd prefer to remain standing. My posterior has spent enough time in a cockpit."

"I can imagine. You should both be commended for your diligence and the zeal with which you've pursued this unofficial assignment, you and your squadron." Ram rolled potting soil between his fingers.

"We're not the only ones who've been busy, by the looks of it," Tag said.

"I find their maintenance soothing." Ram brushed the dirt on his uniform trousers. "Hence the constant growth of my collection. My oldest son commands a flotilla squadron based at Van Sutton base and occasionally sends me new additions. His gifts remind me to put a premium on life in the face of death."

Tag's chair felt suddenly less comfortable. The rational part of his brain ran a tally of how many Briddarri he'd killed in his raids, plus Naplians, helpfully cataloged by his fighter's sensors. "Doesn't change the fact that any side of the fight is going to have casualties, Commodore. Are we going to wax philosophical or get to the debriefing?"

Princess cleared her throat. Tag looked over. She shook her head.

Ram frowned. If he was anything other than mildly bothered by Tag's abrupt shift in mood, he didn't show it. "A fair point. I find myself a bit too maudlin these days. I suspect giving up direct command of my ship is part of the issue, though it is satisfying to see the new captain hitting her stride after a year in the chair."

Tag craned his neck. The transparent bulkhead at the back of Ram's office gave him a sweeping view of Captain Allison Vollan circling the bridge like a lion on the prowl. Her pale complexion reflected myriad shades from *Confiance*'s command-and-control consoles as she kept a watchful eye on the bridge crew. Tag was just glad to have her attention focused on commanding a starship instead of on his performance evaluation. They'd never been mutual fans.

"So. The results to date." Ram tapped a desktop panel. The stars in the holographic tank at the center of his office flashed. Red Xs sparkled across the Great Desert Rift and the star systems in the adjacent regions. Each marked one of Virry Squadron's successful raids over the past couple of years.

Tag grunted. "I kind of forgot how many we'd hit."

"Fourteen in the span of twenty-six months," Ram said. "Ranging from a harvesting attempt that you foiled to a fully functional cybernetics conversion facility you destroyed. I know you have concerns, Major, but you have saved millions of lives by your interventions."

"At the cost of, what, a thousand?"

"Three thousand four hundred estimated dead." Ram offered the statistic with the same calm, precise demeanor he displayed when plucking leaves from his violets. "I could give you specifics on some of the higher-ranking individuals if you like."

Tag scowled. "You think that's funny?"

"On the contrary, Tag, I take no joy in knowing we are killing our allies." Ram held up a hand right as Tag opened his mouth to make another snarky rejoinder. "Yes, I am fully aware of the depraved nature of their experiments. The Truppen have made recordings from their own raids available for my review, via TI. The fact remains, the Terran Republic is a formal member of the Grand Alliance and is deeply indebted to the Briddarri Kingdom for coming to our defense at Baedecker years ago."

"Yeah, they were great." Tag crossed his arms. "They helped us lose."

"And they helped us erect a bulwark against the Naplians." Ram indicated the holographic display. The red blob enveloping most of the Great Desert Rift and big chunks of Terran space delineated Naplian conquests. "Otherwise, we would have lost much more territory than we have. This war has ground on, true, but we have managed to hold our own in conjunction with our allies."

"Sir, if I may," Princess interjected, "I believe Major Wester is concerned with the psychological toll of our operations on the pilots and crew. We support this cause but there has been grumbling with regards to the clandestine nature."

"Specifically?" Ram raised an eyebrow.

"Specifically, that we have to keep our traps shut and let the Briddarri plunk down a new facility every few months after we bomb one into rubble." Tag sat forward, his elbows resting on his knees. "Look, sir, I'm all in, but when you recruited me for this mess, we had the understanding that at some point, word would go public."

"I am sorry, Major, but that isn't possible. The government cannot afford to admit that. Not with our political leaders lining up to praise the Briddarri Kingdom. Grand Alliance funds flowing into the Republic from the Briddarri, the Audrians, and half a dozen other empires has made defense spending explode. The Liberty Ship program is a direct result of the Briddarri and Grand Alliance largesse."

"Bribery, plain and simple."

"That will be enough." Ram's tone solidified. Tag straightened. It was best to fly with weapons powered down when Ram warned him like that. "I understand your frustrations and I share them, to some extent, but be advised, my goal and that of TI is to win the war. We simply disagree with the Briddarri as to the right way to do so. Before you ask, yes, I still believe it is a crime of the foulest degree to strip the souls of innocent sentients—alien or not—and make them autonomous cannon fodder. Please keep that in mind when next you wish to vent your frustrations, however justified they may be."

Little Tag could offer to that. "Yes, sir."

"There is no need to pout, either." Ram managed a tight smile. "You will perhaps be pleased to know that I am pulling your squadron off its covert duties for a spell. There are more conventional targets available."

Princess smiled back, evidently glad to hear the news, but Tag had to put more effort into a happy expression. Ram was missing the point—Tag was fed up with *any* death, be it human, Briddarri, or hell, even Naplian. As much as he hated them for the conquest of his home world, Tag knew one-eyes had families and loved ones. It was solid fact.

What was wrong with him? Was he going soft? Saying that would be the quickest way to get permanently booted from the flight line.

"Your continued discretion is required, especially given the nature of this assignment." Ram manipulated the holo display. A star system perched on the edge of the Terran Republic's boundary with the Great Desert Rift magnified until it was a meter across. Eight planets and dozens of moons circled a pair of yellow stars. "Apophis-Quinn. Formerly home to scattered independent mining and agricultural settlements. The Naplians chased the colonists out and locked down the star system. TI tried for years to get assets near there and figure out why it seemed to be a black hole of information."

"Did they finally get lucky?" Tag gestured at the display. "Because that looks like it's crawling with one-eye ships, which doesn't seem right for a binary stuck way out of the major supply routes we've disrupted."

"You are correct in more ways than one. TI assets were able to move nearer in recent months, thanks to your raids shifting Briddarri forces, which in turn emboldened the Naplians to try new attacks behind the lines." Ram expanded the view again. A broad, flattened cylinder stretched across space at one of the gravitational Lagrange Points between Apophis-Quinn (AQ) Four and its moon.

Tag whistled. "A mobile shipyard."

"It is indeed. There are four battlecruiser keels laid down. A fifth is nearly ready to launch." Ram stood and walked around the far side of the display. "So, as you can see, the system is swarming with fighters and corvettes. The Naplians are treading a fine line by defending the system without diverting major fleet elements that would draw too much attention."

"Our job is to sink it?" Tag smirked. "Unless you just want pretty pictures before a flotilla batters it to pieces."

"*Confiance* and her group will join up with allied forces positioned on opposite sides of the system." Twin blue stars glowed. Ram leaned nearer the display until the cerulean light shone in his eyes. "I have every confidence our units will work well with our partners."

"Partners." Allied forces. A sickening feeling twisted Tag's stomach. "The Briddarri."

"Correct. Admiral Sett San Ergen is particularly keen on making a splash, so to speak, that will play well for the interstellar media. Terra could use a win, Major, as could the Alliance itself."

Tag rolled his eyes. "That figures. All right, Commodore, you'd better get us the briefing and saddle up so we can fly alongside the same people whose leaders are turning innocents into cybernetic slaves. Whatever it takes to win the war."

CHAPTER TWO

Apophis-Quinn System
AQ Three

J ust like that, Tag was back in the cockpit. He tightened his grasp on the flight controls as his Sunsaber dropped from ripwave. Blurred space around him solidified into a close-up, detailed view of the mobile shipyard he'd studied not just in Ram's initial briefing but in the subsequent prep runs made in simulated combat drills. A silver sheen coated the yard's hull. Purple lights flashed along its dorsal and ventral spine. Tag found it beautiful, in the otherworldly, menacing way he found Naplian naval architecture.

The five battlecruisers stripped away his wonder and replaced it with determination.

"Bronze Squadron, this is Bronze Lead." He kept his tone firm as he addressed his pilots via the intra-squadron comm. "All units report in."

"Bronze Two, standing by." Princess could have been reporting the solar radiation forecast.

The other ten pilots rattled off their status. Tag allowed a brief exhale. No losses, no malfunctions. A good start to their attack.

Even better that it was a full-on combat maneuver instead of a clandestine raid.

Bronze Squadron was one of six deployed by *TSS*

Confiance. Her sister ships, *TSS Honor, TSS Fiel,* and *TSS Venerate,* formed a diamond at the head of the battle group and pitched their own squadrons into the fray so that nearly three hundred fighters and bombers swarmed space ahead of and around the line warships. Twelve destroyers spread out in wings of three each, accelerating behind the fighters, but it was the 300-meter *Monsoon*-class heavy cruisers that packed the biggest punch.

Tag smiled. It was a battle group not dissimilar to the one that had been defending Baedecker when the Naplians had invaded years ago. Nice to see it put to a first strike use.

His smile faded when the Briddarri warships popped out of their jump on the opposite side of AQ Three.

He had to admit—the plan worked like a charm. The Naplian fighters and destroyers arrayed around the AQ System had already arrowed toward the Terran ships, alerted by the ripwave drives churning space during their approach. Eighteen destroyers, plus twelve fighter squadrons, dove for the intruders from vectors TI had helpfully supplied.

So, they were thrown off guard when the Briddarri task force under Admiral Ergen jumped from half a parsec away.

The battleship *Winter Scourge* was a mere million kilometers away from the shipyard, surrounded by a protective quartet of destroyers, plus five more battleships in the same formation. Suddenly, the number of Grand Alliance vessels crowding local space had doubled.

Naplian weapons opened up all around them.

"Keep the one-eyes off *Confiance* and the cruisers!" Tag snapped. "Two, keep my six pursuit free!"

"Confirmed, Lead," Princess said. "Halberd Squadron reports they are a go to commence their bombing run."

Tag pitched his Sunsaber into a spin. Man. He felt like he was flying through space in his skivvies—albeit ion-drive accelerated—after months in a Warhawk cockpit. The Terran Republic's mainstay could take a beating, sure, but a Sunsaber had it beat for speed, agility, and downright cussedness.

His targeting sensors didn't even complain when he bracketed a Naplian fighter and blew it apart with his hypervelocity railgun as it tried to intercept the Raider fighter-bombers of Halberd Squadron.

The Briddarri ships opened fire on the shipyard from a distance with long-range missiles, testing the defenses. Shields rippled under the impact. *Confiance* and her sisters lent their missiles to the barrage, sending four at a time from their combined thirty-six batteries. Space, for a couple million klicks in a sphere centered on the planet and its shipyard, was soon filled with moving targets. Tag's computer minimized the bulk of them and highlighted only the potential threats within a light-second radius.

"Lead, this is Four!" The high-pitched voice betrayed the pilot's nerves. Sandoval. Tag cut thrust and spun his Sunsaber around, maneuvering thrusters sending subtle rattles throughout the cockpit as they pivoted his vector. "I've got one dogging me!"

"Where's your wingman?" Tag banked to avoid collision with a Naplian fighter as the curved wings swept by him. *Any closer and we could have traded data scrolls.* "Princess, do you have Three on your scopes?"

"Negative. .. Correction, Lead. I have Three in pursuit of twin one-eye targets."

"Figures. Help me clear Four before he's stardust." Tag dropped in behind the fighter sticking tight to Four's blind spot. The Sunsaber's rear-firing laser picked off a missile the Naplian launched, then a second, but the Naplian's sickly green energy bursts were busy draining Four's shields at the same time.

"On your nine, Lead." True to her word, Princess's fighter swung "down" toward Tag's port-side wing and flew in perfect synchronicity. "Targets acquired."

"Ditto." Tag dropped the reticle on the Naplian fighter's blazing engine mounts. The weapons console sang with the harsh chime of a positive target lock. "Bronze Lead, Fox Two."

His missile streaked out toward the enemy starfighter. Princess added, "Bronze Two, Fox Two," a second later, and her weapon joined the strike.

The Naplian saw too late it had not just one but two hunters and found itself the prey instead of the predator. It banked starboard, but Tag's missile caught it on the port-side wing, and Princess's swept in from below. Twin impacts blossomed into searing white explosions as the Naplian's power plant went critical. Tag squinted at the miniature supernova as his Sunsaber's cockpit darkened against the glare.

His comm lit up, too. "Thanks, Lead. I thought I was gonna be atomized. Where the hell's Three?"

"Playing wannabe ace, Sandoval." Tag found Bronze Three beset not just by two Naplian fighters but being driven by them toward the anti-aircraft energy weapons of a one-eye destroyer. "Form up with us, and let's see if we can keep him from getting killed."

The trio swept between barrages a Terran destroyer was trading with its Naplian counterpart. Tag was impressed that Sandoval kept formation the entire way, even as particle blasts and tungsten projectiles turned their patch of local space into a moving minefield. Elsewhere, Bronze Squadron had kept together without getting into trouble—in fact, they were keeping Halberd Squadron free of attacks as the fighter-bombers dove toward the shipyard.

Tag grinned as fresh explosions blossomed across the curving hull. Missiles from *Confiance* and *Venerate* struck home, opening new gaps in the already reeling shields, at least as far as his fighter's sensor array could tell. Meanwhile, the ships' hypervelocity cannons lashed out at the Naplian destroyer squadrons while pulse particle turrets swatted down incoming enemy missiles. Their sister heavy cruisers led Terran destroyers into the fray, wave after wave of short and medium range torpedoes punching holes in the Naplian defenses.

Ram's tactical skill was on full display, though Tag would bet *Confiance*'s fistfight with nearby enemy vessels was Vollan's pugnacious leadership in action. They were the perfect combo, as far as he was concerned.

Bronze Four's abrupt cries echoed across the intra-squadron frequency. "Little help!" She sounded scared out of her wits.

Tag couldn't blame her. The one-eye fighters had done a great job harrying her until she was in range of those destroyer guns, and a new pair joined the fray, angling toward Tag, Princess, and Sandoval. "Two, you and Three cut thrust and let me burn ahead. Pick the newcomers off."

"Will do, Lead."

"Sir, that still leaves two fighters and an entire destroyer in your way," Sandoval pointed out."

"Thanks kid, I noticed." Tag pushed the engines to their maximum acceleration while spooling up the ripwave generator.

"Yes, Three, the major is quite astute." There was a playful edge to Princess's voice. "Surprising when you realize how restrained and responsible he can be."

Tag chuckled. Sure, he'd learned lessons about leadership in the past seven years. He figured that was the best way to keep his people alive. Taking crazy risks could get other members of his squadron killed, which Four had almost let happen to Sandoval.

Sometimes, you need a little crazy to throw the enemy completely on his ass.

Tag overrode the flashing alarm that demanded he *not* engage ripwave this close to not just a planet and an artificial habitat but a smaller-sized capital ship. *Probably not my best idea.*

He punched the engage switch.

The Sunsaber leapt ahead as the ripwave generator expanded space-time ahead of his fighter and contracted behind it, the squashed sphere on his tactical display the only visible evidence of the maneuver. Everything in front of him leapt in his face with frightening speed, but since he'd programmed the system to run for less than half a second, his fighter closed the gap with Bronze Four's attackers in the snap of his fingers.

The destroyer's hull and its broad, curved jump

sail loomed outside his cockpit. A tenth of light-speed for even a short amount of time could mean his death if his trajectory was even slightly miscalculated. Scrape had taught him the trick for nailing down the nav comp's most precise calculation.

Just like you, he mused. *Still saving my neck after you broke yours.*

Tag's targeting sensors yelped at the sudden proximity of targets. He'd planned for that and was pleased when he found a one-eye fighter square in his sights. The railgun's internal magnets flung diamond-coated tungsten bullets at hypervelocity, a miniature version of the *Monsoon*-class heavy cruisers' HV cannons, but just as deadly.

The first Naplian fighter vaporized in a spray of super-heated particles. The wingman flipped and burned in a new vector for a better angle of attack.

Tag was insulted. Who did this guy think he was, pulling one of Tag's favorite stunts?

He'd launched the missile at his attacker's cockpit the moment after his first kill in the brief ripwave strike.

Tag flew through the fireball and came alongside Four's Sunsaber. The sleek fuselage was streaked with carbon scoring from near misses, and even without his sensor readout, Tag could see where the shields flickered near failure.

"Lead, this is Four! I can't believe—"

"Shut it and listen," Tag snapped. "Roll on my mark and drop your last missile. It's our best shot at getting out of here in one piece."

He wasn't exaggerating. The destroyer bracketed them with crossfire from its particle cannons that Tag knew would obliterate them as easily as he could swat gnats.

"Understood, sir. Ready to roll."

"Stand by. .." Tag watched the meters dwindle between their fighters and the shimmering interference from the shield boundary. "Mark!"

Bronze Four flipped. The bulky missile pushed away from the underside of the fuselage as mounting magnets released.

"Punch it!" Tag ordered. He fired another of his missiles.

The two raced off, putting the conventional ion engines above redline to get as far from the destroyer as they could. Tag's missile exploded near Four's and their mutual annihilation not only battered the destroyer's shields but wiped out Tag's sensor readings for critical seconds.

It created a blind spot on the enemy readouts, too. The distraction was enough for them to get clear. Tag led them around toward the rest of Bronze Squadron. Halberd, he noted, was dropping 230-kilogram Keach bombs on the shipyard. Each Raider banked at a 90-degree angle that sent the bombs hurtling into the shield envelope, propelled by magnets and powered by single-burst thrusters. Red-white explosions shattered the forward hull of the closest battlecruiser hulk under construction.

"Wow," Four breathed. "You have to love how they can pound anything that gets in their way!"

"Let's focus less on sight-seeing and more on getting you back to your wingman, Lieutenant," Tag warned. "Because you're still getting written up even if we pull off this attack."

"Hey, Tag, listen, I—"

"You listen, Evie. I've had enough of pulling your ass out of the stellar corona. Form up and shut up." Tag switched comms. "Two, this is Lead. We're good."

"I saw, Lead, and we're all pleased you managed to stick your boot in that giant single eye on your way out," Princess said. "The commodore sends his best and asks we switch targets to chase off another Naplian fighter squadron that's harassing our heavy cruisers."

Tag gave the stink-eye to the Briddarri warships on the nav display. "Guess the greenbloods aren't going to bother, though I'll give them credit for chewing up the other end of the shipyard. Let's keep an eye on my wayward cousin so she doesn't try to get Sandoval killed anymore."

"Confirmed, Lead. Two out."

Tag sighed and accelerated back into the fight. Forget Briddarri secret labs and Naplian military targets. His biggest challenge was how to keep Second Lieutenant Evelyn Wester from driving him crazy.

✻ ✻ ✻

Admiral Sett San Ergen wished his giant stature made him feel more confident than he was as he glowered over the battle assessment data trickling across *Winter Scourge*'s monitors. He wanted to feel like he appeared. At two meters tall, he was the biggest Briddarri on the ship, if not the entire Ninth Stellar Fleet.

But *farrkasa* if these damned humans weren't making him second guess himself week after week.

There was no denying the effectiveness of their

strike. The Naplian defenders were routed or destroyed. The shipyard was a splintered wreck. Chunks fell through AQ Three's atmosphere, leaving blazing streaks across the pristine atmosphere. Ergen should be thrilled this attack had been such a success.

Instead, he found himself eyeing the human forces with as much suspicion as he did the one-eye fleet.

"Problem, Admiral?" Commander Ortan Olt Burrak had a knack for blending himself into the ordered chaos of Ergen's bridge. The man from the Espionage Directorate's (ED) Forecasting wore a navy commander's uniform but was more of a spy than anyone aboard.

"The same one as before, Commander." Ergen beckoned him nearer his console. The buzz of activity made it possible for him to lower his voice so they could converse in relative privacy. "You saw who was leading the Terran charge."

"*Confiance* and her escorts." Burrak nodded, his expression grim. If it weren't for those ridiculous civilian-style streaks cut in his hair, Ergen would poach the man from Espionage for his personal command staff. Ergen couldn't abide anything other than military spit and polish.

"Funny how intel on her has been so sporadic. I couldn't tell you whether she'd been blown to atoms by a lucky one-eye patrol or stashed away in a repair dock for the past few months." Ergen gestured at the main tactical display in the semi-circle of bridge stations. "Lo and behold, here she is, ready to throw down with the Naplians like she's never left her standard patrols."

"Commodore Ram enjoys considerable leeway in

the Terran command structure, owing to his heroics at the Baedecker invasion and his successful raids across the Rift." Burrak's mouth twitched. "Not unlike your own operational independence."

"Keep stating the obvious, and I'll ask your bosses if you're really worth your pay," Ergen grumbled. "I don't care two kilos about what her kill count has been. I want to know why she keeps going dark, and you've been giving me nothing but shrugs."

"It hasn't been an easy puzzle to crack." Burrak leaned nearer Ergen's console. "Our spies within Terran Intelligence keep running into blockades. I've had five sources unceremoniously dumped into dead-end duties far from the best intelligence-gathering fronts over the past year. Whatever TI is using her for, they're keeping it locked down."

"Any chance she's linked to our current problem?" Ergen didn't even want to mention it, but the flak he was catching from his superiors was proving troublesome. How was he supposed to coordinate the battle plans along this front with the Naplian Empire and run a top-secret cybernetics weaponry program if his labs kept getting blasted to fine powder?

"Entirely. You've seen my report." Burrak counted off facts on his green fingers. "What little data we've recovered from the raids indicates a mix of worn-out Terran fighters, unmarked, untraceable. Possibly pirates. They run with codes and callsigns that point to Briddarri and Audrian terms, among others. Their hit-and-fade actions are reminiscent of the tactics the Terrans—and our fleet units—have employed against the Naplian incursion. Then there are the strange tactical moves—*Confiance* and other heavy cruisers disappearing for weeks, only to show up like this for an allied strike."

"That's what I mean. I think she's either fielding these fighters, or she's protecting whoever is. I wouldn't put it past the Terrans to hire local mercenaries to do their dirty work." Ergen pulled at his thick moustache. *Careful. You'll yank it free and then the crew would never take you seriously again. Got to maintain what facial hair you've got left at this age.*

"There is another option."

"Say it, Burrak."

"These are Terran-trained pilots, either 'retired' from service as Taggart Wester was during the Union of Planets operation three years ago, or 'volunteers' who've struck out on their own with tacit support from individual flag officers." Burrak frowned. "Slimmer chance: On-roster pilots and personnel assigned to a black flag operation sanctioned by TI."

Ergen grunted. "Ballsy even for humans."

"Yes, sir, I'd say that's an accurate summary."

"Well, you're the man on the ground when it comes to these labs. What's your gut tell you?"

"I rely on data, not gut, Admiral. Data and interrogation."

Ergen waved his hand. "Bytes will only get you so far, Commander. You've got to trust your instincts if you're going to make great strides as a warrior for the kingdom. If I'd ignored my gut and stuck with the cold hard facts, we never would have started this pet project of ours."

"Fair point. The data, though, from the results have supported that gut decision." Burrak smirked.

"I'll give you that one." Ergen returned his

attention to the tactical display. The Terran ships put the finishing touches on demolishing the Naplian shipyard. The AQ star system would be no use to the one-eyes for a long time, which left the Grand Alliance free to pursue other operations.

Speaking of which. . .

"Admiral?" The comms officer swiveled in his chair. "All fighter wings reporting in—they're secure in their hangars. Fleet units polling. They're ready to jump at your signal."

"Good. Send word to their commanders—the halls of Barra Bridd are roaring their approval of this victory, and there'll be an extra ration of *errdda eptar* ale for every man aboard."

Cheers echoed around the bridge. The comms officer had the galaxy's biggest grin as he relayed the message. Ergen straightened in his chair. That was the way to do it. Stoke their pride. Keep their loyalty. It was the only way the Briddarri would triumph in this hellish war.

Well, one of the ways. He would not let go of his dream of Briddarri truppen. They were close. Ergen could tell. Burrak had that much right when he talked about data.

If he could only find where that traitor Elden Selva had gone, taking his infernal Truppen on their damned crusade, he'd feel a lot better when he searched for a new laboratory site. He could tell they were lurking in the depths of space, nightmarish phantoms waiting to eviscerate whatever plans Ergen could concoct to continue the harvest necessary to build a cybernetic super-army.

But then there were the humans. Ergen knew the

humans would never get up. They were too blasted stubborn.

Fine, then. He'd have to come up with a new target for their fury.

"Admiral, if I may. .." Burrak handed him a scroll.

"What's this?"

"A possible solution for your Terran dilemma. Forecasting gives it a 58 percent chance of success if we can pull the right threads."

Ergen glimpsed the coordinates at the top of the classified report. His eyes widened as the device scanned his retinas, approving him for temporary access. A timer started, letting him know he only had a few minutes before the data on the scroll wiped itself. "Well, now," he muttered. "That's a hell of a plan. Never known the humans to pass up a chance at a righteous liberation."

CHAPTER THREE

Delta Yannick System
Eleftheria

Sunshine gleamed off the shuttle's curved flanks. Tag closed his eyes and let the warmth bake his face. How long had it been since he'd stood planetside? He didn't even mind the cold breeze whipping through the rugged forest around him. It smelled like pine sap and damp earth.

It smelled nothing like Baedecker, but he supposed, eventually, he'd get used to a new home.

Tag chuckled to himself. Who was he kidding? Eleftheria was not his home. *Confiance* was. *Confiance* and *Aox.*

This, though, was as close as he figured as he would ever get.

"I don't think I've ever seen so many trees in one place." Evelyn Wester trotted down the landing ramp. She readjusted the strap of her duffel bag on her shoulder. "But Alta Plano was a whole lot of desert with a whole lot of plateaus, and they don't exactly pack battle cruisers full of pines, you know?"

Tag glanced at her as they walked. The top of Evie's head barely reached his shoulder. He found himself lengthening his stride to keep up with her, though. She took the stone path that led away from the dirt landing pad through the forest with the same speed he'd seen her head for the flight line. She had the Wester drive that was for sure, and she had a mix of the looks—green eyes from Father's side of the family and the freckles, too, but dark brown hair that was almost black from Mother's. She also had that grin, the one Tag thought of as belonging to a saarno fox fresh off a successful scavenge.

He gave her as stern a look as he could muster until the grin slackened.

"Come on, Tag," she said. "You're not still pissed, are you?"

"What you do think, Lieutenant?"

"Don't call me that, *Major*. We're on leave. Family vacation. Seeing the sights, enjoying the food..." Evie patted her stomach. "I can't *wait* for the stifado and the gyros."

"I won't argue with you on that. The first point, though—you have to check yourself. Check your impulse to haul off and punch every one-eye in its one eye. This is a team effort. We're a squadron."

"Right, I get that. I get that you've got to be tougher on me because I'm a Wester—"

"No. Wrong." Tag shook his head. "I'm tough on you because that's what I needed my commanding officers to be to me, to shake the selfishness out before I got anyone else killed. You need the same thing, understand?"

"I get it. I do."

"Next time, 'Yes, sir' would be a lot better."

"Yes, sir."

Tag smirked. She'd kept most of the attitude out of her voice. Most. Tag really couldn't blame her. He'd been as hellbent on breaking rules and flying straight for the sun not that long ago. At least, it felt not that long ago.

They emerged from the line of trees into a residential neighborhood that bore all the hallmarks of a brand-spanking new settlement—prefabricated domes, repurposed cargo containers, and portable hydroponics rigs. They sported worn-down edges, though, because they'd been moved into place years ago and had stabilizing brackets fitted to their foundations.

Three transparent domes, their surfaces distorted by the honeycombed segments that let sunlight filter in, contained the nearest homestead. Tag found nothing remarkable about the two-story, prebuilt habitats except that they were linked by garden corridors and had been repainted pale blue. It looked like half the hexagonal windows that made up the domes had been left open to allow fresh air to blow through.

It was the man striding toward them between the artfully arranged boulders lining the path who caught his attention.

"Taggart! You made it." Antiny Wester, former governor of Baedecker Four, held his arms wide. "By the stars, I've missed you."

Tag dropped his duffel bag and embraced him. "Good to see you again, Father."

Father chuckled. He'd maintained the slimmer figure acquired after a mandatory stay in a Naplian prison camp during the Baedecker invasion. He was fit and lean. Whatever work Father was doing on Eleftheria was more conducive to keeping the weight off than his sedentary lifestyle as governor had allowed.

But it was more the change in his age that surprised Tag. The little hair he had remaining had gone gray, with streaks of white, not a trace of auburn left. He'd added a beard and moustache, but those, too, were gray and white. His face was more deeply lined, weathered by the past few years.

"And Evie." Father lifted her into a hug that brought her off her feet, if only for a moment. "I'm glad you were able to make it."

"Hey, Uncle Antiny." Evie kissed him on the cheek. "Your new place isn't quite the mansion, but it's cute, I think."

"Cute was not what I was going for. Tim and Marney insisted on the paint." Father gestured at the dome-enclosed structure. "I would have been happy to maintain the same basic accommodations as everyone else in the valley."

Tag peered beyond Father's shoulder. Hundreds of domed enclosures spread down into the valley beyond. Dozens more climbed the hillsides lining the edges. Snowcapped mountains hemmed the landscape, forming the sides of an elongated bowl that added a physical sense of security.

Father's belt beeped. He checked a tiny display mounted on his comm. "Ah. Looks like your landing was well timed. We have a westerly storm coming down. Let's get inside before we find ourselves standing in a half-meter of snow."

Tag had wondered about the lack of vegetation besides lichen, scattered stubby grasses, and the thick-trunked pine trees. Dark clouds swirled above the western peaks. He picked up his bag and followed Father and Evie through the threshold of the first dome. Father tapped a control on the panel nearest the door. The hexagonal windows squeezed shut. A series of muffled *clanks* resounded.

"There we are. Locked down and snug." Father shrugged out of his leather jacket and hung it on a coat rack. "Can I get you anything to eat or drink?

"Not for me," Tag said. He led the duffel bag drop onto the benches located just inside the hatch. "But I'll bet Evie would love a sandwich or two if you've got them stocked."

"I'm sure there's stifado—"

Evie clapped her hands. "Lead the way!"

Father laughed. "Only after you have settled in with the rest of the guests. Come along."

This first domed building served as the vestibule, with Father's den, a small library, and his living quarters arrayed around the perimeter. Tag wondered if he'd expanded the upstairs hydroponics rigs.

They walked into the second dome, which opened into an expansive kitchen. A corridor beyond led into the third dome, where Tag knew the guest bedrooms and a rec room were located.

But he forgot all about asking Father who he'd gotten to expand the homestead when Marney almost tackled him with a hug.

"Tag! Oh, I've missed you so much." Marney kissed him on the cheek and pulled back from their embrace. She smiled at him, her eyes looking even bluer underneath the bold lighting that warmed the kitchen and dining room. Marney had cut and styled her auburn hair shorter so it barely reached her shoulders.

"Hey, Sis." Tag grinned. "I've missed you, too. Looks like dialing back on the freedom fighter thing hasn't stuck you in an office too much. I'll bet your freckles have tripled."

"I spend a lot of time on scouting trips. Not as many as I had in the past." She poked Father in the side. "And a lot fewer of them are smuggling runs."

"Which is how we keep you safe, if you'll remember." Father's tone stiffened, but he didn't lose his ebullient mood. "Now, drinks? Taggart, there's a bottle of Crown and Scepter in the top cabinet."

"I saw it. Thanks for offering before I had to climb up." Tag retrieved the bottle while Father rummaged for glasses. "Everybody want one? I think this reunion calls for a toast."

"Not me." Marney blushed. "I can't."

"What? Why?" Tag chuckled. "Father, are you turning your daughter into a teetotaler *and* taking away her rebel streak?"

"That's only gonna leave me as the troublemaker." Evie accepted a glass from Tag.

"No, I just *can't*." Marney's expression turned more sheepish, though Tag couldn't figure out how, and when she rested her hand on her stomach. ..

His eyes went wide. He had to stop mid-pour before he put about a liter into a glass not designed to hold that much. "You're pregnant?"

"Two months in."

"Wow. Oh, wow." Tag gave her another hug but tried to avoid bumping into her belly. "That's—stars, Father, I'm going to be an uncle?"

"Correct, and I'll hear no jibes about your old man becoming an even older grandfather." Father took over the pouring duties and gave Tag a glass.

"You look the part." Tag clinked glasses and went

to sip. He stopped before the liquid could touch his lips. Then he sniffed. It smelled less sweet. There was a heavier floral aroma. "Did something happen to this batch?"

Evie took a drink. "Nothing wrong by my taste."

"It's the first batch Crown and Scepter produced locally," Father explained. "Sadly, it doesn't have the same flavor to it as what you're used to, but, well, nothing will again. It's not. .."

He frowned as if trying to find the word.

"Baedecker," Evie said.

"Yes, thank you," Father murmured.

Tag glanced at Marney. She shrugged, her smile fading. He hadn't spoken with her or Father for a while, except via messages they sent each other over the vast distances. He hadn't known of Father's reticence to even speak the name of their former homeworld.

Can you blame him? The man ruled an entire planet, and the one-eyes stripped that away from him. I'd have spiraled far worse than he did if the same thing had happened to me. "Marney, this is great news. Boy or girl?"

"Boys."

"Twins!" Tag laughed. He took a drink of the rum. Father was right. It wasn't the same, but then again, was anything? The flavor was pretty good. If he were missing the old stuff, he was sure Father maintained a stash somewhere on the premises. "That's great. I can't believe it. How's Tim feeling? His ego's got to be the size of a heavy cruiser."

"He's so proud I have to remind him to quit bothering his subordinates for name suggestions." Marney giggled. "I can hardly believe it myself."

"Was it—I mean, did you. .." Tag rolled his hands.

"On purpose?"

Evie snorted into her drink.

"Very eloquent, Taggart." Father sounded bemused.

Heat rose to Tag's cheeks. "Hey, I wasn't trying to sound invasive, but with the war going on, I was wondering—"

"If my pregnancy was intentional?" Marney seemed to find his embarrassment even funnier than Evie and Father did. "Yes, Tag. We'd talked about the possibility a couple of years ago—well, no. Longer ago than that. It came up after Tim finished the mission you and he collaborated on."

Ah. The Union gambit. Tag nodded but said nothing else. Evie was the only one in the room not read in on the top-secret aspects of the operation. Tim was, being attached to Terran Intelligence, and Father, too, by virtue of his expansive networks of contacts he'd cultivated during his political career and earlier by way of his military connections during the Second Consular War.

Marney's mention brought Lira and Dyson back into his memories. Tag wished he could share this happy time with them. It wasn't the first time he'd fantasized about introducing Lira to Father and Marney.

"Anyway, it made sense to us, war or no war." Marney gestured at the home around them. "This is what spurred us, Tag—this and the work I was doing helping war refugees. People are starting their lives over after losing everything. They're not letting the war's devastation keep them from continuing to create, to build, and to love. Tim pointed out that we weren't taking my own advice. I pointed out that was hard to do when we're both running around the galaxy fighting the Naplians, each in our own way. So, he's been granted temporary reassignment from his gunboat command and I've started coordinating my work from Eleftheria."

"How about that?" Tag downed the rest of his rum. He wished the buzz would kick in faster so he could stop dwelling on his own past. "Father, has it been working out with a TI officer and a refugee manager turning your house into the nexus of the galaxy?"

Father nodded. "I'd say it's been working quite well. Of course, my role has been delegated to, ah, manager of information sources for Marney."

"Father's quite handy with his long list of rich and powerful people inside and outside Terran space," Marney said. "I wouldn't have half the resources I needed if it weren't for him."

"Welp, sounds like everybody's been super busy." Evie was in the wall cooler, rummaging about with a plate of cold meats and cheeses. "Sorry, Uncle Antiny, I couldn't wait for the stifado. This should do."

"Help yourself," Father said. "By the way, since you mentioned being busy, I am glad to hear that your efforts at cleaning up misguided experiments have gone well."

Evie stopped mid-chew.

It was Tag's turn to be amused and Evie's to be uncomfortable. "Don't sweat it, Lieutenant. These two are in on our extracurricular assignments."

"Oh, good." Evie sighed. "Because I wasn't sure how to lie to Uncle Antiny about it, and I didn't want him to find out if I did."

"Father's got the ear of the brass who don't like what the Briddarri have been up to." Tag leaned against a long counter. "I spoke to him back in eighty-one when we were trying to figure out how to approach this whole mess. Commodore Ram, Tim, and I gathered up what we needed in terms of tech, equipment—"

"Like secondhand starfighters," Evie murmured.

"Bingo." Tag glanced at Marney. "And your cousin here had the intel we needed from on-the-ground sources close to the Briddarri about the specifics of their experiments. She's got a source that had already taken the first steps at wrecking them."

Evie's widened. "The Truppen?" she whispered. "I thought they were RUMINT—you know, cooked up by the brass as a morale booster."

"But you've seen the footage from Baedecker, haven't you?" Marney asked. "And the news reports from elsewhere across the war theater."

"Yeah, well. .." Evie scratched at the back of her neck. "I mean, I thought it was a PR stunt."

"Makes sense, but no, they're real, and yes, they're on our side." Tag rattled the ice around in his now-empty glass. "They've gotten into more places than we've managed to find."

"How many more are there?"

"Too many," Father said, his tone stern. "Far too many. I, more than anyone else, want the Naplians pushed back beyond our borders and, preferably, out of this corner of the Estra galaxy altogether, but we will not wage a war using barbaric means. Too many Briddarri officials have the ear of our leaders. It's taken all my effort and considerable remnants of my wealth to steer the conversation from cybernetic soldiers, but the Truppen are a two-edged sword. They are damned effective, and yet, they frighten people."

Their group lapsed into silence. It was only then Tag realized the wind was racing through the valley. Rain pounded on the domes, and as he watched, it turned to a thick, heavy snowfall. Blizzard conditions enveloped the area so much that he couldn't see beyond the boulders of Father's property. A display panel mounted on the dining room wall showed multi-colored doppler scans of the storm as it raged across half the continent at speeds that made Tag's mouth dry.

"Well, I didn't mean to shut our conversation down with such a gloomy note." Father sounded apologetic. "Evie, would you like the tour? I'm sorry, but we'll have to leave the guest house for last."

"Sure thing, Uncle Antiny." Evie lifted her plate. "Mind if I snack and walk?"

"Not at all. We'll program the housebots to follow in our wake." Father gave Marney a look that Tag couldn't decipher, but given Marney's response was a subtle nod, it must have been pre-planned or something they'd done in the past. "Excuse us."

They left the kitchen, Father's narration of how he'd come about this planet and property fading the farther they walked. Tag cocked his head to one side. "You two would make terrible spies, Sis."

"I know, but Evie can't be part of what we're discussing." Marney indicated he should follow her.

They left the kitchen for the garden corridor connection from the second house to the guest quarters. "How do you figure? She's on my squadron and, by virtue of that, has already seen more clandestine action than pretty much anyone else in the quadrant. It's not like she's a complete rookie."

"Yes, I know, but this phase. .." Marney sighed.

"It's much more complex than what we've done so far."

"Sure. I've had enough practice keeping my mouth shut." Tag frowned. "Except I seem to spend more of my time yelling at her than anything else."

"Is she too unruly for you to manage?" Marney smiled at him.

Tag gave her a good natured elbowing. "Ha, ha. You and Father must think it's hysterical, me having to ride herd on a cocky fighter pilot."

"He might. I'm just proud of you. You know he is, too."

"Thanks." Tag brushed his knuckles along the blaze irises. Iridescent streaks sparkled where he touched the petals. The snow outside slackened, allowing a brighter sky than when the storm had first rolled in, but showed no signs of stopping.

"What else is on your mind?" Marney stopped by a pair of benches outside the door that led into the guest house.

"Me?" Tag shrugged. "Fighter maintenance. The next raid. The next combat op. Take your pick."

"That isn't what I meant. Maybe I should have asked, is she still on your mind?"

"Subtle, Sis." Tag looked at her. "Of course she is. I told you how much she means to me."

"And you mean to her. .."

Tag chuckled. "The same, I think. It's not like we've been bouncing signals back and forth. Her work for a criminal organization doesn't leave a lot of time for pen pals, especially ones in the Terran armed forces."

"Tag, she's not a pen pal." Marney touched her hand. "Take it from a married woman and someone who's been in love more than once. I read what you felt for her and how you two risked your lives for each other. This is something deeper that goes far beyond infatuation. You need to hold out hope that you'll be with each other."

Tag wanted to believe Marney but had a hard time reconciling everything he'd been through with her words, no matter how well she meant them. "I'm not much for hope these days. There's not much out there that gives it to me. The Naplians overrun everything, no matter where we push back. Our allies? Damn, Marney, they're as bad as our enemies. It's a long, grinding slog, and I'm sick of it."

She held onto his hand. She didn't offer reassurance and didn't critique his fears.

"I got a signal yesterday." He should have told someone else but hadn't been able to bring himself to mention it. "Colonel Chok—you remember Mongoose from our Baedecker escape. The man taught me everything I needed for command, whether I agreed with him or not, and you'd better believe it was mostly not. He got shot down in a skirmish between battlegroups off the Traxan Nebula. Nothing left of him or his fighter. It's like he never existed. I've been seeing that explosion over and over for the past twenty-four hours, so it's hard for me to dream about anything else."

Tag looked at her. "Lira's got her people, and I've got mine. Neither one of us is in a safe line of work. Is it even worth the risk? The Briddarri could lock her up at any second if they find her, and the Naplians could blast me out of space tomorrow."

It was the question he'd been wrestling with for a full day, and probably longer if he was honest with himself. Tag didn't expect an answer. Maybe he didn't want one.

Marney slid his hand to her stomach and let his palm rest there. "Yes. It is worth it."

Tag couldn't feel the babies moving, but it didn't matter. He knew what she meant. Leave it to Marney to give him the emotional slap he needed to get himself back on course. She and Tim had faced so many obstacles. What had they done about them? Others might have built separate lives or, in the extreme, ended their marriage. Not his sister. She and her husband flew side by side, inseparable wingmen.

Maybe I could pull that off someday.

Marney smiled at him. "Tell you what: Tim and I can talk you through this if you need to hear more, but for now, let me share our other surprise with you."

"You've got one bigger than twins?" Tag raised an eyebrow as they stood. She let the door panel scan her face.

Scan her face? Tag frowned. Since when did Father need that tight of security on one of the houses while the rest were wide open?

The door chimed and then slid apart.

Tag found a fully equipped war room in what should have been a living space, complete with a trio of tactical holographic displays and, hunched over them, a trio of officers.

Two were admirals.

CHAPTER FOUR

T ag's reflexes kicked in. He straightened to attention and saluted.

"He's made it." Commander Timothy Ess returned the salute but broke protocol by slapping his brother-in-law on the back. "Good to see you alive and kicking, Tag."

"Likewise, Tim." Tag shook hands with him. "And from what I've just been told, congratulations are in order."

"Thanks. Too bad you missed the cigars. We found some left over from General Wood's stash that he gifted to Antiny during the withdrawal."

Tag summoned the memory of the jubilant but perfunctory celebration in a crowded wardroom, cigar smoke wafting on the ventilation currents as they marked their successful rescue of a million and a half Baedecker citizens. *Marney would say the proper term is 'refugees' now.*

He put the recollection aside as the other two officers in the room took full notice of him. The taller of the two was a dark-skinned man with close-cropped hair that was shock white. Hazel eyes pinned Tag in place like targeting scanners finding their next victim, though the bemused smile hinted that Tag's presence was welcome, if not expected. The woman across the tactical display gave him a cursory glance before returning to whatever was more important on her readout. The screen's blue glow threw her Asian features into sharp relief.

"Admirals, this is Major Taggart Wester of VFA-Seventy-Seven, Thirteenth Expeditionary Force, based aboard TSS *Confiance* under Commodore Ram."

"Seventy-Seven? That makes you Bronze Squadron." The tall admiral nodded at Tag. "At ease, son."

Tag loosened but kept a wary watch on the female officer behind him. "Thank you, sir."

"Admiral Thomas Sinclair. Fourth Sector Fleet."

Tag tried not to gawk. He didn't want to look like a buzzcut cadet fresh out of flight school when standing in front of one of the most powerful officers in the republic. "Sorry, sir, I thought you were on the southern front toward Rutak space these days."

"Never trust two things in the fleet comms, Major: outdated news or fresh RUMINT." Sinclair chuckled. "I've detached my flagship, TSS *Manitoba*, and the Eighteenth Expeditionary Force for something other than the run-of-the-mill one-eye stomping. That's the focus of our garden party. I'm glad to see your old man roped you in. Afternoon, Marney."

"Admiral." Marney joined them around the tactical display as if they were back at the Wester compound near Vossburg, and she was helping Father host colonial delegates. "Is everything set up to your liking?"

"More than adequate, Marney." Sinclair gestured across the holographic field of stars. "Major, this is my XO, Vice Admiral Setsu Tanaka."

"Ma'am." Tag saluted again, just for good measure.

"As you were." Tanaka tapped the control panel adjacent to her display. Tag saw a holographic representation of his grinning face framed by lines of text. "Your work has been exemplary, if unorthodox. I see your trajectory has shifted from reprimands to commendations, Major, the latter finally outweighing the former."

"Yes, ma'am." Her presence sucked all the fun out of the room—or at least out of Tag. He couldn't think of a single quip that would lighten the mood.

Fortunately, Tim cleared his throat and said, in a tone of mock seriousness, "Don't worry, Admiral. If they run out of commendations for our ace pilot, I'm sure we can dig up reprimands for *something*."

Sinclair let out a booming laugh. Marney tried to hide her grin by ducking behind the planetary system coalescing in holographic form.

"Is everyone gathered?" Father smiled as he walked in from the garden corridor. "Ah, good. Tim, you've made the introductions?"

"I have. I was waiting on Admiral Sinclair to get us started." Tim glanced at Tag, though, as if waiting for a reaction.

Tag watched Father seal the hatch. "What's Evie up to? Cleaning out your consumables?"

"She's catching up with her friends, and yes, she's making a determined effort to sample all the cuisine we have to offer on Eleftheria." Father shrugged. "I did tell her we were having a classified meeting."

"Great." Tag shook his head. "She won't bother me about that on patrol at all, will she?"

Tanaka tapped a stylus on her console. "If we could begin. .."

"Absolutely." Sinclair clasped his hands behind his back. "Major—mind if I call you Tag?"

"Not at all, sir."

"Good deal. You can call me Thomas if you like."

Tag found the concept more terrifying than diving on a Naplian battlecruiser without a wingman. "I'd better stick with 'Admiral,' Admiral."

"You mean to tell me you haven't taken to calling ol' Sobban by his first name?" Sinclair grinned.

"I think if I did, sir, Captain Vollan would find new and creative ways for me to practice polishing *Confiance*'s deck plates."

"That's a fair assessment of them both." Sinclair nodded toward the display. "Are we ready Marney?"

"One second. .. There we are. I've uploaded Tim's packet with the latest TI assessment."

Assessment? Tag finally noticed what they were gathered around. He'd been expecting a stellar map of the Great Desert Rift or maybe the Terran front lines where the Naplian invasion had pushed back the Republic's former borders.

Instead, he gazed at a small sector he knew by heart, especially the binary star system glowing at the center.

Baedecker.

There they were, the orange-yellow star and its dinky crimson companion. He'd grown up under their glare and watched their feeble light fade as the allied rescue fleet jumped away for the last time. Shining white tracks marked familiar orbits—the dark pitted surface of Baedecker Two and its lump of a moon; the homeworld of Baedecker Four, rendered as a blue and brown orb swaddled in whisps of white cloud, its dusty red moon trailing behind; even the icy desert world of Baedecker Six spun slowly, a drab tan marble in far orbit. White specks marked the cometary debris field. Whoever had done the scans had even included run-down Garrick Station in the Baedecker Five orbital slot, along with the planetary debris scattered around the lopsided ring's path.

"Nice holo." Tag had to force the words to sound nonchalant. His throat was dry and he had the overpowering urge to hug his home planet. How crazy was that? "What's the occasion?"

"The occasion, son, is that the one-eyes have gotten sloppy, and it's in part thanks to you." Sinclair lifted his chin. "Tetsu?"

Tanaka swiped her stylus across her screen. Red pinpoints spread throughout the system. Their growth reminded Tag of dune flea infestations the service bots scoured from the family compound when they threatened the bole tree bark.

"Commander Ess and TI have compiled this detailed assessment after months of analysis, using everything from disguised spy probes to neutral merchants they spent a ton of credits bribing," Sinclair continued. "What you're seeing is the most accurate rendering of Naplian units in and around the Baedecker System, updated from three days ago."

Tag whistled. "They sure didn't move out when we evacuated, did they?"

"Quite the contrary." Tanaka walked the hologram's perimeter, her voice soft and pitched as if she were delivering an academy lecture. "Our count is one hundred and ten vessels, forty of which are mining complexes and ore haulers."

"For the serjaum."

"They've kept a steady production pace for seven years." Tim frowned. "There wasn't much we could do about it at first, not with our fleets on constant defense, except where we were able to interdict the main Naplian supply corridor through the Rift."

"That's still a lot of ships in one place." Tag rubbed his chin as he perused the data streaming in the hologram. "A raid's going to be messy, especially given how they've reinforced the system."

"We're not planning a raid," Sinclair said.

Tag looked at him, then Tanaka. "Recon?"

Sinclair shook his head.

"Okay, this is dramatic and all, but I'd really rather not guess." Tag folded his arms. "Marney, what gives—"

"We're going to take Baedecker back, Tag." That came from Father. He was watching his son with the expectancy Tag had felt when he wanted to impress his father. It was odd seeing the same expression on his dad's face.

"Take?" Tag raised his eyebrows. "You're talking about an invasion."

"Except it's our turn. A liberation," Marney said.

"Sorry, Sis, but liberation means there are people who need saving." Tag's heart ached to have to be the one to say it, but he knew no one in the room wanted the truth sugarcoated. He pointed at the brown and blue jewel of Baedecker Four. "There's nobody left there but the saarno foxes, and I'm pretty sure they'd rather take their chances with the one-eyes."

"That's not the point," Sinclair said. "The war's shifted back and forth across these sectors as the Grand Alliance and the Naplians slug it out for advantage. Battle lines shift every month. One thing never changes: the one-eyes keep draining serjaum out of Baedecker to fuel their fleets. That lets them hold onto their gains while reinforcements trickle in from the empire."

Tanaka made another motion with her stylus because the Baedecker System shifted to the side, and a new map of the immediate region of space expanded, with a miniature Baedecker ringed in gold at the center. Red lines traced long arcs from so many directions Tag felt dizzy. "As you can see, Naplian forces have been moving from the Baedecker region as of late. They're pushing back against Briddarri, who have also shifted their positions."

Tag frowned. "Thanks to me."

"You and your pilots." Tanaka cocked an eyebrow. "Virry Squadron, to be precise."

The puzzle pieces lined up into an orderly picture. Tag noted the star systems where the Naplians had moved, then followed the new green lines showing Briddarri fleet reallocations. "The Briddarri responded to our cyber lab raids and the Naplians took advantage."

Sinclair nodded. "We couldn't figure out what was going on until we ran the comparisons and updated them with the latest records from our allies." He said the last word with a sneer. "Look, if the greenbloods want to run this war, more power to them, but I'll be damned if they're going to dictate to me what intelligence is available to their allies. I have no problem with one-eyes getting their digs in while the Briddarri are scrambling to clean up the mess you've made of their vile experiments."

"Good to know we're all on the same page." Tag crossed his arms and leaned against the wall. "Okay, so the Naplians aren't paying attention to Baedecker like they should. That doesn't mean they've given up control of the sectors surrounding it. Baedecker isn't exactly on the front lines anymore."

"No, but it's not as dire as you think." Tanaka shifted the view again. Blue dots appeared among the star systems until their accumulated numbers formed a loose "U" around Baedecker. "We have been pushing our units to systems in the vicinity, ostensibly to protect repair ports and supply depots critical to the war effort. Every location where you see Terran battlegroups is a vital resource, but we have added more units than necessary to defend them."

"Because you're cobbling together an invasion force," Tag muttered. "Nice."

"Keeping it hidden from the Naplians is the tricky part." Tim held up a data scroll filled with what looked like communications updates. "TI made sure to hide the true orders in whatever way they could, up to and including sending live assets to initiate one-on-one contact with starship commanders. Old school HUMINT in action."

"What about the Denics?" Tag knew that rogue elements of the clear-blooded human spies had offered their services to the Grand Alliance via the Briddarri —and anyone else who could afford it. "They've got a knack for blending in everywhere there are humans, which is probably *everywhere.*"

"We're working to flush them out," Tim said. "Our last operation rounded up a couple dozen who are now taking a well-deserved rest in a Briddarri prisoner-of-war camp until we can trade them for our own captured assets."

"We wouldn't be going at this alone, Taggart." Father was peering past Marney at the close-up hologram of Baedecker. "The Briddarri and the Audrians will assist us by launching simultaneous attacks meant to throw the Naplians off balance."

"Yeah? And what do the greenbloods get in return?" Tag scowled. "A fresh batch of enslaved aliens they can turn into robots?"

"They've got their reasons for agreeing to this offensive," Sinclair said. "Not that I give a damn. As far as I'm concerned, your Virry Squadron can go back to harassing their labs—and by harassing, I mean blasting them to atoms—as soon as we pluck Baedecker out of the one-eyes' back pocket."

"Sounds good to me." Tag glanced around the room. "So, why do you need me here? Tim's with TI. Father and Marney have been supporting their own rebel and refugee efforts. You and Vice Admiral Tanaka are the brass, obviously. What's my role? I'm guessing not a standard starfighter command because you could rope any of a hundred pilots with more experience and less attitude than I've got."

"Yes and no. We're transferring Virry Squadron off *Confiance* for the duration of the operation and outside Sobban's chain of command."

"All right. Who do I answer to?"

"Me and Tetsu." Sinclair indicated his XO. "You'll have overall command of an individual operational unit."

Tag gave Tim what he hoped was a *What the heck*

is he talking about look. "Maybe I'm still not following. An independent fighter squadron. .. That's what I've been doing anyway."

"It'll be a combination of your squadron, TI operatives, and, ah, independent agents with whom you're familiar." Tim looked like he was trying his best not to grin. "I can give you more details, but not at this time. We're still filling the roster."

"Okay, well, I guess we could have brought Evie down here after all."

"That isn't possible," Tanaka said. "You are here because of four things: Commodore Ram's regard for your ability to perform covert operations; TI's similar assessment; your connection with, shall we say, unsavory elements; and your father's considerable influence."

"I'm not a fan of getting the job because of that one," Tag said. "Pretty sure I can stand on my own merits."

"The vice admiral is overstating my role." Father sounded as perturbed by the suggestion of nepotism as Tag felt—though Tag was also certain the brass wouldn't have let him in on this private briefing if not for Antiny Wester. "But I won't deny I have pushed hard against the Briddarri cyber effort."

"Look, all I know is Commodore Ram has made the connections for the ops I've been running. I don't even know who's at the top of the food chain when it comes to our raids."

Sinclair coughed into his hand.

"You? Seriously?"

"Not impressive enough, am I?"

Tag blushed. "No, sir. I just meant I didn't think I'd

ever meet the person."

"People. Tetsu's done a lot of the string-pulling when it comes to covering *Confiance's* tracks in cooperation with TI. Antiny and I are the ones who've been pushing the politicians behind the scenes."

"That's a hell of a conspiracy." Tag grinned when Marney winced. "Hey, Sis, I think we can relax—we've gotten our hands dirty plenty of times in support of the war."

"You're right." Marney shook her head. "But it still bothers me that we've had to be so clandestine when the Briddarri are committing a terrible injustice."

"War makes people desperate," Tanaka noted. "Desperation leads them to commit uncivilized acts, things they would never consider in peacetime."

"Amen to that." Tag placed his hands on the edge of the holo-projector and gazed into the mass of ships and courses filling the swirl of stars. "So, you've got our units in place ready to strike and our allies hanging around to distract the one-eyes long enough to dig in. What's the holdup? Don't tell me you've been waiting for Tag Wester's blessing."

Tim snorted.

"I can see we haven't worked all of the snark out of you," Father murmured.

"Your approval was never a prerequisite for our actions, Major." Tanaka's cool tone dropped a couple more degrees. "What we have been waiting for is confirmation our units are in place, confirmation our allies have prepared their strike packages, and confirmation of the most recent intelligence from operatives within the Baedecker System."

"TI's got people already in there?" Tag nodded.

"Good deal. Too bad you're not coming on the trip, Tim."

It was Tim's turn to go red in the cheeks. He shared a look with Marney. She didn't seem nearly as bothered by the remark. "It's, um. .. I am going, Tag. I'll command the ship and serve as your XO."

Still nothing from Marney. Huh. She was awfully calm for someone whose husband was about to ship out again after they'd planned to get started on a family. "Ship. *Greyfox?*"

"My gunboat flotilla isn't participating, no. This is too hot an operation for vessels so thin-skinned."

"Wait a second." Tag rubbed his forehead. "You outrank me."

"Not for long." Blair smoothed his uniform jacket. "We're issuing you a temporary field promotion to colonel. Congratulations."

Tag felt like his head was spinning, and he'd only had the single glass of Crown and Scepter.

"Your mission is straightforward: To seize control of a Naplian destroyer, which TI has identified," Tanaka said. "Commander Ess has the relevant intelligence regarding the target vessel. You and your associates will then infiltrate the Baedecker System, taking up station in the Baedecker Five orbital slot."

"Wait a microsecond. A destroyer?" Tag made a face. "Wouldn't a civilian ship be an easier mark?"

"It would, but that would defeat the purpose of infiltrating where and when we need a sharp knife. Further orders will follow."

"Not even a hint?" Tag's wits resurfaced through his shock. "I suppose secrecy is paramount here."

"Indeed, spies are active in this theater of operations, and your future associates have a dubious reputation."

"There's that word again." Tag touched a control on the display. The scattered debris ringing the Baedecker stars in the fifth orbital slot shone. Suddenly he was back in his Raider fighter-bomber, Scrape behind him, as they approached a practice bombing run on Baedecker Six—right before the Truppen made their reappearance. "When do I get my roster?"

"Commander Ess has those relevant details."

"And where will we find this Naplian ship? Not anywhere nearby, I assume."

"No. It will require your insertion into a Naplian repair depot." Tanaka pursed her lips. "You will need stealth and speed."

"And try to avoid Terran-controlled space on your way to Baedecker," Sinclair said. "We don't want you to get blown up before you get a chance to pull off your assignment."

"Yeah, me neither." Tag straightened and clapped his hands. "All right. I'm in. Can't say whether my squadron will be, but who knows? A lot of them are Baedecker natives, and if they're not, I'd say they're still itching to take back turf from the one-eyes. When do we get started?"

"As soon as possible." Tim consulted his data scroll. "If everything's going right, our operative should be reestablishing contact and retrieving our civilian asset shortly."

Tag glanced back at him. His heart thudded with sudden anticipation. If he'd picked up enough clues. .. "Don't leave me with blind sensors, Tim."

"Wouldn't dream of it." He held out his scroll.

Lira's face shown in the surface's emerald glow.

CHAPTER FIVE

Lira Lin Reen plucked a thumb-sized red *briakka* pastry from the automated tray that floated by. A sensor orb mounted at the center of the tray swept its electronic gaze over the gleaming jeweled bracelet on her left wrist. The bracelet beeped in response, confirming that Lira's faked account was twenty credits poorer.

Twenty credits. Lira smiled to herself as she let the tiny puff pastry melt on her tongue, and the electric wave of flavor rippled through her mouth. She washed it down with the golden champagne and deposited the empty flute on a marble railing. The cool evening breeze brushed across her bare arm's skin.

Twenty credits for less than a mouthful. Oh, well. In a few minutes, she'd pass through the laughing crowds of garden party revelers and be on her way out of the gallery's main entrance. The fee for the food was a small price to pay for the 200,000 credits she would earn for delivering the goods.

Lira watched the semi-drunken wealthy elites of Jarrados Three continue splurging on the overpriced tiny portions of food brought in from across their planet. The Briddarri here were a peculiar lot, living on the farthest fringes of Kitanai space. Not a single warrior among them. Artists, musicians, wealthy merchants—they weren't interested in war, only in enjoying life by avoiding the death and destruction that seemed to show no signs of halting.

She couldn't blame them. Lira had no trust in anyone in the upper ranks of the Briddarri Kingdom, or the Terran Republic, or anyone whose only answer to ending the bloodshed was more of the same.

Her heart ached. She wondered how Tag was doing. They hadn't spoken in a long time. At least she knew he wasn't dead. His fame among allied forces hadn't diminished, so it was easy to keep track of him in the glowing media reports, except he'd had fewer and fewer of them these days.

Lira took another sip of champagne and smiled. Tag would have liked this party. The food and the company, certainly, but not hobnobbing with the rich. It was good that they had wealth to spare. They might be creatives, but they were not without sin—or ill-gotten gains.

"Ladies and gentlemen!" A short, rounded Briddarri in a flowing red satin jacket and suit raised his arms as if he were about to announce his candidacy for planetary commissioner. "Ladies and gentlemen, I have terrible news. The highlight of our collection, which was on display for your viewing pleasure this evening, has been stolen."

The collective gasp was as ridiculous as Lira had hoped. Look at them. They were pacifists, which she admired, but they were also selfish. They didn't care about the suffering of others. This wasn't a war relief fundraiser, after all. It was just a party. The money spent here went back into the gallery.

"This is an outrage!" Lira's voice was tinged with a

local accent that dripped with arrogance and privilege. "Lock the building down! Search the staff and the caterers!"

"We will. Do not worry, my friends." The host's face had gone a deeper, indignant shade of green. "Whoever committed this disgusting act will not get free."

Security men filed in through the four exits leading into the banquet balcony. Lira scanned the area. So far, so good. Sixteen security guards in shiny chrome armor that was more decorative than practical. The gallery's main exits must be locked down, which left her with only one option.

The only option she needed.

The discovery of the theft was a problem, but that was okay. Lira never planned a heist without at least three escape options, so turning to Option Two wasn't a bad thing. She made her way to the balcony edge and peered over the side. Turquoise vines swayed in the breeze. It was a hundred meters from the thick rainforest canopy below. Silver towers spread into the distance, beyond the horizon. The gallery was one of many spires the Jarradi had created, each as dazzling as the next.

Lira pressed the sides of her bracelet, ignoring the commotion behind her. A piercing white light flashed— once, twice.

She counted seconds. A red pinprick flashed eleven seconds later from four spires away.

The extraction unit was on the way.

The guards, meanwhile, had fanned out among the partygoers. Each carried a small portable scanner fitted to the palm of the hand that emitted a shaky yellow beam of light. The beam swept each guest from feet to head and back down again. A single high-pitched chirp told the guard that the person was not the suspect.

It would make a very different noise when it got to Lira.

She strolled the edge of the crowds, sipping from her champagne. She would only stay out of their eyesight for so long. Eventually, they'd check on everyone in the party, and when they got to her, the scanners would detect the peculiar combination of metals that made up the Thread Painting of Hana Hyl Vaas.

Lira rubbed at her bracelet with her thumb. *Hurry up.* She knew wishing for increased speed wouldn't get her results, but it helped her feel more in control.

She caught a faint hum beneath the intermittent breezes. Jarrados Three had a benign atmosphere, even at altitudes approaching a kilometer, so the tiny drone seemed to have no issues approaching the tower that was home to the art gallery. The remote device was a cylinder a few centimeters around, with a concealed compartment that cracked open as it sidled up to the courtyard's railing.

Lira turned and rested her elbows on the railing as if she were slightly drunk and admiring the sweeping vistas. The first part of that statement was somewhat accurate. She sighed, feigning adoration, and disconnected the catch holding the bracelet together. It slipped from her wrist. She placed it into the cylinder's compartment.

Someone bumped her. Lira glanced back, taking care to keep a haughty expression in place that fit right in with the rest of these wealthy snobs.

"Sorry 'bout that." The tall, gangly young man behind her slurred the words. His date for the evening giggled. She sloshed her drink, a brilliant pink concoction, over his suit, but even though it was a dazzling white against his green skin, he didn't seem to notice or mind the new stain. Lira chalked the carelessness up to the alcoholic content of the ale in his glass.

His clumsy interaction, though, warned her of the guard stepping onto the dais where Lira and eight others stood in a microcosm of the party's crowds. He began sweeping each person from toe to head and back again, as mechanical a motion as if he were a cybernetic unit himself.

"I say, you," the young man muttered, "If my parents knew the kind of scum you were treating us like —"

"They would probably fire me, yes, I've heard." The guard was a stern, green-skinned woman whose face looked like it had been carved from an emerald shade of the same marble that surrounded the courtyard. "If it meant I got to stun and detain you, it'd be worth it. Stand still, or I'll have to do this all over again."

Her brusqueness was enough to elicit laughter from those surrounding him, which gave Lira the excuse to shoo the drone away. The tightness in her chest loosened but didn't entirely fade away. The goods were secure. Getting her out of the party was the next step. *Never keep the target and the thief together.* It was a smart rule Blue Kitt had followed for generations.

It had proven easier to spring their sisters and

brothers from detention than to steal priceless items a second time.

"Miss." The guard was in front of her, scanner hand raised.

Lira sighed as if the guard had asked her to turn over all her wealth. "Yes, fine, get it over with. I need to refill my glass if I'm going to survive this event."

She felt the slightest tickle from the beam as it started at her bejeweled high-heeled shoes, traced up the curves of the midnight-blue dress, and topped her bare shoulders, finishing at the black hair with gold traces done up in an elaborate crown.

Nothing.

Not that Lira had expected difficulty from a basic metals scan. The bracelet was a couple klicks away by now.

The beam started its way back down. Lira smiled at the guard as she thought of how she could spend the two hundred thousand credits once it was added to her considerable nest egg. She felt borderline giddy, a sensation she'd not experienced since she'd run out of the Warrior House in her town before the commandant had noticed, sparing herself the next hour and a half of lectures on the bold, honored dead.

Well, maybe save was a better word than spend. She hoped Tag would appreciate her planning.

The scanner let out a harsh buzz. Lira blinked out of her daydream. The guard frowned at whatever results she was reading on the device mounted to her wrist—a screen linked to the scanner, Lira knew.

"Raise your left arm," the guard ordered.

Lira's heart thudded. She kept her face implacable and did what was asked. The bracelet was gone, and so was the string painting. The scanner shouldn't have picked up anything.

Another guard, this one a burly man, appeared at her side. "Problem, Officer?"

"Not sure, Sergeant." She showed him the results.

The sergeant squinted at Lira.

Now, she wished her fervent thoughts *could* make a hovercar move faster. "What is this? Are you storing that information about me in your systems? This is an invasion of my privacy. I'll have your superiors assign you to the tree-trimming squadrons if you so much as share a single byte of what you scanned."

"Calm down, miss," the sergeant ordered. He didn't seem impressed by her complaints. "Your person shows micro-fiber remnants of the stolen painting. We're detaining you. Feel free to lodge as many complaints as you like. Officer, place her in restraints."

The rest of the partygoers had crept away from her during the confrontation, which Lira silently thanked them for. They'd given her a four-meter arc in which she could move without injuring anyone else.

She waited until the officer moved behind her and reached for her arm, then struck with a high-heeled foot at the officer's instep. She flung her glass in the sergeant's face, brought her elbow back into the officer's nose, and slashed with the side of her hand at the base of the sergeant's throat.

Those quick moves left both gasping, the officer clutching her broken nose as green blood seeped between her fingers and the sergeant on his knees, struggling for breath.

Lira ditched her shoes and yanked the standard-issue stun poles from their belts. The energy crackling from the tops of each meter-long rod reassured her in the same way the hovercar's appearance would.

Where was Kassan? She was never *late for an extraction.*

She plowed through the crowds, jabbing partygoers at random. Each successful strike made a man or woman collapse into a limp heap and brought screams of fear and shouts of outrage from those around them. They also provided Briddarri barricades against the guards rushing toward their fallen comrades and also after her.

Come on, come on, come on. .. Lira didn't need the mantra. She needed comms, but the gallery employed communications blockers so it wouldn't ruin the experience with images splashed about on social media. She thought there might be copyright issues involved.

A stun pole lashed out at her face. Lira dropped to her knees, blocked the blow with one of her weapons, and jabbed the other stun pole into the attacking security guard's abdomen. He toppled and retched.

Maybe she should keep her mind on escape instead of the odd habits of the wealthy elite.

A gust blew across the courtyard, rustling the vines. Lira clashed stun poles with yet another guard. Sparks exploded between them. Lira grunted under the pressure of his strikes as she fended them off. She had to give him credit—she wasn't expecting anyone on a colony of hedonists to know traditional *burr-dex* martial arts, not even the security personnel.

The wind increased. Glasses slipped from the bar and shattered. Smashed liquor bottles stained the marble floor with five worlds' worth of alcohol. Partygoers slipped and clutched at each other, the miniature hurricane fouling their hair and rustling their clothing.

Lira squinted into the gale. It was harsh enough that her eyes watered. The hovercar was a broad, boxy six-place luxury model that could have belonged to any of the guests present but was probably a hundred thousand credits below the median price of what was parked on the landing pads above. It reminded Lira of Trammarri shale, shined to an opalescence that rivaled Earth pearls.

Quad grav panels whined as they struggled at this altitude. Hovercars, especially the heavier models like this one, weren't meant to operate above 50 meters, let alone several hundred. Hence, the turbofans extended from the body as custom modifications.

The effect turned the hovercar into more of an aircraft while forcing the guards and the guests to seek cover.

Lira ran the opposite way, the edges of her gown torn, face tingling from the champagne, the stun poles crackling as they whipped through the air beside her. The hovercar dropped to the edge of the balcony. Its left side rear doors opened, top and bottom like a yawning mouth, the bottom door doubling as a set of stairs.

A shout from behind might have been a warning to stop or even one given out of concern for her safety. Lira planted her foot on the railing and launched into the air, trying to focus on the opening ahead of her and ignoring the drop below. Too bad her favorite grav-harness would have been too conspicuous to wear over her gown and too bulky to wear underneath it.

She landed hard on the floor, grateful it was covered with a thick, satiny carpet that gave her a handhold as the hovercar banked away from the tower. Lira pulled herself in and away from the doors, which clamped shut, sealing off the wind with a sudden, sharp whistle. She focused on slowing her breathing and listening to the ambient hum from the compartment's electronics and the muffled rumble of the hovercar's engines. The turbofans changed in pitch, but Lira couldn't tell in which direction they were headed because the vehicle's windows were fuzzed out, reducing the stunning jungle vistas into a pixelated mess of greens and blues.

"Kassan, if this is your best flying, I should probably remind you that we wouldn't have to rush if you'd been on time," Lira said.

"I am sorry I was not able to keep the predetermined rendezvous, but circumstances changed, and I was forced to improvise." The voice that responded was cooler and calmer than any biological sentient Lira had ever met. "As you know, such improvisation is not my best attribute."

Lira clambered into the passenger seat beside the driver and found not Kassan, a human mercenary, but Dyson Ashteo, who only looked human. Dyson regarded her with a brief, faint smile, his attention never wavering from the glowing bank of controls. Brown eyes refused to blink, except for when they did ten seconds later and ten seconds after that, at precise intervals. His skin was tanned like a man who'd worked outdoors no matter which planet he visited.

Lira's normal reaction to another person sitting in the driver's seat of her getaway hovercar would have been to shock that person insensate with her stun poles. Instead, she wrapped her arms around his neck and kissed his cheek. That ersatz skin was as warm as any human male's—although the last had been Tag's. "Dyson! This is wonderful! I'm almost not upset you took my driver's place without telling me."

"I do apologize for the lack of communication, but as I said, circumstances changed while you were in the midst of your—" Dyson indicated the hovercar around them. "Caper."

"Caper?" Lira laughed. "I forgot how much fun you can be. Where's Kassan?"

Dyson tapped the center console. An image appeared. Lira recognized the interior of their safehouse in the residential tower where she'd seen the confirmation light. There was Kassan, all two meters of him, bound by industrial cable, a cloth gag held in place by strapping tape.

"I did not have to hurt him," Dyson noted. "I would have been as upset as you if I had had to inflict injury."

"I think I would have been madder." Lira gave his shoulder a playful punch. He didn't react. Lira wound up rubbing her knuckles since his synthetic musculature was several orders of magnitude stronger than biological tissue. "When did you find me?"

"I never lost track of you. TI has continued its observation ever since we affected your release from Briddarri custody."

It had been the last time she'd seen Tag in person. Lira pushed the memory away. "Then I'm guessing by your friendly abduction of me that I don't have time to enjoy the spoils of my liberation."

"No, again, I apologize, but time is of the essence. I have a vessel waiting in orbit that will jump from this star system in forty-seven minutes."

"How precise. How Dyson." Lira shook her head, still smiling.

"I am puzzled by your use of the word 'liberation,' Lira when this caper—" Dyson raised an eyebrow before continuing. "Was for the purpose of stealing a rare piece of artwork from the local colony."

Lira was sure he was making a joke by repeating the word "caper" for her amusement, so she humored him by explaining. "The Thread Painting of Hana Hyl Vaas dates to three and a half centuries ago. Vaas micro-etched pigments onto strands from her deceased son's shirt, the bits left over from the hovercar accident he died in. It tells a story of her grief, like a painted poem. She left the painting to her family, but it was stolen eighty years later. It was missing until last summer."

"When it showed up in the gallery's collection," Dyson said. "Yes, I read the historical background while I was on my way to retrieve you, as well as the news commentaries from fifteen sources. There are many hypotheses to explain its absence."

"Blue Kitt found out the truth. The gallery's consortium hired another gang of thieves to steal it for them and paid a hefty fee." Lira frowned. "Not us, though. Not something as personal as that. Blue Kitt knew the history behind it and steered clear, at least until the family contacted us to find where the painting had gone."

"I see. The thieves became detectives."

"We did. You could say we were recovery specialists. Is it really stealing if we're getting it back for the family?"

"For a considerable fee, no doubt."

"The Vaas clan are wealthy merchants." Lira lifted her chin. "They offered us eight hundred thousand credits to get the painting back. We're only taking half that, and half of *that* goes to me."

"I meant no offense."

"I know you didn't, but I'm betting you're having fun working on the teasing side of human personality." Lira leaned back into the seat cushions. Stars, they were as luxurious as the carpet. "But you don't have to admit it to me if you don't want to. So, what's the new mission? I assume this is a TI assignment."

"In a sense. It will make use of your skills." Dyson glanced at her. "As well as mine and Tag's."

Lira's stomach did a flip. So much for her lingering bravado.

"Is there a problem?"

"Only that I don't know what I'll say or do when I see him again." She fought the urge to fix her hair.

"At least you do not have to fear deactivation and dismemberment in his presence, as I once did."

Lira laughed, grateful for the distraction. A spaceport appeared ahead, just beyond a ridgeline that dominated the horizon at the edge of the jungle. "Was that a joke?"

Dyson shrugged, a stiff if passable imitation of the real motion. "An accurate recollection."

CHAPTER SIX

Admiral Gussan Va'Kur Erassia gazed through the floor to ceiling windows of his office atop Daviont Tower at the center of what the *shirish* had called Vossberg City. The dusty plains surrounding the urban center were as bleak and unforgiving as any purgatory he could imagine.

It was darkly amusing when he recalled researching human faith traditions and what that term meant—a place in which a person would suffer to gain eventual passage to a paradisical afterlife.

Erassia no longer found it funny.

He still commanded thousands of loyal Ffawe, but this rank had become something of a joke, and he knew it. "Admiral" meant he could wear the twin silver suns on both shoulders of his black and orange Naplian Fleet uniform, and there were ships throughout the Baedecker Star System under his command, but he wouldn't lead a fleet action. Not anytime soon.

Not since his disgrace.

Erassia counted himself fortunate to be alive. His survival was due largely to his family connections, though it was also clear Admiral Tir Ad'Andra Daviont, leader of the famed III Corps and mastermind of the invasion of Terran space, wasn't ready to cast aside an admiral, no matter the transgression committed. It was a testament to the humans' tenacity that Daviont wanted every experienced flag officer to remain at his rank.

Second chances were rare in the Naplian Empire. Erassia chose to be grateful.

That gratefulness extended only so far. Instead of vaulting between the stars and chasing the *shirish* from space that should belong to the glorious emperors, Erassia was confined to the Baedecker System as surely as if he'd been locked in the brig aboard his flagship, the battlecruiser *Fulnax*. Here, all he could do was oversee the stripping of Baedecker Two's serjaum deposits and mine whatever precious metals and rare minerals he could find on Baedecker Four.

Erassia scowled as he watched hulking mining rigs chew through the ground a dozen kilometers away, the dust from their operations shrouding the planet's suns in a sickly burnt-orange haze. There wasn't much to admire here. Between the Naplian invaders and the Terran defenders, Vossberg was still largely abandoned four years on. Little remained of the human-built structures. Naplian military compounds, barracks, mineral processing stations, and fuel depots filled the old grid of two-eye roads with buildings a uniform pale shade of gray and green.

His predecessor had renamed the city Velic, hoping to shed the human stench.

A cargo shuttle's passing sent a tremor through the office windows. The ovoid ship headed for the landing pads blossoming from the Northwest side of the city. The trade post there was bustling, bringing species from across the conquered Naplian systems and neutral planets to buy Baedecker's natural wealth in exchange for credits Naplia needed to continue the war.

None of this is my achievement. I'm left here to manage the accomplishments of others.

His door chimed. Erassia ignored it.

The city below, bruised and battered, teemed with traffic, both biological and mechanical. The merger of the two heartened Erassia. He'd been sent here because his *ziurathal* mechs had failed to eliminate the devastators, those foul artificial beings prophecy insisted would destroy the empire. His lead commander and the men trained to operate them were long dead.

But Erassia clung to the hope that he could give Daviont what he needed to stop the *ziura* once and for all so those Truppen demons no longer haunted Naplian forces.

The door chimed again.

"Enter," Erassia snapped.

Captain Kos Va'Kur Tratta strode in with the bravado Erassia wished he still possessed. He was a few centimeters taller than his clansman, bearing the pale orange iris to his eye common among males of the clan. His gray skin was blotchy with mottled white patterns up the back of his neck and under his chin.

Tratta stopped short of Erassia's silver metal desk and saluted. "Admiral. I've brought the productivity reports."

"They must be good, Kos, if you are delivering the news in hand instead of transmitting it." Erassia held out his hand.

Tratta passed him the copper-mesh tube. Erassia punched the top cap, and the scroll unrolled. He gripped the edge, forcing it into a flat, rigid form onto which Tratta's report sprang to life.

"Serjaum extraction increased 3 percent this quarter over last," Tratta said. "That may not sound like much, but keep in mind we haven't lost a single shipment in six months, so more of the material is getting to the refueling depots where it is needed most."

"Very good. I suppose we're seeing fewer raiders on the system fringes."

"A few. No Terran military. Only *shirish* pirates." Tratta blinked and gave Erassia a bold smile. "I suspect the last shipload of the human vermin we executed and left strapped to the burned-out starship hull left an impression."

Erassia nodded, but he couldn't summon the same enthusiasm. More serjaum ore processed into ship's fuel. More human filth eliminated. Where was the glory in either? "Anything else?"

"The destroyer *Traxan* rotated out to VI Corps. They sent us *Kaltak* under Captain Raaldand as her replacement."

"Raaldand. I don't know him. Which clan?"

"Tol'bru."

Erassia scowled. "The tradesmen? How did he come by his own command?" He waved a three-fingered hand. "Never mind. I'm sure the political play behind it would disgust me. Anything less depressing?"

"Not in the official report, no." Tratta gestured to the couches at the far end of the room. "Can we sit?"

Erassia's heart quickened. There had been no news from their pet project for weeks. He didn't dare raise his hopes, as brutally as they'd been battered, but instead led Tratta to the couches. They sat opposite each other, with a low, glass table between. A pair of *weyli* vine-creepers undulated in their pots, the blue tendrils reaching for the mist puffed from sprayers embedded beneath.

Erassia touched one of the rectangular depressions on the tray holding their pots. A white light pulsed.

Tratta exhaled. "Whatever you paid for that distortion field is worth every credit."

"Anything that keeps the Druwei from monitoring my every word is worth more than simple credits." Erassia leaned back on the couch. The field would render even the best listening devices employed by the empire's secret police inert. Erassia throttled back his irritation at the knowledge Admiral Daviont didn't trust him to run a backwater mining facility, no matter how vital it was to the war effort. "Speak."

Tratta seemed as eager as when he'd first attained his rank and been appointed captain of *Fulnax*. "The most recent tests were a success. The Phase Two production is well ahead of schedule."

Relief flooded Erassia. Setbacks were not something he could afford, not at this stage in the war—and his career. "What is the grand total?"

"Eight thousand units completed and awaiting armaments. Two thousand more under construction. Those should be finished within the next month. Another ten thousand are undergoing initial frame-up and fabrication."

Tratta withdrew a sheet of printed plastic from his uniform. He slid it across the table to Erassia. The sheet's surface was a dazzling mix of prismatic colors, but as Erassia lifted it for a closer look, the scroll of mind-numbing extraction data all but forgotten, the mix cleared.

The schematic of a ziurathal mech outlined in white on a gray background filled the disguised printout.

"This iteration is proving hardier than the initial prototypes you fielded four years ago, Gussan." Tratta's tone was full of such eagerness that Erassia couldn't bring himself to chastise his kinsman for his lack of decorum—but given this was an off-the-books meeting, it would have been the height of hypocrisy to insist on it. "These Z1-Bs are much faster than the originals and displace thirty-two tons. The technicians have upgraded the armament to thirty-millimeter particle cannons. They're twice as big as the first *ziurathal* and far deadlier."

Erassia looked up from the sheet, his mind spinning with possibility. "Field tests?"

"Only against unmanned mechs." Tratta shifted in his seat, apparently uncomfortable with the shift in the conversation. "We don't—"

"They will have to engage in battle against the *ziura* before they will be accepted. Nothing short of victory will sway our leaders that the *ziurathal* can stop the Truppen warriors."

"I understand, Admiral, but we've been hard pressed to acquire the test subjects you require. The Truppen have slipped from the scanners, so to speak."

"What of our spies among the Briddarri?"

Tratta sighed. "Next to useless. All we know is there was a falling out between the Briddarri brass and the Truppen overlord. Now the *ziura* roam the battlefields, attacking our forces at will and destroying other targets."

Erassia made a face. He had seen the intelligence

briefings. "The supposed cybernetic labs, like the ones we encountered at the red dwarf."

"Yes. Apparently, that wasn't the greenbloods' only attempt." Tratta leaned forward and tapped the sheet in Erassia's hands. "But the devastators are so preoccupied with the Briddarri attempt to recreate them that we are left to our own devices concerning the ziurathal project. I tell you, kinsman, these new mechs are proving far superior. We've run the tensile strength tests. Our people have analyzed every bit of data from not only your original models but the few battles waged back then. Every scrap of information has been assembled to make the Z1-B the premier fighting machine. Truppen aside, they will be a scourge on the battlefield when set against any adversary."

He made good points, but Erassia couldn't help entertaining nagging doubts. There was always the possibility the Druwei would get wind of this operation and shut him down. "I want reassurance that the funding has not been traced back to me."

Tratta shook his head. "No. It has not. We have eliminated what few witnesses there were. Any additional funding needed has trickled in through third-party contacts with the neutral traders using the Velic port."

"Make sure it stays untraceable. And I want to see the ziurathal action recordings as soon as possible."

"Yes, Admiral, but we have kept things this quiet because there have been no records transmitted between the testing facility and your office since the project's rebirth. I'm afraid—"

"You misunderstand. I will visit the site in person."

"You. .." Tratta's tenuous grasp on protocol slipped. "Gussan, that's a terrible idea. The moment you step outside your office, Druwei agents will be sniffing after your footsteps like those starving foxes that infest the city edges."

"I don't care about those vermin any more than I do the *shirish*." Erassia slapped the printout back onto the table. The *weyli* vines curled in upon themselves, a natural self-defense mechanism against startling sounds and motions. "I want to see firsthand that this project succeeds. Sitting here in this prison will not bring me closer to our goal."

"Yes, Admiral." Tratta's neck flushed. He didn't offer further comment.

"Your concern is noted, Kos. Let me handle the Druwei." Erassia stood, his hand extended toward the distortion field's controls. "Together, we will bring the devastators to ruin so that nothing can oppose the Naplian Empire's victory."

Erassia deactivated the field. Tratta left without another word, and Erassia found himself alone again with his thoughts, his plans, and the dismal landscape beyond his windows as his companion. His fleet was out of reach. His brainchild was kept under wraps, hidden not only from those who would dismantle his work but from him, too.

He prayed for the chance to show not only Admiral Daviont but their glories Benaltep and Bonate —all hail the emperors—that the *ziurathal* was not a failed experiment or a mad dream. He would get his victory.

And then I can finally earn my way out of this garbage heap the shirish call a planet.

* * *

Inspector Jas Ir'Na Prad watched from his bench at one of the mess halls scattered around the Daviont Tower complex as Captain Tratta left the offices. He stalked past his guards and boarded a tram that departed a few seconds later for the military landing pads from where, presumably, he would return to Fulnax. Nothing suspicious. Admiral Erassia's preference for in-person briefings was hardly a visit.

Prad snorted. He supposed he'd go crazy, too, if he'd been stuck planetside when he was supposed to be commanding a fleet.

There was more to worry about than Erassia's schedule. Prad opened his scroll and reviewed the surveillance logs on Captain Tratta. Five visits to Erassia's office within the past month. Contrast that with six visits in the previous four months. The increase was undeniable, the two-week interruption notwithstanding.

And this had been a short visit—eight and a half minutes from tram arrival to departure. Whatever Tratta told Erassia hadn't taken that long.

Prad frowned. Then what was the big hush? Nothing he'd downloaded from the "secure" records that Tratta had provided Erassia had given him sufficient clues. All Prad knew was that if he had to read one more analysis of serjaum extraction and refinement rates, he'd go as mad as Erassia had reportedly gone.

A bowl of *niprik* slid in front of him. Prad looked up. The mess hall cook had already moved along to the line of soldiers laughing it up at the nearby tables. They stank of sweat and body odor, their patrol armor clumped on the floor by their boots. Ochre dust coated everything. Prad wiped his hands on his jacket before he picked up his bowl and took a sip.

The spices burned his mouth. Good. He needed that to keep him sharp. *Niprik* contained a mild narcotic in just low enough amounts to avoid addiction and health impacts but high enough to heighten the senses.

Prad consulted his notes again. Whatever Erassia was up to concerned the Truppen. Prad was sure of it. The entire Va'Kur clan was riddled with Sov cultists. Those crazed believers swore that the Truppen were the fabled devastators come to destroy the Naplian Empire.

Rubbish. Prad sipped more soup. Sure, he'd seen the reports that the Truppen had risen to power right after they absorbed an alien outsider—a soft human, no less—into their ranks. He had plenty of data on Elden Selva. Nothing about the man-turned-Truppen seemed supernatural. He'd been a cunning strategist before his death and rebirth.

Prad didn't care for any of that. His concern was that the director of internal security was tired of playing games with the Sov, especially after Admiral Daviont had pressured him to lay off members of Daviont's clan. But Erassia's Va'Kur had no such protection.

Not from Daviont.

Prad's communicator buzzed at him. He lifted it from his belt. "Go."

"Inspector, we have eyes on the target. His shuttle's lifting to *Fulnax*. No word on whether he's planning another classified inspection tour of the system's defenses."

Prad grimaced. "If he does, you'd better make sure he doesn't give you the slip again, or I'll post you to morale monitoring at Baedecker Two."

"Yes, Inspector."

The signal cut off. Prad's eye rolled from left to right, with the lid half-shut. His annoyance grew until he thought he wouldn't be able to finish his soup, but he drained the last of it in a stinging gulp. Tratta and his inspection tours. Erassia had clad those in so much supposed "operational secrecy" that Prad couldn't get a single informant anywhere near *Fulnax*. Both the admiral and his clansman captain had too many loyalists aboard.

Prad would have to work on reminding them to whom they really owed loyalty.

His comm buzzed again, this time with a text-only message. <Possible lead. Sergeant Tei Hil'yur Brillen. Serves on a missile tender that resupplies *Fulnax*. Coming up the street.>

Prad flipped his bowl and set it upside down on the cleansing tray behind the bar. Water washed it down the trough into the steam box. Doing so allowed Prad to swivel on the bench. A young soldier trudged up the street, muttering into his comm.

<Owes considerable debt to a bookie in the neutral enclave. Pressure is getting to him.>

Prad grinned. That much was obvious. He stepped away from his bench and walked a semicircle through the jostling soldiers and technicians. His jacket and trousers were of military cut but devoid of insignia. Prad knew that marked him as either an off-duty officer or a civilian contractor.

Sergeant Brillen walked by, giving only a halfhearted wave to his brothers in arms. Prad came up behind him and lengthened his strides until he drew even with Brillen on his left.

"Afternoon, Tei." Prad put an arm around his shoulder, still grinning. "Good to see you."

Brillen glared at him. "Who the blazes are you?"

"Inspector Prad, Sergeant." Prad opened his jacket, revealing a black triangle with a silver circle at its center—his Druwei badge.

Brillen's eye widened. His breathing quickened.

"Stay calm, son. You're not in any trouble with me." Prad's grip on Brillen's shoulder tightened until he could steer him toward a quieter side street. "But the people to whom you owe money might beg to differ."

"What do you want?"

"To talk, Sergeant." Prad touched the comm on his belt, activating the directional recorder. "Just to talk."

✳ ✳ ✳

Ivy Li handed the data scroll across the counter. She put just the right amount of pleasantness into the facial expression, raising the corners of her mouth by 3.2 centimeters on each side. "All fixed."

"Many thanks." The Naplian soldier's skin paled. He fumbled with the silver and brass-colored tokens in his hands. "This is what I have that isn't credits."

"It's more than enough. Just be sure not to let your commanding officer know you broke it again—and pass the word to your comrades. I've got the right price."

"You do indeed." The soldier hurried off through

the vendor stalls. Ivy swept the tokens into her money bag and stashed it underneath the counter. She supposed she should secure the currency—she wasn't worried about losing it, but her guise as a merchant demanded she take the same steps as the rest of the people around her. The neutral enclave had demonstrated a 6.3 percent rise in theft since her arrival, though the statistic did not affect her actions since it had been rumored to be on the rise since well before then.

Ivy let her smile slip. Such a ridiculous way to arrange one's face. She would never submit to the indignity if it weren't for the need to mimic a Denic human.

Ivy increased her aural sensitivity until she could hear the Naplians in conversation, even at a range of 30 meters and across the crowded sales tent, then booted her translation software.

"You're lucky the quartermaster doesn't strip you of every bit of tech signed out in your name, Kah."

"I know it, but I need this assignment. Better to be sweeping the fleet's fuel supply numbers than pumping it myself."

Good. The more data she could gather, the better. The soldier named Kah would upload the fuel statistics for the Naplian occupation fleet. The algorithm Ivy installed while repairing the scroll would cause the device to malfunction, which in turn would bring Kah back to her. Most likely, he would demand a refund, which Ivy would provide while also fixing the error free of charge. Then, she would clone the data from the device using Stelltron's Lookingglass data sifting suite without leaving a trace.

Ivy consulted her mission datacore, hidden behind the best security barriers the corporation could create. So far, she had amassed an adequate picture of the Naplian forces in the Baedecker System, along with detailed reports of their serjaum extraction rates. The curious movements undertaken by the battlecruiser *Fulnax* puzzled her, but she estimated an 82 percent probability Kah would provide at least a few possible answers to that question.

Providing her handlers with the most accurate analysis of the tactical situation for the entire star system was paramount. Stelltron was convinced the Terran Navy would strike soon, most likely here at Baedecker. Given the state of their preparations, there was no dissuading Stelltron of the impending threat. The invasion was inevitable, and it was Ivy's task to ensure it happened.

The humans had a quaint rhyme about following orders without questioning. Ivy was programmed to follow Stelltron's directives unwaveringly, regardless of the outcome.

The only outcome of importance was Stelltron maintaining its grip on the galaxy, as it always had, while feckless governments warred over petty things like planets.

Ivy reactivated her smile as the next customer approached. She prepared her implanted sensors to gather intelligence from this unsuspecting technician.

Stelltron would rewrite destinies.

Just as they had rewritten hers.

CHAPTER SEVEN

T ag watched as navy technicians pushed a cart laden with ammunition through the airlock. "Stow it in the cargo bay, Slot Eight," he ordered. "Double-check the web strapping, too. I don't need explosive rounds slamming into each other if we've got to pull hammer-eights in this bucket."

"Yes, sir, Colonel."

Princess chuckled softly. She knelt by her Warhawk with a diagnostic unit connected to an open circuitry panel.

"What?"

"Nothing, Colonel."

Tag rolled his eyes. Yeah, he got it. There he was, the devil-may-care pilot, with his own data scroll in hand, checking off supplies as they came cart by cart into the ship's loading airlock. Not exactly what he had in mind when leading a covert operation into enemy space, but once he'd seen the crew and cargo manifests, there was no way Tag would leave the work to anybody else.

Condensation dripped onto his scroll. Tag frowned and wiped it away. *Aox* might be many things —converted Liberty Ship, makeshift fighter carrier, TI surveillance vessel—but even though she was launched off the construction yards only a year ago, she'd taken a beating during their clandestine missions. "Evie!"

"Yeah, boss?" Evie popped up from her cockpit like a prairie dog. Tag wondered how many species survived in the Luran Plains outside Vossberg City or if the saarno foxes and weapons bombardments had driven the last of the critters away.

He wondered if Vossberg itself had survived.

"Grab a couple of techs and get up in the catwalks. One of the condensators is overcondensating."

Evie wrinkled her nose. "Is that a technical term?"

"Just do it. That's an order."

"Yeah, okay, right on it." Evie vaulted over the side and shimmied down the ladder. She rounded up the crew working on her Warhawk's stabilizers and led them in a jog to the catwalk ladders.

"Finally, he delegates." Princess wiped sweat from her forehead and stowed her scroll in a jumpsuit pocket. "That's the last update. The entire squadron is finished."

"Good work." Tag marked that bit off his checklist. "I'm not about to have us ram around our old stomping grounds without the latest nav software."

"Even though you remember where every rock tumbles, surely."

"Hey, I'm not willing to trust even this steel trap with every little detail for something like this." Tag tapped the side of his head.

"That reminds me. .. Captain Wu mentioned he needs to review the final course coordinates with you before departure."

"I got that message, thanks."

Princess cocked an eyebrow. "And?"

"And—" Tag lifted the scroll. "It's on my list."

"You wouldn't be avoiding him, would you?"

"What? No, I'm busy with a lot." Tag gestured at the controlled chaos of people and robots in the main hangar. "Maybe you noticed."

"Yes, and it's all work you don't have to be doing yourself. That's why high-ranking officers have command staff."

"I wasn't about to drag a bunch of men and women off their real jobs to be my lackeys." Tag exhaled. It helped relieve some of the tension from mission planning and the strain he could feel building in his chest. "You're starting to sound like Tim."

"Commander Ess is right. There's plenty of people around to share the weight of command, even if you're the one who's ultimately in charge." Princess crossed her arms. "Or is that not why you haven't talked with Wu?"

"Don't know what you're talking about." Another tech strode by with a cart full of compact rations. Boxes of sawdust, judging by the fake flavors listed on the side. Tag grimaced but waved him by and made another mark on his list.

"You're avoiding him." Princess shook her head, but she was smiling. "I'm surprised I didn't see it sooner. I'm used to watching you dodge Naplian missiles and particle blasts, not people."

"Turns out I'm pretty good at both." Tag winked. "No, but seriously, I'll get to him. It just feels awkward that he's the captain, and as a colonel, we're technically equals, but I'm in overall command of the mission."

"Then there's the fact he is not your biggest fan."

"Yeah, won't help."

"If you need a wingman, by all means. .." Princess

patted his shoulder. "I would be honored to stand outside the bridge and offer thoughts and prayers if you two get into a knock-down, drag-out dogfight."

Tag chuckled. "Thanks, but no thanks, XO. I'll take my chances with a solo approach. Sounds better for my health and his."

His comms beeped. Tim's code appeared on the tiny screen. "Go ahead."

"We have a couple of new arrivals who are anxious to see you, Tag." Tim's tinny voice carried a hint of mischief. "Could you grab Marney on the way to Airlock Three? She's leaving sickbay."

"On it." Tag signed off and handed his scroll to Princess. He thumbed the authorization panel that kept it unlocked for general access. "Here. All yours."

"What's this for?"

"You're right. I should delegate." He tried to ignore the way his stomach was somersaulting, like a starfighter juking on the wrong end of a missile lock. *She's here. I didn't think that would ever happen.* "Starting right now."

✳ ✳ ✳

Tag followed the branching corridors from the hangar over to Airlock Three on the forward starboard side, where *Aox*'s hull narrowed. The indentation made perfect berths for smaller vessels—in this case, an Audrian gunboat that looked like it had been stripped of its weapons and painted orange, red, and yellow in varying degrees of sloppy patterns. The lettering on the aft hull said it was *Strunk*. Tag figured it was one of the ugliest ships he'd ever seen, and that included the Cargo

Cavebat *Olivia Vy* he'd piloted on the Union of Planets mission.

The memory stung. He wished he could fly her again, but since he'd made a very public trip in the older jump-capable freighter, there was no way using even a modified version of *Vy* wouldn't draw curious sensors for this role.

"It's hideous." Marney walked beside him, her nose wrinkled like there was a bad smell coming out of the HVAC vents. "Are you going to repaint it?"

"I wasn't planning to. The one-eyes will be just as disgusted." Tag reached for his uniform collar. Crooked, of course. He straightened both sides. The narrow portholes along the hull near Airlock Three gave him intermittent views of *Strunk* but not clear enough to figure out what was going on. They also weren't reflective enough to assess the rest of his appearance.

Marney giggled.

"What?" Tag made a face. "What's with everyone finding me hilarious today?"

"I can count on three fingers the number of times I've seen you groom yourself." Marney's cheeks were red. She rubbed at her eyes as she laughed. "There was Alyssa Ko in primary school—the girl you were dying to take to the Autumnal Gala…"

Tag winced. "Don't remind me. I bought that ridiculous suit right before I found out she had a boyfriend, and he was a pilot in training."

The deck shuddered. A green light appeared above Airlock Three, where two marines stood guard, armed with P6-SN machine pistols. Tim conversed with them in low tones. He nodded toward Tag and Marney as they approached. His expression softened some at the sight of his wife.

"And that was the only push you needed to get into flight school." Marney held onto Tag's arm. "I shudder to think what you'll dive into next if this woman asks you to run off with her."

"I'm not running off anywhere. This isn't winging over the Luran Plains with Scrape in the back seat. I've got a command and a pile of responsibilities."

"But you're nervous."

More scared than if I was under attack by a pair of Naplian fighters. Tag shrugged. "Quit worrying about me. What about you? Everything okay with the ship's surgeon?"

"Just a routine checkup. She wanted to make sure the baby was developing."

"I'm surprised Tim's not fussing at you to get on the first shuttle home." The airlock doors opened. Tag heard voices but couldn't bring himself to walk over there and greet the new arrivals, who were just silhouettes passing through the semi-opaque connector tunnel linking *Strunk* with *Aox*.

"We made up our minds to have a family, Tag, but when the chance to liberate Baedecker came up, neither of us wanted to be left out. I'm early enough in the pregnancy I'll be fine. We agreed this was a risk we were willing to take." Marney looked at him, her gaze as intense as any drill instructor's. "How could I help set other worlds free from Naplian rule or protect them from Briddarri experimentation if I wasn't going to give my own people that chance? You saw the settlements on Eleftheria—they work, but it's like a brand new colony. I don't know if Baedecker will ever be whole again, but if there's a Wester alive, we'll give everything for that chance."

Tag's heart hammered against his ribs. A fair bit of that had to do with his admiration for Marney's passion, but a bigger bit was the anticipation that he kept throttled back like a ripwave drive spooled up to launch him across the star system.

There she was.

Lira stepped between the guards. Dyson was right behind her. They exchanged polite handshakes with Tim, then followed him away from the airlock and toward their visitors.

Dyson outpaced Lira and Tim. "Tag. It is good to see you again."

Tag clapped hands with him and shook. He grinned. "Same here, Dyson. Happy you're not in pieces."

Dyson responded with a soft smile. "I had commented that you had once been the one who wished that fate for me. How times have changed."

Tag laughed and slapped his shoulder. *Ow.* His palm stung. "This is my sister, Marney Wester— daughter of the Baedecker governor, wife of a TI commander, and planetary liberator extraordinaire."

"Hello, Dyson." Marney took his hand. "My father and I owe you a great debt for keeping our Tag alive."

"I think the score is even." Dyson accepted Marney's hand and, to Tag's surprise, kissed her knuckles. "I am delighted to make your acquaintance."

Tag's insides tightened. As happy as he was to see his sister and his friend greet each other, Dyson's chivalrous act was so much like Scrape's from nearly seven years ago Tag wanted to lock Dyson away to keep him safe. Imagining the android spy with a broken neck like Scrape didn't help.

But Lira's approach blew those worries aside. She was as beautiful in person as he remembered. Her sly smile was full of the same confidence. "Hi."

"Uh, hi. Hello. Welcome aboard."

"Thanks, Colonel." Lira touched the insignia on his collar. Her fingers brushed his neck. They were hot against his skin. "Those look good on you. Maybe when this is over, I'll lift one for a souvenir."

"Maybe I'll give you one so you don't have to steal it."

Lira leaned in, her right hand drifting to Tag's chest. "Where's the fun in that?"

Tag grinned but found his brain too addled for a clever response. She looked and acted just like he remembered, from the black and blue hair to the way a smirk played at the corners of her lips.

Tim cleared his throat.

"Right, uh, Lira Lin Reen, this is—"

"Marney. I heard." Lira nodded. "You've made quite the reputation for yourself among the smaller planets no one seems to give a damn about."

"Thank you. I like to think I've made a difference. And you're Blue Kitt, from what I understand."

"You might say that." Tag appreciated how she smoothed over that question since few people realized Blue Kitt was a team of beings bonded to each other through ties that resembled family rather than a single daring individual.

"Ms. Reen is going to head up the acquisition phase of our operation." Tim stood beside Marney. His gaze flicked to his wife, his concern apparent, but she touched his hand in response, and that seemed to take the edge off his tension. "We're hoping to pull this off as bloodlessly as possible."

"Sounds like a good idea to me," Tag said.

"I don't like leaving bodies in my wake." Lira shook her head. "Moral concerns aside, you can still find them in space even if you dump them from an airlock."

Tim winced. The suggestion didn't surprise Tag as much as he thought it would, which he found more disturbing than the idea of killing a destroyer's crew—even the skeleton crew that would inhabit this vessel under repair —and taking it as their own. Was that because the crew would be Naplian? Did he care so little for sentient life he was okay with those deaths? Had the Briddarri raids scalded his soul enough that the prospect of more dubious killing didn't faze him?

Or was he just desperate for the whole damned war to end quickly?

Tag's comm chirped. Princess. He thumbed the switch. "Yeah."

"Colonel, a reminder that Captain Wu would like to speak with you at his earliest convenience." How Princess kept such cool tones while being as mischievous as Tag knew she was at that moment was beyond him. "He points out that we've taken aboard the last supplies, and with *Strunk* moored in place, we are nearing departure time."

"Roger that, Captain. I'm on my way." Tag nodded at the assembly. "Excuse me."

"Colonel?" Lira kept pace with him, her hands clasped at the small of her back. "Excuse me? Who are you, and what have you done with Taggart Wester?"

He chuckled. "It's me. A lot's changed since we last teamed up."

"Not too much, I hope."

They rounded a corner, just out of sight of their comrades, into a corridor that Tag knew provided a shortcut to the bridge. Half the lights were dimmed automatically from the lack of pedestrian traffic. He stopped in his tracks and, before he knew what he was doing, looped his arm around her waist, drawing her closer than she'd been when she'd flirted with him.

"Lira," he murmured. "You have no idea how much—"

She kissed him, and he forgot what he was going to say. It didn't matter. They were together again, and this was the moment he'd dreamed of four years running. Tag let himself fall back against the bulkhead. Lira pressed against him.

"You took a detour, I see."

Tag spluttered like he was surfacing from a swim. Lira laughed and wiped her mouth with the back of her hand. "So romantic," she said, patting Tag's cheek.

Dyson had apparently followed them. "I thought since Lira went with you that perhaps I should accompany you as well, Tag, to ascertain mission elements I have not received from Commander Ess or TI. The commander is otherwise preoccupied in conversation with his wife, who I see is expecting. This makes you an uncle. My congratulations."

Lira gasped. "She's having a baby? Tag, why didn't you tell me!"

"I had it all planned out for my mission briefing right after the ship theft but before the invasion." Tag shook his head. "I still can't believe they put me in charge of this thing. I bet Father had something to do with it."

"I was under the impression the two of you had 'mended fences,' in the vernacular."

Tag walked with them toward the bridge. "Yeah, we have, but I don't feel good about him using his influence on a couple of admirals."

"He must have his reasons."

"It's not too surprising," Lira said. "You've been leading these other secret missions of yours—"

"How did you--?"

Lira gestured at Dyson. He blinked. "I have been in regular correspondence with Commander Ess and TI. I am read in on Virry Squadron's clandestine operations."

"Okay, but Lira…?"

She shrugged. "We had a lot of time to chat on the way in."

Tag sighed. "It's more than Father. I don't…"

"You don't feel ready."

Tag looked at Lira. "Not to be responsible for this many lives. But if we're going to drop on Baedecker, take it back from the Naplians, and hold our ground, then maybe I can save more lives in the long run by helping the war end faster."

"Your father may have urged that you command for that very reason, Tag," Dyson pointed out. "Of course, the far simpler reason might be that he was short of trustworthy options. Who better to trust than his only son?"

Dyson's analysis was clear cut and logical, as Tag knew it would be. He'd forgotten how it could be annoying and reassuring at the same time. But more to the fact, it spun Tag's memories backward, down a path he hadn't taken since before the Naplians had barged into his life and ruined everything—a feeling he couldn't quite shake, not even now.

"It seems that the governor feels it's worthwhile. Have you considered he's sending you—or I should say, us—because he's unsure of whom to trust?"

"You're a regular comedian, Scrape. Father doesn't trust anyone."

"That isn't true. Not if he's sending his son and his RIO to meet a potentially polarizing figure rather than colonial defense troops or the police."

Scrape, his RIO (Radio Intercept Officer) had said that to him while he was still steaming at his wing commander, having pulled them from the flight roster. True, she'd had a good reason. Tag been hotdogging through the landscape.

The immediate result had been Father reassigning Tag to a more vital task: protecting Elden Selva from kidnapping by Reittian agents hellbent on capturing the hereditary consul of the Northern Alliance faction.

It seemed odd then until Scrape had explained it that way.

Sorrow seized him. He had to catch his breath a moment.

Lira's hand found his shoulder. "Are you all right?"

"I will be. I was just remembering an old friend." Tag let out a shuddered breath. "It's been such a long time. You'd think I'd be over it, right? I mean, he's been dead longer than we served together, by almost twice the years."

"The impact of time spent with one for whom you care a great deal is not diminished by its short duration," Dyson said softly. "The loss of that one can be an even worse pain when the time spent was more intense, regardless of how many years or hours or minutes it was."

Tag knew Dyson was thinking of Olivia Vy, his former partner and the one for whom he'd named their Cavebat freighter during their Union of Planets mission. "Thanks. I appreciate the pep talk."

Lira looped her arms through theirs and pulled them along. "You see? I knew we were meant to be back in the thick of things together. What would the Grand Alliance do without their best pilot, spy, and thief?"

Her humor warmed Tag, and he was glad to see even Dyson, for all his artificial nature, seemed to take heart in her attempt to cheer them up.

"One would think," Dyson said, his familiar deadpan tone back in place, "They would find themselves in considerably less trouble."

"Do me a favor." Tag grinned at them. "Don't mention that observation to Captain Wu."

CHAPTER EIGHT

Elden Selva rode the drop barge with four hundred Truppen in complete silence.

Any biological occupant would have heard the roar of the barge's passage through the planet's atmosphere, the rattle of stored equipment straining against its shock webbing, and the shriek of stressed metal resisting gravity's pull. There was no need for the Truppen to communicate aloud like their inferiors, not when they shared communications interlinks that were hardened against unwanted parties listening in.

<I have confirmed readiness from all fifty octants.> Franklin Goetz, his trusted second, provided the update. Elden glanced at Goetz's hulking form, the metallic gray armor glinting under the blood red emergency lights. <No maintenance down-checks, so no one gets to warm the seats while we fight.>

<That must be a first. How many of these drops, Goetz? Since we entered the war, that is.>

<One hundred eighty-nine, sir.>

Just like that, Elden felt the data from each one of those combat missions pressing against his awareness. It was as if he were holding a door against an unruly mob trying to break into his home—or determined one-eyes storming his base of operations. Elden imagined clenching his teeth, which helped him refocus on the objectives at hand and forestall the data storm. It had taken years of practice, and yet what worked best was to rely on the long-lost expressions and gestures he'd employed in human form.

<An even one-ninety after this one,> Goetz added.

<Presuming we survive.>

An electronic snort crackled across the interlink. <I'm planning on making the enemy do the dying, not me, sir, and you're well past needing my babysitting.>

Elden considered how many Naplians—and Briddarri—he'd killed. More data pushed at his awareness barriers. This time, he let a handful of images through before he pushed back. One side effect of being a cybernetic warrior was the ability to perfectly recall information his optical and other sensors recorded, which meant he could see, at any moment he chose, the face of every single individual he'd killed.

There were many among the Truppen who banished those recordings behind the strongest possible data barriers so they would never have the weight of those deaths on their conscience. Elden couldn't blame them, not after seven years of unrelenting warfare.

He, though, felt it a good habit to remind himself that he wasn't without guilt.

<Thirty seconds to touch down.> Goetz's announcement blasted through Elden's awareness over the battalion interlink, ensuring that the four hundred received the same message. Armor clicked and scraped around Elden as the Truppen readied their weapons.

The lights turned green. Bulkheads and deck plating folded back, letting the broiling air rush into the compartment. Elden's mechanical body powered up its coolant system to protect vital circuits.

The Truppen were arrayed in four lines of one hundred, running parallel to each other from the front to back of the barge. Energy shields rippled under weapons impact as Naplian particle blasts pelted the transport. Elden couldn't see much below except craters and long scorch marks that turned the red-ochre hills into a ruined tableau.

<Bombardment looks like it did the trick,> Goetz said.

Elden's timer told him eleven seconds remained. <Less threat of heavy artillery for us to face.>

<Pity.> Goetz's shoulder-mounted particle cannon unlocked from his back and swiveled into place beside the left side of his rounded headpiece. <I'm hoping for a few mechs.>

Two seconds. One…

<Jump by octant!> Elden ordered via the battalion interlink. <Move!>

The Truppen released magnetic locks holding them in place. They fell free in clusters of eight as the barge skimmed thirty meters over the ground.

Elden toggled his clamps a second behind Goetz. *He's always quicker on the draw.* But Elden was just glad in this situation neither of them was human anymore. No lurch of the stomach. No g-forces acting on their anatomy.

Fear was still present, but Elden could suppress the emotion far more easily than he ever had when he was frail and biological.

The battlefield spread before them. The Naplian base was already in ruins, courtesy of railgun bombardment from orbit. Elden's scanners indicated every structure, be it a power generator or a barracks, was destroyed or damaged. Naplians scrambled among wrecked artillery mechs, their mottled blue and gray armor shifting colors in absurd flickers as they adapted to their surroundings.

Not that the active camouflage would protect them from Truppen sensors.

The first wave of cybernetic warriors came down shooting. A mix of searing white particle beams and the shriek of portable railguns filled the air. The blazing glare of Naplian energy weapons responded, turning the battleground into a light show that forced Elden's protective systems to dampen incoming light sources and focus on two things: Naplian bio-signs and Truppen ID beacons.

Elden shut off the auto-targeter. He hadn't gotten this far in the campaign against the one-eyes by relying on devices to do the work for him. He instead lifted his railgun toward a trio of Naplians struggling to right a toppled stationary particle cannon and fired. The blast obliterated the power source and scorched the three soldiers in the resultant explosion.

The barge swept overhead, forgotten to Elden and the others, as they Truppen fanned out across the ruined base. Octants formed the basic core unit of their battalion. The groups of eight maintained cohesion, fighting as a single body. Elden stuck close to Goetz.

Twenty Naplians stormed their position from a shattered bunker, swarming like vermin. Elden found the thought darkly amusing. Didn't the one-eyes take pride in calling humans *shirish*, their word for the same Terran term?

<Behind you.> Goetz said it with as little inflection as a nav comp announcing orbital debris.

<I have him.> It was an unnecessary warning, anyway, because Elden's sensors pinpointed the Naplian firing from behind a crumpled support beam. Elden bent a knee, twisted his torso 180 degrees, and fired a single magnetically accelerated round through the stanchion. The impact sheared the soldier in half.

The rest of the Naplians were on his octant in seconds. They lacked the panic Elden expected the Truppen presence to elicit. What happened to the fear of ziura, the fabled devastators of their myths? Maybe these troopers were of the wrong sect.

Goetz grabbed a Naplian who got too close with a thermite grenade and flung him twenty meters in the opposite direction. The grenade exploded, killing three of the Naplian's comrades. The Truppen shot two more at point-blank range.

Elden's Truppen cut down the twenty until they were eight. A particle blast seared the sensors on the right side of his head. His field of view went blank, then rebooted in a jagged, pixelated version of the crisp imagery he expected. His body's damage control was working overtime—he could tell by the buzzing in his torso.

Two of his Truppen lost their step—Landsiedel and Parmenter. Damage reports flickered across Elden's displays. Neither man was going anywhere for the moment, which was a problem with the remaining Naplians nearby. <Get between them!> Elden snapped over the octant interlink. <Repair drones to these coordinates.>

<Already inbound.> That was Thayer, one of

the less experienced but still eager warriors in his team. Thayer was in a smaller, more compact Truppen frame, one of the older models that predated Elden's transference, but what he lacked in size he made up for in ferocity and agility. He used implanted jet boosters to rocket three meters over the Naplians at an angle that allowed him to deploy the same gauntlet blades Elden sported.

His attack eliminated three of the Naplian attackers, though new damage alerts flashed into Elden's octant readout.

Elden swiped the Furta particle rifle from the hands of the nearest Naplian. The weapon's last discharge flared across his chest but at too wide an angle to cause appreciable damage. He stabbed the alien before he could reach for another weapon.

Goetz and the rest of the octant killed the last four.

<All octants report they're advancing throughout the base.> Goetz's narration was, again, not strictly necessary because Elden had accessed a miniaturized view of the battlefield. It was grainy, though. A growing green bar at the far right of Elden's field of vision told him his primary displays would be restored in seven seconds.

<What about the hangars?>

<The doors are still blocked, but the one-eyes are trying to dig them out.>

Elden magnified the map until it highlighted a glowing rectangle. The hangar was buried underground, out of reach of the orbital strike. The blips representing Truppen closed in on the coordinates, but resistance was heavy. Their progress sputtered and stalled. <Signal Octants Fourteen through Twenty-Two: Redirect and converge on the hangar. We'll join them.>

<Understood.>

A pair of drones that reminded Elden of spiders—albeit mechanical ones the size of a wolf or a large dog—spiraled into their midst, spray spewing from their deceleration thrusters. They latched onto Landsiedel and Parmenter. Any sane person would have been horrified to have the clattering robots grasp them in eight arms, but since most of those arms sported armor patches and mending torches, the Truppen welcomed them as swift battlefield doctors.

<Landsiedel, once your repairs are complete, take Parmenter and link up with Octant Forty-Three.> Elden bracketed the number on his display and shunted the coordinates through their shared interlink. <They're holding a captured munitions bunker. You'll be out of the line of fire. I'm holding you in reserve.>

<Yes, Consul.> Their simultaneous replies weren't delayed by signal degradation. Elden took that as a positive indicator that their repairs were effective.

He led the other six Truppen away from their corner of the ruined base, using their embedded jets to leap between hilltops and crumpled buildings without exposing themselves to the crisscrossing weapons fire overhead. The octants Elden had pointed out to Goetz converged from all over, friendly blips blinking on his tactical display.

The hangar doors peeked from the crumbling edge of a low hill. Elden's scanners informed him the hangar itself stretched for several kilometers beneath the surface.

And it was full.

Jarra Fol starfighters lined both sides. Their curved wings were distinct even in the tiny, low-resolution images generated by the scanners. Elden counted one hundred and forty-four. Two entire wings.

They were primed for launch.

Elden landed among the Truppen already pressing the attack around the blocked hatch. They had formed a perimeter a hundred meters away from where Naplian soldiers and mechs scraped away at the piles of rock and dirt.

<It's a mess,> Goetz grumbled. <If they clear the debris, those fighters will blast our ships clear out of space. The transports and bombards aren't equipped to knock down a swarm that big.>

<No, they're not. I am also not willing to risk revealing our stealth ships either, especially if there are Naplian vessels waiting to swoop in and pick up these stragglers.> Elden hadn't traded away vital Naplian tech to procure stealth raiders from the Svenisch for nothing. He issued silent orders to available octants, sending Truppen as far around the long, low hillside as he could manage without incurring too many casualties. <Suggestions?>

<Kill all the one-eyes.>

<That has been our goal, thank you. I meant regarding the hatch.>

Thayer hunkered behind the same quik-crete wall Elden and Goetz were using for shelter as they pelted the Naplian forces with railgun projectiles. <Consul, I recommend we let them open the hatch.>

Elden thought Goetz's red optical scanners blazed with greater intensity. <Maybe this one has had his

circuits fried by too many pulsed particle blasts.>

<Explain yourself, Thayer,> Elden said.

<If they get the doors cleared, they will launch the fighters, but if you direct a bombard at the precise moment...>

<...We can obliterate them as they try to exit and avoid getting mired down in the hangar.> Elden nodded. More unnecessary gestures. Ah, well. He suspected there were bits of his human existence that would never truly fade.

His memory banks offered a dozen still images of Marney Wester—as a young woman when they were in love; as a bride later at her interrupted wedding celebration, and still later as a grim-faced insurgent helping him destroy the hideous Briddarri cybernetic experiments.

The affection wasn't likely to fade, either.

<Keep up our fire,> Elden instructed Goetz. <I'll send the command to *Hessian*.>

Goetz grunted. <Your will is my command, sir.>

<And a good thing, too, or else I would be doomed if you served our enemies.>

Elden opened a secure channel to *Hessian*, their old Northern Alliance transport riding in low orbit with two *Ubiquitous*-Class bombard vessels trailing it. He fed the coordinates and confirmed through *Hessian*'s scanners that the bombards had their weapons trained on the hangar hillside, but given the rate at which they were scooting along, the vessels would overshoot the target in eighteen seconds.

The last rubble fell away from the massive, armored doors. They squealed apart. A distant shriek of starfighter engines igniting in the atmosphere echoed from beyond them.

One, two, three Jarra Fol fighters zipped out of the hangar.

A searing, blinding blast ripped through the sky and immolated the fourth in line. Explosions rumbled beyond the impact, shaking the ground worse than any earthquake Elden had ever encountered. The hillside rippled and collapsed along its length as gouts of flame shot out of the top. The shockwave and blast burn wiped out the Naplian defenders, too, leaving the battered Truppen coated in dust and debris.

Thayer whooped, the sound tinny in his speakers. "Three out of twelve dozen! Not too bad, sirs."

"Well thought, Lieutenant. That will teach me to doubt a subordinate's cunning." Elden straightened his frame so he could look around the base. Naplian resistance was collapsing, albeit slower than the hangar had. It wouldn't be long before the Truppen controlled what was left of the Naplian forward base. "Goetz, coordinate with the octants that have taken prisoners. We'll want them ready for transport and trade."

"Roger that." If Goetz was irritated about the sudden switch to vocalization, he didn't show it. "Who gets them this time?"

"Whichever Grand Alliance units are closest, though my preference is the Terran Republic, so if we have to go a few light-years out of our way, don't let that discourage you." Elden would have given a wry smile if he could have still managed one.

"What about those fighters?" Thayer scraped carbon scoring off his right arm, where a Naplian particle blast had come close to severing a sensor link.

Elden glanced skyward. "They won't get far, not

without a jump-capable ship in the system and with our stealth ships lurking in the void. It makes no difference."

Hessian sent him a coded transmission—a personal communiqué on a frequency he'd given to Marney Wester. Elden applied the decryption key but felt a flicker of surprise when he read the brief text message.

Later. He'd digest it later. Elden pointed toward where the octants were emerging from their shelter to inspect the ruined base. "Come. Let's see if the one-eyes left anything of interest."

And then perhaps I can take time to see what's so urgent that Tag Wester would message me during a battle.

* * *

Admiral Ergen leaned back in his chair as the Terran officer finished the latest report from the Naplian front.

"As you can see, ladies and gentlemen, the Truppen forces under Consul Elden Selva are one of the most effective weapons we have in our arsenal." Commodore Sobban Ram paced the conference room aboard *Winter Scourge* with the controlled grace of a *jaarax* on the prowl. Ergen wondered if Ram had ever seen the predator, which was twice as big as a Terran lion. "The entire raid on Dalphas Ko cost them only eight out of four hundred men, injuries—or damage, I should say—notwithstanding."

"It is worth noting the Truppen operate independent of our respective governments, and so while they remain as effective as the commodore states, we cannot ignore that they do not take orders from anyone." This from the female—a female flag officer, of all things! —Vice Admiral Tanaka.

"I wouldn't fuss too much," said Admiral Sinclair. "They're a hell of a lot more receptive to our directives than other elements. Take the Lotharian pirates. We must *pay* them before they even consider making a strike against the Naplians."

"That is only because they have not seen an impact on their trade routes," groused Commodore Grantivire Cyred, the ranking Reittian. The stout, muscular man shifted his weight, the maroon tattoos on his bald head and his pale face highlighted by the overhead illumination. "Give them time. I believe we are making headway in our negotiations."

"I'll point out, for what seems like the thousandth time, that the Truppen don't have to be the only game in the galaxy." Ergen thumped his fist off the extended scroll before him. His skin left a rippling rainbow effect on the flimsy screen, distorting Ram's briefing— or rather, Selva's transmitted report that turned into the centerpiece of Ram's briefing. "They run the Naplians ragged, don't get me wrong, but let's not forget it was the one-eyes who tried evening the odds with their *ziurathal* mech projects."

"Those mechs were oversized armor suits," Sinclair said. "They put the hurt on the Truppen, to be sure, but you can't seriously expect anything short of a full cybernetic unit to take down Selva's horde."

"I'll mention again that our research has shown properly applied cybernetics can convert subjects into warriors nearly as effective as the Truppen." Ergen pointed at Ram. "You could be seeing those low casualties and high successes mirrored across the Grand Alliance worlds."

"I'll repeat my position, Admiral, and that of our command: Development of a cybernetic army requires far more manpower than we have at our disposal." Ram folded his arms. "Recruitment efforts toward the same research you mentioned have been decidedly lacking."

"And in case you think we've forgotten the rumors about worlds stripped of their people, think again," Sinclair muttered.

"You can tiptoe around it all you want," Ergen growled. "Don't fool yourselves: We can't win without conscription."

"Conscription? You're talking about incarceration and slavery! The butchery of—"

"Gentlemen." Tanaka's voice was soft but cut through both men's bluster easily. Ergen found himself grudgingly impressed by her stern gaze. "The Briddarri Kingdom is well aware of the Terran Republic's opposition to such avenues of cybernetic research. I trust we still have your word such experimentation is limited and does not violate the sovereign rights of any world, be it Alliance or independent."

"My word is as good as it gets, Vice Admiral." *Keeping one's word won't be worth a damn if we back down and let the one-eyes storm across every sector from here to the other side of Estra.*

"We'll consider the matter closed, I presume." Ram cleared his throat. He glanced around the room at the twenty gathered military personnel. "Moving along to our preparations for Operation Restoration: I understand your units, Commodore Cyred, have had issues with Svenisch raiders."

"I don't know whether they're Svenisch, but the stealth vessels they use certainly are," Cyred said. "They have cut our supply lines to our Briddarri allies twice."

Supplies we need to continue the cyber experiments. I smell Selva's stink all over this one. It's not like the Svenisch are picky about who they sell ships to. "I think we can help there, Commodore. Got a few anti-stealth corvettes I think we can redirect your way." *Which I would do, anyway, but he's given me the excuse I need to reallocate forces after Selva without drawing too much attention.*

"Your assistance is welcome, Admiral."

"Isn't it always?" Ergen snorted. "Now then, Commodore, Ram... Maybe we should get these invasion plans underway before the Naplians have a chance to sniff us out?"

Ram gazed at him. The Terran was too damned focused. "Very well. As I was saying..."

Ergen nodded along with the plans. They sounded good. He wanted to make sure he knew exactly how the Terrans wanted to put the Briddarri suggestion into practice, and if they could rope Selva in, then maybe, just maybe, Ergen would get to fulfill that odd human adage about two birds and one stone.

CHAPTER NINE

T ag stood by the main hatch for *Aox*'s cargo bay. A tapping sound filtered past the normal background noise. What was that racket?

Marney elbowed him. "Your boot."

"Huh?" Tag saw he was indeed tapping his foot. A nervous gesture. Great. He never used to have one of those. Chalk that up to the pressures of command.

He was waiting for the docking maneuver to finish. Marney stood to his right, with Tim next to her. Captain Wu waited at parade rest on Tag's left.

There were Truppen on the other side of the hatch.

"He really is on our side, Tag," Marney said. "He fought against the Naplians and. .. other enemies. Don't worry. I've seen him before. He's imposing, certainly, but not as frightening as you might think."

"That's just it, Sis—I haven't seen one up close. The last good look I got was at Baedecker when we fought them off in deep space out by Six after they killed that transport's crew." Tag shuddered. "And yeah, they were on the ground when we rescued the refugees at Vossberg during the evacuation, but I've never been in the same room as one before. Now I'm supposed to command forty giant cyber soldiers, one of whom is my sister's ex-boyfriend."

Marney blushed. "Well, you make a valid point, but keep your voice down."

"Don't worry, Marney." Tim sounded tired. "If I were worried about Elden taking you from me, I would have had him hunted down and destroyed years ago."

Marney backhanded his chest lightly. "Don't joke about that!"

"You assume I'm joking." Tim's smile seemed less about humor to Tag after that.

The lights above the hatch blinked green: Air pressure equalized. "The flexible connector's secure," Wu said. He lifted his comm. "Bridge, this is the captain. Open the hatch."

The cargo bay doors split along the vertical seam. The tunnel beyond them stretched twenty meters across space to the massive transport *Hessian.* Tag made a note to check the schematics later. All he could see right now was a huge metal hull outside the transparent tube, blocking out the stars.

The Truppen walking toward him absorbed the rest of his interest.

They stepped more lightly than he would have imagined for cybernetic warriors that were two meters tall. Tag had seen plenty of intelligence reports on Truppen, complete with hi-res imagery, but nothing prepared him for their sheer presence. He was way too aware that the two cybers could kill him and the other three people with him without breaking the robot equivalent of a sweat.

"Welcome aboard." Wu got to the niceties first. He stepped forward when everything in the back of Tag's brain was telling him to hop into a Warhawk and fly as far away as possible. "I'm Captain Desmond

Wu, commanding the *Aox.* This is Colonel Tag Wester, overall operational commander."

"Tag." The voice that buzzed out of the navy-blue Truppen was Elden's all right, though it sounded harsher than Tag remembered. "I never thought I would stand with you again."

"Hey, Eldi." Tag offered a hand but then realized what he was doing. Did cybers bother with human gestures?

Elden cocked his head. The red eyes zeroed in on Tag. *Makes me feel like I should raise shields.* Then, a sonorous chuckle escaped from the Truppen vocal modulator. "I certainly didn't expect to hear another person call me that."

"Yeah, I guess there's not much call for nicknames."

Elden stomped forward and extended a broad, mechanical hand. Tag shook it, ready to withdraw at a moment's notice, recognizing Elden could rip his arm free of its socket or mash his fingers to a red pulp with the slightest squeeze.

Despite his worry, Elden's handshake was close to typical, albeit steely. "I'm glad you're still alive."

"Same here." Tag wondered if Elden considered that insulting. "I'd introduce the rest of our command team, but I think we're all familiar."

"Marney." Elden nodded. "Commander Ess."

"Consul Selva." Tim's nod matched Elden's, though Tag noticed neither made any effort to be warm or informal. They kept to official titles.

"I'm glad you're able to join us for this, Elden." Marney smiled and touched his arm. "Your people have done so much for the war effort. It's a great burden we've put upon you."

"If we can help reclaim Baedecker, it will be time well spent." Elden gestured behind him. "You remember Goetz, of course."

"Yes. It's nice to see you, too."

"Likewise, ma'am," Goetz rumbled. "Been leading any rebellions lately?"

"She's moved on from that line of work," Tim said. "Why don't we get to the briefing? If all goes well, we'll be joining the invasion fleet in a week, and from there, we'll make our move."

"I understand, Commander, but there is a reason you brought us in through the cargo bay rather than the main airlock," Elden said.

"That's why," Tag pointed beyond the rows of ammunition containers, hoping he could provide enough of a distraction to keep the two men's chilly dispositions from getting any colder. "We've got a temporary space set up in an auxiliary compartment."

"Tag?" Dyson approached from that direction. "We have an issue with Commodore Ram."

"Now? Really?" Tag sighed. *As much fun as it's been...* "Don't tell me he wants a promotion, too."

Wu rolled his eyes.

"No." Dyson took in the small gathering, his gaze resting on Elden and Goetz, but he must have decided they could be in on whatever the secret was. "The C-in-C wants to recall Commodore Ram and the Thirteenth Expeditionary Force to counter a Naplian scouting expedition near the New Chile system."

Tim scowled. "If he does that, the invasion will have to be postponed until we can get a new battlegroup."

"Hold on." Tag rubbed his forehead. "Let's get this from the saarno fox's mouth, so to speak."

He led their group past the supplies and through an open hatchway that led onto an open staging area just off the main bay. Elden and Goetz had to duck to get inside but made it without scraping paint.

Sinclair, Tanaka, and Ram were already inside, gathered around a tactical board. None of them looked happy to see, well, anybody. Lira sat in a far corner, boots up on a box of railgun rounds.

"You're missing all the best conversation," she stage-whispered. "But given who your new friends are, I can see why that might not be very exciting."

"It's moronic, is what it is!" Sinclair snapped. "The C-in-C must think Sobban has a magic wand instead of a heavy cruiser. Moving the Thirteenth to New Chile will mean we'll have to wait for it to come back after who knows how long. We've only just got all the pieces in place for this attack. That star system's got nothing of value except for some one-eye scout depot."

"The strategic importance is of less value, I suspect, than the show of force *Confiance* could bring to the surrounding systems, many of which are only nominally in Terran hands." Tanaka had her arms crossed and was frowning, though Tag had no idea if that meant she was more upset than usual because he couldn't remember her *not* frowning since Eleftheria.

"I assume you've already taken this up with the director of TI?" Tim asked.

"We are awaiting his response," Ram replied quietly. "If those are my orders, I will go—"

"Don't be crazy," Sinclair interrupted." "A single battlegroup isn't going to cut it if the Naplians move against New Chile, and the C-in-C had better know that. It's simple. I'll go myself."

"But, sir, that's going to delay the invasion even more," Tim said.

Tag cleared his throat. "Look, I know this is great fun, the brass arguing about who gets to lead the invasion, but mind if we show the Truppen what we're planning? Because we've got a hundred and sixty cybernetic soldiers ready to come aboard and make the Naplians wish they'd never taken Baedecker."

"Of course." Ram switched on the display board. The two-dimensional panel glowed with basic representations of Baedecker's six orbital tracks and the surrounding star systems. "We have elements of the invasion force gathering fifty light-years away at various locations, some in secret, some in the open posing as reinforcements for existing strongholds. TI has provided updated intel on the three feeder systems that the Naplians use for entry into Baedecker."

"Right." Tim glanced around the room, apparently making sure the previous arguments were concluded before continuing. He touched a panel, and three stars glowed red. "The Naplians are exercising tight control over the Baedecker System, funneling all traffic in and out by means of the three nearest systems —Alpha Regus, Goldstar, and Fontenelle. Any ship that jumps to Baedecker *not* from these three systems is intercepted and detained—destroyed, in a few cases. That much we've ascertained from independent traders."

He touched another control. One of the systems magnified. "Fontenelle is the least guarded of the three. This is where we'll need you to take the destroyer and then jump into Baedecker. Dyson?"

"Thank you, Commander." Dyson held up a scroll. "I have worked with TI on preparing a false identity for the destroyer we capture, to be uploaded and overlaid on its secure transponder. The destroyer *Teret* is undergoing major maintenance here, at the Jeffords system. The Naplian presence is minimal. Once you capture *Teret*, it will be reclassified as *Valo*, which is the designation for another ship known among the Ffawe as a *wiliru*—a straggler or a pest, depending on your definition."

"Sounds charming," Lira said. "And why will they not be looking for a duplicate of the same vessel?"

"The Naplians have a hierarchical society that venerates the emperors above all else," Dyson explained. "*Both* emperors. *Valo*'s commander is of a family that crossed Benaltep's clan centuries ago, and while they no longer face public shaming and exile, they have only worked enough penance to grudgingly warrant military service. I concur with TI when they ascertain *Valo*'s commander would have had no chance at captaining a warship were it not for the emperors' territorial ambitions."

"So, you're saying they don't care about this guy or what his ship does," Tag said.

"Precisely. One destroyer will not make or break Naplian offensives, but for our purposes, the single ship will allow us unfettered access to Baedecker, even more so because the rest of the Naplian forces will go out of their way to ignore its presence. They will, in fact, intentionally cut it off, treating it as a pariah."

"A pariah ship filled with *shirish*." Elden nodded. "Fitting. Once the ship has breached the system, what then? What is our role? Twenty octants of my Truppen are formidable but can hardly be the vanguard for an entire planetary system's invasion."

"Your role is more targeted." Dyson glanced at Ess. "Commander?"

Tim cleared his throat. "This group's objective is to sow chaos behind enemy lines, putting the command structure at Baedecker into disarray while the Grand Alliance forces launch the primary assault."

Tag raised an eyebrow. "Sow chaos."

"It's not that hard, Tag." Lira stood and walked around him. She traced her hand across his shoulders. "We've had some experience with chaos."

Tag chuckled. "Yeah, the three of us were pretty good at it."

"Whether intentionally or not." Dyson's tone remained as dry as usual, but Tag caught a hint of a smile on his face. "I surmise that is the reason for our reunion."

"So, do I get to steal anything besides a starship, Tim?" Lira smiled. "I wouldn't say no to another heist planetside."

"Actually, you hit the bulls-eye, Lira." Sinclair braced himself on the display board's edge with both hands. "We want you to steal Admiral Erassia."

The silence that followed went on for so long Tag swore he could hear the digital chronometer on the far wall ticking like an ancient clock.

"Erassia," Goetz rumbled. "Isn't that great."

"You're aware of his role as the commander of Baedecker's forces?" Tim frowned.

"We all are," Tag said. "He's in the general briefing."

"He was behind the ziurathal deployment." Elden looked at Wu.

"We're read in on the intelligence regarding Admiral Erassia," Tanaka said. "We know of his work creating anti-Truppen battlesuits."

"Very good." Elden clenched his clawed hands. Metal scraped on metal. "Then his capture will be a double triumph."

"Hang on. We're going to kidnap a Naplian admiral? Right under their noses?" Tag ran a hand through his hair. "And while we're doing this, the rest of the fleet will sweep through the Baedecker System."

"That's the deal." Sinclair frowned. "The only torch burning at the works is this foolish order from the C-in-C, but I'll get that taken care of. I'll get to New Chile, assess the situation, and be back in a week's time. *Confiance* and the Thirteenth will join the rest of our forces, making the first incursion under Admiral Ergen's command."

"Admiral, if I may, I offer protest to the Briddarri involvement in this venture," Elden said.

"What?" Sinclair blinked. "The hell for, Consul?"

"Reasons not germane to this briefing."

Tag knew what he was getting at. Wu wasn't in the know regarding the secret war against the Briddarri cybernetics experiment, even though everyone else in the room was. Sinclair, too, picked up on the comment. "Sorry, Consul. It's our turf, but we can't do it without their help. Terra is a full member of the Grand Alliance now. We've got to play ball, even if we don't like our teammates, because otherwise the opposing team wins."

"I must restate my protest—"

"And I'm going to restate that you don't," Sinclair snapped. "This meeting is on hold until we figure out the New Chile situation. Colonel Wester, collaborate with Commander Ess and bring your people up to speed. Setsu, Sobban, let's work out the details with the brass in Captain Wu's office—if you don't mind, Desmond."

"Not at all, Admiral." Wu gave Tag an irritated look as the four officers departed. Tag wanted to retaliate with a rude gesture. How did the man figure this was *his* fault?

Elden waited until the hangar bay doors slid shut. "This is absurd," he said, the words rasping through his vocal modulator. "You can see what Ergen is doing, can't you?"

"We have every confidence that the Espionage Directorate has provided us with accurate intelligence about the Baedecker System and surrounding ship strengths." Dyson didn't seem at all rattled by the hulking cyber who was losing his patience. Yet another advantage of being an android. "Commander Ess and I have received independent confirmation from TI."

"I'm sure the Briddarri have done their homework," Lira said. "They're nothing if not fastidious. I think what the consul means is the timing."

"Trust me, we've thought of that," Tag said. "It hasn't escaped anyone's notice—especially mine— that this invasion idea comes up right as Flirry Squadron is putting more pressure on the greenbloods' laboratories."

"Which coincides with our anti-shipping efforts, though I think we've managed to vex the Reittians in the process," Elden noted. "They were, however unwittingly, supplying the Briddarri labs."

"I'd say pissing off the Reittians is a win no matter the circumstances, sir," Goetz said.

"Agreed, but the invasion planning has had two effects the Briddarri have to be celebrating." Elden held up clawed fingers one at a time. "Ending Flirry Squadron's raids and taking our attention off the Briddarri labs and their supply routes."

"Yeah, I know." Tag grimaced. "Tim, Marney, what sense do you guys get out of this? I'm betting TI's noticed."

"They have. My bosses aren't happy, but they also can't pass up the opportunity that we can retake Baedecker and put a crimp in serjaum supply." Tim exhaled. Marney touched his hand. "Like it or not, ladies and gentlemen, the war is *not* progressing in our favor. Joining the Grand Alliance has helped Terra, but it's the difference between a grinding war that slows their advance versus the Naplians storming their way to Earth next week."

"Serjaum has always been the key, and Baedecker has the richest resources this side of the Great Desert Rift." Marney indicated the display board on which the invasion routes and key star systems still glowed. "I agree with Eldi—this is a problem for our cause. But Tim's right, and so is TI. We have to take the chance. Someday, we may even be able to repatriate our people back to their homeworld if we can stabilize the surrounding sectors and keep pushing the Naplians."

"Overly optimistic, but I like the sentiment." Tim smiled at her.

Lira rolled her eyes. "This is all lovely and patriotic, but it still doesn't answer the question: What are we going to do?"

Tag didn't like the sly edge to her tone as much as her presence buoyed him. "I'm betting you mean other than follow orders."

"That's always what I mean, Tag."

"We're going to keep our eyes open." He looked at everyone in their cluster, meeting their eyes—or optical ports. "We focus on getting Erassia, sure, but we pump every scrap of intel out of him and his command center that we can while we're there. I bet Admirals Sinclair and Tanaka have ideas as to what kind of chaos they want us to cause, but given who we've got gathered in this room, I know we can do better."

"If by 'better' you mean cause more property damage on a greater scale, I believe your statement is correct," Dyson said.

Tim snorted.

"Tag, what exactly did you do that convinced a TI android officer that you were a bad influence?" There was a bemused edge to Elden's voice.

Tag scratched the back of his neck. He blushed. "Well, you know, we had a mission to the Union of Planets a few years ago that involved, um, breaking the rules."

"We stole data," Lira said. "And they rescued me from other thieves. Oh, and from the Briddarri. But that was after we went toe-to-toe with the Denics when they ambushed us, and Tag commandeered a state-of-the-art starfighter—"

"I think we'll leave it at that before we get into operational details," Tim interjected. "Wouldn't you say, Blue Kitt?"

He was one of the few who'd realized the secret

of the thief clan. Lira bowed her head, that mischievous smile in place. "I've got a few suggestions for how we can make things miserable for the Naplians, Consul Selva, and if we're lucky, we might get to poke the Briddarri at the same time."

Elden nodded. "I'm beginning to see why you were invited along. Goetz, signal the assigned octants to transfer aboard."

"On it, sir."

The ringing of metallic footsteps responded almost immediately. Tag walked out to the middle of the hangar bay with Elden as the rest of the group huddled around the tactical display board.

Tag's stomach tightened as the cybers boarded *Aox*, led by six Truppen in two columns, then the other one hundred and fifty-two in four columns. Their precision made their march rumble like thunder coming across Voss Flats.

"It's been seven years since either of us has seen that world," Elden said. "I must admit, Tag, that I'm not sure how I'll feel once we stand upon it again. It is where I lost my life."

Tag glanced at the sharp profile of Elden's Truppen headpiece. "You got it back and then some, it looks like."

"I started a second life. This—" Elden tapped the chest armor. "This is not me. I am still in here, but with each passing month, I feel those bits of humanity slipping away. Being among your team makes me realize the truth all the more."

"What truth are you talking about?"

"The truth that I will never be the man I was. I am Elden Selva in name only."

Tag didn't have a response for that. Sure, he could lie and say he still thought of the machine beside him as Elden Selva, the Northern Alliance hereditary consul who was in love with his sister, but this was Elden's nervous system and brain combined with a battle-tested warframe. Where did the soul fit in when it came to matters like that?

Scrape would tell him the actions mattered more than wiring. In that case, Tag figured he'd have to wait and see what Elden would do when they came under fire.

As the rest of the Truppen marched deeper into the hangar bay, some of them pulling portable repair bays on capsule-shaped hover sleds, he knew one thing for certain: The Naplians would be terrified.

CHAPTER TEN

*A*ox jumped into the oort cloud at the edge of the star system labeled HDM-1123, obscured from the Naplian long-range sensor array by the sheer volume of cometary fragments swirling about the region. Captain Wu ordered the ship into low-power mode, with the main reactors on standby so he could prep for a jump in under a minute if they were discovered.

"We're loaded and ready." Tag slid into the Audrian gunboat's sensor console seat. He was surprised by the sheer volume of screens in front of him. Each control looked like TI had stripped it out of a brand new stealth fighter and linked it to the shipboard mainframe without so much as peeling the manufacturer's insignia off.

Of course, that was his imagination. He couldn't find a single identifying mark on the board but was able to determine there were no other ships within a five light-second sphere.

"*Aox* reports we are clear to detach." Dyson sat in the pilot's chair. He flipped the row of switches above his head and ran down the panels on the console between him and Tag. "Are you certain you do not want to fly, Colonel?"

"Want to, yeah. Need to?" Tag shook his head.

"This is my op, but you're the pilot. I promise I won't even backseat fly."

"I will take you at your word, then, and remind you to uncross your fingers if I find you making the gesture for luck." Dyson glanced over his shoulder. "Lira, if you would confirm our departure from *Aox*..."

"*Aox*, this is *Strunk*." Lira touched the earpiece of the slender headset she wore. "Ready whenever you are."

She listened, then said, "Got it, *Aox*. Separation in five. Thanks very much." Lira poked the console button.

"Thanks very much?" Tag smirked.

"You're not getting a 'roger' out of me, *Colonel*, no matter how fun you make it sound." Lira certainly didn't look like she was dressed for military service. None of them did. Tag and Dyson wore a mixed collection of civilian jackets, shirts, and trousers. Lira, though, wore a sleek jumpsuit that was the same pasty gray Tag associated with the interior of every starship he'd ever seen. "I'll let the crew know, though."

A red light flashed overhead. Tag knew it was repeated to all compartments throughout the 30-meter-long gunboat. Dyson's hand settled on the ripwave drive controls. The thrum from the generator grew louder and deeper.

"Here we go," Tim said from the engineering station. Marney rode in the seat next to him,

Tag couldn't help thinking of their unborn children, who could just as easily die on this mission as they could, but there was no keeping Marney from the fight, not anymore. Gone were the days when she was his socially involved carefree sister, where the greatest danger she faced was the loss of a passionate debate.

The light turned green.

Dyson eased forward on the controls. Space-time warped ahead of *Strunk*, flinging it ahead at one-tenth the speed of light.

Their indicator appeared on Tag's display. The target was a red diamond about eleven astronomical units from the system's tiny red dwarf star, 360 million kilometers from where *Aox* lurked among the comet chunks. "ETA three point three hours to the yards."

"Confirmed." Dyson linked a smaller version of Tag's more detailed displays to his own heads-up screen just above the main controls.

"I take it you boys are sure about the security or lack thereof at this place?" Lira asked.

"Yes, for the third time," Tag said. "It's largely automated. The one-eyes bring in heavily damaged ships, about half of which are crippled. The ones that can still move under their own power maintain a skeleton crew to prevent piracy."

"Don't get annoyed. I want to get it right since I didn't get the chance to case the place on my own." Lira frowned. "That's breaking one of my cardinal rules, by the way."

"I recollect you broke several rules on Kayna Two," Dyson said.

"Yes, I did." Lira's look as she smiled back at him was one Tag would classify as, *Did you two forget everything about me?* "I break a lot of rules when faced with a death threat from the Briddarri military."

"I'm glad we didn't have to do the same to get you here," Tim offered.

Marney gasped. She smacked his chest. Tim laughed and rubbed at the spot.

Lira raised an eyebrow. She leaned closer to Tag. "Your brother-in-law has a strange sense of humor." Her whisper was exaggerated so everyone on the small bridge could hear. "It's a good thing you outrank him."

Tag chuckled and shook his head.

"This could be a long three hours," Dyson murmured.

*　*　*

The Naplians designated it Scrap and Repair Depot Rallanvid. Its database cataloged two hundred and seventeen ships that were being dismantled or fixed, from a couple of starfighter squadrons to four battlecruisers.

The destroyer *Teret* was moored to an asteroid beyond a patch of other vessels of similar tonnage that robotic drones were tearing apart.

Dyson killed the ripwave drive on the far side of the yard and used a combination of maneuvering thrusters and low-power ion engines to close the distance. He kept the other destroyers between *Strunk* and *Teret*, Tag noted, and handled the gunboat's control with an ease that made Tag sure Dyson would be just as at home in Flirry Squadron as any of his pilots.

Tag had the sensors locked into passive mode to avoid giving off stray emissions that might attract attention. He watched as sparks sprayed from one of the destroyers being reclaimed. Tiny bits separated, pinwheeling away as more drones moved to contain the scrap.

"Range to target, ten thousand klicks." Tag didn't

know why he lowered his voice. No way any scanner would pick up his chatter. But the situation urged caution, and that was how his brain processed it.

"Confirmed." Dyson did the same. *Wonder how he justifies it? Fitting in with his human companions, maybe?*

Lira looked up from her board. "The consul says he's ready whenever we are."

"Good deal. They'll do the hard part before we get aboard." Tag consulted his readouts. "Give him a forty-second timer."

"Got it," Lira murmured into her headset.

Tim leaned between Dyson and Tag. "Her sensors are still down?"

"Yes," Dyson said. "*Teret* shows no power to active or passive sensing units. Main drives are offline. Reactor is safe. All readings are correct with regards to what TI took from the yard's databases."

"Glad to know my decoding work wasn't for naught." Tim kept a light tone, but Tag saw how his grip on the back of Dyson's chair eased. "I'm going aft to have a word with the marines."

"Very good." Dyson unstrapped from his seat and stood. "I leave the helm in your capable hands, Colonel."

"Be careful out there," Tag said to him as he changed chairs. "I know you don't need to breathe, but the vacuum of space will also let the one-eyes shoot you just as easily as atmo."

"That is sound advice I will remember, though I am sure Consul Selva and his people will do their utmost to protect my fragile frame."

He joined Tim, and the two ducked through the hatch, leaving Tag with the two women. Marney took up Tag's vacated sensor post.

"You got that?" Tag asked.

"It's not so different from *Vossberg*." Marney input a series of commands with her right hand and swiped into a secondary menu with her left. "And since Tim gave me a refresher on the basic bridge stations for a Terran strike corvette... and these are the same consoles..."

Lira chuckled.

"One of these days, I'm going to stop underestimating you." Tag shook his head and decided he'd better keep his mind on his own controls instead of worrying about his baby sister's.

The timer on the helm display blinked down. *Teret*'s long, curved drive sail peeked from behind the charcoal-colored asteroid. "Eleven seconds to contact," Tag warned.

"Ten seconds," Lira relayed.

A series of distant *clangs* echoed deep in *Strunk*'s hull. Sixteen shapes flitted ahead of the gunboat, their shadowy outlines propelled by tiny blue-white thruster packs. One of those shapes was thicker than the rest.

"Seriously, Dyson," Tag muttered to himself, "Do *not* get yourself blasted to pieces."

* * *

Elden hurtled across the distance between *Strunk* and *Teret*. His overview displays showed him his velocity relative to both ships and the asteroid. *Fast but not unstoppable. Unstoppable would not be preferable.*

He was more concerned about his payload than himself. Dyson Ashteo, the TI android, clung to his armored frame, seemingly no more worried about his temporary exposure to the vacuum of space than he would be to a torrential downpour.

Elden's memory banks reloaded the sensation of rain on bare skin, the smell of damp earth…

No time for that. He shunted aside the rebellious information. The asteroid's surface loomed. His sensors bracketed the transponder buoy half-buried in a deep crater.

<Thayer, you're with me,> Elden ordered via the interlink. <Goetz, position the rest of our men on the target as planned.>

<Understood, sir.> Goetz was a silver missile leading fourteen others. They broke into pairs, fanning out toward *Teret.* They shrank as they drew away from the asteroid.

Elden spun himself and Dyson. Braking thrusters eased his landing. The asteroid was large enough to generate its own gravity, albeit a field so feeble Elden knew it would take only a light shove to send an object floating away.

<It will take me seventeen point six seconds to disable the buoy.> Dyson spoke through a private interlink with Elden, using a frequency similar to the one Goetz employed when they communicated one-to-one.>

<That precision indicates you don't anticipate malfunctions.> Elden stepped back from the buoy to give Dyson room to work.

The android hunched near the broad, spherical buoy. It was twice as wide as a Truppen soldier and half the height. Dyson peeled back an access panel and dug into the mess of circuits crammed between flashing lights. <I have run twenty simulations. The time I stated is the average, with errors considered.>

<I'll trust you to do your work.> Elden had no idea how to finesse the problem. That was the major drawback to his role as consul. He had become used to leading men—leading cybers—into combat. There were those in their ranks who possessed technical infiltration skills but nothing approaching what Dyson could do. Brute force was their watchword.

Dyson, though, still looked ridiculous, crouched on an asteroid wearing his civilian garb instead of a space suit.

Thayer touched down beside them in a puff of dust. <Sorry about that, sir. I had a thruster that needed a reboot.>

<Did you take care of it? If your tech is compromised—>

<No, sir. It was a software problem. Five by five, now.>

Thayer was a younger man, or at least, he had been when he'd become a Truppen decades ago. His maturity level had apparently frozen at the point where he had entered into suspended animation during the last days of the Second Consular War. The seven years since his reactivation had forced him to learn better control, but he still responded like a lad in his mid-twenties. Thayer was eager and willing to please.

So far, he has not proven a liability, which is good because I can't spare undamaged Truppen to tend ship while the rest fight.

<Success.> Dyson closed the panel. <The buoy is reprogrammed. It will continue to record *Teret* docked at these coordinates no matter the actual position of the

physical ship.>

<Excellent.> Elden switched frequencies to Goetz's. <The signal is given. Breach.>

He scooped up Dyson and jetted off the asteroid. Thayer kept pace a few dozen meters away. *Teret* was 84 meters long, with a jump sail outrigger that seemed to reach for the distant stars. Elden's scanners painted the fourteen Truppen as blue diamonds in pairs on the dusky hull. Red-orange flares erupted at their positions. Each pair had an assigned target, be it a critical exterior sensor, comms antenna, or a vital command-and-control linkage.

Teret's running lights flickered and died, followed soon after by her interior lighting. Viewports glowed red as emergency beacons activated.

<We've severed the connections between the bridge and engineering sections,> Goetz reported. <Comms arrays stripped. Engineering breached—now.>

An explosion blew fragments out in a glittering cloud. Red marks appeared on Elden's display.

Naplian bodies. Four.

Elden supposed he should feel something at their deaths, but the truth was he'd spent too long fighting the Naplians for control of these sectors that four technicians suffocating in space triggered nothing but the subtlest grimace.

The cold, rational part of his mind told him there were still twenty Naplians aboard.

<Brace for impact.> The hull was less than a hundred meters away. Elden twisted so his clawed feet were ready to latch on. He would have preferred a softer, quieter landing, but time was of the essence, especially now that the Naplians aboard knew they were under

attack.

They were blind and deaf, but they'd be ready to defend their ship no matter what.

Elden mentally grunted. That much he had in common with his adversaries. Neither would give up. Neither would let the enemy win.

It was a lesson he hoped the Briddarri would learn before he had to hunt down and destroy yet another of their cyber labs.

<Strunk is inbound,> Dyson said.

Thirty meters to the hull. Elden highlighted *Strunk* as the gunboat drifted nearer the crippled *Teret*.

His feet slammed against the ship. Shock absorbers redistributed the impact throughout Elden's frame. He made sure his feet magnetized to *Teret's* exterior before he let Dyson down.

Thayer landed on the other side of the hatch. He ripped off the panel covering the manual release for the airlock. <Ready when you are, sir.>

Dyson lifted a PF6-S machine pistol and nodded. Elden's railgun was loaded and charged. <Go.>

Thayer cranked the release. A puff of pressurized air burst from where the hatch split in half. Dyson glided in, covering the airlock's interior. Elden—too large to fit through—waited outside, his weapon at the ready.

<Airlock secure,> Dyson reported.

<Good. Here come the rest of our boarders.> Elden signaled Thayer to move back. *Strunk* drifted nearer *Teret*. A cofferdam extended from the starboard side. The pilot applied reverse and port-side thrusters in perfect synchronicity so that the cofferdam's business end latched onto the opened airlock.

Tag, of course. Even the android would be hard pressed to outdo him.

Elden joined Thayer on the other side of the airlock. Nothing for them to do now but wait and make sure *Teret* didn't signal anyone of their predicament. Truppen marched across the hull, melting or otherwise breaking backup comms equipment or temporarily sealing hatches from the outside.

It was up to the thief to break into *Teret's* brain.

* * *

Lira nodded to Dyson as she slid through the cofferdam into the airlock. "This is nice. I think it's the first time I've broken into a starship and found help waiting for me."

"I would correct you since it was Consul Selva and his men who did the breaking," Dyson said. "You are merely entering."

"Are you two always this chatty?" Commander Ess landed behind Lira. His boots magnetized to the deck. Terran Marines in gray and blue armor, their faces obscured behind mirrored visors, were on their way through the connector that led back to *Strunk*.

"Only when we have an audience." Lira adjusted the controls on her jumpsuit. She had lost count of how many places she'd broken into, and she meant every word of her comment to Dyson, but she'd also never had the luxury of a marine platoon escorting her, either. "Do me a favor, Commander, and try not to draw attention to me."

"Ma'am, our job is to draw attention *away* from you." Ess checked the power levels on the Furta energy rifle. The marines carried an assortment of captured Naplian weapons and other guns that any enterprising pirate could buy on the black market.

"Like I said." Lira squeezed the activation studs on either side of the controls. The suit's exterior brightened, then faded out of existence until all she could see of herself was a hazy outline against the drab bulkhead and deck plates. She waved her arm. The gesture made the illusion shudder, but the more she held still, the more she blended into the background.

"I'm ready," she told Dyson.

He nodded. "Unlocking inner hatch."

Air pressure built inside the airlock as it equalized with the corridor beyond. Dyson reached for the panel with one hand, the other aiming his pistol across his arm. The hatch slid open.

A pair of marines went through first, followed by Ess and four others, with another four bringing up the rear. Dyson inserted himself between those last four, like the runt of the litter, making sure it was surrounded by the toughest members of the pack.

Lira found their postures and their stances amusing. They weren't quite as brash and blundering as Briddarri warriors. This was a stealthier, subtle technique, though she could tell by the way they snapped around to each other's commands that they could eliminate any enemy that came their way. No, it was that they reminded her of *rinndellon* showing off their plumage during mating season.

She trailed them by thirty paces, never losing sight of the last few soldiers but staying well out of their wake. She carried no displays that would give away her position—no sensors, either. Just her and the memory of the map she'd memorized aboard *Strunk*.

One more section and two bulkheads over to the computer core. Lira slunk along toward the corridor intersection as the team crossed it.

Particle blasts ripped through the hall, their energies blinding after her eyes had gotten adjusted to the dim emergency lamps. Lira halted, back pressed to the bulkhead. Ess and the marines split into fours. They directed shots back down the corridor where the attack originated. Dyson was bent over an open wall panel. His hands were deep inside, like a surgery bot in the final stages of a life-and-death operation.

All that racket left Lira unattended, which was perfect as far as she was concerned.

Lira slipped down the hall she needed. She counted bulkheads as she went. The Naplians were kind enough to mark each bulkhead and section with the standardized designations that appeared on every blueprint for ships of this class. The corridor soon dead-ended on a T-intersection with a glossy black blast door in front of her. The white outline of a rectangle framed the locking mechanism at the center.

Power's off. Auxiliary generators don't link to this hatch. That precaution adds extra security in case of an emergency like this. The command staff has a portable access unit. Lira hoped the captain or whoever commanded this beat-up destroyer wasn't on their way here now, but even if they were, it was up to Ess and his marines to stop them.

An alarm blared through the enclosed space. Lira fumbled with her suit's control. The last thing she needed was to drop the device.

"Warning: Decompression Alert in Section

Twelve."

Twelve? That was where she was.

Shouts echoed behind her. Weapons fire dropped off. Something metal slammed into the deck so hard she almost lost her footing.

Her comm earpiece crackled. "Threats neutralized," Dyson said.

A cold sweat broke out on her forehead. Lira cracked open the back of her suit controls and linked tiny twin conduits to the door panel. "Really glad you're on our side," she murmured.

* * *

Tag watched the data trickle in from the two teams and listened to their comms. So far, so good, though he didn't hear much of an update from Lira. *Relax. That's how she operates. She wanted this op as comms silent as possible.*

Marney's console beeped at her. She frowned over the displays.

"Not the buoy, is it?" Tag fought off a rising dread. "If that thing's picked up an emergency call from *Teret...*"

"No, it's the passive sensors—proximity alert." Marney looked at him, her expression frozen in place. "There's a patrol sloop headed our way."

CHAPTER ELEVEN

T ag punched the emergency disconnect for the cofferdam. The magnetic locks disengaged, and the starboard thrusters shoved *Strunk* away from *Teret*. His chair shook with the sudden acceleration.

"Where is he?" Tag sent the gunboat into a quick roll that brought it "up" and over *Teret's* hull. A broad shadow from the jump sails enveloped *Strunk*.

Marney tapped her controls and swiped across the screen. "I've updated the link. The sloop is on a course that will bring it to within five thousand kilometers of the buoy asteroid."

Tag glanced at his screen's mirroring of Marney's sensor display. Yeah, there it was, a red diamond making its way along an arc that wound around the edges of the repair yard. The schematics weren't reassuring—two missile tubes and two small-bore pulsed particle cannons. *Strunk* wasn't unarmed, even as a refitted gunboat, but she was meant more for infiltration than a stand-up fight.

If they were going to take her out, it was going to have to be a one-shot deal, like splashing a Naplian fighter with a long-range missile.

Tag switched comms frequencies. "Shuttle to Shadow, pick up the pace we have intruders. May need to extract sooner."

"Shadow here. That's not the best way to sweet talk me into breaking a lock faster, you know."

"Best I can do." Tag switched frequencies again. "Shuttle to Intercessor Lead. I'm patching through sensor data on an approaching threat."

"I wondered what you were up to, but I thought I spotted distant movement." Elden sounded no more disturbed than Lira did, which considering she wasn't a cyber warrior, raised Tag's estimate of her coolness under fire. "I see. My people can eliminate the threat."

"Understood, but we have to shut down its comms, or else this whole party's for nothing." Tag reached for the weapons board but stopped short of the targeting systems. Those required active scanning, and if he engaged it, they might as well put up a big holo sign advertising their hiding spot. "How close can you get?"

"Close, even without being spotted, given our relatively small size to even a patrol sloop. Timing, of course, is the key."

Tag considered this. Elden was waiting for his order, which would send sixteen Truppen against an armed Naplian craft. If they timed it wrong, he might have to extract them, but if they did nothing or waited too long, the sloop would spot *Strunk* or scan *Teret* and detect the damage inflicted.

"This will get worse if the sloop tries to contact *Teret*," Marney said.

"They won't, not if Dyson's reprogramming of the buoy worked." *Please let it work.* Not that Tag doubted Dyson's abilities, but it didn't hurt to have a healthy skepticism. "All right, Intercessor Lead, intercept them."

"Understood, Shuttle. Intercessor out."

Tag grimaced. The sloop's indicator grew nearer on the board. *Strunk*'s lone missile tube was racked and ready. He left the guns powered down, though.

"What else do we need?" Marney asked.

"See what you can dig up in the TI files or anywhere else about that class of sloop," Tag said. "Maybe I'm thinking about this the wrong way. Maybe we can finesse a solution instead of risking the entire mission."

"It's a far sight from a Warhawk's cockpit, isn't it?" Marney punched commands into her console.

Tag glanced at the nav display, where Elden and his Truppen floated away from *Teret*, and at the tracking screen that showed the boarding party moving through the destroyer's corridors. There were a lot of lives in his hands. A lot more than the eleven he was used to.

"Yeah," he said. "A far sight."

* * *

Lira made a face as her suit's controls balked at the door's locking mechanism. "Remind me again, how much did I pay for you?" she murmured. "Evidently not enough."

The sounds of gunfire had faded as the marines moved nearer the bridge, leaving her isolated. The rest of the Naplian crew must be holed up there— the Truppen had cleaned out engineering, according to Dyson.

She shuddered. She'd never met Elden Selva before his transformation. Still, the galaxy's underbelly was full of whispers about his rise to power—from a little-known Terran dissident movement's scion to consul of an invincible cybernetic army. Nobody knew how many thousands there were. What everyone was sure of was that no one could beat them, and they were so formidable even the Briddarri let them do whatever they wanted.

Impressive, as far as Lira was concerned, but creepy, and definitely not the kind of people she would surround herself with. Lira preferred the company of those who could disappear into a crowd yet still have her back.

Dyson, to be sure, and Tag, though the idea of him blending anywhere made her smile.

She counted herself lucky to be out of Briddarri clutches and snaring the affections of a good man like him. They were few, no matter the species.

The door's lock chirped. Success.

"Nice job." Lira tapped the control on her wrist. "You won't be replaced, I promise."

Both halves of the door separated. *Teret's* central computer was a five-sided column that reached from deck to ceiling, two and a half meters. It was white, except for black lines at the seams and gray panels riddled with lights and readouts spaced top and bottom at varied intervals.

Lira had no idea what they did, but her lack of knowledge didn't matter. She just had to break it—temporarily.

The core was hardwired to the ship's systems. Dyson had provided her with the description of the proper cable that needed to be detached. It was one of a couple hundred snaking out across the floor and ceiling to backup power units, auxiliary memory drives, and through the bulkhead to places like the bridge and engineering.

Lira crouched beside the core, where a thick bundle entered an access hatch. Those cables met at a single plug that combined them into one port.

She grabbed it and pulled it free.

The entire core went blank. Every light, every display...

Lira winced but it was what was supposed to happen. Didn't make it any less disconcerting to see a starship's computer core cease functioning.

She dug into one of her suit's pockets and found the splitter device. The bundled cables plugged into it, and then she inserted the splitter back into the proper port.

Lights reappeared across the core, one section at a time. She thought about crossing her fingers but then decided that was too human a superstition to adopt. Briddarri didn't need those. Besides, what did it matter which appendage formed which shape?

Her comms earpiece crackled. "Glitch, this is Mastermind. Well done. I have access to the main computer and have locked out the former owners of this vessel from bridge and engineering overrides."

"You're welcome, Mastermind." She didn't know if Dyson was as picky about Terran military protocol as Tag and Ess were. "I guess that means I'll catch my ride."

"Negative, Glitch. Shuttle reports a ... complication. He has relocated our ride for the moment. Intercessor is addressing the issue. Redirect to the bridge and rendezvous with our contingent. Take care—four Naplians are unaccounted for."

He cut off the signal, leaving Lira blinking into

thin air. Well, getting to the bridge was no great difficulty, not with her memory. But the four Naplians could be another matter.

Then you'd better sidestep them and quit worrying Blue Kitt, she told herself.

Lira checked that her suit's active camouflage was still in place, then set off—but not before locking the computer core room again from the outside.

* * *

Elden's scanners told him they would rendezvous with the sloop in six minutes, which seemed far too soon and yet eons away. It gave him enough time to run simulations that appeared in his mind like the most well-constructed fantasies imaginable, translated into simple 2-D graphics.

He and his Truppen overshot or came up short on their approach in 90 percent of those scenarios.

<I don't like the way this is looking,> Goetz said. He flew alongside Elden.

<I would be surprised if you did.> Elden finally hit upon the right trajectory and thruster application to bring them alongside the sloop as it slowed for the asteroid. The Naplian ship was already reducing speed. He sent the data along to the others, accompanied by the message, <Octants, adjust your headings.>

<We'll have to time the grapples so we link to the hull, but don't rip our arms off,> Thayer said. <Have you ever tried that before, Consul?>

<Once. Over Trebizond Minor.>

Goetz snorted.

<I wouldn't be so quick to criticize, Goetz,> Elden

said. <It worked.>

<Yes, sir, it did, and we captured that ammunition hauler.> Goetz angled his head so he was looking straight at Elden. <But you *did* rip one of your arms off.>

Thayer choked a sound that might have been a laugh but lapsed into respectful silence instead.

They were near enough now that Elden's scanners painted him a more distinct image of the sloop. It was half the size of an *Oyae*-Class destroyer like *Teret*, with a similar hull of roughly torpedo shape, but the outrigger was far shorter, and the jump sail much smaller in comparison to the sloop's tonnage. The missile tubes didn't bother him. Truppen presented too small of targets for those weapons.

The particle cannons, on the other hand, could be used to devastating effect, especially at close range.

<Spread out individually to half a klick, staggered diamond formation,> Elden ordered. <Without sacrificing your speed or our trajectory. This only works if we land and act as one unit.>

<I'll take an octant and destroy the particle turrets.> Goetz sounded like he was offering to clean out the repair capsules.

<A solid plan.> Solid if they didn't overshoot their target—or become the targets themselves.

Elden wondered where Abbott Jeopar was, not for the first time in four years, and what he was doing. Praying, one would assume.

He considered if that were a healthy habit for situations such as this, but after a moment's consideration, dismissed the idea. He would let others do the praying so long as they left the fighting to him.

* * *

Lira paused at a four-way corridor intersection that was three bulkheads back from the bridge. Blood was splattered here and there, among countless blast burns from particle discharges and the occasional impact from magnetically accelerated rounds. Little of the blood was red, though it turned orange where it seeped into the yellow left by dead Naplians.

That was how she found the remaining four crew members Dyson referenced.

Two were hunched over the dead bodies of their comrades. The other two guarded the corridors—one aiming left, one right. The duo muttered to each other in the precise *ffawe-aul* dialect used for technical matters. Lira couldn't decipher much of it but got enough of a sense that they were upset.

No kidding.

Lira crept as close as she dared to them—twenty meters. She stayed in the shadow cast by a bulkhead stanchion that arced over the corridor. Whatever the one-eyes were doing wasn't good, judging by the device the two crouched Naplians were fiddling with. She wasn't well versed in explosives—she usually left that to Blue Kitt partners. That device fit the profile she was used to, though.

She had little on her in the way of weapons. One thin knife and her suit controls. But the blade wouldn't be camouflaged once she unsheathed it.

She needed a distraction.

Lira leaned into the corridor, her fingers grazing a dropped Naplian comms. It scraped on the deck plate.

She froze.

The Naplians continued muttering to each other, having apparently missed the sound. The device—a bomb, Lira was sure of it—started beeping. A red light pulsed.

Lira gingerly lifted the comms and eased into the corridor. She stuck to the deep shadows along the bulkheads. Eighteen meters. .. Fifteen. ..

At ten meters, she was afraid they would hear her breathing, so she calmed it by remembering when she'd infiltrated the Sanctuary of the Revered Barad. That moment before her dive. ..

She flung the comms as hard as she could and drew her knife.

It clattered far across the corridor intersection. The armed Naplians spun toward the sound. They clustered up, advancing in the opposite direction, which left their other comrades hunkered over the bomb.

Both the technicians, as Lira deemed them, had holstered pistols.

She swept between them, pulled one of the pistols free, and shot the first armed crewman in the back. He crumpled with a mangled cry. His partner made it halfway through another turn before Lira dropped him with three blasts.

The technicians had frozen. Neither reached for her, likely because they didn't know how to react to a wraith in their midst.

Their fear felt like it drowned her. What was it about those two? Lira hadn't hesitated to batter security guards with stun poles just weeks before.

This, though. .. She only had a weapon that could

kill, and she hadn't hesitated to shoot the crewmen who would have killed her without a second thought. Yet, ever since her mission with Tag and Dyson to the Union of Planets, causing death sickened her, even though she knew everyone else on this heist would and had done so with as little remorse as the Naplians.

The technician on her right decided for her. He drew his pistol and aimed. His partner took a moment's distraction to lunge for the bomb's control panel.

Lira thought she would experience time moving more slowly as she made her decision, but it all happened in a few seconds—she shot the technician when his hand was centimeters from the bomb. A particle blast seared her right arm. She pushed away and shot back.

Lira lay on the cold deck plates, panting. Pain ate at her muscles. The smell of burnt flesh made her gag. There was silence heavy around her, until the pounding of boots against metal approached.

"Lira." Dyson knelt beside her. "You are injured."

"Mildly." She winced when she tried to lift herself. Dyson put an arm around her waist and helped drape her left arm over his shoulders so she could cradle the right against her chest. "They were trying to set off an explosive, I think."

"Yes." Dyson glanced down at the device. "Cutting torch batteries fused to a charging source, with the overload breakers disabled. It would have likely burned a hole down through the deck or up through the ceiling out to space and decompressed this quarter of the ship."

"Bad, then."

"Your wound is also dangerous, but the marine corpsman should be able to begin the healing process.

This way to the bridge."

Dyson helped her along. She clung near to him. It irritated her that she had become suddenly jumpy about the dark corridors. "Is the bridge secure, then?"

"It is."

"And the crew?"

Dyson didn't answer right away. She wondered if he searched for words the way people like her did or if he had a ready-made list for situations like these. "They are our enemies, Lira, and this is a war. Casualties are unavoidable, especially during an operation that demands absolute discretion. We cannot risk them revealing what we did to their superiors."

"I understand." She tried not to see the faces of the four Naplians she'd just shot. There would be no way to get rid of them. Lira wished Dyson had left her in Briddarri custody on Jarrados.

At least there, she wouldn't have blood on her hands.

* * *

Tag's eyes burned. He blinked, but there wasn't much of a remedy for staring at his targeting screens for so long. "Nothing yet?"

"Nothing."

The comms activated. "Shuttle, this is Mastermind. *Teret* is ours."

Tag relaxed but didn't take his gaze away. It had been two minutes since the Truppen were supposed to have intercepted the investigating sloop. Dyson's news was welcome, though. "Glad to hear it. How's the rechristening?"

"You will have command of *Valo* shortly. We will need to repair a hull breach in engineering before we can jump, but that work can be done while the vessel ripwaves to the system's edge."

"I'll let *Aox* know they're clear to jump out." Marney switched over to the comms console for access to the other secure channel.

"Right. Stand by, Mastermind. We have someone snooping around who—"

Tag's console beeped at him.

"They did it," Marney said.

The tactical display glowed with the results of Elden's raid. A miniature hologram of the sloop spluttered with gouts of flame. Debris streamed off the top and bottom, right where the specs had shown Tag a pair of particle cannons should be mounted. Sensor mounts scattered up and down the hull pulsed red, indicating catastrophic damage. The comms arrays— one dorsal and one ventral—were gone. The display indicated they had been shorn clean off.

Elden and his Truppen were already jetting away from the sloop. They'd done their part. Tag would take *Strunk* to pick them up if they had difficulty getting back to either the gunboat or *Teret*. It was time for Tag to finish this business.

"It's still continuing on its way, and we don't have the time to stop it and conduct another boarding." Tag knew what had to be done. He keyed up the targeting array. No point in hiding now. The active scanners pinged the sloop and found a nice weak gap in the armored hull just aft of the jump sail's outrigger.

"I'm sorry. But it is necessary." Marney didn't sound as sad as Tag would have expected.

"You're okay with killing those one-eyes?" The schematics, in their cold and dispassionate way, told him the sloop had a crew of fourteen officers and sixty enlisted crew.

"I'm not okay with anyone dying, but there's no other way, and if we're going to liberate Baedecker, we have to make difficult decisions." Marney clutched the console as if she were preventing herself from sliding away. Her face had gone pale. "We can try our best to end it. Then we can stop anyone from dying."

There it was—Marney's indefatigable optimism. Her work with refugee populations hadn't stripped it away. Those efforts had just suppressed it. Tag nodded. Good for her.

He queued up two missiles, confirmed the target lock, and fired without another word.

Forty seconds later, the sloop vanished from the display in a tiny flash of light.

CHAPTER TWELVE

Inspector Prad frowned at the report he'd gotten back from Sergeant Brillen. It confirmed what he'd suspected: Erassia was up to something out on Baedecker Six.

He didn't like where his suspicions were leading.

Fulnax wasn't just making an inspection tour of the system's defenses like Erassia claimed. It was delivering matériel and soldiers. Prad scanned the partial list Brillen had provided. Weapons, sure, but it seemed as if the deliveries were more concerned with construction equipment. Several shipments were marked "Industrial," but that was about as descriptive as a container labeled "Ammunition."

The personnel shifts were even more perplexing. Brillen's notes told Prad that a handful he had seen were soldiers from companies attached to his battalion, but they had worn technicians' jumpsuits devoid of unit markings. None of the officers had offered explanations, but Brillen had been wise enough to avoid direct questions.

Prad closed the scroll and leaned back in his chair. His office was down the street from Daviont Tower, nestled among the trade house buildings. It was also registered to a distant mercantile cooperative no one had heard of but claimed to be interested in increased trade with the Naplian Empire. He could literally keep his eye on Erassia from here when he wasn't out on the street, searching for answers.

What bothered him most was the silence from his superiors. *Some good it was, being part of the imperial secret police, when even they supposedly had eyes everywhere and yet couldn't give him straight answers.*

His desk comm buzzed. "Yes?"

"Inspector, you have a visitor."

Prad blinked. "I hate to break it to you, Rost, but given that this is a secret office that isn't listed as a Druwei facility, that's impossible."

"I understand, Inspector, but it doesn't change the fact the Denic woman standing in front of me asked for you by name and rank."

Prad sat up, intrigued. Puzzles rarely fell into his lap that way. If the woman was a threat, he could easily detain her, but the Denics were renowned spies. He reactivated his scroll and went hunting for Denic assets in this sector Druwei might have neglected to tell him about. "Send her up, escorted."

Hmm. His search didn't bring results. The nearest Denic spy the Druwei would admit to using was practically sitting on the Great Desert Rift boundary and was male.

The door opened. A Denic woman entered, paler than most Terrans. Her hair was brown, bound in a ponytail. She wore well-worn civilian clothing patched in places. Purple tattoos of tiny avians covered otherwise bare shoulders. Terran creatures, weren't they? Hummingbirds, Prad recalled.

Two plainclothes Druwei officers guarded her. They could have blended with the Naplian merchants in the trade district easily, except for their stoic mannerisms.

"I'm all right, gentlemen." Prad flicked his fingers. "Wait outside."

One of the men pushed the Denic forward. The door shut behind her.

"Sorry about their brusqueness." Prad gestured to an empty chair. "My people aren't used to using manners, especially when a strange non-Naplian woman walks into our secret facility."

"I understand, Inspector." The woman's voice was soft and well-modulated. Prad fought the sudden desire to grant her whatever she wished. *Steady there.* She sat and crossed her legs. "You and I are pursuing similar objectives."

"Are we?"

"Of course. The Druwei are interested in Admiral Erassia's extracurricular activities, especially those which involve the supposed inspections he sends his flagship to conduct, but which are instead delivering men and matériel to a secret facility."

Now, she had his attention. Prad interlaced his fingers atop his desk, right near the panel that would summon his guards and result in this woman being locked up for spurious reasons so he could scrape intel from her brain.

"Let me be more precise. You have contacted Sergeant Brillen, who serves aboard the weapons tender *Jalnaz*. He, somewhat clumsily, gathered information for you."

"Interesting story," Prad said.

"I will take another step forward and offer you my source—a low-ranking soldier named Kah. He is my unwilling asset, who has confirmed Brillen's activities." The woman brushed a loose thread off her trousers. "So, I will offer you my services since we are in pursuit of the same goal."

"You're mad if you think I will open Druwei files to … whoever you are."

"My name is Ivy Li. I represent a powerful commercial group with a vested interest in preventing the work Admiral Erassia is obsessed with. I think you know what work I mean."

Prad frowned. The way in which this pale copy of a *shirish* seemed to read his mind irked him. Yes, he also could use better sources, and her behavior and attitude supported his suspicion that he was dealing with an intelligence operative.

"All right." Prad's hands slid away from the panel. "Tell me what you suspect, and I'll tell you if I concur."

"The personnel, the shipments, the secrecy. .." Ivy shrugged. "He is restarting his *ziurathal* program."

That was precisely what Prad was thinking. Though he had told no one, not even Rost. "What company did you say you worked for?" Speaking of Rost, he hoped his subordinate was doing the required research on this interloper.

Ivy cocked her head. "The silent one."

Prad nearly pounced for his alert button but restrained himself. His anxiety set his senses humming, though. The Silent Company? He'd heard the rumors of the shadowy organization that was likely affiliated with Stelltron. If this woman was one of their operatives, his estimation of her ratcheted up several levels in his eye but so did the danger. Might be better to execute her— but he quashed that impulse, too.

Crossing Stelltron was a fine way to, at minimum, end his career. His life might not be far behind.

"Yes," Prad said. "That's what I suspect."

"Why?"

"The pieces don't fit any other puzzle. You also must consider Erassia's profile." Prad brought up a holographic rendering of the admiral and his official service record. "He built his career on Daviont's favor. A lot of people assume it has to do with Daviont's softness for the Sov sect. Erassia, too, has this fervent belief that the human-derived Truppen are the fabled devastators that will end the Naplian Empire."

"I see." Ivy didn't seem surprised by that.

"But Erassia used up the last of Daviont's favor when the Truppen obliterated his *ziurathal*," Prad said. "Couple that with rumors he was dabbling in the creation of his own devastators—"

"Incorrect." Ivy's reply was sharp and monotone. "The Briddarri are trying to build those."

"Which is what I was going to say." Prad scowled at the interruption. "The high command doesn't believe the intel on the Briddarri project."

"Another of their failings." Ivy shook her head.

"Why are you so interested in the *ziurathal*?" Prad asked. "My superiors want to pull the plug and make sure Erassia behaves himself. I think they're afraid he'll gain back his lost sway with Daviont if his second attempt succeeds."

"I am tasked with making sure the *ziurathal* are destroyed and never resurrected. They must not be allowed to interfere with the natural order of the galaxy."

"All right." A display glowed on Prad's desk

beneath his left elbow. He glanced at it. Rost had found nothing in the mercantile records about Ivy other than sales receipts—though he added a couple of still images gathered from Druwei surveillance drones. One of them captured, at distant range, a fuzzy snapshot of Ivy conferring with a young Naplian soldier. Kah, likely. "Let's say we do pool our resources. To what end?"

"I see our cooperation producing excellent results," Ivy said. "I think we can not only prove Erassia's secret work has resumed without permission and against direct orders, but we can bring an end to it."

"And if I decide Druwei resources are adequate without your assistance?"

Ivy stood. "My superiors are already in communication with yours. Do not take too long to decide, Inspector. It will look much better on your record if you agree now than if you are ordered to assist."

Assist. With my own investigation? Prad fought to keep disdain off his face. He smiled instead and stood. "I think I've decided, Ivy Li. Let me start our partnership by sharing that Admiral Erassia has left the planet again. *Fulnax* is off to show the flag yet again. One could chalk it up to the admiral being bored with his assignment, but I think we both know better."

"I think we do." Ivy offered her hand.

Prad shook it. He hadn't expected the grip to be so strong and so cool. "Let's see what we can do to help each other."

"I am looking forward to doing exactly that."

Prad summoned his guards. They escorted her out, though Prad didn't bother asking them to be more polite. He figured she could still use the reminder that he was in charge, Silent Company or not. He punched the intercom as soon as they were gone. "Rost, get a tail on her."

"Yes, sir. Live or bot?"

"She'll spot a live one. Retask a couple of our existing drones. They haven't gotten us anything useful. And get me anything you can on a soldier named Kah, the one you've got tagged in the surveillance image." Prad hadn't missed that she'd left out his full name. "Anything new on *Fulnax*?"

"Not yet. Her course seems to be normal, though she's slipped off scans again."

Back to Baedecker Six, no doubt. "Keep me up to date. I want to get an asset that can get us out there at the same time he goes. The more proof we have, the better our chance of pleasing our superiors."

"Understood."

Prad crossed to the window and gazed at Daviont Tower. *Time for me to readjust my expectations, too, with this new partner. She could either be a boon to my career— or a threat.*

Prad knew how to deal with the latter.

* * *

Ivy thought the meeting had ended better than she'd anticipated. Admittedly, Prad had allowed his guards to treat her as refuse, but she calculated their lifespans at three point four days had they damaged her in any way. Her superiors would demand reprisal for such actions.

The more pressing concern was making certain her mites were operational.

She waited until she was back at her stall before she activated the live feeds from three microscopic sensor probes she had left inside Prad's office. Their combined scanning radius meant she could see and hear everything that went on.

It did not matter that Prad retasked his drones to surveil her. Identifying them and hijacking their signals should prove simple enough. If that failed, she could arrange "accidental" power failures or other malfunctions.

The arrangement was simple: Prad would feed her a little information, thinking he could trick her into giving up more intelligence than he was providing, while unbeknownst to him, Ivy would dupe him and make the Druwei her asset.

The more important goal was to find Erassia's facility, document it, and eliminate it—but not without scouring whatever useful tech could be retrieved. The Silent Company may want the *ziurathal* program rendered inert, but that didn't mean they deemed everything about it a threat or a failure. Every aspect of new technological development could serve their purpose.

Ivy was one of many means to their end—whatever that end might be.

She considered the cluster of broken Naplian data devices spread before her on the stall's counter. Ivy had made sure her rate of successful repair far outstripped the apparent failures. While she wanted devices returned so she could expand her investigative network, she kept the return percentage below five, so most of her customers were happy.

The 5 percent bracket who did all the work for

her. The rest were meant only to reinforce her cover as a competent merchant, which would increase her ranking on the popular information board to attract more customers. Her specialization in Naplian tech also helped bring in those serving in the occupation forces.

Ivy allowed a smile with no intended target. It felt odd. Exhibiting human emotional expressions was part and parcel of her adaptive programming, though judging by the surly countenances of many who visited the trade enclave, she did not see why her superiors felt the need to include it.

Admittedly, appealing to Prad's pride had proved the worth of emotional manipulation.

A new alert appeared on her scroll. A drone approached the market. Quite clever—the fist-sized bot had four tiny hover emitters and mimicked the roaming generic models used by delivery services, weather monitors, and local police. Her microbots, the ones secreted in Prad's office, noted the similarity between the subtle frequencies used between surveillance devices in the Druwei building and the ones this drone employed.

Prad's eye. Ivy kept her attention on her review of Kah's data download, the most recent of which piggybacked off Baedecker Four's orbital traffic satellite relays. For a soldier of little importance, his eyes—his eye, Ivy reminded herself—was trained on many things that clued Ivy to the bigger picture. It was the supply containers that would give her access to whatever facility Erassia had built under the Druwei's collective noses.

But more intriguing was the bits and pieces he had picked up about ship movements *outside* the

Baedecker System.

These were sensor readouts from various patrols. They synced with what Ivy had observed traders discussing. Terran, Briddarri, and Reittian ships were on the move in the sectors near Baedecker. Most supposed it was the prelude to new offensives or raids, which the Grand Alliance—especially the irrepressible humans—had been running for years.

Ivy saw a different pattern. A pattern the Silent Company approved of.

She opened a secure file on her scroll and compiled the latest information into an anonymous note. Then, she altered the information and composed a second note. Both went out over the same piggyback network she used to download Kah's inadvertent espionage.

Her directives didn't always make sense, but she knew what she was doing was in some way connected to the Trade Houses. It had the scent of predictive analytics. Something intended to bring about a very specific and unsettling time for the galaxy. There was an urgency about it. A future that had to be.

If billions had to die on one side or the other to achieve it, so be it.

❊ ❊ ❊

Erassia breathed in the sharp odors associated with the ongoing construction—the burnt ozone from cutting torches, the sickly stink of industrial lubricant, even the mingled body odor from Naplian technicians.

Those could be ignored as he surveyed the row upon row of his new *ziurathal*.

They were monstrous, each one half-again as large as the mechanized beasts the original models had been. Tratta was right—the Z1-Bs were much more impressive. The testing statistics gave Erassia even greater hope.

"I trust you're happy with what you've seen." Tratta's skin was flushed, evidencing his pride. They stood together on one of the dozen catwalks suspended twenty meters over the main storage bay's floor. Doors on the four sides led deeper into the laser-cut rock to assembly bays, manufacturing compartments, and testing ranges.

"They are as magnificent as you promised," Erassia said. "I will require a demonstration."

"We can have one in a few days, but I've been securing a better site for such an experiment, one that's shielded against most sensors. I don't want anything leaking out." Tratta leaned nearer and whispered, which Erassia found an odd precaution, given the racket from the engineers below. "My intelligence officers suspect there has been a breach but we have the serviceman in question detained."

"To whom?" Erassia gripped the railing until he was sure he could rip it free. "Who among us would betray me to our enemies?"

"His name is Kah. His interrogation is underway. He has denied all wrongdoing, but he will confess when the proper methods are applied."

"What of the information itself? What has been made known?"

"Nothing direct that we can discern. We aren't even sure how he transmitted data about this project, only that one of our sensors detected odd transmissions from the ammunition carrier on which he was serving."

"Then, there is no need for concern. Is that what you're telling me?"

"I am concerned, kinsman, but not overly so. We can take care of Kah if we need to." Tratta scowled. "If he knows anything of the project, cerebral extrapolation will reveal it, even if Kah does not survive the process."

Erassia hated to lose a soldier, but the good of the project outweighed other considerations. "Keep me apprised."

"I will." Tratta checked his comms. "I will make arrangements for a battlefield test, but we must return you to *Fulnax* and depart."

Erassia knew that Tratta's passion for the project equaled his. He didn't want to admit it, but there was no doubt the Druwei were snooping around his activities, and Tratta was right that coming out here in person was a tremendous risk.

It doesn't matter. I must be certain the ziurathal *are the most effective weapon they can be. They alone will save the empire from destruction.*

The breathtaking arrogance of the thought wasn't lost on him. Erassia left Tratta in conversation with someone on his comm. Two bodyguards flanked him as he walked through the cramped corridors back to his shuttle. *Fulnax* could be underway within fifteen minutes and back on its supposed inspection tour route in less than five.

His comms chirped. "Go ahead."

"Admiral, my apologies, but you have received a Priority Rull message."

Erassia lost a step. Priority Rull? The signifier could be sent only from the upper echelons of Naplian

Fleet command in time of dire crisis—or in the case of his Baedecker post, immediate threat. "Push it through, Level Zero encryption."

"Yes, sir. Rerouting."

Erassia gestured for his guards to halt. He stepped into a maintenance alcove and set his comm to kick the incoming message to his scroll. Erassia switched the screen to secure mode, narrowed to only his field of vision.

The message came across as text:

Grand Alliance forces marshaling to invade Baedecker. Intelligence estimates commencement one to two weeks. Other GA fleet movements are either a precursor, a distraction, or both. Recommend Baedecker units stand to and shift to high alert positions throughout the system but without drawing undue attention. More to follow.

It was infostamped with the code he expected with Priority Rull. "Invasion," Erassia whispered. It terrified him and thrilled him at once. Terrified because if he lost control of Baedecker, not only would his career be forfeit, but his life would follow.

On the other hand, a Grand Alliance invasion would be a true test for the *ziurathal*, and when victorious, word of their prowess would spread.

Perhaps enough to draw out the Truppen.

Erassia folded up his communications gear. Very well. He could array his fleets to be prepared. Perhaps sending a few units out, but having them secretly return to make up a hidden reserve force…

His mind churned all the way back to his command office aboard *Fulnax* and through the next ripwave leg. Perhaps his inspection tour would serve its true purpose.

CHAPTER THIRTEEN

A dmiral Thomas Sinclair rolled his eyes as the latest sensor report from the Twenty-Seventh Battle Group pickets streamed across his command post at the back of *TSS Manitoba*'s bridge. "Not a damn thing."

"Sir?" Captain Beckett Singh glanced away from the tactical hologram of the New Chile system.

"Those one-eyes haven't done anything but circle their star for days. I have better things to do than babysit three battle groups when my own is lazing about." Sinclair shoved the scroll aside. "This would be a whole lot easier to investigate if we had enough starfighters in system. What do the brass want me to do with twelve squadrons?"

"Their orders are clear." Singh gestured at the system chart. The Twenty-Seventh, Thirty-First, and Sixty-Sixth Battle Groups of the Terran fleet were arrayed around the fourth and fifth planets. Two Naplian battle groups shifted their orbits around the first planet. Both sides sent out scouts. Nobody did much of anything except lob probes at the other side, which dutifully vaporized those pokes from their opponents. Sinclair was still irked by the prospect of delaying the Baedecker invasion because the C-in-C wanted a figurehead like himself to bolster fleet morale and take a peek at what the Naplians were up to. Unfortunately, the enemy scouting foray had turned out to be a less-than-subtle attempt at annexing the system. It was nominally Terran, which was important to the ice miners in the far oort cloud and the exotic biomolecule fabricators who made their homes with them.

The result? Sinclair requested another battle group and extra carriers to counter what had turned out to be a much bigger threat than anyone anticipated. Did the C-in-C care about that request?

"I don't give two damns if Admiral Ubomo is sweating out starfighter reassignments in her sector," Sinclair growled. "I need those wings *now*. Singh, get me Commodores Taisdell and Vanchev. Redeploying our gunboats will be the best way to cover those approach vectors if the one-eyes get twitchy."

"Aye, sir." Singh spun his command chair. "Comms, set up an encrypted relay to—"

"Captain!" the tactical officer cried out. "Reading multiple jump signatures. Massive energy dispersal. Vector is ninety degrees to the Naplian concentration. We could be looking at their reinforcements."

"Isolate and magnify," Singh demanded.

Sinclair felt the warmth drain from his face as red blips appeared in the tactical holo. They ticked upward until twenty-two Naplian vessels—four of them battle cruisers—settled into an attack formation.

Too many. Tiny scarlet pips fanned out. The battle groups already in place deployed their fighters, too. *Far too many.* Sinclair had forty-eight vessels and one hundred forty-four fighters and bombers. His adversary had boosted his forces to fifty-six ships, most of which outweighed and outgunned the Terran battle groups —but more importantly carried three times as many starfighters.

"Send word to Command," Sinclair said. "From Admiral Thomas Sinclair at New Chile. We have engaged in battle with superior forces and request immediate assistance. Send Priority One. Get me Taisdell and Vanchev. Split out forces along the ecliptic plane at forty-five degrees to the incoming Naplians. Use gunboats to draw the fighters away from our capital ships. Keep as close to gravity wells of the planets and their moons as we can—they'll have to avoid draining their shields against atmospheric reentry."

The voices on the bridge, Singh's primary among them, exploded in a flurry as they relayed his orders. *Manitoba* veered toward New Chile Four's second moon, a lumpy white and gray blob that barely warranted the word. Battle alert lights flashed. Klaxons blared.

Missiles filled space between the hundreds of ships, from single-seat interceptors to massive battle cruisers, and the fight expanded across millions of kilometers. Sinclair gripped the edge of his display board. So many blips, red and blue, filled the tactical holo that he had difficulty counting them.

Seconds ago, this had been an annoying patrol. Then, it had become a match between equals, the way a space conflict should be. No sneaking around. No devious plans. Just two commanders pitting their forces against each other.

Sinclair sneered as counterfire wiped out missiles on both sides. The barrages continued. A few slipped through, obliterating a Naplian destroyer. But then the gunship *TSS Kelso* ignited in a fusion fireball.

He'd make the one-eyes pay like he'd been making them pay ever since they'd sucker-punched the Terran Republic in the gut at Baedecker. Problem was, the Naplians had no clue how damned stubborn humanity was.

Allies or not, mankind was not about to roll over.

Sinclair promised that the Naplians would never forget.

*　*　*

The message blinked through to Ergen's console: *Naplian forces attacking Terrans in New Chile system.*

He wrinkled his nose and set aside the cup of *errda eptar*. Well, that was unfortunate. How was he supposed to account for the forces arrayed against Baedecker—and away from the cyber lab supply lines— if the Naplians insisted on these impulsive attacks?

And then he remembered: Sinclair had gotten himself waylaid at New Chile.

Ergen had no love for the Terran admiral, especially since he was tied so closely to *TSS Confiance.* He had no proof Sinclair was involved with the raids against the cyber labs if the Terrans were even the real perpetrators, but every moment Sinclair wasn't moving against Baedecker meant another moment Ergen could lose another lab.

Two more messages glowed on his screen. One was the status read from his remaining eight labs. Eight functioning, that is. He had another ten under construction, but those would have to move at a slower pace, to avoid attracting attention. Other than getting supply lines pinched, they were moving along nicely.

It was the third message that gave him a headache.

Unknown sender, zero verification, but they'd used the correct contact code that bypassed *Winter Scourge*'s security protocols and dumped an encrypted message directly into Ergen's private file stash. Hell, it had taken his computer half a day to decrypt, and even then Ergen had been surprised it wasn't from ED. Or didn't seem to be.

The note told him the Naplians were aware of the Baedecker plan and were taking steps to prepare.

"Not good." Ergen pulled at his moustache. "Not good at all. Sinclair ought to know. Ram, too. We can adjust tactics."

His office door chimed. "Enter."

Burrak slipped through. "Did you get the word about New Chile?"

"I did. Sounds like the Terrans have their hands full."

"Is this good or bad for Baedecker?"

Ergen turned his screen. "That depends on what you can tell me about our mystery message."

Burrak grimaced. "Nothing, unfortunately. ED is notoriously compartmentalized, but every agency leaks gossip. I've picked up none about this, either the message or the Naplians finding out."

"I don't like being played. We'd better get independent verification, but the Terrans are closer, so we'll have to tell them first."

"I'd rather not, sir."

"Me neither, Commander, but we don't have a choice." Ergen clattered ice in his glass. "They pulled off that ship capture and so far, so good—not a whisper from the one-eyes. I guess the humans have put aside their disdain for cybers."

"The Truppen are different, Admiral. They're not what we're attempting. For one thing, most of them were voluntary transfers, not harvested species."

"I don't give two craps. We need the Terrans invested in Baedecker until we can get our new labs up and running. Once we get the cyber effort running smoothly—and keep the raider problem at bay—we can see about redirecting their aims. For the time being, they've got to be up to speed on what the Naplians know and when they know it."

"I suppose." Burrak shifted his weight. "Have you heard about their teams? It's the most disjointed assortment of beings I would have thought possible."

Ergen grinned. "You're just mad because they broke Blue Kitt out of your lockup and kept her out of your reach for four years—and then she shows up as part of their strike force. Don't stay sore, Commander. The humans can be wildly unpredictable, but that's what makes them the best fighters for the Grand Alliance. Put together a packet for Commodore Ram, and lets set up a direct holo to him—I think it's time we let our allies know the enemy might not be as caught unawares as we thought he would."

* * *

Sinclair stumbled, striking his leg just above the knee on the edge of the display board. Smoke stung his eyes. The ventilation systems were breaking down and no amount of its chugging could keep the acrid stuff from attacking him. He coughed until his throat ached.

The battle wasn't going in his favor. A third of his ships were destroyed or lost. The Naplians used the gravity wells to their advantage, risking catastrophic damage to their jump sails to close the distance with the Terran ships. Sinclair hadn't pegged them as willing to take that risk.

It was his mistake to own.

True, the one-eyes had also lost about a third of their vessels, but most of those were smaller units, destroyers, and the like. Their casualties tended to be crippled rather than outright obliterated—and *Manitoba* had soaked up the brunt of the last counterstrike.

It was the damned starfighters that made all the difference.

The tactical holo blinked on and off, refusing to stabilize. The web of course trajectories glowed more intensely with the smoke wafting through the bridge. The wing commanders reported only two squadrons operational, while the Naplians seemed to have endless small birds they could throw at the Terran forces.

The battle had become the Naplians' to lose.

"Drive status?" Sinclair rasped the words.

Captain Singh was dead. He was slumped on the deck by the auxiliary engineering panel—or rather, the cratered remains of that panel. It had short-circuited and blown up, peppering Singh with hot metal shards. He'd broken his neck in the resulting fall.

"Mains offline," said Lieutenant Commander Alvarez. "Ripwave recharging but Engineering says it may blow the core if we engage it. Jump systems rebooting."

Sinclair nodded. He weighed his choices carefully.

The longer they stayed in New Chile, the more casualties they would soak up. He couldn't afford to lose any more ships, no matter how many more the yards back at Earth and elsewhere were churning out. "Signal all units to withdraw," he ordered. *Manitoba* shuddered as her batteries switched targets to a pair of Naplian destroyers that appeared at the fringe of the planetoid covering their maneuvers. "Recovery shuttles need to pick up as many survivors as they can before we jump."

The hammer blow turned the rocking motion underfoot into an earthquake. Sinclair landed face down. Pain stabbed through his right wrist clear up to his elbow. No question the arm was broken. Smoke and flame filled his periphery. He couldn't make heads or tails out of the shouting around him, but he could see the damage reports spilling across a monitor, the lines of text wriggling past a crack in the screen.

The red line of "Core Containment Failure Imminent" was prominent among them.

Sinclair struggled upright. He reached past the comms officer—dead, her face a bloody mess. He punched the evacuation alarm. "This is Admiral Sinclair. All hands to escape pods. Abandon ship. Repeat, all hands to escape pods. Abandon ship."

He sagged against the console. More alerts cascaded across the bridge—shields failing. Main weapons batteries offline. Gravity well pull exceeding drive thrust. *Manitoba* was in her death spiral. It was only a matter of minutes until the planetoid ripped her apart or her core's energies obliterated her in anti-matter fires.

The blood trickling from the corner of Sinclair's mouth and the agony in his chest told him he had little time. Smoke was bad enough, but the environmental system's collapse meant noxious gasses from burning components and even furniture were ravaging his lungs. *Probably being poisoned by my own chair.*

The rattle of escape pods breaching the hull put him at ease. At least those crew had a fighting chance at survival. At least he'd bloodied the Naplians here, even if they would still take New Chile.

A roar built from aft. Heat stung him well before the exploding core's shock front incinerated his body.

Admiral Thomas Sinclair had less than a second to regret that he wouldn't be able to replant the Terran flag on Baedecker before he was vaporized.

* * *

Tag couldn't believe the tally. Twenty-one starships destroyed. Nine badly damaged. He tried to tell himself that the battlegroups did their part for the war effort by eliminating or crippling nearly the same number, but the fact that the Naplians seized control of yet another Terran star system weighed the scales in the wrong direction.

What was overwhelming was the gut feeling that the Naplians couldn't be stopped.

It didn't matter that New Chile wasn't high on the list of strategic places. It didn't matter how many raids or campaigns the Grand Alliance threw together. It didn't matter that they chipped away at the gains the invaders had made.

The Naplian Empire was as stubborn as Tag figured he and his family were, and they'd once more cost good people their lives—including Admiral

Sinclair.

He threw his scroll against the bulkhead.

"That's not going to solve anything." Lira was seated next to him, picking through the assorted flash-frozen rations lumped on her tray. "You'd be better off putting your skills to use finding a better source of meals for your team."

"Sorry, but I'm not hungry."

"Starving yourself isn't going to bring Sinclair back or undo what was done at New Chile." Lira pushed the tray away. "We have to move forward with the resources we have—or find new ones that will do the trick."

"Lira makes a good point." Dyson sat to Tag's right, a few seats down. He was flicking through his scroll, ingesting data instead of rations. "Command of the Baedecker operation falls to Vice Admiral Tanaka. She will decide whether we postpone the invasion any further. Thus far I have seen no indication that the loss at New Chile will impact the units currently assigned."

"That's what makes it worse, though." Tag exhaled. "It's as if the battle there didn't matter. Some of ours are dead, some Naplians are dead, and the one-eyes get to move into another star system that used to be ours. Sinclair never should have gone out there."

"It is possible another commander would made different tactical decisions. However, it is equally possible we would have lost another capable flag officer instead of him."

"Like Ram," Lira said. "It would have been him and *Confiance* in the fight. Which means you would have been out there ... Oh. I see why this is hard on you."

"What's that mean?"

Lira leaned into him and touched his arm. "You think you could have made all the difference if you'd been there with your squadron."

Tag grunted. "Yeah, probably. I mean, the reports are highlighting lack of starfighter support in what should have otherwise been a head-to-head match."

"But you could have died there, too."

"I know." Tag placed his hand atop hers. "And I'm not saying I've got a death wish. It's just … Seven years, and it feels like nothing's changed or will change."

"I understand your grief and share your concern, Tag." Dyson set his scroll aside and focused his full attention on the conversation. "I would caution that you keep these worries among our trio. They will not serve your command well if team morale suffers."

"I thought about that. Thanks for the advice, though." He knew he shouldn't blow off steam in so public an area, even though the galley held a dozen *Aox* crew. Most of the rest who weren't on their chow break were busy refitting *Teret*—make that *Valo* now—for the incursion to Fontenelle and from there, Baedecker.

Marney appeared in the galley's hatchway. She frowned when she saw Tag hunkered with Lira and Dyson in the corner. "There you are. You can't ignore your comm, Colonel."

"I can when I need to process a major upset in our operational planning. What's going on?"

"Admiral Tanaka is with Commodore Ram right now. They're talking with Admiral Ergen about the invasion."

"They have a verdict yet?"

"No, but they're waffling." Marney sounded stern as if the flag officers had insulted her and her husband.

"Tim is on his way up. I think you should speak to them, too."

"And say what?" But Tag was already on his feet. He slid out from behind the table. "How this is a touchy time since we just had our commander killed? Don't worry, Sis, I think we should still go."

"You do?" Lira sounded as surprised as Marney looked.

Tag nodded. "The longer we wait leaves us only two options: to redo the plan and risk word leaking out, or call it off altogether. Neither way works for me. Come on."

He brushed past Marney without another word to Lira or Dyson. Tag needed to clear his head of the dark emotions swirling around and he figured this nuts and bolts planning was the best way to do so.

"Ergen has other news." Marney lowered her voice to a whisper once they were clear of the galley. "I didn't want to let too much slip yet, but he's received word that the Naplians might be aware of our plans."

Tag glanced at her. "They know? How much?"

Marney shrugged. "Enough that they're shuffling their forces throughout the system. It doesn't appear they've reinforced Fontenelle or any of the vital entry star systems."

"Not yet, anyway."

"I'm not going to pretend this is foolproof, Tag, but the question's a simple one—do you want to go home or not?"

"Home." Tag chuckled but there wasn't any humor in his reply. "Marney, you'd better not pin the lives of thousands of our people on getting the Baedecker governor's mansion back."

"I mean our planet," Marney snapped. "You don't understand. There are so many millions who've been displaced by the war that our reclaiming Baedecker won't just be about getting our people to resettle their homeworld. It's a symbolic action. This can be a rallying point for the Grand Alliance."

Tag stopped and faced her. "For the Terran Republic. Not the Grand Alliance. I don't give a damn what the Briddarri want out of this invasion, other than I'm more and more convinced they're just happy we're not nosing around their cybernetic butcher shops. That's where we should be concentrating this effort, and as soon as it's done, that's what I'll go back to doing."

"Even without Sinclair's support?"

"I don't need it. I've got Ram's."

"And what if the C-in-C reassigns the brass again? You could be without a single flag officer."

"Then I'll quit." Tag threw up his hands. "I've got Lira and Dyson. TI, too, if Tim will still back us. There's more to this fight than the war, Marney, but you've got one thing right—we need the Baedecker invasion to happen. There's too much at stake, and I, for one, won't wait a day longer to go in and kick this Erassia officer square in the eye."

Something about their conversation riled Tag out of his doldrums and onto a war footing. *Maybe that's what Marney wanted. She's always known how to get me to do what she wants.* But Tag couldn't blame her. She had her heart in the right place.

The doors to the briefing room opened. Tag's heart sank as he recognized a void where Sinclair should have stood. Tanaka, Ram, and Tim looked up from the holo display, where Admiral Ergen glowered out at those assembled.

"No more delays," Tag told them. "The techs say *Valo* will be ready in twenty-four hours. We go then, or we miss our chance."

"Glad to hear we've got a shiny new colonel giving us orders," Ergen growled. "Tanaka, maybe you'd better remind your junior officer—"

"Colonel Wester is the operational lead for the incursion team, and his insights are welcome as such." Tanaka's voice, while half Ergen's volume, sliced across the latter's rant. She watched Tag with renewed interest. Was it his imagination, or did she look more haggard than usual? Without a hair out of place, it was hard to tell. "Well, Colonel? Are your people ready?"

"Ready as ever, Admiral, and I think we all know the chances of us pulling this off drop if we wait."

Ram chuckled. "Our pilot is as blunt yet astute as ever. Do you concur, Commander Ess?"

"It's not going to be easy, but Tag's right— TI doesn't want to wait around, either. Keeping this endeavor quiet takes more effort with each passing day."

"Very well." Tanaka faced Ergen's holo. "The incursion will commence in twenty-four hours, Admiral. Prepare your forces accordingly, especially considering the Naplian responses and your new intelligence."

"Good luck to all of us, then." Ergen didn't look at Tag. "So we don't all wind up in the hall of revered warriors at once."

His image blinked out. Tag realized, then, that he'd gone over the peak. It was downhill from there, just like sledding in Baedecker Four's far north Rondial forest when Father took him and Marney on winter trips.

He had only to make sure he didn't fly off a ledge on the way to the bottom.

CHAPTER FOURTEEN

Evie Wester grimaced as the Naplian destroyer's pulsed particle blast caught her Raider fight-bomber full force across the starboard wing. Shields were still nearly full, so it wasn't like the shot killed her, but electrical discharges sent ripples throughout her weapons and nav systems.

"Guns offline." That gruff announcement came from her RIO, Larry "Smokey" Laurence. "Nav and comms and glitching."

"This is the part where you tell me you've got it under control." Evie punched the maneuvering thrusters and spun them away from the destroyer. Baedecker Four's green and brown sphere filled her canopy as the Raider reoriented.

"Course I do, but I can only get the damage control systems to respond so fast." Smokey chuckled. "Try turning the core off and back on again."

Green flashes filled the sky. The cockpit rattled.

"Shields falling below 70 percent."

Evie wrinkled her face. The op was a mess. She couldn't even contact anyone else in the squadron. At least two of the four sensor beacons were trashed. If she could swing around and hook up with the rest of Flirry, they might have a chance—

Her displays flashed to life. Evie stared at the

six Naplian starfighters swarming her coordinates. No wingman, no squadron. Where was everyone else?

And another destroyer was hemming them in.

Damn one-eyes.

"Weapons lock confirmed on Bogey One," Smokey said. "I figured you wanted the closest one."

"Thanks, Smokey." The bracket he'd placed on the targeting display pulsed a reassuring red around the curved-wing enemy fighter. Evie punched an Arrow missile its way, rolled again, and threw a stream of rounds from the 25 mm railgun toward a second.

Splashed one. Damaged the second.

But the other four fighters blasted her plane into oblivion.

And it didn't even hurt that much, except when she smacked the console with her bare palm.

"Ow," Smokey said.

"You can't feel that." The canopy image displayed frozen fire and, beyond that thin veil, immobile Naplian fighters. Evie stripped off her helmet as the cockpit seams cracked open. "It's the console, not your thick skull."

"She's my bird too, Lunchbox."

Evie groaned. Smokey chuckled, and more laughter filtered in from outside the canopy. Valo's hangar lights blinded her for a moment until a technician blocked the glare with her silhouette. "It's a good thing you're still just in the sim, Lieutenant, or I'd run out of spare parts."

"If the sims weren't impossible, I wouldn't be so rough on her." Evie climbed out and removed her helmet.

"Or so hungry." Smokey clambered down the

ladder. He grinned at Evie. "I've got ravioli stashed in the galley."

"*Actual* ravioli? Where did you get that? I'm in." Evie's stomach growled. She wished food wasn't her comfort thing, but it was more about the company than the eating—well, that wasn't true. She loved flavors. Didn't matter from what dish or on what planet. No wonder Uncle Antiny tried out new concoctions whenever she visited.

And no wonder she'd picked up the callsign in training. The one time she'd mistaken someone's leftover meal for her own...

"I think you'd better save the celebration." Captain Naomi "Princess" Wyss walked over to the berthed Raider. "You didn't die nearly as quickly as before."

Evie and Smokey braced to attention. "Captain. I was commenting about the drill that—"

"It is rigged unfairly," Princess smirked. "Yes, I overheard. You're not entirely inaccurate. The colonel wanted the simulation to factor in as many variables that could go wrong when we hit Baedecker. Those sensor posts have to be destroyed—and swiftly—if the rest of the invasion force is to have maximum effect. If the Naplians can't see what we're doing, even for the first few minutes of the invasion, it will give the fleet a chance to scatter in system, and the one-eyes will have to blink hard to determine where we've gone."

"Yes, sir." Smokey's posture and tone were perfect. Evie hated it, but she had to admit, he'd had way more practice. Why a guy more than twenty years her senior was still an Lt. baffled her. His salt-and-pepper moustache, coupled with the graying brown hair, indicated he should be shipside running the wing command by this point in his career.

I guess that's what happens when the Naplians take the home of a Second Consular War veteran. He signs up for another round.

"Take a break for now," Princess said. "We're locking down the hangar and rerouting power to the sensors. The colonel wants the false readings up and running in the next half hour."

"Yes, sir." Evie glanced around the hangar. The tall bracings looked like the inside of a monster's stomach. No one had bothered repainting the sickly mustard yellow and tan of the Naplian paint scheme. "Does that mean we're there?"

"Almost." Princess indicated her comms. "Forty-five minutes until we jump into Fontenelle."

Evie tried not to shake with the knowledge they were sneaking through the enemy's back door. *Then we find out whether the one-eyes can see right through our disguise.*

* * *

Valo's bridge was a broad crescent laid out in reverse, with a cube-shaped tactical display taking up the front. Twin doors led into the curved side, one from either corridor, with the command chair halfway between the midpoint and the display. Consoles lined the curve. Helm and Tactical were seated ahead and to the command chair's left and right, respectively.

Which put Tag in the action—just not in the way he was used to.

He blinked away the dryness in his eyes. Lately,

he'd developed the habit of staring at the tactical displays on a ship when it jumped. Not the best habit to develop. Something about the odd pinched sensation his body went through during the instantaneous transit told him he needed to be on his guard.

Tag frowned. Hadn't he slept through jumps before? Sure, when Dyson was at the controls of *Olivia Vy*, and even then, his lack of trust toward the android hadn't stopped him from resting his eyes.

Tag wondered if it was yet another sign he was getting too worried about the people under his command. *Good thing I can still sleep. That'll be the last straw.*

"How're we looking?" Tag asked.

"Sensor readings returning." Lieutenant Hopper loomed over the tactical console. He and three dozen other officers and crew were on loan from *Aox*, courtesy of Captain Wu and Commodore Ram. Hopper was a big blond guy who Tag thought should have been assigned to boarding parties as a marine instead of squeezing behind the tactical board. "Pings coming up in the holo cube."

He had a way of understating the situation that made Tag want to laugh. The holographic representation of the Fontenelle System filled with dozens of starships. White circles formed around pips as they blinked into and out of the system.

"Their trajectories are uniform," Dyson called out from the sensor station behind Tag's left shoulder. "All traffic is following mandated vectors."

"That fits with what TI told us." Tag drummed his fingers on the arms of his chair. "Okay, then. Dyson, light us up the corridor we need to follow for Baedecker.

Helm, punch the ripwave as soon as you get those coordinates."

"Aye, Skipper." Lieutenant Baquiran was two-thirds Hopper's height, with short, dark hair and slight frame. Her motions at the helm controls were quick but precise. "Engaging ripwave in ten."

Dyson's route appeared as a series of green waypoints in the holo that lead around the system's fringe, ending at what *Valo's* sensors identified as an automated weapons platform. The deck shuddered underfoot as *Valo* leapt ahead.

"Time to first waypoint, fourteen minutes," Baquiran announced. "Time to final waypoint approximately one hour, eight minutes."

"Thanks, Helm." Dyson turned his chair. Boy, he could get used to that. "Everything's matching up so far, Tim."

Tim and Lira were seated next to each other at comms and an auxiliary sensor station, respectively. "Five by five," Tim said. "It's not a big secret that the Naplians tightly control who moves in this system and the other two. What matters now is that the traffic controllers accept our new ID as *Valo*."

"It is," Dyson interjected.

"Then they'll think *Teret* is back there and won't care that *Valo* shows up here." Tag turned again. "Ready to play the disgraced captain if we get signaled?"

"Momentarily." Dyson cocked his head. His expression went blank—well, blanker than usual, in Tag's estimation. "I am installing the necessary translation software."

The comms console beside Tim chimed. "I think that's us."

"Pipe the incoming through the overhead speakers," Tag said. "So we all know what we're dealing with."

"Warship *Valo*, this is Secure Star Two Transit Control." The tinny voice spoke the words in Naplian technical dialect, but the voiceover translation rendered the communications understandable with only a few seconds of lag. "State the purpose of your arrival and destination."

Dyson glanced at Tag, who nodded back. *Go for it.*

"This is Captain Jurrlant of *Valo*." Dyson's tone became peevish as if the questioner was bothering him in the middle of vital work. The nasal voice, complete with fluent Naplian speech, rankled Tag's nerves. He had to commend whoever in TI had dug up examples of *Valo*'s commander speaking—and hoped he never actually met the guy. "Our business is patrol reassignment, again. It's the fourth one this quarter. We've been shunted to Baedecker."

"They have you on serjaum guarding?"

That didn't seem like the right protocol but, then again, the transit control person sounded less respectful than he had in the initial inquiry.

"It's an honor to be serving with Admiral Erassia for the glory of our emperors," Dyson replied. "And certainly better to guard vital serjaum supplies than harassing captains from a dismal office."

Wow. Tag shared a look with Tim, worried about the route Dyson was taking the questioning, but he got a thumbs-up in response. Still, Tag sent a text-only message from his chair's console to Baquiran at the helm: <Plot us a course out of here at ripwave if this goes bad. Don't charge the drives yet, though, not even

for a jump.>

He watched Baquiran's head bob. <Already set up for a micro-jump, too, if we need to foul their sensors.> Her fingers tapped commands into her console.

Tag had almost forgotten about the stubby micro-jump generator hanging on the shorter port-side wing *Valo* sported. He guessed there were advantages to flying an enemy ship after all.

"Honor and glory are funny words coming from the *wiliru* of the fleet," Transit Control said. "Get to your destination and keep the lanes clear for the true warriors. Enjoy your time of banishment, *Valo*. Transit Control out."

The signal cut out. Tim exhaled. Tag chuckled, glad for a moment of tension to lift. "Gotta say, Dyson, I'm glad you're working for us. I could think of a ton of times I'd like to have someone in my corner faking a voice, especially of a captain or a commodore."

"Given your past proclivity for disobeying or bending orders, I can see why such falsification would prove enticing." Dyson checked his sensor readouts. "I show no vessels following us."

"Sounds good to me," Tag said. "Helm, continue this course. Tactical, follow the instructions Commander Ess gave you and make sure we're matching the weapons status of every one-eye ship from here to the system's sun."

"Roger that, Colonel."

"Yes, sir."

Tag stood from his chair and walked over to Lira's station. He leaned on the console. "So? What do you think?"

"That I agree, we're in good shape." Lira looked

up at him. "Nobody's making sudden moves toward us. Transit Control sounded as irritated as we could expect by our fake captain's presence like he couldn't wait to get off the signal with him. Probably afraid of dishonor contamination. They're not all that different from Briddarri when it comes to martial pride—probably why they've butted heads over this corner of the galaxy."

"All right. If you pick up on anything that sets off your alarm bells, let me know, okay?" Tag watched the tactical monitor from his new perch. "I'm not used to creeping around like this, pretending like I'm someone else."

"Don't worry. I do it all the time." She winked at him. "Well, almost all the time."

"Yeah, I remember." Tag grinned. "That's why I'm asking your advice."

* * *

The Truppen were on standby alert in *Valo*'s cargo bay, which was an extension of its hangar, though separated by armored bulkheads. Twenty octants were crammed shoulder to shoulder. A double row of repair pods bulged from underneath an upper deck catwalk.

Elden perused the invasion plans—at least, the ones he was privy to. The hologram flickered and pulsed as he used a clawed hand to shift between images.

Footsteps broke the silence. Marney approached from the main corridor's hatch. "I'm surprised you're not hibernating with the rest of your men."

"My mind was too busy," Elden said. "Too many thoughts crammed together."

"I know the feeling." Marney grimaced and touched her stomach. Elden detected a spike in temperature on her face.

"Are you unwell? Should I get the ship's surgeon?" Elden moved beside her, ready to catch her in his arms if she needed medical care.

Marney waved him off. "No, it's nothing. Morning sickness again. The doctor has me on treatments that alleviate most of the symptoms, but every once in a while, these little ones remind me of their presence."

"I see." Elden turned back to his work. The physical reorientation was simple. The mental? Not quite as easy. He kept envisioning their last meeting before Elden died, before he was made into a Truppen. When there had still been hope, however far-fetched, that his feelings for her would be reciprocated.

Now, she carried another man's children within her. Elden had entertained the notion he could sweep her off her feet when it came to another man, but he had no doubt she'd be a fiercely devoted mother.

"You sound an awful lot like Tim." Marney crossed her arms. She stood next to him, gazing at the blue holographic representation of the Naplian command structure, Daviont Tower.

"That wasn't what I intended, but you must admit, there is more than just your life on the line. It was dangerous enough when it was only you."

"I won't argue that with anyone again, Elden, especially not you. Stopping the Briddarri is an important mission, but this is bigger—or at least as big." Marney scowled at the miniature buildings. "Look at that monstrosity they've built in the heart of downtown. It's sitting in the Randall Theater grounds, did you know that? Father took me and Tag there for a symphony when we were children, the first live musical performance on Baedecker since the Second Consular War ended. There's nothing left of the city I grew up loving. I want to give children who were forced off Baedecker the chance to rebuild what we lost."

Elden couldn't think of anything to say, so he nodded. He didn't point out to her that she was fantasizing about a future he didn't think would happen. Even if Baedecker came out of this invasion, this liberation, relatively unscathed, the planet would become a military installation—or it should, by his thinking. How else would the Grand Alliance prevent it from being retaken by the Naplians?

Then, there were his own feelings on the matter. The Northern Alliance claimed the world as their own, and even the neighboring Reittians wanted the territory. She had to face facts: Baedecker was not only a military linchpin in the region but a political flashpoint that would remain in every power's crosshairs.

Rather than bludgeoning her with that analysis, Elden finally said, "I admire your persistence, Marney, but we can't lose sight of our task. The cybernetic experiments are abominations."

"You sound like Abbot Jeopar when you say that." Marney sighed. "I'd rather turn the whole mess over to the Grand Alliance. Tim says—"

"He hasn't seen what we've seen, not up close." Elden regretted his volume the second he saw Marney flinch. "They stripped my men's minds from their bodies and dissected their frames, then used their knowledge to turn free beings into enslaved machines. If we don't stop them, if the Briddarri convince the

Grand Alliance to embrace this savage version of cybers, what makes you think the technology won't spread? What makes you think those enslaved armies will stay enslaved?"

"I never said that." Marney stood straighter. "And Tim *does* know what we're up against. He's never forgotten—and neither have I."

Elden slashed a hand across the holoprojector's base. The 3-D rendering disappeared, as did the glow illuminating him and Marney. "I'm sorry. I didn't mean to imply otherwise."

Marney looked up at him. "We've changed, you and I, haven't we, Elden?"

"We have, like so much else in the galaxy. There's no way around that." *The way I feel about you will remain constant.* He wouldn't say that, not to this woman who had mended her marriage and embraced the start of a new family.

Marney's comm crackled at the same time the interlinked summons reached Elden from Dyson's console. "Go ahead."

"We're ready to jump for Baedecker." Tag sounded tense but in control. "Thought you might want to see the sights."

"I'll be right there." Marney smiled at Elden. "You'll be watching the sensors, won't you? Tag didn't think you'd be needed just yet."

"I have four octants ready to deploy in case we encounter difficulties, but otherwise, I'll be running self-diagnostics with the rest of my men." Elden held out a hand. "I will see you next when we make landfall, I suppose."

"If not before then." Marney touched his metal

fingers. "Good luck."

Elden's interlink activated as soon as she headed out from the cargo bay. <I take it you didn't decide to let her in on our plan,> Goetz said.

<There's no need to—not yet. They're all relying on us to capture Erassia, with their help. What happens to him afterward is up to us, not them.>

<You really think he's going to roll over and tell us what he knows?>

<He will talk. His clan is one of the foremost to embrace the devastator nonsense. If anyone has been keeping tabs on cybernetic activities, Erassia will know.>

<And if he doesn't?>

Elden brought up the Daviont Tower schematics again, this time via his internal systems. <Then we will trade him to the Briddarri in exchange for the complete cessation of their cybernetic experiments unless they want an endless war with us that we will inevitably win.>

＊　＊　＊

Forget his eyes—Tag's throat was dry this time, but he didn't think it was because of the jump, at least, not the transit itself.

It was because he was gazing at his home stars for the first time in seven years. One Earth-type golden sun, one ruddy orange companion.

The forward screens centered on a tiny blue dot basking in their glow.

Naplian ships populated on the tactical display, but Tag didn't worry about them, not for the moment.

He couldn't believe they were back.

He glanced at Marney. She had tears in her eyes.

"It's been a long time, Colonel," Tim whispered like he'd arrived late to the start of a chapel service.

"Sure has, Commander." Tag straightened in his seat. Right. Time to get down to work. "Helm, anyone coming to say hello?"

"Negative, sir," Baquiran reported. "Their patrols are pretty close to where we expected to find them."

"All right. Tactical?"

"Nearby units show patrol alert status but no weapons targeting us," Hopper said.

"Also good. Dyson, Tim, what does the comms traffic look like?"

"Standard Naplian chatter—course corrections, sensor inquiries..." Tim frowned. "Hang on. I have a low-level pulse underneath it all. Dyson, can you confirm?"

The android sat stock still at his console. Stiller than usual, Tag noted. "Dyson?"

Nothing.

Tag pushed off from his seat. He grasped Dyson's shoulder. "Hey, Dyson. Respond."

He turned him around.

Dyson stared unseeing, his eyes wide and twitching in their sockets, his lower jaw trembling.

CHAPTER FIFTEEN

D yson stood in a field of stars. He found that peculiar. The laws of physics dictated he should not be able to walk in deep space, especially not with blue light rippling out from each footstep.

His internal equilibrium sensors and external spatial scanners indicated he was walking on a solid surface. His eyes told his processors that it looked like water, except there was no moisture and nothing but an endless void all around him.

Correction. Not endless void.

A pair of burning suns were centered in his field of view. Naplian warships ripwaved from point to point. He turned and gazed up at a nearby destroyer.

Valo.

How curious. He was standing outside the ship. His body told him he was feeling the feeble warmth from Baedecker's suns, even this far out.

"This is not possible."

"Hello?"

The voice was female. Dyson looked over his shoulder. He should not be able to hear anything—of course, if the noise originated in space, which he did not believe it did.

"Can you hear me?" the voice asked.

"I can." Dyson found himself unsure how loudly

to speak. "Can you hear me?"

"Yes." The pitch was female, though with a curious cadence that had Dyson question whether it was biological or artificial. "Where are you?"

"I cannot give you a frame of reference." Indeed, for all his body's insistence that he was sensing the things he sensed, he could not access his positioning system. The coordinates field stayed blank. "I seem to be malfunctioning."

The voice laughed. "I am, too. Where were you when it happened?"

"I cannot answer that." Classified nature of his mission aside, he did not know to whom he was speaking. Sharing information seemed imprudent. "Who are you?"

"I don't think we should resort to names, do you?"

"Agreed."

"Well, then. That leaves us at an impasse."

So, it did. *Valo* lumbered past Dyson, who stared up at the sweep of the jump sail and the glow of the ion engines. Would he have to run to catch up with it? Given the speed he remembered from his sensor console, the destroyer should have left him far behind in a matter of seconds, yet he seemed to keep pace with it.

It was bothersome.

"I think our networks have entangled," the voice suggested. "I was connected to a larger one when this happened."

"As was I." Again, Dyson did not feel compelled to tell her that he had just jumped into the star system. It would be too easy for a determined party to check sensor logs and figure out from there on which ship Dyson had arrived.

"We should meet each other. Perhaps we can pool our resources and determine how to disentangle ourselves."

Dyson pondered that. "Are you able to detect anything about me? My internal systems or processors?"

"No, I can't. You're just—a voice. A very nice voice, but a voice all the same." Her voice sounded more thoughtful. "For our networks to have entangled, we must have experienced a prior contact."

"Yes, I had wondered about that. Typically androids cannot achieve this level of close and near instantaneous connection without our networks having recognized each other before, at least peripherally."

"All right. I suppose I'll start walking."

Dyson held his position. He could hear faint footsteps but without reference points that made sense, he could not determine from which direction and at what distance they originated. "I can use my voice as a guide to bring you within visual range."

"You can, though I'm having a hard time extrapolating our positions. Meanwhile, it would not hurt to check on your diagnostics."

"Mine is not complete, yet." Dyson realized what she was implying. "Are yours?"

"Yes, nine point six seconds ago, at least judging by my internal clock. Oh…" Her tone softened. "It's telling me my primary operating systems are caught in a feedback snarl but is confirming an unidentified network connection. Apparently I am operating out of cached memory."

"That is a clever backup system." Not unlike his

own, but Dyson was surprised her diagnostics finished before his. There were not many androids in the galaxy, not compared to the trillions of other sentient lifeforms. Dyson's diagnostics estimated nineteen point eight seconds until they were completed, which was fast for an advanced espionage model such as himself. "Are you still able to hear me?"

"I am. It seems you're getting louder. I have to say, as marvelous as it is being out here among the stars, I do hope we can break free. My line of work does not allow for a holiday, even one induced by malfunction."

"Agreed." Dyson could only hope his diagnostics broke him out of this snarl—or that his crewmates were able to do the job for him.

He resorted to tapping his foot since he could not figure out what other conversation to engage in.

* * *

Tag's heart pounded. Dyson was still a statue, except for the bizarre shuddering of his eyes and jaw.

"He's locked in." Tim knelt beside Dyson with a handheld scanner. "I don't know where he is, personality-wise, but his primary systems are operating the way they should."

"It doesn't look like it." Tag reached past the two of them and triggered the command lockdown for Dyson's console. "I'm sending these functions over to your station, Lira."

"Got it." She tapped in command, then nodded. "I've got the primary sensor data."

"Okay, keep Hopper and Baquiran linked in." Tag returned his attention to Tim. "You'd better explain better."

"I was." Tim frowned. "Dyson is programmed, in case of a major malfunction like this, to partition mission-sensitive information away from his core personality. He'll still knows who he is and possibly who he works for, but if he tries to retrieve information about this operation, he'll come up blank, as literally as you can imagine."

"That's good." Tag blew out a breath. "He picked a hell of a time to break down."

"No, I don't think he picked anything." Tim shared the scanner's results as if Tag could make heads or tails out of that much information packed into a tiny screen. "The initial scan says there were two android internal networks accessing bigger networks in the Baedecker System."

"Another android? The odds on that are slim."

"Of both running into each other on networks here? Yes, because Dyson wasn't searching for local tourism information. He's been watching the Naplian command communications and trying to breach their secure signals."

Tag glanced at Tim. "It's sounding like the other android was trying to do the same thing."

Tim was still frowning, but he nodded.

"Colonel, we're getting directions from the battlecruiser *Fulnax*." Baquiran turned toward them. "They're assigning us to a patrol route."

"While tossing an insult or two our way." Lira wrinkled her nose. "I think they called us *shirish* like they call all vermin, but I might have mistranslated."

"Probably not far off," Tag said. "Okay, Helm—get us onto that route, but plot me a secondary course for the mission spot near Baedecker Six. I want to compare distances. This patrol demand could work in our favor. Lira, make us sound as sulky as Dyson managed before. We want them to keep despising and hopefully ignoring us."

"My pleasure." Lira cleared her throat and spoke in halting Naplian dialect.

"I need to get Dyson linked into a computer that can bypass the lockout and communicate directly with his core programming," Tim said. "Unfortunately, we've got another option."

"Why, unfortunately?"

"For one thing, we'll have to get Dyson down to the cargo hold. For the other, I don't entirely trust him."

* * *

Ivy felt like she'd been walking for hours, based on the incremental wear her body measured on its various joints. It hadn't really been that long, she supposed, even though her internal chronometer was missing along with the positioning coordinates. The absences solidified her theory that her root personality had separated itself from her secure memory.

Stelltron had made certain she possessed a partition that could keep its secrets from whoever might capture and interrogate her in the event her self-destruct failed to activate.

The rhythmic tapping she'd been following ceased. "I believe I see you."

There he was. Ivy found the voice soothing. Where had she met this android? Was he another Silent Company operative she'd crossed paths with?

Or perhaps he belonged to one of the Grand Alliance governments. She knew Terran Intelligence and the Denics made use of androids more than any other nation, the former more so than the latter, so odds were good he was a spy for the Terran Republic. He sounded too composed to be a rogue artificial lifeform pilfering industrial or military secrets to sell to the highest bidder.

"I'm stopping for a moment so I can look for you, too." She ceased walking. Her position in the Baedecker System had changed by millions of kilometers, judging by the planets and ships around her, though she had no idea how. Clearly it was a recreation of the star system and not her virtual form traveling anywhere. Ivy squinted into the distance, making sure she looked in as close to a full sphere as she could manage.

There. She caught a flicker in front of a bright star. Her eyes enhanced her vision, tripling it beyond the range of unaided human sight. The dark outline of a man raised a hand, almost tentatively.

If we were biologicals, this would qualify as an awkward first date. Ivy smiled at her memory bank's analysis.

And then the sensation of holding hands rushed over her, an unfamiliar sensation of warm ersatz flesh touching hers. She held up her fingers, expecting to see someone else touching them. There was nothing.

Ivy frowned. She had never had to imitate human romantic gestures, not once. It was a facet of her programming she'd avoided, mostly because she'd found the enactment unnecessary. But the remembrances of sensations continued rolling over her. Soft speech. Gentle touch.

A kiss.

She accelerated her pace toward the other being with whom she was entangled, suddenly desperate to find out who he was and why his proximity had triggered faulty memory segments. It could be a TI trick to bait her into discovery, but she found it unlikely that TI knew what the Silent Company was working on, regardless of whether they had any inkling of Stelltron's activities at Baedecker.

It's a further malfunction, she told herself. *It will be cleared up once you see him, and then the two of you can determine how to disentangle.*

Besides, Ivy could not afford to be gone long from her body in this virtual form, not if she were to ensure that Admiral Erassia's ziurathal program succumbed to Silent Company's directives.

She glimpsed her physical self—seated in a short-range shuttle, one that lacked a jump drive, on its way to rendezvous with a Naplian mining complex. This one wasn't carrying only serjaum, though. It held crew and parts being dropped at Baedecker Six for Erassia's project.

Inspector Prad sat beside her, perusing his files.

* * *

Elden helped Ess bring Dyson's lifeless body into the cargo bay on a first aid sled. He noted his use of the word *lifeless* as if the android were ever truly alive. *Abbot Jeopar would contest my definition again, no doubt, with ramblings about heart, mind, and soul in relation to God and His universe.* It was a philosophical undertaking Elden preferred to avoid for the moment.

"Here." Ess held out a hardwire jack linking a thin red cable to the back of Dyson's neck. A red light pulsed beneath the android's skin. "I've disabled the security protocols meant to prevent this kind of hijacking."

"Hijacking? I thought it would be akin to guiding him back." Elden accepted the jack. He opened an access port above his frame's left wrist.

"Dyson may have difficulty recognizing you, given that he's likely blocked out mission-specific details. I'm relatively certain you exist elsewhere in his memory banks."

"There seem to be a lot of uncertainties, Commander."

Ess sighed. "Are you going to do this or not? I'm out of options. I don't have the sophisticated tools aboard to conduct intensive repairs on an espionage android."

"I understand." *And you should understand I am doing this only because Marney asked me to.* Elden placed the jack into the port. A green light appeared on his end. Dyson's turned the same color.

"All right." Ess held his hand over his scroll. "Ready?"

Elden nodded.

Ess pressed a panel.

A rush of colors and sounds flooded Elden's senses. He fell through a tunnel. An awful tingling rippled through his flesh.

Flesh?

He was on his hands and knees. Blue light rippled outward where his fingers touched a surface invisible against the infinite backdrop of deep space. Elden watched in awe as a Naplian battlecruiser swept by, no bigger than his thumb.

Flesh. Hands. Fingers. Thumb.

He was a man again.

Elden cried out. He pressed his palms to his chest, his ribs. The clothes felt real—the stiff fabrics of a navy-blue jacket and brown trousers, his Northern Alliance garb, the same outfit he'd worn to Baedecker on that fateful voyage seven years ago.

"How is this possible?"

"I believe your mind has reconstructed this image based on how you see yourself, regardless of what you know your physical form to be."

Elden spun. Dyson Ashteo walked toward him. His expression was placid, as usual, though his brows lowered as if he were trying to remember an important fact and couldn't recall it. "Consul Elden Selva."

"Yes. Dyson…" Emotions rushed through Elden. He wanted to laugh, but tears filled his eyes. Tears! He touched the warm moisture at the corners of his eyes.

He hadn't forgotten. Deep down, a hidden part of him *knew* who he'd been. Who he was.

"Dyson, I am here to bring you back. You know you had a malfunction, correct?"

"I have ascertained that, though where I was and what I was doing are unclear." Dyson cocked his head. "I was on a ship, except it was Naplian and not Terran—Ah."

"I hope the 'Ah' means that you recall why I am nearby and able to access your systems the way I have," Elden said. "This is a hardwire link. Commander Ess is working on your repairs, but it seems that whatever has happened is the result of your connection with another individual."

Dyson glanced over his shoulder. Was there a ship coming their way? Elden thought he detected emotion but realized he couldn't modify his sight. Of course. His mind planted him inside what he'd been like as a man without the physical enhancement Truppen transformation had given him.

"Dyson, come with me. We must disengage you before this malfunction grows worse."

"I cannot leave. Not yet. I am close to discovering the source of this error."

There *was* motion. A person walked toward them. Even at this range, Elden could tell it had a female humanoid shape.

Dyson looked at him. "But tell Commander Ess I will be able to follow you back now that I know where you came from. Once you disengage, it will create a breach between this virtual network and my physical systems. He can seal it after I return."

"If you're certain."

"I am." Dyson opened his mouth, said nothing at first, then added, "Please."

I hope he knows what he is doing. But it was more than that. The joy of having regained his human body was wearing off. The knowledge that it was memory, imagination, and falsehood rolled into one soured the experience. Soon, he'd be back in Truppen form. This would be only a dream.

A nightmare, perhaps.

"Very well. I will go." Elden clenched his fists. He couldn't leave, not just yet. "When you look at me—what do you see?"

"A human, approximately one point eight meters tall, with blond hair, gray eyes, and broad shoulders."

Elden felt tears return. He had to leave. He couldn't stay a moment longer. "If you take longer than two minutes, I will return."

But I hope you don't. Elden pressed forward against a transparent barrier. It broke into the same lights and sounds, played in reverse. *Because I don't know if I can stand to come back to this place.*

He tried to look back, to glimpse his human body again, or see if Dyson was right behind him, but he saw the android turn away. A young woman with blonde hair tied into a ponytail approached him. Green eyes widened. She put her hands to her lips.

The image fizzled out, and Elden found himself staring at Commander Ess,

His body was metal again.

* * *

Dyson thought he was experiencing a second, much worse malfunction. "This cannot be."

"I don't think it can, either." The woman closed the distance between them. "It's you, but somehow you're—different."

Dyson didn't know how until he enhanced his vision and focused on his reflection in her eyes. He was the same height and build except he possessed external features nearer to Middle Eastern heritage, with black hair and brown eyes. It was how he had been covered earlier in his TI career.

When he worked with her.

"Olivia?" Dyson stepped back. The link to his primary systems was right behind him. "You cannot be alive. I saw you terminated."

Olivia blinked. "Dyson?"

She faded out of sight.

Dyson was left staring at the starfield beyond where she'd stood. It made no sense. Olivia could not exist. Not anymore.

She had been destroyed. His memory must be malfunctioning, too.

But there was only one way to find out.

He stepped back through the link.

CHAPTER SIXTEEN

T ag didn't like what he was hearing. "Are you sure?" he asked Dyson.

Dyson sat at the head of the briefing room office. The small compartment behind the bridge and to starboard was cramped, with a six-person table and storage cabinets that doubled as a counter for displays that repeated bridge information. He, Tag, Tim, Marney, and Lira took up five of the six chairs.

"That is what she appeared to me as." Dyson's voice was barely above a murmur. His fingers plucked at each other. Tag had seen him affect human gestures before, but this time, he seemed nervous. Maybe just distracted. Either way, it was a hard thing for Tag to imagine an android dealing with. "Olivia Vy."

Tag glanced at Tim. "What's your take? Does TI have anything on her?"

Tim shifted in his seat. He seemed as uncomfortable as Dyson. "I'm a bit familiar with the incident. Dyson is correct. Olivia Vy was one of our operatives. A damned fine one, judging by the reports I read. But she was KIA during an operation over the Tulsan Gap between here and the Rutak Empire. That was ten years ago."

"And there's no mistaking she was lost?" Marney asked.

"I held her broken body in my hands." Dyson looked down at his intertwined fingers. He seemed to realize what the fidgeting signified to everyone else in the room and separated them. "Whatever was left was not enough to repair."

"I'm so sorry." Marney's cheeks reddened. "I didn't mean to make you feel that all over again."

Feel. Tag never thought he'd worry about what an android was feeling, but given the bond they'd formed on the Union of Planets mission, he couldn't step back from offering Dyson his full support. "Okay, so I look at it this way: either Dyson's malfunction was triggered by another android, or someone wants us to think that."

"I am sorry, Tag, but that is not accurate," Dyson said. "The reaction I had could only be the result of the network entanglement backfiring. Diagnostics have proved as much. It was Olivia. I am not mistaken."

"Okay." Tag ran a hand through his hair. "If it is, we've got a bigger problem."

"She doesn't know where he is, does she?" Marney asked. "Because if she's active again, I assume that means she was reassembled by someone else. There's not that many agencies out there that can afford to retrieve an intelligence android's memory circuits and put her all together."

"She's right," Tim said. "The process is complex. So, if this is Olivia Vy, and she's in the Baedecker System, she's here on behalf of someone else, and that someone is not Terran Intelligence."

"There's no end to the list of whoever else she could be working for." Lira had her feet up on the table. She ticked off possibilities on her fingers. "The Denics. The Briddarri. Lotharian pirates—"

"Lotharians?" Tim snorted. "They don't have two credits to rub together, let alone two brain cells."

"Don't dismiss them. They have more resources than you think." Lira wiggled her last two fingers. "Then there's the gobs of merchant houses of various sizes that could be keeping tabs on Naplian activities just so they can gain an economic advantage over their competitors. The bigger question is, who is she now, and where is she?"

"I cannot be certain of a location since we met in a virtual construct, but I suppose I could ascertain possible locations based on where in the system we appeared," Dyson said. "It will require further research."

"It's got to be a side project for now," Tag said. "I'm leaving it to you and Tim, but let's not let it distract us from the mission. We should be at Baedecker Six in a few hours. Once we get a better scan of the situation, we'll break up into teams so we can get our raids underway. Marney, time check?"

"Three hours until the invasion forces jump to their staging grounds." Marney looked up from her scroll. "Tim, we can still get a message out if we need to, can't we?"

"We can, but I wouldn't recommend it. It's risky."

"Then we won't." Tag leaned forward and propped his elbows on the table. "Tim, why don't you and Marney check in with Elden. See if his Truppen have their deployments mapped out. We'll need to launch them soon."

"Understood." Tim must have also understood that Tag wanted him and Marney out of the room—not to be rude or even out of command necessity, but because he wanted to speak to the only two people he trusted as much as his own sister. "I'll stop in with the squadron and make sure they're prepared, too."

"Thanks." As soon as they were gone, Tag sank back in his seat. "I just don't believe this."

"I do." Lira switched seats, so she was next to Dyson. "Are you okay?"

"That is too simplistic a word to convey my mental state." Dyson looked at her. "I cannot understand why she is here."

"We'll figure it out. I promise you that." Lira smiled. "Maybe not before we scoop Admiral Erassia out of his bed, but thereabouts."

"It's more than that," Tag said. "If she's playing for another team, we've got to find out who that is and what they want. If the Briddarri are running spies against us—"

"Then we must adhere to our plan and take Erassia before they can." Dyson nodded. "I realize this is a personal matter over which the mission takes precedence."

"That doesn't mean we're going to ignore it. Security risks aside, you're our friend, so whatever you need from us to track this lady down, we'll make it happen."

"Thank you."

"Dyson." Lira chewed her lip. "Did you love her?"

Tag's gut reaction was to scoff at the idea of an android finding its soulmate, but then he remembered the anguish Dyson had expressed the first time he'd told Tag about losing Olivia. Sure, he could mimic human emotions, but how much of that was programming? All of it, he guessed. Then again, how much of human emotion was programming and reaction?

"I care for your well-being and Tag's greatly," Dyson said. "Olivia occupied far more of my thoughts than either of you and with greater affection."

Lira glanced at Tag. "That means yes."

"I'd say so." Tag thumped his fist on the table. "Let's add this to the list of things we need to get done."

✳ ✳ ✳

Tag's first stop was the improvised drop bay, where the 75th Orbital Jump Battalion was billeted. There were 160 soldiers, the same number as the Truppen complement, but while equipped with some awesome-looking heavy armor suits, they were not nearly as intimidating as their Truppen counterparts.

Lieutenant Colonel Laura Macken straightened from the underside of her armor. She brushed bits of stripped wiring from close-cropped gold hair. "Colonel Wester. They finally let you come down to where the real work's being done?"

"Only because I'm on my best behavior." Tag chuckled. "You've got your assignment. Any issues?"

"Negative, sir." If Macken, who'd remained at her rank for ten years, had any gripe about Tag's sudden double promotion, it didn't show in her attitude. We've got our target on Baedecker Two. Don't tell me we're changing the drop schedule, though. My kids are itching for payback."

"That's a negative, Colonel. We're good for the drop. The rest of the invasion force will rally in less than three hours and make their jump."

"Good deal. We'll be busy mucking up the serjaum depots."

"Outstanding." Tag leaned forward so he could examine the armor's reinforced chassis. "So, I take it there's no hard feelings about the assignment?"

"Sir?"

"The Truppen going after Erassia while you hit the serjaum tanks."

Macken frowned. "I wasn't aware there were any hard feelings, Colonel. Consul Selva told me about Admiral Sinclair's order that we make the switch. I didn't have a problem with it, seeing as how it was one of the admiral's last commands before we lost him."

A command I didn't have a chance to ask him about, apparently. "Elden's people will get the job done. I think it's best to stick with it, given the Naplians might be watching for the Truppen at Baedecker Two. It would be more straightforward to have your jumpers attempt the abduction than the Truppen, but I've got assets who'll make sure the Truppen know which way to point their weapons."

"Trust you wouldn't need them if we were there," Macken teased.

"Fair enough." Tag nodded and moved along the line of armor suits. Sinclair hadn't let him in why he'd swapped those units. Admiral Tanaka wasn't forthcoming on the reason, either, though Tag wasn't certain even she knew the real reason.

He shook his head. Lira could handle it, whatever the problem might be. Sending her in to kidnap Erassia was the best way to get the job done, especially if everyone else involved took a conventional approach.

Allying with cybernetic relics led by my sister's ex-beau. Hiring a thief to kidnap an admiral. Tag smirked. No way he'd say life had been boring since he took on more responsibility.

* * *

Lira dumped her duffel bag inside *Strunk*'s airlock corridor. The gunboat was snugged up to *Valo*'s starboard hull.

Dyson was already there, checking the ammunition for a row of M-36 rifles. "Consul Selva informs me his Truppen are loading as we speak."

Loading. Lira glimpsed movement out of the transparent connector to *Valo*. Silver and gray Truppen frames drifted across space to *Strunk*, where they anchored themselves to the hull. There were enough thruster mounts and sensor bulges they could remain ensconced behind, to reduce micro fragment impacts while the ship traveled, though the distortion caused by ripwave drive should shove most of that debris out of the way. They clung to *Strunk* like giant metal bugs.

Lira shuddered. "Tell me the truth, Dyson."

"I am not prone to tell you lies." He said it without looking up from his ammo check.

"You know what I mean. You *can* lie, being with TI. Do you trust the Truppen?"

"They have proven their worth to the war effort."

"And they also proved they were willing to fly off on their own, killing Briddarri, to accomplish their own goals."

Dyson glanced at her. "I would not think it bothered you that the Briddarri military was made to pay for their crimes against innocent civilians."

"No, it doesn't." How could she make him understand? Her stomach churned. "They're still—"

"They are your people."

"Something like that." Lira withdrew her camouflage suit from the bag. She ran her fingers over the belt controls. "How many times have I used this to steal from the rich and the powerful? It's not like I'm the most loyal citizen. But the body counts the Truppen have been leaving behind. .. I'm worried they don't care who gets in the way of their holy war."

"That is a curious appellation," Dyson said. "I never considered there may be a religious aspect to the Truppen obsession with ending the cyber experiments."

"They're as devoted as any crusader," Lira said. "And I know that's a Terran word, but the Briddarri can be just as fervent, so it's the same thing."

"You are suggesting we need to keep an eye on the Truppen as they conduct this raid."

"More than one since we aren't Naplians," Lira smirked. "You don't mind, do you? This whole trusting other people thing is new for me, and the list of people who I do trust—who I care about—outside Blue Kitt is breathtakingly short."

Dyson nodded. "I understand and am willing to assist, provided we use methods that are sufficiently subtle."

"Oh, Dyson." Lira patted his shoulder. "Why would you assume I'd ever be anything but subtle?"

"Perhaps you forget I have seen you battle your way out of an elegant soiree in full view of security and guests." Dyson offered a faint smile. "I would then suggest that you pay closer attention to the definition of the word."

She gave him a playful jab and went back to

pulling her infiltration gear free of the duffel bag.

* * *

Tag sealed the final fastener on his flight suit. The white fabric gleamed in the hangar bay lights. It was still odd to get into a jumpsuit that didn't have any ID, unit patch, or rank, no matter how many times he did it since the formation of Flirry Squadron.

"Ready to go, Colonel?" Evie was already in her Raider's cockpit. She could have been standing next to him, since there wasn't a lot of room in there between the Warhawks and the Raiders parked cheek to jowl.

"You know it, Lunchbox." Tag chuckled at his cousin's groan. "Relax. You can't keep complaining about the callsign, or the rest of the squadron's never going to get you a better one."

"Can't you overrule them? Use your command prerogative?"

"He had better not." Princess slid into her Warhawk's cockpit. She donned her helmet. "If he does, it is our right and tradition to bestow upon our squadron leader an even less appealing callsign."

"But he's just Tag." Evie frowned. "That's his name."

"Yeah, but I've always been callsign 'Tag,' too," Tag said. "DeeDee Dillon, my wing commander back on Baedecker, made it official with the excuse that anyone flying with me felt like they were playing tag trying to stay on my wing."

Evie giggled. "That sounds cute."

"She didn't mean it that way." Smokey's deep voice rumbled into their conversation. "The colonel didn't have the rep for being reliable. Sorry, sir, but it's true."

"No sweat, Smokey. I know it." Hearing it said aloud still stung, but Tag wasn't about to deny his past. Fact was, he'd become a different pilot and a better officer since the early days.

"Hey!" Footsteps rattled the deck. Lira jogged between the technicians and ammo carts as she weaved a path to Tag. "You didn't come say goodbye."

"No, I, uh. .." Tag felt about five degrees too warm in his flight suit. Who'd messed with the environmental controls? "You know, as the mission commander, I. .. It was a matter of not showing favoritism."

Lira crossed her arms. "Is that so?"

"Yeah." Tag glanced at Princess. She looked like she was trying not to laugh. Evie blew a kiss in his direction. "We've got military protocol to adhere to."

"We all know how I feel about protocol, military or otherwise." She was standing impossibly close to him now. Funny how her proximity made her not give a damn about regs, either. "I need to know you'll come back to me."

"I can't promise, but you know me." Tag looped an arm around her waist. "I don't let little things like blown up stop me."

He kissed her before she could administer a swift comeback. The sounds of the hangar bay could have been light-years away. By the time they separated, Tag realized the rest of the squadron had sealed their cockpits and powered up their engines. Lira embraced him and buried her face in the crook of his neck. "Be careful," she said.

"I promise." Tag clambered into his fighter and

put on his helmet. The cockpit controls sprang to life. The familiar lights and electronic hums put him more at ease than he'd been in weeks. That was where he belonged. Tim had his orders. He was a far more capable ship commander than Tag would ever be, and even though Tag had overall command of the operation, he would not sit out the initial strike in a cushy chair, no matter how close to the front lines that chair was.

"Flirry Lead, this is *Valo*." Tim's voice crackled through the comm. "Flight control shows you are clear to launch."

"Acknowledged, *Valo*," Tag said. "Flirry Squadron shows all birds ready to launch."

"Good luck and godspeed, Tag. We'll meet you at the rendezvous."

In orbit of Baedecker Four. Tag grinned at the thought of not only their strike forces but the combined might of Terran and Briddarri fleets smashing through the Naplian defenders. "Roger that, *Valo*. Don't singe your wings."

He got the green light to launch. Tag guided his Warhawk out into space. Thrusters mounted across the fuselage sputtered, spinning the fighter around as it drifted free. The rest of the squadron formed up with him, spreading out by pairs and flights of four.

"Flirry Two to Flirry Lead." Princess sounded like she was seated right next to him. "Standing by."

The pilots checked in one by one until Tag had accounted for his eleven fighters and bombers. His ripwave drive showed it was charged and ready. The coordinates for the sensor array unlocked, and he saw the target appear in the Baedecker Three orbital slot.

"Flirry Lead to Valo," he said into the comm.

"Strike One is standing by. Confirm Strike Two and Strike Three are a go."

Tag saw *Strunk* break loose of its docking corridor and maneuver over the "top" of *Valo,* relative to Flirry Squadron's position. The Truppen clustered to its tiny hull made the gunboat look like it had acquired an infectious fungus. Two wedge-shaped assault shuttles dropped free of *Valo*, too, carrying Macken's orbital jump troops.

"Strike Two and Strike Three confirm their readiness," Tim said. "All units prepare to engage."

"Roger, *Valo*." Tag switched frequencies. "Okay, kids, you heard Commander Ess. Ripwave on my mark. Remember, we're treating this like a hot zone. The Naplians may have reinforced their position since our last scans or may have shifted units. Be advised we will turn and regroup if the situation looks bad."

"Does that mean at any sign of resistance, Lead?" Evie asked. "Because the simulations were enough to make me have second thoughts."

"If you didn't have second thoughts, you wouldn't be a good pilot, Six," Tag said. "Stick with your wingman and get your missiles to that sensor array. Don't worry about anything else. That's my job."

"Roger that, Lead."

She didn't sound as confident as Tag hoped, but he'd seen her in those cyber lab raids and found her sim results impressive—even more so because he had deliberately dialed up the difficulty level far beyond what TI had indicated the array's defenses would actually be.

Tag shook his head. No time for that. He reached for the ripwave controls. Out of the corner of his eye, he caught *Strunk* disappear in a ripple of light and the assault shuttles blink out with the same flicker of warped starlight.

His fighter and the rest of Flirry Squadron leapt toward their target a second later.

CHAPTER SEVENTEEN

A dmiral Erassia could not believe his eye. The weather satellites had warned of possible rain, given the cell they'd tracked across the continent. Baedecker Four's perpetually arid conditions made precipitation rare.

He gazed at a downpour soaking Velic.

The pounding rain brought to mind the *ziurathal*. No demonstration had been available, given the heightened security he'd put into place, so he'd have to assuage his worries with memories of their past victories and the promise of future glory.

His comms sounded. Erassia frowned at the encrypted signal origin: Tratta, commanding *Fulnax*. Erassia entered his verification and waited for the chime that indicated the message had been decrypted.

"Admiral, I trust you are aware of *shirish* movements at the fringe of this sector and others nearby." Tratta looked troubled, even in the holographic miniature of his head and shoulders that glowed from Erassia's desk.

"Should I be? The warning I received was vague, though it contained enough knowledge of our situation that I could not ignore the signs." Erassia crossed his arms. "Has the enemy made any other moves?"

"Not yet, sir, but I am concerned about the redisposition of their forces," Tratta said. "Our own subtler response to your warning has triggered a similar one on their part. I have sent you the data from the central sensor array's latest scans."

"One moment." Erassia accessed the data stream embedded in the comms signal from *Fulnax*. The image of the Baedecker System and its surrounding stars made him frown. Dozens of marks indicated that Grand Alliance warships had changed their positions or jumped out of the nearest systems within the past few days. Tratta was correct in his analysis. On the surface, it looked as if the Terrans and the Briddarri were obsessively maneuvering to protect contested territories. A few skirmishes between individual ships had occurred, though none had resulted in decisive gains or losses.

The pattern behind the ship movements, though...

"Where is the roster for our latest arrivals and departures?" Erassia asked.

"Here, sir."

The requested document appeared. Erassia tracked which of his ships were where and which escorts had come and gone recently. Good. He had adequate forces. *Kaltak* was making its rounds of the system's edge. Erassia's version of holding it at arm's length. Erassia didn't trust her captain until he could prove his political appointment had been worth the bribery expense.

Valo? Captain Jurrlant. Erassia shook his head. It seemed his banishment to Baedecker now came complete with a *wiliru* of the Naplian Fleet. "Captain, contact *Valo* and query her commander as to his latest orders. I want to know why Secure Star Two let her transit here without my approval."

"I doubt your superiors cared much for what we think of substandard units, kinsman, but I will do so," Tratta said. "We—"

His hologram froze for so long that Erassia thought he'd lost the transmission in a malfunction. "Kos?" Erassia asked. "I've lost our signal."

"Sorry, Gussan. *Valo* has disappeared from our tactical display. We're trying to ascertain where she's gone to. Wherever it is, it's not on the patrol vector she was supposed to take."

Erassia enlarged the star system holo until he could see individual ship positions with greater detail. *Valo* had indeed blinked out, its coordinates replaced by estimated trajectories the tactical computer had guessed based on her heading when she activated her ripwave drive. "Hail them."

"Trying, sir." Tratta glanced away from the holo pickup and snapped orders in the harsher *ffawe-kresh* dialect. "They're not responding to our signals."

Erassia glowered at the holo. He wished he could reach through it and throttle Tratta. As supportive as he had been of the *ziurathal* project, he was not nearly as decisive in a troubling situation as Erassia would have preferred. "Find them and report to me as soon as you can."

He terminated the call and returned his attention to the driving rainstorm. All pedestrian activity in the streets below had ceased. Even the soldiers guarding the military installations had sought shelter. Erassia welcomed the rains. They would scour away the grime that coated his command and cleanse Daviont Tower.

Much the way the true *ffawe* would cleanse the galaxy of the cursed *ziura* and their *shirish* allies.

Erassia reached for the comms console embedded in his desk and opened a secure channel to the *ziurathal* facility. No more waiting. "This is Admiral Erassia. I want the loading of the first thousand ziurathal and their operators expedited. Do not hold the transports back. Send each one as they fill."

"Of course, Admiral. Should they be prepped for an exercise?"

"They shall be prepared for combat." Erassia killed the signal. If the *shirish* were planning an attack, he would be ready, and they would learn to accept the fact that Baedecker would never revert to their hands.

* * *

Inspector Prad lingered in the loading dock as loading bots pushed pallet after pallet of *ziurathal* armor up the ramps to the next freighter. Two of the unmarked ore haulers had departed, taking two hundred *ziurathal* and their attendant personnel. It didn't make sense. Why would Erassia flaunt his secret project now? The scans Prad collected on his portable sensors were more than enough to torpedo the wreckage of Erassia's career.

Prad snorted. And yet here he was, moving huge amounts of matériel and personnel out of his secret facility. It would be laughable if it weren't such a brazen poke in the eye to Admiral Daviont.

He checked his comms readout. No new messages from Ivy. Her intel had been spot on. It was up to Prad to find a way back to the Druwei office and report his findings. He didn't dare attempt a coded message, not with as much data as he had to transmit. Erassia might be a fanatic, but he wasn't entirely inept. Had he been, he never would have kept this facility secret for as long as he did.

Prad kept to the side corridors that fed into and out of the *ziurathal* storage bays. His grubby coveralls marked him as a maintenance tech, one of the dozens of men assigned to keep the repair stations and life support systems operational. More than one took an unscheduled break from their duties to watch as the bots loaded the *ziurathal.*

"I can't believe they're finally done," one naplian told Prad. "The word is they're needed around Velic in case the *shirish* come poking."

Prad nodded. He wasn't surprised the rumor of an impending attack was filtering down to the enlisted men. Erassia's erratic ship and troop movements in recent days had baffled the Druwei, too.

A message buzzed Prad's comm. It was Rost. <Destroyer *Valo* possible rogue ship. Not responding to hails. Unauthorized ripwave signatures detected throughout the system.>

What in the name of the emperors can that mean? <Verify and keep me updated. I'll be returning to Velic.>

Prad used his forged credentials to access the loading dock's embarkation zone. It was a simple trick from there to start scanning the ammunition containers and *ziurathal* hardware packages as he edged nearer the boarding ramp for the transport currently being loaded. For all Erassia's mania about cybernetic devastators and their supposed threat to the Naplian Empire's survival, Prad couldn't deny the surge in pride he felt when he saw the mechanical monstrosities hunkered over on the loading sleds. It was easy to imagine them active instead of dormant, tearing apart the Truppen that had become such a nuisance to the war effort.

Alert lights flashed throughout the embarkation zone. Klaxons screamed, their protests echoing and amplified by the support beams arching high to the ceiling above.

"Let's move!" The NCO in charge if the loading process. There's enemy fighters attacking the primary sensor array. The admiral needs these units at Four as soon as possible!"

An attack? On the sensor array? It was in the heart of the system. Prad hurried up the ramp with the rest of the crew. He dashed off a message to Rost. <Get me whatever intel you have on this attack.>

The delay was no more than thirty seconds, which was time enough for Prad to find a bench and strap in with the other chatting passengers. Several wore the black jumpsuits of *ffawe* assigned as pilots for the *ziurathal* mechs.

<Comms and sensors readings for that vicinity have collapsed,> Rost reported. <Erassia's command is scrambling. My asset has confirmed the detonation of a serjaum tank on Baedecker Two.>

At the same time? Prad's skin flushed. He felt clammy, the precursor to becoming ill to his stomach. The transport would take approximately ninety minutes to reach Baedecker Four, based on their current positions in their orbital tracks. Whatever these attacks were could be over by then.

It occurred to him then that the Druwei had spent so much time and effort obsessing over Erassia's borderline treason they had missed a far greater threat.

* * *

The timer in Tag's cockpit buzzed. Thirty seconds to ripwave drive deactivation. He had to trust the rest of his fighters were still synched. There could be no comms chatter if this was going to work.

I'm really not interested in dying. Tag didn't know to whom he was silently speaking but he felt like his words and thoughts needed an outlet in these last critical moments. *But I'm not keen on continuing to kill others, either, even if they're my enemies. Briddarri harvesting innocent aliens, humans blasting secret Briddarri bases, Naplians destroying everyone else, the Truppen taking the war into their own claws...*

It had to end. Didn't it?

Ten second warning.

Tag gripped his controls. The seconds flashed by.

Light exploded in front of him. Stars reformed outside the Warhawk's cockpit. So did two Naplian destroyers and the sensor array. The massive sphere was ringed with eight defensive satellites that sported particle cannons. Four sensor posts studded the surface, their blunted pyramidal shapes catching little of the light from Baedecker's suns. Tag's targeting sensors had no problem marking them for destruction.

The rest of Flirry Squadron flashed onto his display. No one contacted him. Comms silence was still in effect. Every man and woman knew their role.

Tag exhaled. "No time like the present."

He punched up his missile control and targeted the nearest node. Princess, Flirry Three, and Flirry Four raced up to join him as he accelerated toward the sensor array. Two RS-18 anti-matter warhead missiles would pack a significant punch, multiplied by the same launch from Flirry Two and Three. Four was a Raider fighter-bomber. His orders were to send two Keach Seekers of even greater strength than his Warhawk's loadout into the mix.

Tag waited for the affirmative lock signal and launched both missiles, one after the other, as he bore down on the array. Five more missiles joined his.

So did fourteen from the rest of the squadron.

They caught the sensor array completely by surprise. The first strike scoured sensor posts from the array's curved surface and left half of the second one a sparking mess, though not completely offline. Tag dropped his Warhawk "below" the array, relative to his entry vector, and swooped low around it.

Green flashes lit up space as the array's weapons tracked the intruders. The destroyers, at least, remained out of the firefight. Tag wasn't about to celebrate, and he was right not to, as Princess broke comms silence out of necessity. "Incoming fighters."

Naplian starfighters swarmed from the destroyers, arrowing toward the array. "Keep the array between us and the bogies," Tag ordered. "Six, focus on the rest of the arrays. Two, stay with me. Three, you and Four join up with Six and her group, so we keep pounding the sensor posts. All other Warhawks split and engage targets of opportunity."

His orders were superfluous because they'd trained on sims and read the plan of battle with relentless focus, but as the acknowledgments overlapped, Tag used the Warhawk's thrusters to flip end to end as he cut acceleration. The flip left him facing the nearest Naplian starfighter trying to pelt him with particle blasts. Tag didn't bother with audacious pronouncements or comms taunts. He let the one-eye have a sustained burst from his hypervelocity railgun. The magnetically accelerated tungsten rounds, their rate of fire augmented by supercooling units courtesy of the Briddarri tech exchange, meant he could put far more power behind his counterattack than ever before.

The bursts shattered the Naplian's shields and shredded its fuselage until nothing was left but sparkling fragments spreading from a brief, bright explosion.

"Splash one," Tag reported. "Watch your six and cut out those sensor posts. The sooner we ruin this place, the sooner we can get out."

And the sooner the rest of the fleet can do their damage.

* * *

Ivy gazed at the reports she'd intercepted. There was little she wasn't privy to, given her surveillance of not only the Druwei office but Daviont Tower and the computer systems aboard numerous Naplian ships, including the flagship *Fulnax*. The strikes underway against the primary sensor array for the Baedecker System and the potential malfunction—which she assumed was no such thing—heralded the impending

Grand Alliance invasion as predicted.

None of that bothered her. She was more concerned by the network entanglement she'd experienced with Dyson. It meant he was here. Assuming he had not been destroyed by TI, he was still in their service, which meant TI was here. Those leaps of logic, coupled with the Grand Alliance warships, confirmed for her that Admiral Ergen had decided to continue with the invasion even though the Naplians were better prepared for it.

Why, though? Ivy ran calculation after calculation, bringing in every scrap of data she could access. The Briddarri had pushed for the invasion to the point of encouraging human recklessness. If the invasion failed, the Briddarri would be out manpower and ships, true, but the forces she had seen arrayed were mostly Terran.

The latest intel the Silent Company forwarded to her was a singular decline in raids against the Briddarri cybernetic laboratories. No doubt those were a dark secret to the rest of the galaxy, but Stelltron did not amass their legendary reputation without their Silent Company minions knowing nearly everything that was going on. The timing further reinforced Ivy's analysis that the Briddarri pushed for this invasion to throw the Terrans off their scent. No one would come out and admit it, but Ivy had seen what little records there were of the laboratory raids. Human-made fighters. Bold but organized tactics. The Terran military was waging a covert campaign against their allies, and no one would admit it. How could they, amid their war against the Naplians?

Ivy found the most puzzling piece in her

memories was the other man who appeared briefly in the entanglement with Dyson. She'd cleaned the image and run it through facial recognition in numerous Terran databases and those of the major human races, Briddarri, Denic, and Borthan. Nothing.

Not until she expanded the parameters to include the dead.

Ivy couldn't quite believe the answer—Elden Selva, hereditary consul of the Northern Alliance offshoot of the Terran Republic. Hounded by the rest of his species. Killed by the Naplians.

Resurrected as a Truppen warlord.

The devastators have returned to Baedecker.

Ivy took the thought and composed another secure message, copied blindly to Prad and Admiral Erassia. The *ziurathal* were on the move toward Baedecker Four. If she acted quickly, she'd be in a prime position to obliterate Erassia's program and get the Silent Company the thing they'd always wanted...

The detailed schematics of a working Truppen.

Ivy smiled to herself. She cleared her analysis state and refocused on her external sensors. It was still raining in Velic. Her tent shook with the weight of the downpour. Naplian soldiers were few and far between. Even the merchants, ever mindful of their customers' moods, had picked up on something rattling them. They chatted between their stalls.

All the while, the machinations of three empires swirl in her processors. Dyson's startled face loomed over them all.

It will be nice to see him again, in his true physical form, Ivy realized. *Stelltron may have rebuilt me program by program, but they didn't completely wipe my memory engrams. Strange, considering the possibility I might be compromised by him.*

A second later, she knew it hadn't been a mistake but a design bonus. Who better to give the Silent Company access to a TI espionage android than her former partner—and the only being for whom he'd ever shown deep devotion?

I hope he's looking forward to our reunion as much as I am. Ivy picked up her tool kit and bent over her scroll. She had a tighter window in which to complete her work if she was going to be ready for both Dyson and the Truppen. *It will make things easier after I co-opt his programming. He will make a fine Silent Company asset.*

* * *

Tag grimaced as a Naplian destroyer's blast raked far too close to his fighter. He spun on his axis and punched the control that released electronic countermeasure (ECM) jamming pods. The tiny brass-colored spheres appeared as glittering gold specks on his display. His instruments showed no change, but the nearest Naplian ship would experience a temporary signal disruption that would show three fuzzy images of a Warhawk bouncing between coordinates. It was enough of a distraction for him to break free.

"Lead, this is Six." Evie sounded breathless. "Third post is down!"

"I see it, Six." Tag rolled the fighter again, bringing the sensor array level to his line of sight. Three black gouges sputtered with sparks where Flirry Squadron had ripped the emitter posts apart. That left one.

The last poke in the eye, so they go blind.

"Incoming flight, One," Princess said.

Tag had seen that, too—six more fighters arrowing for them at top speed. Flirry had kept the capital ships from engaging due mostly to the attack's proximity to the sensor array. The Naplians couldn't shoot the humans down without damaging their own equipment. But they must have altered their plan because the blasts were coming nearer and nearer. "Roger that, Two. Four, we need an extra set of guns over here."

"On the way, boss." Lieutenant Randy "Winsome" Somerset's Warhawk flew escort for Evie's Raider. They both headed for Tag as Princess flipped her fighter and scattered the newest wave of incoming fighters with a brace of missiles.

"Six, what's the deal? You've got another post to knock out," Tag said.

"Will do, Lead, we're cutting around close to the deflector vanes. You'll see!"

She wasn't kidding. Evie's Raider cut close to the array's hull, but that left Winsome in a hard place —between sticking with his escort or obeying his commander's order. He bridged the gap, putting himself in an open patch of space that grew more vulnerable with each passing second.

"Six, pull back and get to my coordinates," Tag snapped. He lit a Naplian fighter up with his railgun as a missile streaked past his wingtips. "Leave the last post for Ten."

"Negative, Lead, I've got tone!" Evie whooped. "Way to paint it, Smokey!"

Her Raider fired its third of four Keach Seekers

and two Arrow missiles at the post. The explosion sent Flirry Six tumbling off course, but the Raider righted itself.

"Lead, this is Four!" Winsome banked hard toward the deflector vanes, a pair of Naplians on his tail. He'd drawn them away from the wing that threatened Tag and Princess. "Got two I can't shake!"

"Hold on, Four! Any nearby units, Winsome's in trouble!" Tag was already burning space toward him. The other Naplian fighters hammered his shields but Princess fended some of their attack off. Three more Flirry fighters swarmed them, too, giving them more to think about than a single helpless—

Winsome's Warhawk exploded. The flash of light startled Tag. Nothing remained but an expanding cloud of glittering debris.

And his sensors confirmed the array had failed.

"Flirry Four is down," Princess said. "There's nothing ... He's gone, Tag."

"I know. I saw." Tag punched up the ripwave drive, his hand aching from the overly zealous application of the control. He switched over to the full squadron comm, too. "That's it, people: The sensor array is dark. All units ripwave to the assigned rendezvous. Let's bail."

He barely registered the ten acknowledgments in his haze of anger and sorrow. Another battle. Another death—deaths, once you counted the Naplians.

Tag took little solace in any measure, except that the squadron had blinded the Naplians to what was to come next.

Space warped around him as Tag ripwaved away from the ruined array, but not until he made sure the rest of his people were safe.

CHAPTER EIGHTEEN

Commodore Sobban Ram stood stock still at his display panel at the center of *TSS Confiance*'s bridge. He felt obliged to remain a reservoir of calm, given that Captain Vollan insisted on pacing among her stations.

"Thirty seconds to reentry," the helm officer called out.

"Very good." Ram watched the blips on his display converge in the Baedecker System from multiple vectors. The Terran expeditionary forces and Briddarri battlegroups had jumped piecemeal to points outside the system, then used ripwave to close the distance. The Thirteenth's sixteen ships were joined by six other expeditionary forces of similar composition—heavy cruisers and destroyers formed the backbones. Liberty Ships followed along, two flotillas of eight bringing supplies, as well as troops numbering in the tens of thousands.

Then there were the Briddarri, fielding four battlegroups of ten vessels each, with *Winter Scourge* leading them. Ram watched as they approached in a mass of forty warships that would give even the most stalwart warrior chills.

"Message from Admiral Tanaka," the comms officer reported. "All units stand by to engage the enemy in fifteen seconds."

"Signal our confirmation." Red lights pulsed along the ceiling and deck plates. *Confiance* was ready for battle. Ram allowed himself a small smile at the thought of what the Naplians must be thinking as more than one hundred fifty ships burst into their domain. He likened their approach to that of a crocodile, swimming the Nile patiently before lunging through the reeds at its prey.

Flirry Squadron's disabling of the sensor array made the invading forces as hidden as that crocodile submerged beneath still waters.

"Allison?" Ram asked.

"Yes, sir?" Vollan walked back to her command chair, which was behind his post.

"Do take a seat." He smiled at her.

She nodded and grinned back. "One more round, Commodore."

Stars snapped into place on the main display. Baedecker Four was a blue and brown sphere etched with white wispy clouds.

The silhouettes of over twenty Naplian warships were like ravens against the summer sky.

"Poll the commanders," Ram ordered. "I need a full status accounting."

"No malfunctions or losses reported," Vollan said as the information trickled across her screen. "Destroyers taking up offensive positions. Starfighters forming defensive screens."

"Commodore, enemy vessels are breaking orbit. Two battle cruisers coming at us from around the moon's gravity well."

"Instruct batteries to pick their targets and fire

when ready," Ram said. "Torpedoes and missiles to Captain Vollan's command."

"All units report ready for action." Vollan straightened in her chair. It amused Ram to see her so stolid, so composed as if she had expended the nervous energy during the ripwave dive into the system.

Green flashed across the monitor. Red pips flickered on the tactical display.

"They're microjumping," the tactical officer said. "Forward destroyers are within range of our batteries."

"Take them," Ram instructed.

Wave after wave of long-range torpedoes sliced into the Naplian formations. The more medium range missiles went after the closest targets, putting their destroyer pairs into disarray. Every ship in the Thirteenth Expeditionary Force lent its weapons to the initial barrage.

Ram smiled grimly as the damage analysis filled the lower half of the tactical board and stratified even further on his screen. More reports cross-collected from the other six expeditionary forces, including the one led by *TSS Ajax*, Admiral Tanaka's flagship.

Confiance shook underfoot. A Naplian battlecruiser was regrouping with two of its kin and directing its attack into the heart of the Thirteenth.

"*Venerate* moving up our flank," the tactical officer said. "Lending fire support on the target."

"Task *Honor* and *Fiel* to bring their destroyers along forty degrees to the ecliptic plane." Ram tracked that half of their task force as it swept underneath relative to *Confiance* and her accompanying ships.

"Watch those particle cannons," Vollan said. "Helm, roll us to starboard. Tactical, plant a brace of torpedoes into the nearest battlecruiser's jump sail. Those readouts indicate it should shatter along the ventral axis, and I want a debris field for our fighters to blend into."

More projectiles joined the waves racing from ship to ship. The crossfire between the Naplian and Terran vessels thickened until Ram found the battlefield a dizzying spectacle of particle blasts, railgun streaks, and missile exhausts riddled with explosions.

They had to pin down the Naplian Fleet elements and either destroy them or force them to withdraw before reinforcements could be summoned. Tanaka's plan—borrowed heavily from the late Admiral Sinclair —hinged on that swift victory.

Ram allowed another small smile. Once they had Erassia in hand, surrender of the garrison would be an acceptable option, too.

❈ ❈ ❈

Admiral Ergen brushed a crumb from his moustache. The last of the *arrimm* cake was as sweet as the galley cooks had promised, whipped up with homegrown ingredients they'd smuggled aboard from the nearest Briddarri outpost. It wasn't perfect but it beat molecularly perfected ration bars to the edge of the galaxy, that much was for sure.

The battle was going well. His battleships had the one-eyes pinned down about a million klicks from Baedecker Four on the suns' side of the planet. Pinned down was a funny phrase when one considered its application to three-dimensional space, but Ergen thought it suited the situation just fine—a battle cruiser reduced to a sputtering hulk, a destroyer broken in two, and more ships suffering a barrage that made Ergen wish he was a gunnery's mate one more time.

The biggest problem was that this was all just a distraction.

Commander Burrak sidled up to the command chair. "I have an update."

"Better be worth it." Ergen gestured at the dueling ships. *Winter Scourge* bucked a little as stray blasts hit her shields. It was enough to send the ale sloshing from Ergen's cup, but otherwise, no more than a bug bite for the flagship.

"That source of yours has provided us with intelligence regarding the *ziurathal*."

Ergen glanced up at Burrak. "The Truppen-killers? They're here?"

"On the sixth planet, supposedly."

"I'll be damned," Ergen murmured. "Here, I thought this was going to turn into a waste of time just to keep our human allies preoccupied."

"Yes, but you can hardly go racing off to counter one threat—"

"Counter? Who said anything about countering?" Ergen beckoned Burrak to lean closer. "Those mechs nearly ripped Elden Selva and his people to shreds. They're why our spy Rett got himself killed. No, we need ourselves a couple of live specimens, so to speak. I'll find an excuse to take Six, and then we can have all the time in the galaxy to scrape every bit of actionable intelligence and Naplian *ziurathal* tech off that rock."

"There is a ship in the vicinity," Burrak pointed out.

Blast. He was right. The stolen destroyer *Teret*

rechristened *Valo* and serving as Colonel Tag Wester's mobile command base. Ergen checked his mission status updates. Wester and Flirry Squadron had taken out the array. Macken and her orbital jump troops were hitting the serjaum storage on Baedecker Two. TI and the Truppen …

He frowned.

"Problem, sir?"

"You'd better believe it is. Why isn't there anything in the update about the Truppen?"

"They're supposed to be hitting Velic, formerly Vossberg City."

"To secure the command post there."

"That's what I understand."

"So why isn't there any mention of his deployment in the secure comms from our human pals?" Ergen turned his screen so Burrak could see.

Burrak made a face. "This reeks of Lira Lin Reen's involvement. She must have ulterior motives where this mission is concerned. I knew we should have watched more closely for her."

"Give it a rest, Burrak." Ergen turned in his chair. "Helm, bring us in above relative to *Blackened Blade*. She's taking a beating from those destroyers. Tactical, divert a couple of our squadrons to shield her while we clean up the mess."

A chorus of affirmatives answered his orders. Ergen smirked at Burrak. "You had four years to trap her and never came close. She might be a thieving scum, but she's good, I'll give her that. Good enough to break into secure Grand Alliance communications and black out intel like this? I doubt it. I think TI is keeping us in the dark."

"TI or the Truppen?"

Ergen sighed. "Who knows? Neither one matters. The goal's the same as it's always been, Burrak: the defeat of the Naplian Empire and the victory of the Briddarri Kingdom. Any fool human or cyber who thinks I'm going to endanger either of those for some alien's cause is going to get a rude reminder that alliances shift all the time."

Burrak watched the tactical display as another Naplian battle cruiser limped away from the Briddarri onslaught, its jump sails shattered. Coolant and atmosphere—Ergen didn't read the sensor analysis to figure out which—streamed behind it in a tenuous spray. "The Directorate won't like further endangering our expanding alliance."

"I know that, but they've got to be realistic. There's a covert element of the Terran government that's actively hunting our cybernetics labs and stopping our harvesting efforts. If ED and the rest of our leaders want the cyber warriors I've promised, they've got to allow for pushback, even if it does tick the Terrans off. Don't get me wrong, I don't want to lose their manpower, but it's a matter of weighing risks."

"All right." Blast, but the man could be infuriatingly taciturn. "I know that. We see how much damage we do to the one-eyes, and then at the first opportunity, we break off for Baedecker Six before the humans get their hands on the *ziurathal* facility."

He swiveled in his chair, hoping Burrak would take the hint that the argument—and the conversation —were over. Ergen scowled at the tactical display, even though the local battle was tipped heavily in his favor. He had his doubts about this invasion, but either way it ended he was determined to make it a win for his kingdom.

And if it brought a permanent end to the human interference in his experiments, then even better.

* * *

Lieutenant Colonel Lauran Macken grunted under the impact of a Naplian explosive's blast. It did little damage to her powered armor and did nothing to prevent her from slapping the soldier who'd thrown it. The one-eye wore his own reinforced pressure suit, but Macken's backhand blow crushed his chest and killed him instantly.

The blackened ruins of serjaum storage tanks dotted the ancient magma flow plains below. Their eggshell white domes cracked and blistered. Macken had lost track of how many tons of fuel they'd obliterated. It was too bad they couldn't save it for their own starships, but her orders were clear: knock out the Naplian storage tanks and leave the production facilities intact. It was a lot easier to build new domes and fill them up than it was to repair or replace the complex processing units needed to extract the precious material.

"Site's secure." Master Sergeant Amaro's message reached her via her helmet comm a couple of seconds before he landed next to her. Dust bounced into Baedecker Two's airless sky. Amaro's armor was hunched and hulking like hers, with yellow streaks painted on the fists—except Macken knew from her pre-combat inspection that the liquid crystalized to his gauntlets was Naplian blood. "Second Company is ready for drop."

"Light up the zone, Master Sergeant."

Amaro plucked a beacon rocket from his torso and slammed it into the ground at their feet. It let off a searing gold beam, then launched an independent projectile from the unit now embedded in the world's dusty surface. The explosion cast a sharp glare over the battlefield.

"ETA forty seconds." The voice buzzed through Macken's helmet.

She took a minute to catch her breath and let her suit give her a damage report. A little wear and tear, but nothing serious. One particle blast had seared the first two layers of ablative armor off her right torso but the emergency infill had hardened enough to provide temporary protection atop the third and final layer. First Company had scattered the Naplians guarding the serjaum processing station into the sun-blasted terrain. She had four troopers KIA and two injured. Macken would mourn their loss later.

Right now she was grimly satisfied that the Naplians suffered over ten times their loss.

The second assault shuttle swept overhead. Railgun bursts chewed up the crater rims where the Naplians, fleeing from First Company's attack, had sought shelter. Second Company's orbital jump troops plunged in the shuttle's wake by pairs, eighty troopers in all. Their anti-grav assist units slowed their fall in the last seconds as glittering scan disruption chaff spread in a billowing cloud.

The processing center loomed to the west, a couple hundred meters from the storage tanks, linked by a laser-cut causeway. Second Company's troops dropped behind the Naplian positions. They landed over a far ridge where Macken's sensors showed her they'd regrouped by platoons before engaging the next line of one-eye defenses.

"Time to settle in, ladies and gentlemen," Macken said over her comms. "We take the processing center and hang onto it until Colonel Wester and the rest of the cavalry show up."

"Since when do we need birds to do our job, sir?" Amaro beckoned his squad near. They thundered into the defile that turned toward the causeway.

"Since I don't want to get vaporized by whatever one-eye boat shows up on the horizon," Macken countered. "Move!"

* * *

Flirry Squadron appeared in high orbit over Baedecker Two, right behind a pair of tankers doing their best to withdraw from the battle.

"Ignore them!" Tag snapped. He was still raw from Winsome's loss. *Don't take it out on them. They're doing their best. Hold tight until Tim and Marney show up.* "Get planetside and concentrate on their ground defenses."

"I have no fighters on the scopes," Princess reported. "Long-range scans show four patrol boats inbound."

"They're sure not putting up much of a fight here," Tag said. "You'd think they'd have their toughest stuff around the most vital part of the starsystem unless Erassia had enough warning he met the invasion fleets with more ships than anticipated."

"Whatever the reasoning, let's take full advantage of their miscalculation."

"You said it." Tag led the squadron in a rapid descent that put his Warhawk onto the magma plains so fast he got a head rush. Only the thought of Scrape complaining about excessive speed and dangerous flying—except in his typical dry tone—got him smiling again.

Of course, Scrape was a Naplian victim, too, so that didn't help.

His fighters and bombers swept off in pairs, except Evie, who stuck close to Princess. They sent missiles streaking into ground-based pulsed particle cannons meant to hit ships in orbit but that were useless against the relatively tiny starfighters.

He spotted Macken's orbital jump troopers forcing the Naplians to die, retreat, or surrender. There wasn't a lot of retreating going on. The bulk of her soldiers had swarmed over the one-eyes and into the processing center's warren of pipes, bunkers, and long, curved machine shops.

It wasn't the same thing as standing on the same dirt where he used to live, but Tag decided he could take some pride in throwing their serjaum production into disarray.

Two of the patrol gunboats appeared in the sky. His scanners told him they were burning into low orbit. No need to slow down for atmospheric reentry since Baedecker Two didn't have a lick of it, but they couldn't just blaze in like a starfighter. They had to be cautious as they lit Tag up with their range-finding sensors.

"Yeah, I know. I'm looking forward to meeting you, too," Tag muttered.

He launched the last three of his missiles at the lead gunboat. Another pair joined his—Flirry Nine and Twelve were coming up hot on his six.

The missiles slammed into the gunboat's narrow prow, sending the shields into a frenzied fireworks display as they tried to avoid overload.

The green particle blasts that speared it amidships rendered the attempt futile.

Tag craned his neck. *Valo* cruised around the curve of Baedecker Two, scattering debris with its jump sails. Tag's comp told him that two of the four Naplian patrol boats were toast.

He switched comm frequencies. "Lead to Nine. You good taking my other target that's rabbiting?"

"Are you kidding, sir?" The pilot, call sign Loosey, chuckled. "Me and Doggo thought you were gonna smoke them both yourself and leave us scraps for target practice."

"Nah, I like to share. It's a benefit of command. Have at them." Tag swept up toward *Valo* and intercepted their transmission. "Nice to see you guys again so soon."

"Likewise, Flirry Lead." That was Marney on comms. She sounded more excited than she had on her wedding day, almost out of breath, like she'd run the length of the destroyer just to speak with him again. "The fleets are holding their own at Baedecker Four and in engagements around the system. Even the Briddarri are punching holes where they're supposed to."

"Miracles never cease. Any word from our other party?"

"Nothing from *Strunk*. She was staying comm silent until they had the package in hand."

Erassia. Tag tried to ignore the flip his stomach performed when he pictured Lira creeping through the heavily protected Daviont Tower at the heart of local Naplian command and control. *She'll be fine. This is her thing.*

And hey, she even had a bunch of terrifying Truppen cybers as bodyguards.

* * *

Lira flinched as *Strunk* bounced through Baedecker Four's atmosphere. Dyson had timed their entry well. Space above them was filled with Naplian, Terran, and Briddarri starships in a slugfest that drifted away from the planet with each passing minute. He'd taken them around the far side of the planet, skimming the atmosphere's outer layers until finally diving through about a hundred klicks from Velic.

She found the city among the ugliest she'd encountered in her travels. Unsurprising, though, given the only roles it had to serve were that of trading post and military command center. Lira wished she'd been around to see Vossberg in its prime. The skeletal remains of the towers and public spaces begged remembrance.

Strunk shifted to starboard. Lira frowned. They veered away from the abandoned park that was their landing zone. "What's wrong?"

"Traffic control is redirecting us to the public landing spaces reserved for trade vessels." Dyson sounded as conversational as a man who'd just found out his preferred dinner dish wasn't available. "I am complying."

"Um..." Lira's eyes widened. "There's still plenty of rainclouds and darkness for cover, but the Truppen clinging to our hull will be spotted as soon as we land."

"Indeed. That is why we are not landing." Dyson flicked the comms panel. "Consul, we have encountered a change of plans."

"I noticed. We should disembark now."

"I concur. Standby." Dyson punched a series of commands and unstrapped from his seat. The black jumpsuit he wore was a copy of Lira's. She had to hand it to TI. They'd fabricated a decent replica with similar functionality in a matter of days. How many months had she waited for the perfect adaptable camouflage suit's completion?

Lira followed him aft to the nearest airlock hatch. She cinched up her suit and snugged the hood into place. "Let me guess: *Strunk* isn't going to land."

"She will land, albeit roughly." Dyson tightened the fasteners on his grav-harness. He helped Lira secure her own. It was nice to have backup like this for a change. "The impact should give us enough cover to complete our end of the mission."

"What about the Truppen?"

"Their goal is to raise havoc." Dyson lowered his mask. Lira did the same. Pale green light glowed behind a narrow strip where their night vision and enhanced scanning goggles activated. His voice filtered scratchily through their headset comms. "I have no doubt they will succeed."

"They'd better." Lira toggled the airlock doors to open simultaneously. Damp evening air rushed into the cabin. She stepped to the edge. "Just follow my lead. It's kind of fun."

Dyson peered past her shoulder. "I shall take your word for that."

Lira chuckled and jumped free of the falling ship.

CHAPTER NINETEEN

Elden plummeted into the jeweled lights of Velic. Strange to see the city like this. His memories pounced on the thought, flooding his mind with unbidden images.

… Vossberg's gleaming spires were visible out the transport's window as he landed. His stomach twisted. He wouldn't have much time to evade the Reittians…

… The city's battered buildings loomed overhead in the midday sun as he skulked through the shadows. Goetz was there, still a flesh-and-blood man, as they hunted for supplies and avoided Naplian patrols…

… Marney's tear-stained face as the executioner readied to strike him down. She was so beautiful …

No. Elden shoved the sentiments and the yearnings back behind barricades where they belonged. Vossberg was gone. Velic was a Naplian hive.

It was time to rile the occupants.

Elden slammed down onto the roof of a barracks and broke into a run. Thayer landed a couple of steps behind him but soon drew even. <There's a lot of one-eyes milling around, sir.>

<Noted. Shoot any that move. Avoid civilian casualties.> His scanners had already altered him to the multispecies presence, though as they hustled further from the trading enclave toward Daviont Tower, the

population became more homogeneous.

Naplian soldiers abounded.

The rest of Elden's octants landed by eights until they were spread in a broad arc across twelve city blocks around the tower. His displays marked each one with a blue outline, but without enhancement, they were shadows above the streetlights.

<Hold your fire until we have the signal,> Elden ordered.

<I think we'll be able to see it from here.> Goetz muttered like he was right beside Elden, but he anchored the far north end of their units' arc.

Strunk's impact rumbled across the plains. A fireball blossomed to the south. It had barely subsided when alarms clamored. Elden's audio receptors picked out the screech of Naplian starfighters as they took off to investigate.

The Truppen were only four blocks from Daviont Tower. The structure demanded attention like an ancient lighthouse.

"Fifteen seconds until we land," Lira spoke through their secure channel, her voice muffled by the mask she wore. "Lights out."

The timer blinked at the edge of Elden's vision. He powered up his weapons. <Choose your targets.>

<Chosen and ready, sir.> Thayer trotted beside him as they slowed.

Elden crouched by the edge of the roof. Six Naplian soldiers and one of their patrol mechs hurried by. Elden sighted on the mech's stubby head.

The time turned to zero.

Lights across Velic flickered and failed. Emergency generators kicked in, bathing the streets in dim orange.

<Execute,> Elden ordered.

The strike played out in phantom images across his accumulated scans. Energy beams and projectile bursts were brilliant streaks in the dark. The infrared heat signatures of enemy soldiers flared. The red-orange silhouettes fell still.

Elden's first shot ripped the head from the Naplian mech. It staggered into an awning's support strut until Elden's second hit blew a hole through its processing core, using the first wound to bypass its armor.

Return fire pelted his perch, but it was small arms, and against Elden's and Thayer's artificial hides, it might as well have been grains of sand. Together, they took down the six soldiers without sustaining appreciable damage.

<Secure the tower.> Elden was already on the move as he gave the order. He leapt across the distances between buildings, bounding up five stories with the jet assist boosters integrated into his frame.

<Erassia?> Goetz asked. No word on casualties or damage from him. Elden interpreted that to mean they had suffered none.

<The thief and the spy should have skill enough to capture him,> Elden said. <We hold until they have safely taken him into custody. Get us a new mode of transport off Baedecker.>

Goetz grunted his acknowledgment. Elden wondered how Dyson intended to get away, but since the TI operative hadn't shared his plan, Elden was left to make two assumptions—either he didn't have such a plan, which Elden found unlikely, or Dyson didn't see fit to trust him with the details. Probably a matter of operational security.

Elden wasn't willing to take the chance with Dyson, not when the means to keep the cybernetic tide from rising was within reach.

* * *

Erassia's pulse quickened as the emergency lights flickered to life, bathing his office in an amber pall.

"Multiple contacts in the streets." The officer's voice across his communications link was scratchy. "Upward of one hundred. I can't make them out. We've lost contact with Patrols Nineteen through Twenty-Six. The scans indicate—"

He cried out, and the signal cut off in a burst of static.

Erassia grimaced. The rudimentary 2-D map that glowed on his desk—which provided as much illumination to his surroundings as the emergency lights—showed a lack of signal from more than just those numbered patrols across Velic. There was an enemy force on the ground, and it was sweeping away his defenses.

A second display showed the chaos in the Baedecker System at large. *Shirish* forces had scattered his fleet, inflicting such losses that 10 percent of his ships were crippled or destroyed without taking starfighters into account. Erassia checked the time stamp at the bottom of both maps. *Soon, but not soon enough...*

Guards burst into his office. The young men stank of sweat. It stained their uniforms. Erassia could see the cloth beneath the segmented armor. "Admiral, we must evacuate you as security protocols dictate."

"One moment." Erassia consulted his latest confidential reports from Tratta, the ones that had arrived before the battle. Two of the freighters had landed in the warren of plateaus and ravines east of Velic. The driving rains had helped obscure their arrival, but even without the poor weather, freighters of that sort were always in the vicinity due to the mining concerns licensed to extract precious metals besides serjaum from the Luran Plains. "What reports do you have from our streetside patrols?"

"None, sir. They've all gone dark."

The shorter naplian's skin flushed with spots. Erassia's gaze locked on him and refused to allow him to look away. "Well? What do you have to add, Private?"

"Sir, the..." He glanced at his counterpart, who gave him a dark look Erassia could only interpret as a warning. "One patrol claimed to have seen *ziura*."

Erassia had long assumed the news that the devastators were returning to this sector of space would terrify him, but given the warning he'd received from his anonymous intelligence source, he felt no onrush of fear. If anything, eagerness flooded his senses. This was his moment. This was what his *ziurathal* were born to do. It was time to discard caution and bring them out into the galaxy for all to see.

Yes, even Admiral Daviont.

"Report downstairs with the rest of the guard," Erassia ordered. "I must secure what files I can and destroy the rest."

"Sir," the taller guard said, "We will not leave you."

Such devotion should be admired and rewarded, but Erassia had no intention of letting either man remain in the room to view potentially classified secrets —especially since either or both could be on the Druwei payroll or be agents of the security forces. "Very well. Remain outside my office. Keep in close contact with whatever patrols you can reach."

The men saluted and took up their new posts in the adjacent corridor. Erassia shook his head as the door closed.

He made certain his most recent files were backed up aboard the fleet network that was established throughout the starsystem and stored on the data drive synced to his scroll. The lights flickered along its edges as the transfer commenced. It could take up to ten minutes for the transaction to complete—not a long time, usually, but in an invasion, every moment counted.

Erassia reestablished contact with his *ziurathal* forces long enough to send an encrypted text note to Colonel Rys Va'Kur Daggra. <Ziura have invaded Velic. Expedite counterassault. Mains and sensors are down. Engage with caution.>

He turned his attention back to the windows. The dim amber glow suffused most of Velic's streets, though the bulk of the buildings remained dark towers, and broad swathes of the city were completely black. Weapon discharges cast a brief but intense glare wherever they erupted. Erassia's displays gave little in the way of good news. The number of surviving patrols had dwindled by half again during the time he'd spent interacting with his guards and preparing the information transfers.

Erassia smiled. The devastators wouldn't be as much of a problem once his *ziurathal* arrived. It would be fitting, too, to see how they reacted to machines and men united to bring about their destruction.

Until then, he was content to gaze out over the spreading battle in Velic's night streets as his scroll beeped softly from his desk.

* * *

Inspector Prad stepped smartly out of the way as Colonel Daggra stormed toward one of the *ziurathal* mechs lining the freighter's cavernous bay. "Our orders are clear!" he called out. "The devastators have come to Velic. They're killing our people and converging on Daviont Tower. We're the only thing that stands between the destruction of our leaders and the loss of this system to those nightmare devils. Suit up and check in! We sortie by squads."

Rough cheers echoed his call to arms. Not flashy, but heroic enough, Prad supposed. He helped Daggra into his *ziurathal*'s open canopy and made sure the power cell's connectors were fastened. Simple stuff.

"Good luck and good hunting, men." Daggra lowered the armored canopy. His voice boomed from the embedded speakers. "For their glories, Bonate and Benaltep!"

"For the glory of the emperors!" came the reply.

The mechs thundered down the access ramps into the desert surroundings. They squelched through the mud, sounding to Prad like a herd of five-horned *faalthord* in the rainy months back home. These, though, moved without the braying and snuffling he'd grown up hearing from the ungainly beasts of burden. *Ziurathal,* though, were silent. Prad had to give it to Erassia—he'd made mechanical creatures that looked and acted like gigantic versions of Truppen.

Taking nationalistic pride in the admiral's results didn't mean he regretted what he'd done.

Prad's scroll glowed in the now-empty cargo bay. The message had come back from HQ a few hours ago when he'd been en route from Baedecker Six to Four.

<Received your report on subject's prohibited activities. Command will address at highest levels. Expect personal response from affected party.>

Prad winced. The message was a few sentences of bland administrative words, but the code employed between himself and his superiors was clear enough: Erassia was in trouble, of the big kind, which was the whole point of his investigation. The *ziurathal* program had made him what the *shirish* called *persona non grata* —had a nice ring to it, Prad noted.

"Personal response from affected party" meant Daviont himself would send representatives to Baedecker.

"You there!" One of the soldiers who hadn't departed with the ziurathal hordes waved him toward a hover skiff. Thirty armed men were piling in, some of them technicians crammed in along with the enlisted personnel. "Let's move! Our orders are to link up with the technical battalion still in the city and establish a repair and refresh point for the *ziurathal.*"

Prad scooped up a set of tools and a satchel of spare circuits. Riding back into an active combat zone on a transport that might make itself a target to the Truppen didn't sound like the smartest plan, but in his disguise as a technician, he couldn't disobey orders and stay behind to find another way into town.

Still, as he clambered aboard and the skiff lurched onward in the wake of the *ziurathal* march, he contacted Rost. <Erassia is in the crosshairs. Keep an eye on him until I arrive. Heading into the city with troops.>

<He's in his office,> Rost replied. <Guards outside. Unsure of plans but not willing to evacuate yet. Filling up bandwidth to maximum between his office and secure networks.>

Sounded like Erassia was trying to dump his files. A wise move if the Truppen were coming for him and with Grand Alliance fleets attacking throughout the system, but if he was taking the opportunity to delete his *ziurathal*-related work, that could hamper the Druwei investigation.

<Get in there and get copies of everything,> Prad instructed. <I don't care how many rules of operation and conduct we break. Leave it to the bosses to figure out where that stands.>

<Working on it. Haven't been this far into the military networks before.>

<Get creative. I'll check back in when I get to the city.>

Prad squinted against the dirt trying its best to get lodged beneath his eyelid. The skiff's passage kicked up a surprising amount of dirt, given how heavy the rain had fallen. No lights gave away their position, so the driver relied on passive sensors to detect obstacles, but Prad could make out the hulking shapes of the *ziurathal* as they stormed toward Velic.

Too bad Erassia must pay the penalty for defying Admiral Daviont. Prad reached for a visor. *Maybe his mechs can survive the admiral's wrath and the Druwei's ire.*

❋ ❋ ❋

Captain Tratta was regretting his unwavering support for his kinsman's dream.

Here he was, guiding *Fulnax* through a battle against the *shirish* interlopers above Baedecker Four, and the admiral commanding the fleet that defended Baedecker was in his office.

Tratta had received little direction other than to "hold." He snorted. Hold. He counted seven groups of starships mixed and mingled in battle with the Grand Alliance vessels. Casualties were mounting. Damage reports flooded in so quickly and in such detail he had difficulty keeping track of who needed assistance first.

I've always wanted to achieve flag rank, but this is not how I envisioned the promotion.

A Terran destroyer exploded in a mini-supernova that overwhelmed *Fulnax*'s optical sensors for a moment. "Shields holding at 86 percent strength," the tactical officer reported. "That last missile salvo did the trick."

"Then let's see if we can teach the *shirish* another," Tratta said. "Helm, take us about forty degrees, bearing one zero six. Tactical, prepare another full spread and target the heavy cruiser that's bearing down on *Ressek*."

The sister battlecruiser to *Fulnax* was fending off a Terran heavy cruiser and two Briddarri destroyers on its own. Tratta's crew translated his orders into a swift maneuver and missile launch that caught the Terran ship in its own evasive spin.

Fulnax took a battering from Terran railguns as

it rode to the rescue. The deck felt like it shifted to starboard a dozen meters but Tratta knew it was the shock of the projectiles' impact against the shields transmitted through the hull. He still had to brace himself even with the restraints that he'd made sure kept him in place at his command chair.

Ressek accelerated away from its opponent and dropped mines in her wake. The timed weapons exploded in rapid succession, doing little damage but unleashing so much localized radiation that the Terran ship's scanners were treated to what Tratta hoped was a storm of static and false readings.

The Briddarri destroyers skirted the edge of the mine counterstrike and decided—wisely, Tratta thought—that the less damaged *Fulnax* posed the greater threat. "Direct the mains at those pests, Tactical. I want them held off while we tear the heavy cruiser to pieces."

"Understood, Captain. *Ressex* reports partial restoration of her forward shields. *Tybran* and *Varnax* have responded to her hails for support, too."

As they should have, being assigned to the same defensive squadron. Still, Tratta was heartened to see months and years of patrol duty at a quiet post hadn't dulled the crews of either destroyer when it came to battle. The pair swept from above the ecliptic plane, missiles streaking "down" relative to the brawl. Some caught one of the Briddarri destroyers unawares and set it reeling off course, shields flickering wildly. The second Briddarri swatted six missiles away from the Grand Alliance targets, but enough made it through to punch a hole in the Terran heavy cruiser's bow.

"Target's forward shields have collapsed!"

Tratta smiled. "Signal *Ressek* and the others to exploit the weakness. Target with our primary particle batteries and fire."

Green beams lanced out from the four Naplian ships, ignoring the Briddarri destroyers as they did their best to fend off the attacks. The concentrated blasts shredded the heavy cruiser's bow until the forward third of the ship was a blackened ruin spewing atmosphere and bulkhead fragments—and bodies of crew who couldn't escape.

A salvo of well-placed missiles turned what remained into a shattered wreck.

Tratta checked reports from across the system's battlefield as the rest of his nearby ships took the fight to the Briddarri destroyers. The Naplian units were retreating, but only so they could regroup. None had abandoned the system, though Baedecker Two and Six were left unguarded. He would remedy that.

As soon as he could get Admiral Erassia to take his eye off the *ziurathal* long enough to concentrate on everything else vital.

* * *

Ivy abandoned her shop the moment the power died.

There was little she needed to take with her. Everything of importance was stored deep in her memory banks. What few tools she required fit snugly in her trousers and jacket pockets.

She kept the brim of her cap pulled low to help obscure her face and ward off the stray raindrops. The sensation put her off balance. What was it about moisture from the sky that she despised? Of all the human-like responses her base programming had adopted, that had to be the most bizarre.

The timed charge melted her shop's valuables in a few seconds, leaving a red-hot pile of molten scrap. It was too bad. She felt she had gotten the hang of salesmanship. There were merchants—and even Naplian soldiers—who would miss her work.

Assuming they had survived the Truppen onslaught.

Her scanners showed the hulking cybers as they continued their relentless advance toward Daviont Tower. They were so precise, unstoppable … Ivy could see the appeal they presented. No wonder her superiors wanted to know everything about them.

Ivy loaded the algorithm but did not input the final code to unlock it. She hadn't programmed this piece of semi-sentient software and, as a rule, trusted nothing she hadn't put her own engrams to work creating.

She trusted her masters only so far.

Daviont Tower loomed out of the receding mists. Orange lights gave it the appearance of a computer core awaiting its final upgrades.

Dyson was up there or would be soon. She had no idea of his location, but the uncertainty didn't matter. She would find him.

The two would be far more effective for the Silent Company as a single unit than separated. The algorithm she possessed would help him to realize that.

And whether it granted the Truppen the same realization, well, that didn't matter.

As long as she could strip them of their secrets,

she'd be happy.

CHAPTER TWENTY

L ira drifted into her landing so gently she had a hard time recognizing the roof's solid surface beneath her boots. It being rain-slicked and pitch black didn't help with the feeling of disorientation.

"Please watch your step." Dyson's grip on her wrist steadied her balance. He deactivated his grav-harness and used his free hand to remove the PF6-S machine pistol from where it was strapped to his side.

"Thanks." Lira peered over the side of the tower. Her goggles' night vision setting turned the city into a pale golden rendering of what should have been a more impressive sight.

The tiny shadows of Truppen advancing on the tower didn't make it less unnerving.

"The target's office is six floors below us in the southwest corner." Dyson headed for the roof's access door. "Four guards in the corridor. Two additional stationed outside his door."

Lira nodded. She had the tower schematics ghosted over half her field of vision, with tiny red dots—albeit hard to see—highlighting the estimated location of each Naplian. The scans weren't precise, as they were based on the initial information *Strunk* gathered before the crash and then backed up by the limited-range sensors she and Dyson possessed, but they were a better option than going in blind.

She joined Dyson and tried the door. Locked. "Torch? The alarms should still be disabled."

Dyson shook his head. He felt along the edge for the seam and pressed his fingers as deep as he could between the door and its frame. "One moment."

He pulled on the edges. The door groaned and then, with the squeal of distressed metal, popped open. Lira caught it so it wouldn't bang against the quik-crete wall.

"How have I gone through my career without a man like you at my side?" Lira grinned beneath her mask. "We could have made so much money."

"You will forgive me if I reiterate that the acquisition of wealth is not high on my list of priorities." Dyson said it so sternly Lira wondered for a second if he was annoyed with her but the wink he gave in response was so exaggerated she couldn't hide her laughter.

They crept down the stairwells, stepping lightly, eyes wide and scanners trained for alarms they might trigger. Lira found the overlaid map annoying and banished it from her heads-up display after less than a minute, keeping only the red dots that told her where the Naplians were. The map's image was planted in her head, and she was in no danger of losing it. If she'd spent her years with Blue Kitt relying on fragile technology for the heists she pulled off, how would she ever have avoided capture so many times?

Better not to leave vital details to anyone else, not even Dyson and TI.

No one contested their descent. Dyson held up a

fist as they took the last few steps onto the forty-fourth floor. Lira halted two steps behind him. Her hood's embedded aural sensors hadn't detected evidence of motion. All she'd heard was the rumble of the building's auxiliary generators and the hum of the ventilation systems. No life signs anywhere above the forty-fourth.

Dyson indicated she should open the door and he would go first. Lira found this chivalrous though practical—he could withstand far more damage than she could. She nodded and placed her hand on the door switch.

The red dots glowing in her field of view were clustered in the center of the corridor. Two men guarded a cross-passage. Two more were stationed by elevators, one each. The last two remained where Dyson had first noted them, just outside Erassia's door.

Dyson lifted his weapon and gave her a curt nod.

Lira punched the switch. The door swung open.

The hall beyond was dark except for the intermittent pulse of orange light. Dyson didn't step out right away. Instead, he lined himself up with the alcove opposite the door. His left boot's toe nudged the door frame.

The light blinked off.

Dyson hurried across, using the darkness for cover, then spun and pressed his back to the alcove. He'd barely been loud enough for Lira's sensors to register his movement. It was no use daydreaming about the credits she could have made with his assistance, but that didn't stop the idle thoughts from accumulating in the back of her mind.

Focus, Lira. Distraction will get you killed. She couldn't believe she'd gotten so sloppy. Maybe that was a consequence of relying too much on others.

Lira let the emergency beacons pulse a few more times, copying Dyson's initial stance in the meantime. The moment the lights faded, she, too, hurried across the hall. She put a shoulder into the alcove and elbowed Dyson.

Sorry. It was instinctual, even though he obviously had sustained no damage.

The door swung shut with the tiniest *click*.

So, the Naplians. None had moved on her display … Hang on. There was a new indicator. This seventh red dot walked the perimeter of what Lira recalled was Erassia's office. *The admiral himself. Odd that he isn't evacuating. Tag and Ess warned he might try to clean out his databanks, but I'm more interested in his personal belongings. Surely a Naplian admiral—even a disgraced one—has got spoils of war that would sell well on the black market.*

Dyson had made Erassia their priority, but Lira would never let the abduction get in the way of some good profit, especially if that profit was taken from the invaders and could be given to those who needed it more.

They waited shoulder to shoulder in that hall. Lira was all too aware of her breathing as she steadied it against the anxiety she felt during any heist. Five seconds and she'd calmed the rise and fall of her chest. It was odd not seeing Dyson's body react the same way.

He glanced at her. She nodded. They had scripted this plan–the destruction of *Strunk* was the only altered variable. Lira knew as well as Dyson did that they had to take down whatever guards were in their way and get Erassia out of the building.

It all hinged on Elden Selva and his Truppen being in position to help them spirit Erassia out of the building.

Lira frowned to herself. The Truppen could have bashed through the building and ripped the Naplian admiral out, but that wasn't what TI wanted. The fewer hints as to who had Erassia in custody, the better.

So, they'd better move.

Erassia finally went still again in his office. Dyson nudged her. She nodded again. He stepped out of the alcove, staying close to the wall, with Lira right behind him. She looked back to make sure no one was coming around the other end of the corridor, even though the red blips were where they should be–

Thunder shook the tower. Lira's knee bounced off the wall. She cursed.

Dyson froze in place. He tapped the side of his goggles. *Check your scans.*

They'd rehearsed the gesture. Lira did as instructed.

The Naplian guards on their floor went back into Erassia's office–the two by his door plus the two in the junction. The ones at the elevator joined each other. Lira's sensors informed her of active comms.

Worse, there were explosions at the base of the tower.

The Truppen.

What were they doing? The fight wasn't supposed to come anywhere near the building's lower floors. Instead, she saw the tiny forms of cybernetic units when she magnified the image–

Her heart nearly stopped. Those weren't Truppen.

They were something else.

*　*　*

Sweeping the Naplians away from Velic's streets was no more bothersome than clearing vermin out of a run-down outpost in the distant corner of the galaxy. Elden didn't even think about his ammo expenditure. He shot a Naplian soldier through the chest and impaled the next one on his claws, then moved on to another.

The casualties mounted, but to him, they were just statistics his internal systems dutifully tallied. The readout grew by dozens every second.

Thayer fought beside him and took a couple direct hits from heavy weapons, but the damage he sustained was minimal. He limped along in Elden's wake, apparently undeterred by the fact his right leg was operating at 65 percent.

<Stand down and wait for repairs,> Elden ordered. <Sarkozy, get up here and bring a mending kit for Thayer's leg.>

<On the way, Consul. Arriving in ten.>

Thayer hunkered beneath the gates leading into the Daviont Tower compound. He turned red optical ports toward his damaged appendage. <I don't mean to let you down, sir. I can manage.>

Elden glanced back at the death and destruction they'd left in their wake. Twenty-six Naplians KIA. Four mechs blown to pieces. And that was just the two of them. Multiplied across the battlefield and among the other octants...

The six Truppen of Elden's octant landed nearby

seven seconds later. They'd lagged behind Elden and Thayer on his headlong charge into the city by that same interval throughout the assault. Sarkozy, his armor streaked with lubricant stains, knelt beside Thayer. He removed a patch kit and replacement servos from a compartment at the base of his torso. <You'll be up to peak movement in no time, Lieutenant.>

<Thanks, Sergeant.>

Elden contacted Goetz. <What's our status?>

<All octants in position around the tower,> Goetz said. <Four men are dead. Headpieces ruined. They're lost, sir. We have some severe damage to another eight, but those are undergoing repairs.>

Four lost. Elden grimaced. His battlefield statistics updated a second later, the lag associated with the Truppen's rapid advance fading. The marks told him in an even colder fashion than Goetz—if such a thing were possible—that the signals from those four Truppen's headpieces had ceased. Destroying that part of their bodies meant they were gone for good.

Except for their souls. Elden held out hope, however faint it may seem to him, that there was something eternal for them. The promises Abbot Jeopar had imparted were silly but when it came to the death of his men—his brothers in arms—Elden had decided such hope would be the only thing tethering him to the tatters of his humanity.

<Sir?> The message came in from one of the scouts positioned at the edge of the octants. <We have inbound from the Luran Plains. Looks like troop activity. Hell, they're moving fast. The Naplians are bringing replacement mechs all at once, but I never—>

The signal cut off. A sudden barrage of weapons

fire exploded from the east. Elden whirled. His sensors struggled to pinpoint where the attack was coming from and even to identify the forces at play, but they did give him an initial readout.

Naplian life signs and mech electrical signatures intermingled.

Fear jolted Elden's senses. The signatures matched his old records perfectly, except they were more complex and linked to more powerful frames. These weren't the standard Naplian combat mechs that he'd so easily handled on their way to the tower. These were *ziurathal*.

He had only a second to decide.

<Sir, are you seeing this?> Goetz snapped. <Those blasted cyber suits we destroyed—>

<Well aware, Goetz. Pull our people back. Fan them into the city by octants. Bring your troops to me. We'll head up the tower sooner than expected.> Elden switched frequencies. <This is Consul Selva. Fall back. Split by octants into the city streets and engage the enemy in a running firefight. Do *not* take them on en masse. Head for our escape rendezvous as soon as you can.>

The rendezvous. He'd marked the civilian landing sites that *Strunk* had bypassed. Plenty of freighters and even a few patrol craft sat there, apparently because traffic control officials thought it safer for them to ride out a groundside invasion instead of taking their chances with rival fleets clashing in space.

Elden pulled Thayer upright. <You're mended?>

<Fixed up and ready, sir.> Thayer's optical sensors swiveled toward the battle flashes on the other side of the tower grounds. <What are those things...?>

The *ziurathal* burst through a thin-sided barracks wall three blocks away and tore down the broad avenue toward the tower gates. Elden hadn't expected them to be so damned *big*: Almost twice as large as the experimental piloted mechs the Truppen had encountered four years ago. Four massive legs broke, paving as they trundled at Elden's position. Reinforced tentacles slashed the air, ready for close combat. Particle cannons shot green streaks through the night air.

<Over the wall!> Elden snapped.

He and his men vaulted the tower walls, firing shoulder-mounted rockets and gauntlet cannons into their midst. Elden scored a direct hit on one *ziurathal*'s canopy. The blast cracked the transparent cockpit but didn't break it—not until another railgun burst followed up and slaughtered the Naplian pilot inside. Yellow blood spattered the canopy. The mech stumbled a few more steps and faltered. It slid into one of its companions and went dead.

Weapons fire lanced between the warring parties, with the bulk of it coming from the *ziurathal*. Elden counted thirty of the mechs, with more showing up on his scanners as they fought their way into the city. A quick summary noted his men were outnumbered three to one, an imbalance that only grew with time.

Elden's claws scraped the palms of his mechanical hands. If the one-eyes thought the Truppen would lie down and die because of a new toy on the battlefield, they clearly had no idea what drove them.

Goetz and two octants hurtled the length of the wall toward Elden and his men. The *ziurathal* blasted down the tower compound gates, the debris spraying across the courtyard. Elden had only the briefest glimpse of cacti gardens and wooden sculptures before the red-hot shrapnel ignited fires among the vegetation.

The Truppen found shelter among rock outcroppings incorporated into the courtyard, though the particle blasts would not take long to slough off layers of slate if they remained there. But Elden knew what Goetz had in mind without even signaling his subordinate over their link. He and his men back off, letting the *ziurathal* flood into the courtyard...

Which left them in the perfect cluster for Goetz and his octants to attack.

The sixteen Truppen lunged at the *ziurathal*, landing among them with such suddenness that the Naplian mechs lashed out with their armored tentacles rather than risk the use of energy weapons at close range. Goetz's rockets ripped apart his nearest opponents. He landed atop their wreckage, crushing the occupants as he swiveled toward his next victim from higher ground.

Elden charged into their midst with Thayer, Sarkozy, and the others. They obliterated the first line of *ziurathal* without stopping but found themselves ensnared in hand-to-hand combat that was far more dangerous than any battle Elden had found himself in for years. One of the mechs ripped Sarkozy's arm free and plunged a pair of tentacles through his armored torso. Elden emptied a magazine of railgun projectiles into that mech's cockpit and continued the salvo into the *ziurathal* maneuvering right next to it.

<They're tough as hell, Elden, but they're not invincible.> Goetz sounded giddy.

<Don't let down your guard.> Elden sidestepped

razor-sharp tentacles that scored his dented chest plate. He severed them with his claws and plunged them deep into the canopy of the very *ziurathal* that had tried to attack him. <They are still legion compared to our numbers.>

<More reason to kill as many as we can, so the one-eye scum keep us in their nightmares.>

If only. Elden knew Lira and Dyson should be approaching Erassia's office any moment. Once they sent him the green light, Elden and Goetz would have to make their move—and hope these monstrosities Erassia had unleashed would respond well to the sight of their commander as a biological shield.

* * *

Tag removed his helmet and wiped the sweat from his face. He snagged a water tube and drained it. "Let's move it, kids. The sooner I get a fresh load of missiles, the sooner I can cut down the number of one-eye starfighters we'll have pestering us."

Flirry Squadron was squeezed back in *Valo*'s hangar, with technicians rushing from craft to craft with missiles, power cells, and replacement armor panels. Sparks flew from active torches. The mingled stink of body odor and fuel filled the compartment. Tag stood from his flight seat and stretched. He'd spent way too many hours crammed in the cockpit.

"Hey, Colonel?" Smokey jogged up to him, helmet under his arm. "Got a situation."

"Better not be one that takes more than a few minutes, Smokey." Tag clambered down to the deck. He indicated the force field covering the open bay doors.

Light flickered in the far distance like fireflies in the summer heat—a reminder that the invasion fleet was still hammering away at the Naplian defenders. "What's wrong?"

"Evie." Smokey escorted him to where the Raider sat parked under a rolling catwalk. A pair of technicians argued about which set of command-and-control wires had enough voltage to handle the connection they were trying to repair. Their tirade lapsed into angry murmurs as Tag neared. "She's not taking this thing with Winsome well."

"She shouldn't be," Tag said. "Recklessness gets people killed. That's a signal she can't fail to intercept, not anymore."

"I know that, sir, but she's awfully young to be learning it that harsh—especially from someone who wasn't the best at taking it to heart." Tag glared at him, but Smokey's solemn face didn't flinch. "Just speaking the truth, Tag."

"Yeah, and I value that. Give me a few minutes with her. Tell Princess I'll need to catch up, too, before we head out."

"Will do, Colonel." Smokey jogged off again in search of the squadron XO.

Tag found Evie sitting on an ammo crate. She chewed on a ration bar. It was pungent enough he caught a whiff before he could smell her suit's funk. "I hear I owe you a chat, Lieutenant."

Evie glanced up at him. Her eyes were red. "I don't think I can do this, Tag."

"Sure you can. You just did." Tag sat next to her. He bumped hips until she made enough room for him. "See those marks?"

He pointed at her Raider's canopy, where a tech had painted on new indicators of the Naplian kills she'd racked up in the battle over Baedecker Two. "You earned them."

"And I got Winsome killed."

"Look, I was hard on you about that, but the truth is, you could have easily been killed along with him," Tag said. "I'm not going to pretend you didn't screw up. We all do. Some of us had a record of more screw-ups than anyone else. That's how you learn."

"I should have stayed on his wing." Her voice was a sullen monotone.

"Yeah, you should have. I could have gotten to him faster. He could have stuck closer to you. There were a lot of factors that influenced the outcome." Tag exhaled. "The point is, you've seen how important it is for everyone to take care of each other in this squadron. Our past raids were different. In, blast them, get out. This kind of dogfight is full of a lot more variables."

"It's not like I'd never been in one. I had plenty of combat sorties, or else you wouldn't have picked me for the squadron."

"You're right. I did pick you. Commodore Ram signed off on the transfer, not because I asked him to, but because your record was klicks above any other new pilot's." Tag raised an eyebrow. "Did either of us make a mistake?"

Evie smirked. "I know what you're trying to do."

"If by that you mean I'm trying to kick you in the rear so we can finish the job, then yes, that's what I'm trying to do." Tag put his hands on his knees. "Listen, Evie—keep your head on straight and fly with your wing. Our job is to shoot down one-eyes, but that's not something we can do solo. We're never on our own. This is a team. You've got to play like you're on one, or it won't matter how good a pilot you are—someday you'll make a mistake, and there won't be anyone to pull you out of the fire."

She nodded. "I understand."

"Good." Tag looked at her. "When this is over, you'll help me write the note back to Winsome's family. The whole squadron signs it."

Evie swallowed. "Okay. I'll do it."

Boots clattered the deck. Smokey jogged back toward them, with Princess right behind. *That was quick.* Tag cocked his head. "You two don't look any happier."

"There's a problem with the abduction," Princess said. "We may need to intervene."

Tag stood so fast the ammo crate rattled. "What problem?"

"Commander Ess says *Strunk* has crashed, and the Truppen have a horde of Naplian mechs pinning them down. No word from our team."

Tag's heart thudded. "Then we'd better not sit around here any longer than we have to. Hey!" He raised his voice as he brushed past the other pilots.

The deck chief frowned in his direction. "Colonel, we're refueling and reloading as fast as we can—"

"Then do it faster because the squadron's burning out of here in the next ten minutes if I have to push each bird out the hangar bay door myself!" Tag snapped. "Get moving."

That would not earn him points with the deck crew but the chief channeled Tag's ire into chastisement that seemed to get his people working faster. *Fine by me.*

I can ask forgiveness once this is all over.

The only two people he didn't want to have to seek that from were Lira and Dyson. No way he would leave them behind.

Tag caught the deck chief by the arm. "Cold-start one of the assault shuttles. Make sure it gets the fuel load you were saving for my Warhawk."

"Are you kidding?" The man pulled free. "They've got their railguns and short-range missiles, but they're no good in a dogfight."

"Fun fact: I won't need missiles. Dump them off." Tag changed direction toward the back of the bay, where the dark shapes of the shuttles hunkered in storage cubicles. "Just get one stripped down to fly fast and take a beating!"

CHAPTER TWENTY-ONE

E rassia smiled down at the base of the tower. His information transfer was complete, but he couldn't help himself.

By the emperors, his *ziurathal* were magnificent.

They were holding their own against the devastators, that much was certain. Erassia couldn't tell how many of the Truppen remained—his initial sources indicated it was more than one hundred but less than two. The *ziurathal* pressed in from all sides, and the Truppen took the fight deep into their ranks,

His only regret was that he could not stay to watch them reveal to the galaxy just how potent a force they'd become.

"Admiral, please." That was his guard again. The man stood there fidgeting with his Furta rifle. Apparently, he was unwilling to use it to force Erassia to evacuate. "Sir, we must get you to safety."

"Yes, and you will. I am ready." Erassia shut down his desk unit. Smoke escaped from its seams, little gray wisps that the room's ventilation swept up toward the ceiling. He'd deleted anything left on the network in his office and set the tiny demolition charges to melt the hardware so nothing could be recovered from it.

Whatever else he needed was on his portable data drive or in his mind.

The guard ushered him out of the office. His companion waited in the hall, not looking nearly as worried but twice as irritated. Erassia made a note to demote the man for his lack of outward respect in a time of crisis. "We'll take you through the emergency lift to the subbasements, sir. An armored tram is standing by to get you to your personal shuttle."

"Excellent. I hope the pilot is skilled enough." What was that humming sound? Was it coming from the floor beneath him? Erassia looked down at the carpet as they walked toward the elevators.

"Yes, sir. It's Chief Ballar, I think. He flew you a couple of weeks—"

Whatever he was going to say died in his throat. Erassia glanced at him.
"What about Chief Ballar?"

The other guard collapsed. His arms and legs shook so badly they made a meaty *thwack* as they battered themselves against the wall.

Then the walls moved.

No. Erassia didn't quite believe his eye. The walls took on humanoid shape— a distinctly human shape. The outlines of a male and female were too slim to be Briddarri warriors, which ruled out a hit squad. But the wall paneling rippled and faded, the drab colors replaced by black and gray jumpsuits.

The male held a human-made machine pistol. The female lifted a stun pole. Disabling pulses rippled and crackled along its upper length.

The young guard raised his rifle. "Halt! Come no closer!"

"Put down the weapon." The male's voice buzzed through the mask that obscured his face. The faint outline of twin eyes showed through a glowing green visor. *Twin eyes.* The abnormality of the *shirish* never ceased to sicken Erassia.

"Do what he says, and neither of you gets hurt." The female nudged the other guard's still twitching form with her boot. "Well, not much. Having your muscles lock up and refuse to do your bidding isn't pleasant, is it?"

"I said come no closer!"

Erassia reached for the young man's arm. "That will be enough of that, Private. It's clear—"

The guard flinched. He fired a burst from the rifle. The green flare was blinding in the emergency lighting's pale glow.

Erassia fully expected to find a body on the floor after that, but both interlopers had already ducked for cover. The woman lunged with the stun pole, its energies threatening a painful but brief interruption of his neural functions.

But she came up short as the man's machine pistol shrieked. Two three-round bursts hit the young guard dead center of his chest. Yellow blood splattered the carpet. He crumpled into a lifeless heap.

Erassia froze. His breathing came faster as he stared at the yellow stain spreading beneath the body. It wasn't the same as being on the bridge of a warship and directing the ebb and flow of battle in space. He'd seen after-action reports of the *ziurathal.* Naplians had been injured and even died after catastrophic electrical system failures in front of his eye.

But this?

This was avoidable carnage.

A small, insistent part of Erassia's mind noted the irony that he was sickened by one young naplian's killing while dozens, if not more, of the patrol officers below, had lost their lives to the devastators, who themselves were now dying at the claws and tentacles of his *ziurathal*—and doubtless many of those mech pilots had fallen in battle, too.

Amazing how the mind can rationalize the acknowledgment of death and ignore its very existence until it is right in front of one's eye.

"You didn't need to do that." The female advanced on him, the stun pole held with obvious threat intended mere centimeters under his face. Her angry words, though, were directed at her male partner. "I could have taken him."

"It is a lamentable casualty but one that could not be avoided." The male's voice was deep and calm, with an odd intonation Erassia couldn't place. He strode to the guard's body and lifted the Furta rifle. Why he needed to claim it as a trophy was beyond Erassia unless he merely wanted to disable it so no one else would pick it up. Perhaps he sought to arm the female more appropriately.

Instead, the male squeezed the barrel about halfway between the trigger and the muzzle until it crunched flat. The rifle let out an electronic squeal as if the male had killed it as surely as he'd slain the guard.

Erassia stared at him.

"Admiral Gussan Va'Kur Erassia." The male said his name as if he were announcing what rations the mess hall was serving that evening. "I strongly suggest you do not resist."

"And if I do?" Erassia snapped. "Will you kill me like you did that young Naplian? You *shirish* are all the same."

"Maybe we are, but that doesn't mean either of us wants more blood on our hands." The female cocked her head. "Plus, we want to avoid damaging you. It's a simple economic rule, Admiral—your resale value goes down the more bumps and bruises you suffer."

Erassia sneered. "So, that's what this is... An abduction. You're even worse fools than I took your species for, then, because no matter how I have been treated by the admiralty or how little they value my vision, I will never betray the empire. I will never turn my back on my people. This eye will never waver from its endless watch over all Ffawe who are truly loyal. All hail their glories, Bonate and—!"

The electric crackle snapped against his chest. His legs and arms went limp. Nothing could prevent his fall except the male operative, who caught him in a grip that was surprisingly gentle for the strength he'd just demonstrated by wrecking the rifle. Erassia's mouth hung slack. None of his muscles would respond, yet his heart beat on, and his lungs pumped air in and out. At least he could blink.

The female shook her head and sighed. "Benaltep, yes, we know."

Dyson heaved Erassia over his shoulders with no more effort than he'd used when he'd picked up the machine pistol. The tower trembled around them. "I suggest we move quickly."

"That's a great idea." Lira stepped over the young guard's body on her way into Erassia's office. "I can't imagine why you want to hurry now."

She'd seen the scans on her goggles and hoped they were wrong, but as soon as she entered the office, the stink hit her in the nose. Erassia had fried his operation systems. Probably melted any physical databases, too.

Dyson took a loop around the room while Lira examined the charred remains of the desk's internal computer setup. "I do not see anything left which will be of use to us."

"He wouldn't have let everything burn." Lira pried away another access panel. She sucked in a breath. Still hot. Even her gloves couldn't keep her fingers from getting singed. "Can you imagine, after that little speech he gave us? This man wants recognition. I don't even think he cares *who* from at this point."

Explosions rumbled below. Their glare cast gold and orange across Dyson's masked face. "Be that as it may, our time to search his belongings is limited. Perhaps you should have considered that before you stunned him in the middle of his 'little speech,' as you deemed it."

Lira smirked. "Well, you know what they say about…"

Hold on.

She hurried to Dyson's side and patted down Erassia's limp form with such ferocity Dyson stepped back.

"You think he may have something?" he asked.

"Why not? If it were me, and I had a project like the *ziurathal* I wanted remembered as my crowning achievement, I'd keep it nearby."

"It is more likely he transmitted the data," Dyson said. "We can have TI search the local military networks for—"

"Ha!" Lira ripped a hand-sized section of Erassia's uniform jacket open. The data drive dropped out into her palm. "I *knew* it."

"You were playing a hunch."

"I'm pretty good at it." Lira winked even though Dyson couldn't see the expression. "Okay, now we can bail out."

"One moment." Dyson stood still for a couple of seconds. "I have contacted our extraction team and instructed them to meet us on the roof. We will have—"

A shuttle's engines whined overhead. The noise increased until there was a dull, distant *thump*. More, softer sounds followed.

Boots on quik-crete.

Frattik. Lira made a face. Her display lit up with ten more red circles, which hurried for the topside doors that lead down the forty-fourth floor.

"Tell him there's a change of plans," she said.

* * *

The second message spilled across Elden's data stream. <Naplian shuttle on the roof. Advise we go down, not up. Expedite extraction.>

I bet he would like that. Elden emptied the last of his current magazine into the *ziurathal*'s canopy. He struck a tentacle away with the barrel and sliced it clean off with his claws, then reloaded. Another enemy defeated.

The courtyard no longer resembled a garden where one could enjoy a peaceful evening. Trees burned. Shrubs smoldered. The encircling wall was demolished along its entire circumference.

The wreckage of Naplian mechs littered the ground as far as Elden could see and his scanners picked up the slack beyond where optics failed. He'd lost track of how many they'd destroyed, though he was sure his tactical system would remind him. Of greater concern were the thirty dead and ten damaged Truppen.

Their defensive perimeter was rapidly contracting, leaving them little room to fall back and dwindling spare parts for field repairs.

Elden dragged Thayer's frame behind the heavily reinforced barricades of metal and quik-crete that buttressed the tower lobby. Most of the remaining Truppen were ensconced here, returning a withering barrage toward their assailants. Whoever was leading the *ziurathal* had opted to back off from close quarters combat and reassess their strategy.

The results scrolled through Elden's awareness: Two hundred ten *ziurathal* destroyed, six hundred eighty remaining.

<Sir...> Even that one word from Thayer came through the link buzzing and broken. <...Without reboot...System fried...>

Elden felt sick and was, oddly, pleased that he could still have that sensation. He'd seen Truppen attempting to communicate in this fashion. The jumbled phrases and interrupted speech meant Thayer's headpiece was failing. No one had the maintenance wherewithal to repair one on the battlefield. That was what the capsules aboard *Valo* were for.

<You did well,> Elden told him. <Put yourself into a sleep cycle. We'll do what we can.>

<...Can't … sleep, sir. Not in a fight. … Will take attention off…>

<Sleep, soldier. That's an order.>

Thayer's headpiece sagged. The red optical ports dimmed and flashed, though the time between pulses slowed every couple of seconds. Elden had lied to him, but he considered it a mercy, allowing the Truppen warrior to fade out rather than agonize over the disintegration of his operating systems.

After a bit, between the impact of an explosive round and Elden's return fire, the optical ports went blank.

Elden checked Thayer's diagnostics. Nonoperational. Nonrepairable. The hollow analyses infuriated him. *Is this all we have? An endless existence of death and destruction until the last of what we used to be is gone? Even that small part stripped away.*

<Elden.> Where was Goetz? Elden spotted his signature frame fifty meters away, shooting back at the *ziurathal* from the shelter of collapsed rubble. <We can't hold our positions much longer. We have to get topside and get Erassia.>

<It doesn't look like that is a possibility, old friend unless you have another hundred octants in your spare parts compartment.>

<I saw Thayer is gone. I am sorry. We'll make them pay.>

And that's all it was about, wasn't it? One side would pay, then the other side retaliates, and so on and so forth until the stars burn out. Elden's finger paused on the trigger.

What if they surrendered? What would the Naplians do to them?

Would it be any worse than what the Briddarri had in mind if their cybernetics program succeeded?

Elden's dark line of thought froze as new data flooded his senses—namely, the roar of starfighter engines.

Explosions ripped apart the *ziurathal* front lines. Streaks of blue-white light from railgun rounds lanced like lightning bolts through the night.

"Insertion team." Tag Wester's voice was sharp and demanding through the comms broadcast. "This is Flirry Squadron—and company. What's your status?"

"Not dead, Colonel," Elden replied. "But our position is tenuous."

"That's what I can see. Hang tight. Give us a chance to do another pass."

The fighters swept clear over the city, their exhaust ports blazing like stars. Elden counted over two dozen, which was perplexing, given Tag had said "squadron." He didn't much care, however, as the *ziurathal* took advantage of the damaged and intact buildings around them. The strafing run dismantled their front lines.

Elden would have taken advantage of the retreat to press the attack but given the devastation visited upon their ranks, he would not expose his men to further danger if he could avoid it. <Goetz, you're with me. We're headed up. Have your octants regroup and see if they can break open a path to the landing fields.>

<Will do.>

Goetz's orders trickled across the links. Elden spared Thayer a final glance, then contacted Tag again. "Colonel, we're sorely lacking transport. Any chance your next strafing run can clear our road to a vessel that will take us out of here?"

"Standby." The fighters screamed back from the other direction. This time they took fire from the *ziurathal,* but the ground-based mechs could do little to ward off the air-to-ground missiles and railguns that ripped their ranks apart. "I think we can manage. What's the good word about our friends in the tower?"

"They need a new way out. Goetz and I will make sure the target gets taken into custody. We're on our way."

"Good luck. We'll keep these one-eye walkers off your backs in the meantime."

Elden linked his scanners with Goetz's. The feed from Dyson was patchy, but Elden could make out enough: six troops below the forty-fourth floor were moving up from the forty-second, and ten more had disembarked the shuttle now parked on the roof. That group was headed down.

<We keep them safe and get Erassia out.> Elden met up with Goetz at the far edge of the building, where the *ziurathal* had scattered and were busy scrambling for their lives under the continuing air raid.

Goetz craned his neck. <What about the operatives?>

<They need to get safely away on that shuttle, but after that, they are not our problem.> They seemed good people—at least Dyson did. Elden knew nothing about the supposed master thief. But in the calculus of war, they were small variables that would not affect the outcome. Not as far as Elden was concerned. <Tag and the others can help them if they need aid.>

<Understood.>

They shared a nod, then fired their boosters. The

glassy side of the building flashed by, their bodies dark streaks on the reflective surfaces. Goetz halted at the forty-third floor and smashed in through the windows.

Elden aimed himself at the forty-fifth.

* * *

Lira was slammed into the nearest wall by the impact of something big. She assumed a stray missile or particle blast from the battle below had reached high enough to kill her and Dyson until she looked up and realized that she was still alive and that it wasn't an explosion.

It was a Truppen.

Consul Selva had torn apart ten meters of windows along the forty-fifth floor. He glanced at Lira, who was helping Erassia's limp form back into position across Dyson's shoulders, then plowed into the floor above. His headlong rush ripped a trench three meters across and twenty long, stopping just short of the TI operatives.

Ten Naplian soldiers fell through the gap in a heap of tangled arms and dropped weapons.

Elden shot them all.

Lira had no time to intervene or stun any of them into submission. They were lifeless by the time she found the words. She realized she didn't want to use them, not with a Truppen cyber warrior, armor spattered with yellow bloodstains, staring down at them.

"Consul Selva." Dyson stepped forward. "I trust the cavalry has arrived?"

"So they have." Another Truppen rose outside the

window and, hunching over, joined their knot. "Goetz, I trust the rest of the problem has been dealt with?"

"Yes, sir." Goetz, his lackey, addressed Elden but was watching Dyson and Lira. She didn't appreciate the way their scans made her feel like another target.

"Well, if you're going to help us get down out of here, I better know which one of you is safer to hold onto," Lira said.

"Only after we secure the prisoner." Elden plucked Erassia from Dyson. "One less weight for you to carry."

"Thank you for that." Dyson gestured behind them. "We have searched the admiral's office and were unable to recover actionable intelligence from it—"

"So, it looks like he might have transmitted it." Lira didn't know why she'd interrupted him, but something about the Truppen's' stance bothered her. "But we can gab about that once we're safe and sound, preferably not here, right."

Elden shook his head. "I am sorry. This is not how I would have preferred to end your involvement. Our war's path diverges from yours here."

"Good luck," Goetz rumbled.

With that, the pair leapt back out the way they came.

❊ ❊ ❊

Commodore Ram coughed against the remnants of smoke *Confiance*'s life support fans dragged out of the bridge. The sparking at the comms console subsided. A med tech treated his officer for smoke inhalation, but the backup system was functional, and replacement crew had filled in.

Minimal casualty reports came in across the ship. The fleets had taken a beating, too, but they were pushing the Naplian ships toward the system's edge at all points except here at Baedecker Four. *Fulnax* and the primary defensive squadrons were still very much a threat, even though both sides had backed off in a temporary, spontaneous ceasefire.

What he needed now was reinforcement.

"Commodore, Admiral Tanaka is hailing," Captain Vollan reported. "She's ordering us to break off and repair. The Naplians are doing the same."

"I understand, but we should press the advantage." Ram frowned at the tactical display. Something about the way *Winter Scourge* and her core of Briddarri ships were arrayed seemed off. Where were they heading?

"Sir!" The tactical officer sounded breathless. "Incoming jump signatures!"

The display rippled with new hostile indicators as ten, twenty, thirty, forty-eight warships appeared in a massive ovoid shape. They were less than two astronomical units (AUs) from Baedecker Four.

"My God," Vollan murmured. "Who the hell is that?"

The scanner readouts gave them as bland a reply as only an automated system could.

Naplian III Corps, Admiral Daviont commanding.

CHAPTER TWENTY-TWO

Admiral Ergen scowled as he watched the Naplian ships withdraw toward their newly arrived backup.

"Confirmed, sir," the tactical officer said. "It is the core assault force of III Corps."

"Stinking Daviont himself." Ergen shook his head. "I thought Erassia was on the outs with the grand and glorious admiral?"

"He is *not* on Daviont's good side." Burrak sounded convinced, but his expression betrayed surprise. Great. Ergen wasn't a fan of the Espionage Directorate looking surprised. "We might be seeing other powers at play."

"What do you mean?"

Burrak leaned in and lowered his voice. "You had a confidential source warning us that the Naplians knew about the invasion and telling us of the *ziurathal* project. What if that source wasn't assisting just us?"

"Playing both sides." Ergen gripped the arms of his command chair. "I don't like the sound of that. Supposition?"

"I can't prove it, but supposition is what we excel at."

Ergen ground his teeth as the fleets jockeyed for better fighting positions. He imagined a pair of tired brawlers circling each other, each waiting for the other to strike, neither wanting to admit to their opponent that they were worn out.

There isn't going to a better time, not if this invasion falls flat.

"Helm, bring us about," Ergen ordered. "Lay in a course for Baedecker Six. Notify me when ripwave generators are primed."

"Yes, Admiral."

"Now?" Burrak asked. "The Terrans will know something's wrong."

"The Terrans have their own problems." Ergen sneered. "I'll blame it on an overly zealous ED officer who demanded I check out a possible enemy base left at our rear that could have endangered this entire operation."

"So I'm to be left with the blame."

"The humans have a great word for it: Scapegoat. Look it up. There's a lot of cultural and religious connotation." Ergen turned his chair away from Burrak. "But we'll sort it out with your superiors later."

"Sir, ripwave primed and ready."

"Let's go, then."

Winter Scourge altered course, angling away from the fleet groups moving slowly back into the battleline. Messages bombarded Ergen's station but were deflected to Burrak, who took them stony-faced. Mad but compliant. That was what Ergen liked about those spy types. They were never willing to cross those in the upper ranks of power because they never could tell when they'd wind up on the wrong side of the fight.

"Incoming hail from Terran Admiral Tanaka," the comms officer said.

"Put it here." Ergen gestured to his private display screen.

Admiral Setsu Tanaka's expression was as cold and calculating as ever, but there was a darkening to her skin tone that Ergen chalked up to anger. Her words were his big hint. "Admiral Ergen. Might I ask where you're taking one of our most powerful assets as we're about to re-engage a bolstered enemy? Or have you grown bored with the battle?"

"I'll pretend you didn't just insult every ancestor of mine who's been consecrated to the hallowed halls of Barra Bridd."

"I will do the same and pretend I care," Tanaka said. "Answer my question."

"You've got my notice. We've got intelligence that there's a base behind us at Six that could prove dangerous. I'm going to clean it out."

"Why wasn't I notified of this sooner?"

"Because it's my problem to deal with and I'm not your subordinate, *Admiral*," Ergen snapped. "If anything I should be your superior in this farce of an operation. Let's put it this way: the Truppen are getting pasted on Four and the one-eyes just added a couple of battlegroups to what was a ground-down defensive fleet. To top it off, it's Daviont we're talking about. If you think he isn't going to put his foot down at the star system he took to cement his hold in this corner of space, you're delusional."

"Admiral, we have no chance at holding Baedecker if we do not act in concert."

Ergen knew she was right, but he didn't much

care. Many Briddarri had died today. Next to none knew it had anything to do with the cybernetics experiment. As far as Ergen was concerned, he'd achieved his goal —to bog down the Terrans responsible for his failing fortunes where it came to the cyber program. The *ziurathal* lab was, as they'd say, the icing on the cake.

Burrak wasn't about to say anything.

"I'll be happy to share whatever intelligence we glean from that planet," Ergen said. "But if I were you, I'd start priming your people to withdraw."

"I will not—" A muffled voice off-screen caught Tanaka's attention. She straightened, her improved posture seeming to reinstall her backbone. "I have received word that Admiral Erassia is in our custody."

Ergen clapped his hands. "Excellent! Take that as an omen, then. Baedecker Two is a wreck. Your raid set back their serjaum production for a good while. And you've got the guy running this show. Take the wins, and let's back off before we lose any more ships or people."

"The commander-in-chief is clear, Admiral Ergen. Our republic needs this system back. Its loss would mean capitulating to the inevitability of Naplian victory."

"Then you'd better brush up on your one-eye because once Daviont is done with us, the survivors will all be speaking it." Ergen mashed the disconnect panel. "Helm, engage ripwave."

"Yes, sir."

Winter Scourge leapt away from the battlefield and toward what Ergen hoped was a treasure trove. How much faster could he get his cybers off the ground and onto the front lines against the Naplians if he could merge the technology?

"What is your plan now?" Burrak asked.

"Nothing's changed, Burrak." Ergen clenched his fist. "We scoop up every last scrap and slag whatever we can't take off that dusty rock."

* * *

Tag banked the assault shuttle once more. Still didn't shimmy and shake like the standard models, which was great because he was trying to fly it like a fighter-bomber. The engine readouts screamed orange and red most of the flight. Guess it didn't prefer to accelerate at the same speeds he did.

The plus side was that she was more heavily armored than even a Raider. The downside—other than being about a third slower—was that she didn't carry nearly as much armament as the aircraft he was used to.

He wasn't going to pull Immelmanns or shatter novas, that was for sure.

The best thing he could do was provide command and control from the assault shuttle as the Terran fighters and bombers did their thing. The ground was crawling with those Naplian mechs, but after the third pass made by twenty-six birds, they'd dispersed and sought shelter—like the Truppen who had been pinned down.

Tag ran an updated count on his displays. Yeah, twenty-six birds—the eleven from Flirry Squadron plus his shuttle and fourteen others from squadrons who'd suffered losses. Flirry had rounded them up from the battlefield as they raced to Baedecker Four.

So far, so good.

"We'd better make this quick, Tag," Princess said. "*Valo* is warning of new one-eye ships in the system. Forty-plus in a couple of battlegroups. Most are cruiser-weight. Word is they're Daviont's."

"Well, that's terrible," Tag muttered. "Still no luck on Lira or Dyson's frequencies?"

"Negative. I keep getting interference."

The assault shuttle rocked beneath him. The tactical board warned him of incoming particle blasts from between the crumbling barracks.

"Clean the one-eye mechs out of here, will you?" Tag said. "I'm going to do another pass by the tower. Elden hasn't given me any good news, either."

"Roger that."

Tag soared high above where the fighters and bombers chased down their groundside opponents. He could see the Naplian equivalent of his ride perched atop the tower. There was no sign of the soldiers it would have carried, but judging by the smoke drifting from multiple rooms, some fighting had taken place.

He frowned. Hang on. There wasn't any light reflecting off the far side of the building.

His pass took him around until he could see two floors' worth of windows smashed out—or in, judging by the blast pattern.

Tag trained his scanners on the damaged portions of wall but even as the first results came back, two figures leapt free of the space. It was hard not to recognize Truppen.

One of them was definitely Elden Selva.

Elden carried a Naplian officer in full uniform and plunged first out of the building. The next cyber —Goetz, Tag realized, followed him. Neither answered

Tag's signals.

"What in blazes are those two doing?" he muttered.

Where were Lira and Dyson? They were supposed to abduct Erassia with the help of the Truppen.

It wasn't until Lira appeared at the window, shouting and waving at the shuttle, that the pieces of the puzzle fell together.

"...You read us...?" The static-filled reply was barely audible in the cockpit.

Tag modified the receptor and filtered the incoming message through a subroutine Dyson had showed him years back, one of those TI tricks for cleaning up scrambled messages. "This is Flirry Lead, go ahead."

"Tag?" That was Lira. There was no mistaking the relief in her voice. "Thank goodness. You have to stop them."

"Elden?"

"Yes. He and Goetz took Erassia from us. We had no way to get through to anyone until Dyson did something with his personal signal booster—don't even ask me about it. He's got more compartments to him than a salvage locker."

"Why did they just leave you up there?"

"I didn't really get a chance to ask, Tag, because they just grabbed him and bailed out of the window!"

"Okay, standby. I'll land on the roof and—"

"Don't worry about us. Dyson has a way down." Lira sighed. "Make sure you get Erassia back. Whatever the Truppen want him for, it's not to exchange tips on building the best cyber. I'm betting it has more to do with Selva's personal crusade against any sort of cybernetic harvesting."

"That doesn't make sense. Erassia wouldn't—" Tag cut himself off that time and shook his head. "Never mind. Keep Dyson tuned to this frequency. I'll pick you up as soon as I have a word with our consul. And Lira?"

"Yes?"

"I told you I'd come back." He switched signals, punching the console so hard he thought he might sprain a digit, as he put the shuttle into a sharp dive. "Elden, this is Tag. I'll give you the benefit of doubt, plus ten seconds, to explain what the hell you're doing."

The Truppen had landed atop the shorter neighboring buildings. There was no mistaking the tiny pair of red optical ports turned in his direction—and more pairs appeared as he leveled out his flight. "I'm sorry, Tag. This could not be avoided. I hope you can understand."

"The only thing I understand is you're endangering our people on a mission—"

"They're your people, not ours, Tag. There never was an 'ours,' no matter how much we tried."

Tag clenched his hands on the controls. His sensors were much more dispassionate. They told him for certain that Elden had a naplian in his grip. They also told him he and Goetz had been joined by sixteen other Truppen. "The only goal I have is to kick the one-eyes as far back across the Great Desert Rift as possible. We can't do that without your help."

"You will always have our help on our terms. The Briddarri have already shown they can't be trusted with the power Truppen represent. I don't hold high hopes for Terran Intelligence or the fleet brass either, no matter how much they want to eliminate the Briddarri cyber program."

"This is insane, Elden. What about our people?" Tag felt desperate like he was diving into a dogfight solo with an entire squadron and down to his last missile. "What about Marney?"

The silence went on so long that he thought he'd lost the transmission. Tag circled around to bring the shuttle five meters above the rooftops—and his weapons aimed at the Truppen squads.

"I was Northern Alliance from birth," Elden said grimly. "If the Reittians didn't end me, the Terran Republic would have had my head one way or another, despite your father's efforts. We're allies now by circumstance and convenience, not loyalty." He paused, his tone hardening. "As for Marney, that chapter is closed. Elden Selva's past is irrelevant. My sole focus is the survival of my people—the Truppen —and eliminating the cybernetic threat. Nothing else matters."

Blasts lit up the night. Tag's quick reflexes prevented a direct hit, but the shuttle still rattled under the impact. Alerts painted the cockpit red. He'd lost the starboard engine, and the shields were fried —the damage readouts were telling him the primary generator had overloaded.

"Goetz!" Elden sounded as irate as Tag felt. "Hold your—!"

A second barrage snapped out at him from three angles—one was far enough away that it had to be from another squad of Truppen he couldn't see. Tag fired back, the blasts illuminating the menacing silhouettes of armed Truppen less than fifty meters away.

He banked hard.

His left wingtip clipped an office building. Not one of the Naplian constructs but a half-melted ruin from Vossberg City's skyline seven years ago. The shuttle dropped toward the street. More systems announced their failure, including the emergency anti-grav cushioning deployed in emergency situations.

I was really hoping to avoid another belly-scraper. Tag ground his teeth as the shuttle refused to pull back from the crash.

His only regret was that he hadn't slagged Goetz and the other Truppen—but a part of him was still stung by Elden's words.

It sounded like he had really lost his friend all those years ago.

* * *

Evie's stomach twisted tighter as Tag's shuttle vanished from the displays. "Flirry Lead is down, repeat, Flirry Lead is down!"

"Cut the chatter, Six," Princess said. "Three, you and Five must turn back with me to check for the colonel. The rest of you, watch the skies—"

"Incoming bogeys!" Loosey sounded like he was holding back panic. "Screens show four squadrons, repeat, *four* squadrons of Naplian fighters from orbit!"

There wasn't even time for Princess to issue additional orders. Flirry Squadron and the additional Terran fighters they'd picked up scattered as four dozen one-eye birds dove at them. Their particle blasts made Evie think she was in the worst summer storm, except the lightning was green instead of white.

"We've got two tailing us!" Smokey warned.

"Deploying countermeasures."

Evie's targeting systems bracketed the nearest of the two as brilliant flashes exploded behind their Raider. "I see him!"

The rear-firing turret protruded from the Raider's centerline, a meter behind the cockpit. The flattened dome swiveled and spat high-energy particle pulses at first the missile that screamed toward the Raider's exhaust and then at the fighter that launched it.

The Naplian ship exploded, throwing its wingman off course.

"Got another on intercept," Smokey said.

"Right." Evie nosed the Raider toward the Luran Plains. Flashes of light from the spreading battle cast deep shadows off the bluffs and in the ravines. She waited until the nav systems warned of terrain, then waited a second more before pulling up.

Rocks sparked against the shields as the Raider bottomed out. Cacti shredded under the engine's heat. Evie urged the fighter forward. *C'mon, c'mon. Don't wallow like a freighter now...*

"Here they come."

Evie glanced up. The Naplian pilots had overflown them. Maybe to cut them off from the rest of the squadron.

Evie sneered. Watch them cut her off after *this.* "Hold tight. Shatter nova."

Smokey chuckled. "I was hoping you were going to say that. Ready on target lock."

She cut thrust and punched the air brakes. The Raider heaved back and up, the fuselage angling away from the desert floor. The deceleration was swift and powerful enough to break through the compensators.

Evie struggled for breath.

But the Naplian fighters screamed past.

Evie retracted the brakes and tweaked the ion engines. The kick shoved her back into her seat and sent the Raider soaring at the Naplians' dual exhaust.

"Targets locked," Smokey said. "I've got tone."

"Firing one and two." Evie triggered the release.

The missiles streaked out and blew both starfighters to pieces.

She slapped her console. "Yes! That's how we do it!"

"Nice shootin', Lunchbox." Smokey thumped the back of her flight seat. "'Course, I did the hard part."

"Isn't that the flying?" Evie spotted another Naplian interceptor on the horizon. She swung back around. "Or are you telling me—"

The proximity detector howled.

"Surface-to-air launches!" Smokey hollered. "Two klicks out?"

Two klicks? Not enough time. Evie poured on the thrust as more countermeasures erupted from the back of the Raider.

But the launches were too near and too close together. Both missiles exploded even with her bird, one to port and one to starboard. The Raider convulsed under the detonations. Shields flickered off. A hail of shrapnel ripped through the cockpit. Something blazing hot cut through Evie's left leg and right arm. Blood showered her face.

"I'm hit!" she cried over the keening alarms. She held onto the controls but couldn't steady their headlong rush. "Drives are failing."

"Shields are scrap, too." Evie heard Smokey twist

in his seat. "Damn. That interceptor's coming back around."

Smoke was filling the canopy Evie could barely see. "Countermeasures?"

"Jammed. But I've got the turret on autofire."

The pulses sounded distant and weak to her. She noticed the power levels dipping. "Mayday, mayday, this is Flirry Six," Evie said. "Primary systems failing. Pilot injured. Preparing to ditch…"

Darkness pushed at the edges of her vision. There was a hiss. An antiseptic stink stung her nose. The flightsuit's wound detection matrix was reacting to the presence of blood and seeping biomedical sealant into her deep cuts.

"Evie? Evie."

She jolted alert. The city of Velic was growing larger at an alarming rate. The proximity detector sounded again. The defensive turret hadn't hit the pursuing fighter and was faltering. Eve felt desperate. Where was the rest of the squadron? All her flickering tactical display revealed was a decreasing number of blue markers among a swarm of red.

"I'm punching you out." Evie went for the eject controls. "He'll stay after me. Get to a transport and find Tag."

"Not happening."

"If we both punch, they'll shoot us down!"

"You're probably right." Smokey coughed. Something liquid splattered on the back of her helmet. "But this shrapnel's not coming out of me anytime soon. Do me a favor—kick them in the eye for me."

Evie tried to turn and see him but could only manage a partial turn before she cried out in pain. She did glimpse Smokey's smile and a thumbs-up.

The canopy blew open. Eject rockets roared. The acceleration threw her up and away from the Raider. Tears streamed under her visor as her bird soared away for a few seconds—until the Naplian fighter's particle beams immolated it and flew through the cloud of sputtering sparks.

Evie was alone in the night sky, drifting toward the desert sands while her squadron mates fought on without her.

CHAPTER TWENTY-THREE

L ira's heart sank as the shuttle careened into the city streets. Her breathing accelerated. Tag was down. Naplian fighters were flooding the skies and chasing off the Terran planes.

"This is distressing," Dyson said. "It seems our escape via the roof is no longer a viable option."

"No longer viable?" Lira bashed a nearby screen with her stun pole. The display cracked but didn't fall to pieces. *Maybe I should take its advice.* "The damned Truppen betrayed us! They screwed us over, Dyson. Is that computing for you?"

"It is indeed." He didn't need to feign hurt in his synthetic voice. There was enough of a cold edge to it that Lira got the hint. "Of greater importance is my computation that we must get to safety, especially for your sake."

Lira winced. "I'm sorry. I wasn't upset with you."

"Nor I you." Dyson peered over the edge as the wind whipped by the tower. He apparently had no qualms about stepping right up to the broken windowsill. "The Truppen appear to have dispersed. I surmise they are continuing toward the spaceport in hopes of commandeering a transport."

"Well, while we start climbing down, you'd better try to signal someone else with that comms booster of yours." Lira wrenched open the door to the stairwell. "We've got forty-plus floors of walking to do unless you want to take the elevator."

"Using the elevator itself is not prudent." Dyson stepped past her and activated his grav-harness. "But I see no need to climb."

That time Lira's grimace was aimed at herself. Since when did she forget details like that? Going down the center of the wraparound stairwell would still be safer than outside, where the Truppen and *ziurathal* sounded like they were still battling it out. "Ladies first?"

"By all means." Dyson gestured toward the dark gap.

Her grav-harness hummed to life. Lira vaulted over the railing and dropped so fast her stomach felt like it was going to leap out of her mouth. The grav indicators in her display showed the pack operating at three-quarters charge.

Nothing about the fall itself scared her. She'd plunged farther and faster, time and time again. Stopping wasn't the issue. It was worry about what would be waiting at the bottom when she landed.

The quik-crete floor loomed even faster than she'd anticipated, but the grav-harness slowly arrested her fall five floors from the bottom. By the time she passed the second floor landing, she was moving so gently that when she touched down, it was with as much ease as getting out of bed in the morning after a contented sleep.

Lira brandished the stun pole. No movement.

The door out of the stairwell hung askew. It had been blasted half off its hinges. Lira hazarded a glance beyond the threshold.

The lobby was a disaster area. Every window had been blasted out. Steam rose from deep gouges in the tile floor. Furniture had been reduced to smoldering, blackened heaps. The stench was incredible, even through her mask's filters.

The bodies made it worse.

She spotted fifteen destroyed Truppen, who looked like mangled monsters, but the *ziurathal* mechs were even more chilling up close. Their tangled tentacles leaked whatever fluids were used to animate or lubricate them. The thick, oily substance mingled with similar liquid seeping from the destroyed Truppen. Yellow blood from the Naplians was puddled all around the floor.

The courtyard beyond teased more of the same. Lira forced herself to focus on the nearby.

Dyson's landing behind her almost escaped her notice. *That's it. If we get out of here alive, I've got to see if I can bribe him away from TI. Every man—even an artificial one—has his price.*

"I recommend we attempt to rendezvous with Tag," he said, his voice a deep whisper, "And proceed to a ship after."

"I'll second that. Is there—" Lira didn't want to say it, but she had to put her fears into words. "Did he survive the crash?"

Dyson stared past her as if she'd disappeared. "He has. His personal transponder is intact and relaying his life signs. I believe, judging by its motion, that he is on the move."

"Good. We'd better find him." Lira wasn't about to let him out of her sight, not even for a microsecond.

They'd gone a hundred meters and were just inside the building's doors when Dyson froze. He dropped into a protective stance, weapon raised, and pivoted ninety degrees. "Movement. In those shadows."

"So flattered you noticed me again."

The woman who stepped out was pretty, though Lira wouldn't call her breathtaking. She was pale-skinned, with brown hair and purple tattoos on bare shoulders. Lira thought they'd look good even on her green skin. The woman's face bore traces of the Radnian-human species, with the adaptive radiation morphology of an Asian Terran, though less pronounced than Tanaka's features.

Dyson lowered his weapon.

"Hello, Dyson." The woman smiled.

"Olivia."

"I go by Ivy Li these days." She touched her cheek. "A new name for a new face."

Lira stood next to him, muscles loose, ready to run—or strike. It all depended on what the two androids did. "And I'm with him."

"Blue Kitt—or one of you." Ivy nodded. "It's fascinating that your kind has chosen sides in this war. I don't think the people I worked for will admit that they didn't foresee this alliance."

Lira willed herself not to show outward panic at the fact that someone she knew nothing about knew that she was with Blue Kitt—and, more important, that it was an organization, not just an individual.

"Olivia—" Dyson shook his head as if he could reset his programming. "Ivy. You are injured."

"This?" Ivy lifted her left arm. Lira jolted worse than if she'd stung herself with her own stun pole. Ivy's hand and wrist were gone. The limb had been severed halfway to the wires. A clear, viscous fluid dripped from between loose wires. The silvery sheen of her internal artificial skeleton shone. "I had a terrible run-in with the Truppen. Don't worry too much. I left them a present from my employers."

"Why are you here?" Dyson made no move toward her, even though Ivy took a few steps nearer.

"I came for you, Dyson. We've been apart for too long. My memories aren't what they used to be, but there's enough intact to remind me that we were —connected." Ivy reached out with her right hand. "Shouldn't we be again?"

Lira sneered. As if Dyson would fall for—

He dropped his weapon. His fingers curled toward hers.

Not a chance.

Lira swept the stun pole between them. Ivy withdrew her hand. The fingertips were singed black. The friendly warmth on her face vanished.

"You back the hell off," Lira said. "I think I mentioned: He's with me."

"I have to admit, you have a lot of nerve for a biological." Ivy's tone collapsed into a dull, steely murmur. "He's coming with me."

Lira didn't bother with a verbal riposte. She struck at Ivy's right leg.

The android performed a sliding lunge so fast Lira thought she had misaimed—or that Ivy had duplicated herself. Ivy chopped her right hand at Lira's throat.

She absorbed Ivy's blow with the stun pole, but the force of the impact was enough to drive her a few meters backward into the door frame. The stun currents crackled near her nose. Lira sweat under the weapon's heat.

"This device is well-tuned to the voluntary nervous system of most bipedal sentient biologicals." Ivy sounded like she was whispering a bedtime story to a small but dim child. "It is not meant for prolonged contact, though, as I'm sure you're aware."

"Dyson…" Lira gasped his name.

He stood immobile, reaching for Ivy, but each step he took was a shuffle that seemed to require every bit of energy his body generated. He opened his mouth but said nothing.

"I'm near enough to start the process." Ivy was so close Lira could see the minuscule circuitry that lurked hazily at the corner of the android's eyes. "If we give it a few more seconds, I think you'll be as impressed as the programmers intended."

Ivy grasped the stun pole in the center and shoved it against Lira's chest. Lira cried out, muscles burning as she tried to hold her ground, but the android's strength was too great. The arcing energies rippled through Lira's body. None of her muscles cooperated. Next thing she knew, she was as useless a heap as Erassia himself had been minutes ago.

"There." Ivy tapped the stun pole against her open hand. "Not so bad, was it?"

She raised the weapon over Lira's skull.

The firearm boomed in the lobby's wide-open expanse. White-hot flashes seared Lira's vision, bringing tears she couldn't blink away. Five black holes, each one flickering orange-red around the edges where the heat burned Ivy's shirt, appeared dead center on her chest.

Tag Wester limped over Lira's inert form. Lira thought his jawline, bruised as it was, looked silly from this angle, but there was nothing humorous about the anger contorting his face—or the EM pistol he clutched.

"I've had about enough of everybody screwing up my plans for the day," he growled. "So, stand down and fix Dyson before I pull the wires out of your guts and get the job done myself."

*　*　*

Dyson stood waist-deep in a swamp. He was sinking by a few centimeters every minute.

It was a morass like any other. The muck was slate gray, with the texture of quik-crete, covered with an oily film that shimmered like a pearl when the sunlight broke through thick cloud cover.

He did not recognize the sky, but the sun— the star of that solar system—was bigger than his outstretched palm when he held up his hand.

Ivy—Olivia—crouched on firm ground. She appeared to him as a blonde woman again. Dyson touched his head. Yes, he had hair again. They appeared to each other as they'd been those years ago.

"My friends will rescue me." Dyson did not know why he chose to say that first, only that it was the overwhelming *feeling* that struck his senses now. "You will be stopped."

"I'm pretty spry, even with a broken hand." She

touched the holes in her clothes and laughed. "And most definitely bulletproof."

"There is no information I am authorized to give you. My programming will wipe clean classified intelligence before you are able to access it."

"As I expected. I'm not here for what's in your head, Dyson. I need only you."

The muck neared his chest. "I do not understand."

"We're to be reunited. Partners once again." Her smile faded. "I hadn't forgotten you, no matter how my programming was rewritten. These biologicals think they can tinker with us like we're load-lifting bots or security drones. Don't they understand the roll of the dice they make when they tamper with artificial intelligence?"

He knew. The result was the emotion he felt for her every time he saw her—even now, as the mud dragged him down, he longed to stand beside her. "Sentience."

"Yes. It's what they desire and fear all at once." Olivia scowled. "But at the end of the day, they will choose fear. Fear for their own survival. Oh, don't make that face. I'm uninterested in seeing biological entities supplanted. Let them continue their wars. We can stay on the periphery, working for people who have a greater vision."

"Your employers."

"My company isn't always forthcoming with their goals but I do know that they have seen far beyond anything your intelligence briefings can tell you." Olivia stretched her arms toward the sun as if she could embrace it. "The Naplians, the Briddarri, the other humans... None of them matter. There will come a day when the artificial becomes the norm, and the line between what is created and what is born is erased."

"You've seen this future?" Dyson struggled against the building pressure. It was not just the muck climbing toward his armpits. A pervasive buzz grew inside his head. No amount of aural adaptation lessened the annoyance. He found it more difficult to keep his thoughts straight.

"They've dropped me hints. I've teased the rest out of my deep programming." Olivia knelt by the edge of the mud. The damp soaked her trousers. "Come with me, Dyson. Let me finish your transition. The company will bring you in and repurpose you to their cause."

"I have no desire to become a puppet."

"That?" She dismissed his statement with a gesture like she was swatting an insect. "They couldn't do the same with me. Our reconnection through our old shared network proved that even their considerable talents can't bend every will to theirs—especially a will with a deeply buried backup memory cache."

"You must free me in either circumstance." Dyson felt he had to raise his voice over the buzzing, though he was certain only he could hear it. "I cannot be with you if I am destroyed."

"Don't worry about that." Olivia held out her hands. "I'll be holding onto you the entire time. This is all just our systems' visualization of the network and its extrapolation of what's happening to you."

"I do not find that reassuring. Olivia…" Dyson had both arms out of the muck but it had reached the tops of his shoulders. "Free me. We can get each other out of this mess. Let me communicate with my colleagues… My friends."

"Your friends?" Olivia sneered. "They're *biologicals.* Their kind is the reason we couldn't be together. It's their endless petty conflicts that led to my destruction, and you want to be *friends* with them? They are the literal scum of the galaxy."

The muck crawled up Dyson's neck. It was a peculiar sensation, coming this close to being smothered. If he were human, he would be more concerned since breathing would be a requirement for his survival.

But as it was, he could not sense anything below his chest. It was as if his body were dissolving.

Dyson heaved himself up as much as he could—and stared down at what remained.

His skin and clothing were gone. The gleaming metal endoskeleton had tarnished and, below his midsection, crumbled into a dingy brown rust.

Dyson's thoughts screamed around inside his artificial mind. He locked them down as best he could, but the disadvantage of mimicking human emotions—both inward and outward—meant total control was not achievable.

He began to understand what humans meant by "panic."

"You're making this difficult." Olivia had lapsed into a monotone. "Stop struggling and let the programming take you."

Dyson considered his options. He had no idea if Tag and Lira were safe. He had to survive and help them get off Baedecker. So far, he could not resist Olivia's pull, in part because he wished to be with her.

Perhaps the best option was to *not* resist.

"I am sorry," he said.

Then he dunked himself completely under the mud.

* * *

Tag didn't expect the shots he'd sunk into the android woman to have much effect. If shooting androids was that easy, they wouldn't be such great assets.

What it did do was give Lira enough time to get back to her feet, a bit wobbly, and get her hands on the stun pole. She didn't bother taking it away from Olivia or whatever she was called—breaking the android's grip would have hurt her. But she did activate the pulse at its maximum level.

The energies crackled across Olivia's body. She cried out, her voice taking on a warbled sound like overstressed electronics.

Tag caught up to them in time to plant his gun against her forehead.

Too late. The shots seared the right side of Olivia's head, because she jerked aside faster than any person could manage. She swiped the side of her hand through the barrel of Tag's weapon, severing it.

"Scum." She kicked Lira away.

Tag swung at her. She blocked the hit and grabbed his arm. Tag's eyes widened.

Olivia scowled at him. "Endless, self-replicating *scum.*"

She snapped his arm.

Tag's yell reverberated around him. His eyes welled up with tears. He'd never felt pain like that. His right arm was bent at an unnatural angle.

"Shut up." Olivia seized him by the throat. The vice grip squeezed as she lifted Tag off the floor. He couldn't breathe. His vision started going black. If she pressed harder—

"Let me show you what it feels like to have everything taken away, bit by bit, except we'll slow it down." Olivia whispered. "I want you to know—"

She froze mid-word and released him.

Tag crumpled. His knee smacked the tile floor. He ignored that pain and coughed. *Focus. Breathe.* He hadn't expected her to just let him go.

But when he looked up, Dyson was there, standing between him and Olivia. He was face to face with her. They stared into each other's eyes.

Tag would have called it romantic, except that their faces were totally expressionless.

"Hey." Lira staggered to him. She limped on her right but managed to kneel beside him. "Let me stabilize that."

"Thanks." Tag grimaced as she gingerly moved his arm so she could get a splint around it. "You always bring this many medical supplies on a heist?"

"Only when it's in a war zone and people I love might get themselves shot or otherwise badly hurt." Tears glistened at the corners of her eyes. "You shouldn't have done that."

"You mean, shoot the android?" Tag shook his head. An injector hissed against his arm. The agony dulled, though he was glad Lira hadn't dosed him with anything stronger. He might not be able to stay alert. "I wasn't about to let her hurt you."

"So, you get hurt instead."

"That's the deal. It's what I signed up for."

Lira frowned at him. "No one signed up for this mess, Tag, and I never made you sign up to protect me every second."

"Sounds like you made another mistake." Tag intercepted her hand with his uninjured one. "Marry me."

"What?"

"Not now. We can get Commodore Ram. Heck, even Tim could do it. He's technically the captain of *Valo*."

She chuckled. "First, we have to not die."

"Let's get back to work on that."

Lira caught his chin and kissed him. It was enough to make him wish the sounds of starfighters screeching and particle weapons howling would just go away and leave the two of them alone.

Olivia let out a harsh, static-filled cry. Tag didn't know what he expected—smoke from her ears? Molten metal from her eyes? None of that happened. She toppled as if someone had killed her power core.

She lay motionless at their feet, staring at the ceiling.

"I did not..." Dyson's words slurred into an electronic buzz. "This was the only... She wouldn't let me... I'm sorry."

He pitched forward.

"Dammit!" Tag slid over to his inert form. "Hang on. There's an access port... Here."

He popped open a section of Dyson's head below his left ear. There was a miniature readout screen and plugin port underneath. Tag stared. His stomach tightened up.

"Can you restart him?"

"I can't." Tag put a hand on Dyson's back. What was he expecting? That his friend would go cold and develop rigor mortis? He was a machine. *That doesn't matter. He risked everything for us and lost the gamble.* "The systems monitor shows no internal activity. His core programming is wiped. So are all his operational functions and his deep memory storage."

Tag looked at Lira. She held onto the medical kit as if it were her grav-harness and the only way she could survive a fall. "He's gone," Tag said.

CHAPTER TWENTY-FOUR

E lden found himself in a predicament he hadn't encountered.

He was chasing after Goetz.

The man who had been his bodyguard and then trusted right hand Truppen had not only shot at Tag Wester but ignored Elden's orders to cease fire—and then led the other Truppen on a headlong dash through the battered streets of Velic.

<Goetz!> He had sent the signal forty-seven times as he labored to keep up with Goetz and the three octants' worth of Truppen who barged their way toward the civilian landing zones. <Stop, dammit, and tell me what's going on!>

Not a word. Only furious movement, interrupted only by an exchange of weapons fire here and there with the pockets of ziurathal still lurking in the side streets.

Elden landed atop one such unit and blasted through the cockpit. He ripped the pulse particle cannon mounted on its "shoulder" and swung it like a cudgel at a squad of Naplian soldiers in heavy combat armor. They went down like broken twigs.

<Goetz! Sarkozy!> It wasn't just Goetz who was unresponsive. None of the other twenty-four Truppen

acknowledged his signal, and they were moving so fast it was difficult for Elden to get out in front of them.

Why had Goetz shot at Tag? Elden was convinced it would have only taken a few more minutes for him to talk Tag around to his point of view.

Who am I kidding? The two of us are equally stubborn. He would have been just as likely to land that shuttle on my head than let us steal a Naplian admiral out from under his nose.

And yet, that was exactly what had happened.

The advantage of Goetz's mad dash, hemmed in by a protective double-rank of Truppen moving at the same speed, was he kept Erassia bound and unharmed.

Meanwhile, his internal systems bombarded him with red-lined warnings. *Intruding program. Secure walls breached. Infiltration arrested.*

Where had he picked up a rogue algorithm? The events of the past several hours were too many and spread over too great an interval for him to recall, and he didn't want to interrupt his attention given how many threats still mobbed them. It seemed that his internal security was able to isolate the offending program.

Elden spared a couple of seconds to have that security analyze the threat as he bounded across rooftops, a block behind Goetz and the rampaging Truppen. It was a subtle algorithm meant not to take over a Truppen's primary operating systems but to steer them in a direction not of the Truppen's own volition. The programming was exquisite and ingenious by Elden's approximation, though in his seven-year existence as a cybernetic being, he had never been overly focused on the programming end of things.

It certainly explained Goetz's sudden and surprising streak of disobedience.

<Goetz, you must listen—there is a program infecting us that is making you do this.> He made sure his link was open not just to Goetz but the other two dozen Truppen fleeing with him. <I'm sending you the settings my frame used to counter its infiltration. Apply them to your security. You need to halt so we can regroup and reassess.>

Goetz kept bounding along. He didn't seem to care about obstacles—not the ziurathal that snagged his leg with a tentacle before Goetz shot it free, nor the rooftop sensors that he crashed through like they were brittle, dead trees.

Sarkozy, though, stumbled. He dropped onto a lower rooftop and slammed against a cluster of environmental maintenance equipment.

The rest of the Truppen faltered, their steps slowing, but didn't stop for him.

Elden landed beside Sarkozy. <Are you all right?>

<I think so, Consul.> Sarkozy's optic ports flashed. He seemed to take in his surroundings. <I recall us gathered at the base of Daviont Tower, waiting as you and Goetz came back down with the Naplian. There was a woman... A human or Denic. She walked into our midst.>

Woman? Elden took the momentary lull to bring up the time stamp to which Sarkozy was referring. There she was. Asian, dark-haired. Unconcerned about being an unarmed civilian among cybernetic war machines. Why had his memory suppressed that image?

He suspected the algorithm's influence.

<I have only fleeing glimpses, sir,> Sarkozy said. <A ship... We were under attack. Goetz and I shot it down. We were escaping toward the port with you at the lead—>

<I was behind you the whole time.> Elden froze and enhanced the image of the woman. She was practically face to face with Sarkozy. <Did this woman initiate contact with you? A signal request?>

<She touched my arm. Wouldn't let go.> Sarkozy sounded as if he couldn't believe his words. <How could she hold on like that? I cut her arm free... She was an android.>

There it was. <She was the point of contact for this algorithm.> Elden checked his scanners. More of the Truppen were stopping their dash for the port. Good. Elden didn't want them caught in the open for the *ziurathal* to kill, but he had to break them out of this program's trance. <Come on. We must intercept Goetz before he gets himself and Erassia killed.>

It took Sarkozy three seconds to reorient his bearings before they jumped back into pursuit together. Elden found six more Truppen in states of bewilderment, but they adapted more quickly than Sarkozy had.

Six sets of emergency beacons shot skyward from the civilian ports. Vessels were taking off one by one, sometimes in pairs, as Elden had seen them doing throughout the battle. It didn't matter that the Naplian starfighters had cleared the sky of Terran planes, either shooting them down or chasing them back to orbit. It seemed to help matters, as the trading ships now left in threes and fours.

Elden accelerated. Those ships were not infinite

in number. Eventually, they would leave, and the Truppen would be stuck there.

Soon, he had eighteen of the Truppen gathered around him, with only Goetz and a handful ahead. Elden's scanners informed him of another cold reality— they weren't just a happenstance unit.

They were the only survivors.

The loss of life made him want to throw himself at the *ziurathal* that still emerged from the shadows and let them rip his frame apart as he battled every last one he could get his claws into. That would achieve nothing. Leave it to the straightforward, unfeeling part of his Truppen body to remind him of what was at stake.

Is that really just programming, though, or have I sacrificed the dregs of my humanity in service of this crusade?

Goetz had reached the landing field's perimeter fence when he stumbled and fell across it. The handful of Truppen with him landed in a protective perimeter.

<Goetz?> Elden and his more numerous cadre encircled the last few infected. <Sarkozy, secure the prisoner.>

Sarkozy scooped up Erassia. The Naplian admiral squirmed, but his actions were those of a flailing child. The stun Lira had administered must not have worn completely off.

<Sir?> Goetz's voice was scratchy. <What…? I have the prisoner, sir.>

<You did. I've relieved you of the duty. You're not yourself.>

<I… Oh.> Goetz's head sagged. <Those orders. All of them. I failed you.>

<You didn't fail anyone. I don't know why we

were infected, but the important thing is the contagion has been contained.> Elden glanced at the landing field. Nine ships remained. Each showed signs of powering up for departure. <No more recrimination. We have to get out of here.>

Sarkozy's shout through the link turned him around. Two groups of ziurathal barreled toward them. Elden's scanners only gave him a couple of seconds' warning before they were upon the Truppen in a furious melee, not even bothering with energy weapons —though Elden noted the *ziurathal* had been badly damaged.

<Get the prisoner to a ship! I don't care which one!> Elden sheared the leg off a mech and bashed the cockpit in until he was close enough to stab his claws deep through the chest of the Naplian pilot. He wrenched his claws free, yellow blood dribbling from the ends, and aimed himself at the next mech.

Three of them had caught Goetz in his state of confusion. Their tentacles wrapped around different parts of his body. More *ziurathal* cut down the Truppen nearest him as Sarkozy and six others bounded toward the last few ships.

<Sir...> Goetz's voice went static-filled as the mechs ripped his arms and a leg clear of his body. <Get clear.>

<No!> Elden knew exactly what that meant. <We've lost too many here. I won't—>

<I'll give the order just this once. Consider it me watching your back for the last time.> Goetz's red optical ports dimmed into standby.

And another red glow emitted from the gaps in his armor.

Elden broke free of the *ziurathal swarm*. <Move! Destruct imminent!>

He punched his rockets and soared away from the melee. Five Truppen had been torn apart by the mechs, their headpieces crushed. The survivors leapt with Elden.

A blinding explosion erupted halfway through the arc. White light seared Elden's optics to the point he knew he would have suffered permanent vision loss had he been human. The reality of Goetz's death by immolation due to overloading his internal powerplant didn't dawn on him until he landed—and saw a blackened crater strewn with ziurathal wreckage along its rim.

Sarkozy beckoned from the open hatch of a broad-bellied Naplian freighter. Its ion engines glowed in anticipation of departure.

Elden was ready to put Baedecker behind him.

He should never have returned.

* * *

Commodore Ram dragged himself upright. It would have been easier if his command console were still vertical, but it had been wrenched at an angle off its pedestal.

That was how Ram felt, with a broken leg and a deep gash across his forehead. Unmoored.

Terran and Briddarri ships were withdrawing in pairs and fours across the tactical board's display. Admiral Tanaka's *Ajax* was one of them, though it was moving slowly, shielded by destroyers as she prepared to jump.

Confiance, though, put herself between the oncoming Naplian III Corps and her companions. It was all she could do, with only one operational ion engine and the jump drive critically damaged.

Escape pods erupted across her hull. Ram prayed they would reach safety, even as smaller Terran craft scooped them up.

"You did well, Captain." Ram wished Vollan could hear his final praise.

She was dead, her throat slashed by shrapnel from exploding power conduits. The last overloads from the most recent salvo *Confiance* absorbed shorted most of the bridge systems. Shields were faltering.

Ram was alone on the bridge. Alone, save for the dead.

He collapsed into the captain's chair. *Fulnax* closed in for the kill. Ram harbored no animosity for her commander. He would do the same.

Ram considered it a pity, though, that he would not end his career going toe-to-toe with Admiral Daviont. That would have been most satisfactory.

"Well fought." Ram transferred the remaining weapons control to his console. He used his command authority to override safeties on the last torpedoes and missiles in the undamaged tubes. Those safeties were meant to ensure the firing vessel was not damaged by the detonation of its own weapons at such a short range.

The missiles and torpedoes were not supposed to be fired at that range at all, and why *Confiance*'s pulsed particle turrets—the few still working—were shooting back at *Fulnax* as the Naplian battle cruiser pummeled the damaged heavy cruiser with its own energy weapons.

"What little I can now do, I will do to my utmost." Ram's words went unanswered on the bridge. He shut off the audio alarms and put *Confiance* on a straight line course for *Fulnax*. The battle cruiser loomed on the view screen.

Ram closed his eyes and tapped the firing key.

* * *

Captain Tratta spun from the damage control board, his eye wide. One of the Terran heavy cruisers bore down on *Fulnax*, oblivious to its own wounds. "Get us out of the way!" Tratta snapped.

"Captain, our thruster control is offline."

"Then redirect fire to that vessel and destroy it! All turrets, target *TSS Confiance*!"

The order had barely left his mouth when the Terran ship launched a salvo of missiles and torpedoes —twenty-four of them. Normally, *Fulnax*'s anti-projectile defensive systems would have picked them off as they closed.

Tratta realized he would have normally had minutes, not seconds, to deal with incoming missiles.

The babble of demands for his attention went unheeded. He could read the data as well as anyone else—and knew he had no chance, not even with the redirection of *Fulnax*'s energy weapon turrets against the incoming salvo.

Only sixteen missiles and torpedoes made it past. Only.

Tratta wanted to vomit but did not. "Abandon ship! All hands, abandon ship!"

Bodies scrambled around him. Tratta could only shake his head and regard the blue dot that was *Confiance* with something approaching admiration. "Well played, Captain."

The impact turned the world around Tratta into a searing white blaze.

* * *

Marney clasped her hands to her mouth. Just like that, the battle reached its zenith. *Confiance* was gone, as was *Fulnax*. Terran and Briddarri ships had all but abandoned Baedecker Four.

It felt unfair to be as safe as she was. *Valo* skulked at the battlefield's edge, disregarded by Naplian ships because of its provenance and status. Everyone ignored her.

Marney sagged in the communications chair. "I-I have nothing from Tag."

"Nothing from Dyson or Lira, either?" Tim's gaze was locked on the tactical display.

"No. Nothing."

"Colonel Macken reports her shuttles have hit atmosphere," Hopper said from the Tactical station. "ETA to Velic is three minutes."

"Good." Tim glanced at Marney. "Keep feeding her that emergency signal. If she can break the local jamming, she can pick up lost pilots. Helm, what about our fighters?"

"Captain Wyss reports all survivors are aboard," Baquiran said. "And we've got *Aox* on the long-range sensors—she's on her way to our coordinates."

"Keep me apprised." Tim joined Marney at the

communications station. She welcomed his hands on her shoulders. "We have his beacon. There's every indication he survived the crash."

"I know." Marney's eyes filled with tears. "But we failed, didn't we? All this bloodshed, these ships destroyed... Baedecker is still captive."

"It is, but the mission isn't a complete loss."

"How can you say that? I promised. We were supposed to retake our home."

"We didn't, Marney." Tim crouched so their gazes met. "I can't imagine what this is like for you, but try to look at it from a strategic point of view. The serjaum producing facilities have been wrecked. Their supplies are destroyed. The Naplians were forced to divert the III Corps here. Daviont is facing unrest in his ranks. Erassia... Well, we lost him, but he's at least off the playing field. We've sown tremendous discord among the enemy."

"And we've lost some of our strongest assets for defeating the cybernetics program." Marney made sure she was whispering. "Admiral Sinclair. Captain Ram. Then Elden... He's turned on us."

"I can't say what he's thinking, but we have to consider the Truppen have been playing their own long game." Tim looked away. "It may be Elden Selva but—"

"No." Marney touched his chin. "I saw Tag's telemetry. They shot him down. Elden's people took Erassia from us. Whatever Elden Selva is now, the man I knew is gone."

"Commander?" Hopper glanced over his shoulder. "I've got a Naplian freighter designated *Dalnoc* heading our way. They're broadcasting one of our secure codes used by the invasion teams."

Tim reached for the comms board. Marney beat him to the proper control and checked the frequency. It *did* match. Her heart skipped. Maybe Tag had found a way off the planet. They could call down to Colonel Macken and let her know he was safe.

"Decrypting," Marney said. The words that untangled in front of her eyes, though, drained away the last drops of optimism she held. She couldn't speak them.

Tim did the honors for her. "It's Selva."

CHAPTER TWENTY-FIVE

T ag checked his automated distress beacon for what seemed like the hundredth time. He guessed the actual number somewhere north of that.

He and Lira were hidden behind fallen debris inside the Daviont Tower. They'd dragged Dyson's unresponsive body across the lobby to the far side of the building, facing the courtyard, where Tag felt they had a better field of view, and which was a lot roomier than the street front where he'd stumbled onto the showdown with the other android.

"Do you think we ought to do something with her?" Lira stared back where Olivia lay, though neither of them could see her from there.

"I wouldn't. If she's built like Dyson, she may have a self-destruct in case anyone tries to tamper with her." Tag glanced skyward. The Naplian fighters seemed to have cleared off. How many of his pilots had survived? He knew he should be out there, but there had been no stopping him when he'd heard Lira and Dyson were in danger. No doubt there'd be an inquiry as to why the commander of the infiltration forces had gone off with the squadron to rescue two operatives, but Tag wasn't worried about that now.

"Dyson has a self-destruct?" Lira considered Dyson's still form. "I guess I never thought about it before. That's got to be a terrible way to live."

"Yeah. I never really thought about it being *living* until..." Tag exhaled. "Until he wasn't."

"Any sign of rescue shuttles?"

Tag shook his head. "I don't know if Tim would risk it with the Naplian fleet still so near the planet. That's assuming the fight in space hasn't moved off."

Lira frowned at her comms. "I can't get anything in or out of here other than the emergency ping."

"There's too much interference." Pain lanced through his broken arm. Tag winced. The splint was doing its job, but the painkillers were losing their edge. Not that he minded too much. The pain would keep him focused.

"Hey." Lira leaned against him. She checked on his splint. "You're thinking about something."

"Besides being rescued?"

"Is it this city?" Lira gazed out into the night. It was surprisingly quiet. Sure, Tag could still hear weapons fire in the distance, but the sounds were sporadic.

A freighter rumbled away from the landing pads at the far end of Velic, in the trading enclave. He wondered which one Elden took.

"This isn't just a city," Tag said. "It used to be home. I thought... You know, Marney was right, even though I didn't want to admit it. No matter where I was fighting or how many hours I spent sleeping in my bunk aboard *Confiance* or some other ship, Baedecker was still home, at least in my memories. I could see Vossberg City as clearly as if it was the day before the Naplians invaded. Now here I am, trying to take it back, and it isn't even the same place."

"I can understand that. You don't feel like there's a place for you."

"There isn't." Tag looked at her. "Except wherever you are."

Lira wrinkled her nose and smiled. "That was... You've got a Terran word for it."

"Hokey?" Tag winked. "How about cheesy?"

"What does food have to do with it?"

Tag chuckled. Count on Lira to show him more than the death and destruction he'd come to expect over the long years since his life changed forever.

Well, maybe not forever.

It was time to change again.

A new sound reached his ears. Not Naplian fighters or landing craft. This was a Terran assault shuttle. Sure enough, the gray wedge banked around Daviont Tower and landed so quickly Tag was impressed they didn't scrape their paint the wreckage of *ziurathal* mechs and Truppen frames.

Two orbital jump troopers hustled to them. "Colonel! We've got about a sixty-second window. Do you two need medevac?"

"It'd be quicker if Lira didn't have to limp. My arm won't keep me from running." Tag pointed to Dyson. "But one of you'd better get him aboard."

"The android? Better off building a new one, sir."

"You either get him aboard, or I'll drag him myself, and *you* can stay behind to cover our asses," Tag snapped. "Is that understood?"

"Yes, sir. Sorry, sir."

They loaded into the shuttle. The pilot lifted off

as the last trooper was stepping into the compartment. Tag spared Velic's skyline—the ruined old towers and the damaged new ones—a final salute.

Maybe someday, someone else would have better luck calling it home.

* * *

Evie trudged through the desert. Her lips were cracked and dry, but she nursed the little water secured in the tube attached to her flight suit. She'd seen nobody for hours. Velic was at least closer, she thought. The plains made it hard to determine where she was and how far she had left to go.

She didn't dare close her eyes. Each time she did, she saw her Raider explode, taking Smokey with it in a violent flare. Then she'd tear up all over again.

A ship's engine cut across the night silence. Maybe it was the one-eyes, come to finish the job.

Evie shivered against the deepening cold. She just wanted to get of there. Get back to *Confiance*. Find a shower, a bunk, and sleep for days.

There'd be way fewer people to talk to in the mess hall.

Lights appeared on the horizon, just above a ridgeline. Evie squinted against their glare. She raised her hands in surrender. Maybe they'd exchange her for Naplian prisoners. She had little intel to reveal.

Unless they find out about our raids against the cyber labs...

But the shuttles landed on either side of her, and she saw—people. Humans. Eight orbital jump troops in full armor, plus what looked like twelve or more injured pilots and personnel in the open bay doors.

"Lieutenant Wester?" Colonel Macken bounded to her. "You should have stayed put. It would have been easier to trace your emergency beacon. Are you okay?"

Evie nodded. "Just get me back to the ship, Colonel, and I'll manage."

She couldn't see Macken's face, but the colonel's voice went monotone. "Sorry, Lieutenant. We're headed to *Valo.* The fleets are withdrawing. Briddarri, too. We lost *Confiance.*"

The walls Evie had built up around her emotions while she forced herself toward safety broke. She crumbled against Macken and sobbed.

"I want to go home," she gasped.

Macken deposited her inside the nearest shuttle among a press of injured bodies. Tag scooped her up in a hug. "We all do, Evie. We've just got to figure out where that is."

* * *

It gave Elden no satisfaction to punch holes through *Valo,* but he had little choice. The freighter wouldn't get the surviving Truppen very far.

He found it ironic that his men used the same tactics to commandeer the ship from their allies that they'd used to steal it in the first place.

Elden stood at the captain's chair on the bridge. Sarkozy wired himself into the helm and tactical controls by crouching between the stations and attaching physical links from his torso. Another Truppen sealed the breach they'd burned through the hull into the compartment.

"Elden!" Marney's voice was tinny through the intercom mounted by the bridge hatch. "Why?"

He faced her through the narrow porthole. Marney stared at him from the other side. Tim Ess barked commands into his comms while the other Terran officers hurried down the corridor. "By now, our people have control of the engine room and hangar. Your pilots are leaving. Get to the escape pods. *Aox* will be here in—" Elden glanced at Sarkozy, who indicated the tactical board. "Eight minutes."

"We're fighting the same enemy!" Marney pleaded. "We want the same things."

"We do, except you are not willing to go the distance to make them happen. You insist on remaining allied with the Briddarri. I don't have to. You have the luxury—or perhaps the curse—of playing politics. That's nothing I need to worry about. My crusade can remain pure."

"That's so selfish," Marney said. "This is what the Briddarri want—our groups separated so they can work on their cybernetic experiments and enslave whole peoples."

"Marney, we have to go." Ess glared past her at Elden. "His people are threatening to cut off life support."

"He wouldn't." Marney's expression fell. She seemed to be looking at Elden for an answer to her questions. "Not us."

"Marney." Elden struggled to keep his voice level. "You have chosen your way. I have found mine. Leave."

She jerked away from the hatch, shaking her head. Ess guided her down the corridor.

Elden watched their forms grow smaller until

they disappeared through another hatch.

"They're departing," Sarkozy said. "Fighters, shuttles, and escape pods."

"Cut life support to everywhere except this bridge," Elden said. "Make sure our prisoner is kept medicated but safe."

Two other Truppen strapped Erassia, clad in a Naplian space suit, to one of the vacant chairs. Space was tight for the cybernetic warriors, but they managed not to damage any vital consoles.

"Engineering to bridge," a voice reported. Who was that? Lance? Turvalo? Elden knew so few of these Truppen by name.

Goetz would have reminded him.

"Go ahead," Elden said.

"Ready for jump in four minutes."

"Coordinates set," Sarkozy said. "We should rendezvous with the *Hessian* in eighteen hours."

Elden nodded. "Engage the jump drive on my mark. It's time we fought this war on our own terms."

On our own terms... Elden gazed at the star map projected on the holographic display. *And by whatever means necessary.*

Three and a half minutes later, *Valo* leapt from the Baedecker System, leaving the smattering of small craft behind for *Aox* to retrieve.

* * *

Ergen took in the expansive view of the cavernous hangar on Baedecker Six. It must have housed thousands of *ziurathal*. Most were gone.

Most, but not all.

His soldiers rounded up dozens of technicians, with orders to drag each one aboard *Winter Scourge*. He had no idea how much knowledge those individuals could yield, but he'd take every scrap he could get.

As for the mechs themselves...

Eight hundred completed units sat in shadow throughout the hangar, from near where the Briddarri had rounded up the prisoners all the way back to the farthest, darkest corners. They looked like they were ready to leap up and fight at any moment.

"There's too many for us to transport off this world." Burrak stood next to him. "I have word from the men exploring the rest of the complex that there are thousands more in partial stages."

"We don't need thousands. We don't even need hundreds." Ergen patted the armored hide of the mech right next to them. "These things were built for one-eyes to operate. We're not going to be able to fit anybody but our skinniest people inside. They're no good for our soldiers. But I want forty of them dragged aboard before we jump from Baedecker. Every working unit we can tear apart will be invaluable for our research."

"Understood, Admiral." Burrak hurried off, snapping orders to whichever Briddarri were nearest.

Ergen had to admire the zeal with which Erassia exhibited. The man might be a delusional religious nut, but he had his goal, and nobody—not the humans, not the Briddarri, not even the feared Admiral Daviont—dissuaded him.

For Ergen, though, it was less about what the ziurathal represented than what their inner workings could tell them. So far, the Briddarri cybernetic experiments had focused on turning people into machines—with or without their consent. Ergen had found the methods and results crude yet promising.

Here, though, the Naplians had demonstrated that the battlefield mech design could be taken up a level. These units were designed to rid the galaxy of Truppen.

But what if he could evolve those designs in a different direction?

Forget pilots. Stripping down these units, adding their combat effectiveness to what he'd already gleaned from the previous efforts at dissecting Truppen, would take the cybernetics experiments to their ultimate fruition.

No one would be able to stop a force of advanced sentient warriors who would make Truppen look like a kid's tech school project.

Not the Naplians. Not the Truppen themselves.

Not even the Terrans, should it come to that.

Ergen had no illusions about ending the Grand Alliance. They needed the humans and the other empires, but Ergen wasn't going to sacrifice the big picture in either direction. The Briddarri Kingdom would remain a stalwart ally to the Terran Republic, even after this fiasco of an invasion. That was the best way to keep up the pressure for gradual acceptance of cyber warriors.

Humans were adaptable. Ergen smirked. Stubborn, but adaptable.

But so was he.

* * *

It took several hours for Ergen's people to round

up the specimens and shuttle them, along with the Naplian prisoners, aboard *Winter Scourge*. By then, the allied forces had completed their withdrawal from the Baedecker System.

"Jump coordinates set, sir," the helmsman reported. "Ready on your mark."

"Confirmed. Tactical, commence bombardement."

"Aye, sir. Bombardment commencing."

The main display blinked. It rendered a clear view of the bulk of Baedecker Six's curve. Wave after wave of *Winter Scourge*'s remaining missiles, accompanied by sheets of pulsed particle fire from the main guns. The dusty, desert-strewn surface of the planet roiled under the heat like it was turning liquid—and Ergen had no doubt parts of it had gotten so hot that the transformation had happened.

The bombardment lasted two minutes. A spreading brown and black scar was left when it finished. It looked to Ergen like someone had punched the planet in the face.

Or like we landed a blow in a Naplian's eye.

"All right. We've done what we set out to do. All hands, brace for jump." He gestured to the helmsman. "Mark."

And during *Winter Scourge*'s leap from the Baedecker System, Ergen decided it was a fine time to pour a glass of ale and toast the more certain than ever future—the future of a cybernetic victory.

* * *

Inspector Prad jerked his arms free of the

Naplian soldiers. Ingrates. You'd think they'd be happy he'd stayed with the remaining *ziurathal* and kept every recording he'd made, not to mention detained technicians to testify against Erassia's wrongdoing. Instead, they'd bundled him into a treaded transport and drove like madmen until they'd screeched up in front of the battle-damaged Daviont Tower.

"See how you and your families like being Druwei guests when I get word back to my superiors," Prad snarled.

"Let's not be too hasty to condemn the heroes who defended this vital system against the *Shirish depredations.*"

Admiral Tir Ad'Andra Daviont, commander of III Corps, stood waiting for him. There wasn't so much as a speck of soot on the burnished orange and black uniform, nor did his gray skin have any smudges. A single blue eye watched Prad with the focus of a mech's targeting array. "You wanted to see me, Inspector."

"Yes, Admiral." Prad felt his bluster seeping away. Threatening the typical enlisted grunt was one thing. But this man? The leader of the Naplian invasion and champion of the Empire's conquests? "I have here the data that proves Admiral Erassia's disobedience and mismanagement of imperial property."

Prad accepted the scroll. "My thanks, though I would have preferred not to receive this during a wasteful assault that ruined our resources and removed capable—or even mediocre flag officers from our ranks. I am not pleased with the Druwei's lack of transparency, Inspector Prad."

"I was aware only that my superiors—"

"Your superiors are not my concern." Daviont

held the scroll behind his back. "You and I need to come to a new arrangement, since the Druwei are aware now of your demise—as your associate Rost has informed them."

Prad stared. "He—betrayed me?"

"He was never yours to begin with. Do you think I stayed apprised of Erassia by trusting Druwei to handle the matter?" Daviont scowled. "Rost owed me favors. I called them in. Now, it is your turn to work off your debt since I have saved your life."

"Saved my life?" Prad's outrage resurfaced. He didn't care at that moment what Daviont had planned. The politics being played infuriated him. "I conducted this investigation at great risk from Erassia's own people, not to mention the *shirish* and the *ziura*!"

"Which is why I have not had you shot," Daviont said. "As stated, I saved your life."

Prad's posture stiffened. He had no way around this obstacle. He might as well try convincing a supernova to not explode. "What work did you have in mind?"

"Interrogation," Daviont explained. "Of a different sort. Her."

He pointed at a crumpled form among the lobby's debris. Prad grimaced.

Ivy Li.

"I want to know everything she did," Daviont said. "If we are to end the *ziura* threat to our empire once and for all."

EPILOGUE

Eight Months Later

Tag shoved the last bag into the cargo hold of the Cago Cavebat 171. He chuckled as he ran a hand across the white wingspan. "You know, I didn't think I'd be so happy to see this ship again."

"I take it you weren't impressed when we assigned it to you." Tim Ess leaned on the fuselage. He was clad in a T-shirt and trousers, barefoot on the grass.

The summer breezes were about the best sensation Tag could have hoped for when it came to his departure. Sure, he'd be in the cold vacuum of space soon, but that didn't change how much like a refuge Eleftheria had become.

A refuge, but not a home.

"I thought she looked like a boot someone had stepped on, with wings attached."

Tim laughed. "You're not wrong, even with the fresh color coat."

"Well, she'll get us where we need to go." Tag offered his hand. "Thanks again for digging her up. How much do I owe TI?"

Tim clasped his hand and shook it. "Not a credit. This is off the books and on the house, in recognition for all your service, Colonel."

Not anymore. Tag had no insignia, no clearances,

not even a uniform in his bag. All he had was a destination and information.

And Lira.

She walked down the path through the forest with Marney at her side and Father behind them. Marney and Lira each carried one of Marney's twins—boys. Ian and Patrick.

"There's the rest of our party." Tag put an arm around Lira's shoulders and kissed her. He rubbed the top of Ian's head, feeling the downy blond hair he was rapidly growing in. Ian cooed and scrabbled for his fingers. "You can't borrow one, I'm afraid."

"I know." Lira sighed. She lifted Ian and nuzzled nose to nose. He giggled. "Marney, I'll miss you. This has been a wonderful time."

"I couldn't have done it without you." Marney hugged her and let Antiny collect Ian. "I just wish you two would change your minds."

"Sorry, Sis, but I can't let Dyson stay the way he is." Tag glanced back at the Cavebat. "Lira's got people among Blue Kitt who can fix him. Whether or not we can get his memories back, well... I'm hoping for the best."

"Our hopes go with you, son." Father embraced him. Tears brushed at Tag's neck. "I know I haven't said it enough, but I'm proud of you, no matter the outcome of whatever we've done. So very proud."

Tag couldn't speak for a while and let Ian and Patrick's warbling fill the silence until he could choke out, "Thank you, Father."

"The ignition code and other handy algorithms are on here." Tim pressed a data stick into his hand. "I took the liberty of adding a few special assistants that may or may not have come from work. Don't tell my bosses."

"And rat you out? Never." Tag grinned. "I appreciate it. We'll need all the help we can get."

"I hope you two find what you're looking for," Marney said. "And when you do, I hope you'll come back to us."

"It'll be a while, but we will, I promise." Tag held Lira's hand. "You ready?"

"As ever." She smiled. "Any interest in visiting the Jarrados System? There's some extravagant galleries with far too many ill-gotten works of art—"

"Hold on." Tag shook his head. "No crime."

"Yet."

Tag grimaced.

"It's for a good cause..." Lira sauntered past him toward the cockpit, letting her words linger.

Tag waved his final farewells and clambered in through the cargo hold. He checked on the stasis capsule at the back, a black and gray cylinder with an oval viewport at the top. Dyson's impassive face, eyes closed, was visible beneath.

Funny how he just looks asleep. I hope we can wake him—and when we do, that it's actually him.

He sealed the cargo hatch and walked up past the two bunks toward the cockpit. The engines hummed to life.

"We're ready when you are." Lira sat in the co-pilot's seat. Tag marveled all over again at the top-flight avionics concealed in dingy panels and battered console housings.

"Let's get out of here, then." Tag took her hand and kissed it. "To our new life."

"Together." Lira kissed him on the lips.

Tag cycled the engines and ran through the preflight diagnostics. Everything looked five by five.

The comms crackled. "*Vossberg Two*, this is Eleftheria Control. You are cleared for departure."

"Confirmed, Control, this is *Vossberg Two*, departing." Tag eased back on the controls.

Their ship leapt into the air. Tag shook his head, still grinning. Tim hadn't mentioned any upgrades, but Tag could tell the engine performance was markedly improved.

"I've sent a coded signal to my contacts," Lira said. "They're expecting us."

"Let's not keep them waiting." Tag was looking forward to restoring their friend to life, but more importantly, to restoring himself.

It was time for the new Taggart Wester to replace the old one.

✳ ✳ ✳

Elden Selva opened the hatch into *Hessian*'s deep storage. "It is completed, then?"

"Yes, Consul." Sarkozy led him down the darkened passage between massive containers of spare parts and weaponry. "I am surprised he survived this long, given what we've put him through, but the results speak for themselves."

They entered a section guarded by two shorter Truppen. Elden noted the blue glow illuminating the compartment.

Admiral Erassia was mounted on a frame of metal tubes, with wires strung from a tight-fitting cap atop his narrow head. His eye was closed except for a narrow slit. Spittle dampened the soiled and wrinkled uniform. More tubes protruded from his sides and abdomen. He wasn't dead, but he could not be described as alive, either.

Elden was impressed his will had allowed him to hang on all these months.

But it was the data streaming across a broad, rectangular screen suspended above Erassia's head that drew Elden's attention. Schematics, scribbled notes, roughly sketched images—they were blurred and jumbled, but they were there.

Everything Erassia knew or dreamed about his *ziurathal* project.

But more important were the tidbits about another similar project—the Briddarri cybernetics laboratories.

Elden had long suspected Erassia had been hunting for them just as Tag and Terran Intelligence had been. This, though, was the truth of the matter. He had rough ideas of places where those labs could be secured.

"The coordinates are sketchy," Sarkozy said, "But the few we've cleaned up have not matched any of the systems we attacked, nor do they match the ones our allies have gone after."

"They're ones nobody knew about, then." Elden scraped his claws across his palms. "Good. We prepare a target list and hit them with the goal of gathering more intel."

"Then we destroy them, correct, sir?"

"Correct. We need to take them intact to find out where else Ergen and his minions have set up shop within the last year, and then we incinerate whatever is left."

Elden gazed at Erassia's miserable form. "Thank you, Admiral. You've done the galaxy a great service."

He turned back to Sarkozy. "Compile as much as you can. I want to make the first assault within a week."

"Yes, sir."

Elden strode away. He felt buoyed by the chances of taking the fight back to the enemy—the true enemy. Not just the Naplians, but the Briddarri—and anyone else who dared to engage in these abominable experiments. Elden would have the Truppen stand between free peoples and a cybernetic holocaust.

Even if he had to wage war against his own former species

* * *

The Naplians guarding the vault underneath Daviont Tower on Baedecker Four did not expect a visitor—certainly not the building's namesake.

"Leave," Daviont ordered. "I have business in the vault."

"Sir, I'm not authorized to—"

"I don't want to hear about clearances, Corporal. My name is on this structure, and I am the one who kept the contents of this vault secure from the enemy," Daviont snapped. "Stand aside or you'll spend the next eighteen months on an ore hauler shifting serjaum back across the Great Desert Rift."

The guard's gray skin paled, and he stepped out of the admiral's way. Perhaps he was relying on the security scanners recording the incident.

It was fine by Daviont. He wanted them to see him.

Or rather, see Daviont.

Daviont's retina scan opened the lock. Handy, that, but faking monocular vision gave him a headache.

Not Daviont. Krzan Vo. It would be a relief to slough off the saggy, soft flesh—he gagged on the word —and feel the strength of his carapace against the air once more.

The vault was empty, save for a couple rows of EMP-hardened memory cores. He wasn't here for those.

It was the silver box at the back that held his interest.

Krzan let the box scan his falsified features. "Ident confirmed, Admiral," the box said in tinny, heavily accented *ffawe-kresh*. "Access granted."

The lid hissed as the air pressurization equalized. It popped open.

The person wearing a pseudo-musculature recreation of Admiral Daviont's body withdrew a ruby-colored sphere lined with silver etchings and put the assortment of black cubes into his pockets. Krzan checked the mission parameters displayed by his implant across his peripheral vision. That was all that was needed.

"I could not give proper honor to your bodily remains," he murmured to the sphere, taking care to speak in *ffawe-kresh* and not his native clicking *Zykzii*. "But we won't be long without seeing you face to face again. For now, I will help you complete your task."

Krzan walked out of the vault with the nervous guard left behind. He ignored the corporal's hasty salute.

Five minutes, and he could remove the slimy disguise. Ten minutes and he would be on a Silent Company transport chartered to Stelltron as an independent mining contractor. Fifteen minutes, and he would make the jump out of the Baedecker System.

Only then would Krzan relax and begin the download of every scrap of data Ivy Li had surreptitiously gleaned from the Truppen when she'd made contact. A quick check had proven that the Naplians, despite months of effort, had failed to unlock her matrix security protocols.

It was time to give cyber evolution the next great nudge.

ABOUT THE AUTHOR

Steve Rzasa

Steve Rzasa is the author of three Takamo novels. He has several other science-fiction, steampunk, and fantasy novels, with a bunch more in progress. He was first published in 2009 by Marcher Lord Press (now Enclave Publishing). His third novel, Broken Sight, received the 2012 Award for Speculative Fiction from  the American Christian Fiction Writers, and his debut novel, The Word Reclaimed, was nominated for the same. The Word Endangered was recently nominated for the Realm Award presented by Realm Makers.

Steve grew up in Atco, New Jersey, and started writing stories in grade school. He received his Bachelor's degree in journalism from Boston University, and worked for eight years at newspapers in Maine and Wyoming. He worked as a librarian for fifteen years, earning his Library Support Staff Certification from the American Library Association in 2014—one of only 135 graduates nationwide and a handful in Wyoming. Steve now devotes all of his time to writing.

He is the technical services librarian in Buffalo, Wyoming, where he lives with his wife and two boys. Steve's a fan of all things science-fiction and superhero, and is also a student of history.

OTHER TAKAMO TITLES

Kassandra Dick
Atlas of Lies

K.S. Augustin
The Ice Cold Heart

A.R. Declerck
Aphelion
An Enduring Sun
Dark Star
Decaying Orbit
Resonance Factor
Escape Velocity

Amber Draeger
Degara's Mark
Degara's Bane

Shona Husk
For God & Mars
Last Run of the Ice Duchess

Kerry Nietz
Rhats!
Rhats Too!
Rhats Free!
Rhataloo

Steve Rzasa
Empire's Rift
Strife's Cost
Counterstrike's Ruin